KINCAID

The Dragons Of Justice

LANA L HUGHES

Edited by
http://www.onevoiceliteraryagency.com

Cover by
https://www.instagram.com/lemoncreativemedia/

Follow DCI Evander Kincaid here
https://www.instagram.com/dcievanderkincaid/

Follow the author here
https://www.instagram.com/nirosta/

Kindle Direct Publishing (KDP)

Available in formats hardback, paperback and Kindle e-book

First Edition 2022

978-1-7398941-1-5

FOR LYDIA AND JONATHAN

ACKNOWLEDGEMENTS

Graham McMillan - your advice on police procedure, technical process and due diligence has been invaluable.

~~~~~~

Lemon Creative Media - for the fantastic artwork on the cover.

~~~~~~

My literary hero Dean Koontz - while my self doubt persists, I took your advice and worked page by page until I was confident in it. You continue to inspire, and your work is a constant reminder that stories are powerful tools for the imagination. Don't stop creating worlds, mayhem, memorable characters and good dogs through the magic of words.

~~~~~~

My friend Rosalind Winton - editor, critic, guidance system and cheer leader all rolled into one. Your support and belief in my ability (especially when I doubted I had it) has been unwavering. In difficult times your encouragement to 'finish the book' has been motivational.

~~~~~~

"Come not between a dragon and his wrath"

Shakespeare

CHAPTER ONE

Detective Chief Inspector Evander Kincaid stands with hands on hips, looking up at London's Tower Bridge and the body of the man who has been crucified.

The crime scene is bathed by intermittent blue flashing lights from police cars at both ends of the bridge and from police boats on the river. The lights cast shadows that leap and dance in macabre merry patterns across Tower Bridge and the victim. The occasional short burst of police sirens drift across the ether in a distorted wail, that adds a bizarre context to the scene before him.

There is a gentle breeze and though it is not raining, the sun kissed clouds of twilight complicate visibility.

It's difficult for Evander to see from his obtuse angle and in this light, what the cause of death may be. He realises that one cannot assume crucifixion was the way this man met his demise. Sometimes, not everything is black and white where crime is concerned.

The occasional toot of car horns from frustrated motorists, who are stuck in Thursday evening traffic punctuates the scene. A man has been murdered, yet it seems all people care about are congestion charges and making it home for the start of the long Easter weekend.

The timing and staging of this murder scene were deliberately planned for this weekend, apparently.

Evander surveys the scene. He looks around observing people who watch from the embankment, two river cruise boats and from the windows of nearby lofty buildings. Broken pieces of conversation and occasionally audible words find their way to him across the air, as the sound of the crowd travels, drifting in and out of hearing, like an ocean tide that rushes in as the surf breaks the beach and recedes on the ebb.

Although people have been moved back by the police perimeter, it doesn't stop onlookers finding a prime spot to watch the goings on. You always get gawkers at a public crime scene, and you can't get much more public than this.

Evander looks back to Tower Bridge and tries to work out why the blood-stained victim was placed here of all places. Shoeless and dressed only in trousers and a hat, he is otherwise naked. Evander thinks he looks vaguely familiar, but he can't be sure from this distance. Additionally, blood stains on his face distort his features and Evander can't recall where or even if he has seen him.

The hat - a Fedora - looks like it has been pulled tightly onto his head. Blood that had seeped from under the brim, now marks his face in congealed patterns of varied shades of red. His head rests – or is it lolls? – to the right and does not cause the hat to dislodge. The body, spread eagled like Vitruvian man, is held in position below the walkways but above the bascules of Tower Bridge. He is held in place by wires, which have been driven into his hands and feet and are evident even from this distance.

The wounds, though they serve a purpose, are also symbolic imitations of Jesus Christ's crucifixion; though the arrangement is not quite in the same style, the message is clear enough to be noted, even by those who are not religious. Crucifixion is, in some faiths a willing sacrifice by the subject, like the one made by Jesus, offering salvation to humanity. That is not the case here. This, Evander feels is symbolic in respect that the murderer believes that this person, whoever he was, is an example of what is to come. This is too elaborate to be a one off. He feels sure more murders will follow. Here, the killer presents his victim's soul in a *state* of crucifixion, a different type of sacrifice.

Evander already profiles the killer as a religious man and a vigilante. Great - just what London needs right now during the Easter holiday.

Evander suddenly realises why Tower Bridge was the set for this stage; Jesus was crucified in public and this in the modern world, well... It's as public as you get in London.

Even without knowing all the facts, or who the victim is - was - Evander is confident that the person strung up above him, on show for the whole world to see, deserved to be there. It is too elaborate a plan for the victim not to be made a spectacle of. At the very least that is what the killer will believe.

This also smacks of someone looking to gain attention. Most likely from the police and perhaps the media and they have used the most famous bridge in London, as a stage to set out their agenda.

This is a '*look at me, look what I can do*' crime, a kind which Evander loathes so much. It is as audacious as you can get and seemingly, the killer has got away with it by avoiding detection. No doubt he - no, shouldn't assume it's a man at this stage; Evander corrects his train of thought - or she, will be buoyed by the success of this plan, now it has successfully unfolded.

The clever ones always think they are invincible and immune to capture and that is usually their downfall. They become complacent, messy and ultimately sloppy, so therefore susceptible to mistakes and then inevitable capture, they all slip up eventually.

Scene of Crimes Officers - SOCO - are complete with

documentation and photography of the crime scene. Evander does not envy those that are tasked with removing the corpse; he also wonders how they will get him down. It must have been a nightmare for SOCO to orchestrate sketch and shoot for forensics. They would have used video on this one, so even more documentation complexities.

Raucous laughter drifts across the embankment and Evander looks in the direction it comes from. People may be appalled by murder, but they are also fascinated by it, and some have an unhealthy interest in it. He notices people with their backs to the victim, they hold mobile phones out in front of them to take selfie photos with the victim in the background. No doubt some will record the scene and it will inevitably end up all over social media outlets, going viral. 'Humanity can be a strange, nauseating breed'. Evander thinks to himself, but what can you do? people are… *people.*

The victim is held in place by what looks like a series of wires and pulley cables and God knows what other hidden connections, gadgets and gizmos that keep the body firmly in place. Yet they are flexible enough to afford some give, so that the victim was not torn limb from limb when the bridge bascules were lowered.

The bascules - a great piece of British ingenuity and engineering brilliance, as Evander was informed by one of his team - are raised and lowered accordingly, to allow passage for tall ships, cruise liners and oversized vessels of one sort or another. It is quite the tourist attraction on its own but, given its proximity to the Tower of London on the other side of the Bridge, it is guaranteed a large audience. Granted, it's not quite the 'Changing of the Guard', but none the less, it has always been a highlight for tourists from all over the world, so more people would be present at the time this spectacle unfolded.

It was while the bascules of the bridge were lowered, that the system was triggered, which pulled the victim down from the walkways hovering above street level. Obviously, great care and attention was given to this, so that the display was a spectacle, as opposed to a disaster.

Evander is reminded of a spider, catching prey and the victim looks as though he has been caught in a web by a killer spider. Whether that was metaphorical, unintentional, or by design he is not sure, but it is, Evander thinks, appropriate that it appears this way. Somehow, Evander feels as though he is about to be tangled up in the gossamer as well.

The distant but nearing sounds of a helicopter reach Evander's ears. He looks up and tries to pinpoint the source of the sound, he expects it will likely be a police helicopter.

When he finds the bird in the sky, it is silhouetted by the setting sun, which makes it appear darker and more sinister than it actually is.

The helicopter creeps in from the distant West and edges closer to Tower Bridge. Once close enough, Evander can read the distinct letters of a news logo on the front of the nose and doors; they spell out B.B.C. 'Oh, great - the Papanasty!' He thinks. Evander sighs heavily, disdain evident in his wordless disapproval of the press. Now Aunty Beeb has gotten hold of this, it won't be long before the rest of the vultures arrive.

From his peripheral vision, Evander notices someone rushing towards him, which turns his attention to the figure. The petite frame of Violet Jackson, the Forensic Pathologist approaches with documents in hand. Evander had not seen her going back to the SOCO van, as is her custom, to begin

writing her notes, but she must have done so and she hurries towards Evander, obviously with something important to tell him.
"What is it?" Evander asks, anticipation in his mellifluous baritone that is clear, calm, warm and gentle. His Scottish brogue has an elegance that is pleasing to the ear and hypnotic; sensual, intelligent and disarming.
Through puffs of breath, which blows the fringe of her blond hair out of her eyes, Jackson tries to control her breathing as she speaks. "We… have a… serial killer."
"Are you sure?" Evander inquires.
"There was… a note left. We thought it may be... a suicide note, but it's not. Look."
Jackson hands Evander a clear, sealed evidence bag, which contains the note. Written in neat, typed calligraphy, it reads:
'Do you see me now Scotland Yard?'
Evander turns over the bag. On the back of the note is the picture of a dragon. Not just any dragon, but a London dragon. Only, instead of a shield in the dragon's claw, there is a victim. The victim in this case, represents the one currently hanging on Tower Bridge.
"He's taunting us." Jackson muses.
"No, no". Evander replies. "He's pissed off with us. We've obviously missed his previous attempts to get our attention, so this here..." Evander waves his long fingers towards the bridge... "Is his affection for us. It's as elaborate as you can be to get the attention, not just of the police, but the nation. Oh, and let's not forget the 'Papanasty'. The press will have a bloody field day with this; they're here already. Look."
Evander jabs a long accusatory, slender index finger to the offending metal bird in the sky, which hovers near the bridge.

"We'll have to arrange a press conference at some point too and sooner than we'd like, because they'll have questions on behalf of the nation on how something like this could happen right under our noses, blah, blah, blah. It'll be like Easter, Christmas *and* New Year for them. God, I hate that gleeful bunch of bastards."
Evander sighs, looks around at the gawping onlookers.
"According to this"... He says, as he raises the note in his hand. "We missed the others, however many there may be and this, the dragon, it's his calling card, his autograph..."
"TWO!" Jackson blurts out.
"What?"
"You're right about the dragon being a calling card. The victim has two dragons on his chest and from what I could see, it looked like they were carved into his torso. I think the killer may be using them as a way of numbering the victims and this is his second victim."
"Damn it!" Evander exclaims. "How the bloody hell did we miss the first victim? We'll have to go back through previous case files of murders within the last year, maybe two years to see what we missed that he previously left for us. If this is his second victim, I'm not surprised it was so public a display. It's not just a... *'here I am, look what I can do'* message he is sending us, this is a *'you'll never catch me, because I'm better than you'* slap in the face for us. Okay, so how did he die, was it the crucifixion that he succumbed to?" Evander asks.
"Can't really say what cause of death was, or the extent of his injuries till we get him to the mortuary." Jackson replies.
"Okay, if you don't know C.O.D. yet, do you have any idea how long he's been dead?"
"I think between 36 and 48 hours, probably longer, but will be

more accurate when I can fully examine him unhindered. It'll be…"
"In your report, yes, yes - I know." Evander interjects flippantly.
They both look up at the victim in silence. Evander looks out to the West, to the river. The setting sun so low now, it casts a dappled red-purple-pink hue across the Thames. It appears that the river bleeds in sympathy with the victim.
Evander breaks the silence and ponders. "How did they get the body up there? To stage it so elaborately without anyone noticing a man - a dead man at that - was being dragged around. How did he get all the hooks, wires and gadgets into place without anyone noticing?"
Jackson opens her mouth to say something, but Evander continues with his own line of thought before she can give voice to any of her own.
"There's a shit load of cameras all around this area, plus visitors to the city gather here daily. There are hotels and restaurants all around us. People wandering around on both sides of the river, the bridge itself and look at all the buildings, all the offices here and apartments there and across the river. City Hall and the Tower of London… How the hell did everyone miss him?"
"That's what we're all wondering." Jackson says, as she takes the evidence bag from Evander, then turns on her heel and walks away.
Without looking back, she calls out. "Will see you back at the mortuary."

CHAPTER TWO

While they wait for Jackson to conclude the autopsy and file her report, Evander and his team make themselves busy. The team have been given preliminary findings from the autopsy however, Violet Jackson has a work ethic that is obsessive. She begins her notes while at the crime scene, usually in one of the SOCO vans. Once she has table space at a mortuary and conducts the physical autopsy, she records her findings and observations via Dictaphone and also makes notes with pen and paper, in a shorthand only she seems to understand. After the prelim, she will review her recordings and her handwritten notes and corroborate them. Sometimes, that means she will re-examine a body.

Given that there has been a murder in the last 72 hours, while that is the main focus for the team, it also makes sense to have some people from the smaller teams search unsolved chronological cases for any missed links and connections. A small Intelligence Cell (I.C.) of about eight people of varying ranks are filtering through the HOLMES system. They report to another team who work closely with Evander's team. They are all helping review files on all unsolved murders from the last two years. Instruction has been given for cases where a dragon or an animal of some description, has been linked with a murder in some capacity, as something that should be bumped to the top of the list as a case of interest and reported to Evander's immediate team for further in-depth review.

Evander and his team then sift through all the evidence associated with each unsolved case, that is passed up the chain from the I.C. team as a case of interest.

They scrutinize evidence, crime scene photos, autopsy reports, victim profiles, which include backgrounds, family, friends, colleagues, associates, places of work, hobbies, known haunts, adverse media searches - literally everything is researched in their quest to either eliminate cases, or link them together – no stone is being left unturned now in the review of escalated cases.

The only thing they have to work with is what links any of the cases together so far; the victims were all murdered. Not a great deal to work with, even more so when you don't know, with any great certainty what you're looking for, in order to join the dots that would forge that connection. All they have to work with is a murder victim and a dragon, or some form of animal, be it fictional or real.

Everyone has their role to play, including Evander, who digs in to help. He designates his most senior team member, D.I. Adam Eastwood to take charge. The I.C. team report directly into Evander's POD of officers, they in turn bring cases with potential to Adam's attention. Adam then distributes files, tasks and further research responsibilities to other team members, while he searches through his own share of folders. Adam has been with Evander the longest and understands what Evander wants from a team and he guides them with aplomb. Adam is a quirky no nonsense, shoot-straight-from-the-hip Scouser with a love of music, movies, football and history. He has that trademark Scouse humour, a killer smile and a cheeky chappy disposition that could charm the birds from the trees.

Now that they know who the second victim is – was – strung up on Tower Bridge, Adam wonders if the victims they are searching for, may be guilty of one or many crimes and that this should be their focus of attention. Other than that - the victims have so far not been linked, or they would have known sooner than now that they had a serial killer. As any previous victims can't be easily connected, it makes the task at hand a lot more difficult.

While conducting his own research, Evander notes the strange case of a hanging at Leadenhall Market in the City of London. This is a historic location, although the current structure was designed in 1881 by Sir Horace Jones and if he remembers rightly from one of Adam's many history lesson ramblings. The market dates back to the 14th century and stands on old Roman London. Fortunately, it is now also a Grade II listed building, which means it will be preserved for the rest of time, so any potential changes that may happen in the future, will need to be approved.

The structure of the market houses a rather distinct central dome of glass, with supporting cast iron columns painted maroon, cream and gold. It was here that the victim in this unsolved case was positioned, right in the middle of the market. Initially, it appeared to be a suicide, but was later classified as suspicious and upon autopsy results, murder. While Evander looks at SOCO photos and reads reports, he is alarmed to see that the hanging took place with the use of the dragons, situated on the market pillars. Here the rope - from which the victim hanged, under the lights in the middle of the dome - had been carefully threaded through or around the dragons. The killer had thoughtfully protected the dragons by inserting a crude padding of Poly Styrofoam between the dragon and any connections that formed the link to the noose. On closer inspection, Evander notes that the rope threaded through or around the dragons is not actually rope at all, but wire - just like the wire used on Tower Bridge. No doubt this is the reason for the protective padding. It is only the noose around the victim's neck that is rope.

Evander counts the dragons connected to the wires. Four have been used - could this be the fourth victim? This realization hits him like a freight train. If this is the fourth victim, that would mean the Tower Bridge victim is the fifth. Yet, there were only two dragons at the scene, which were carved into the victim's torso. Or were there?

Evander gets up from his desk to retrieve the file for the Tower Bridge victim from a table in the corner of his office. He thumbs through it and pays close attention to the photos from the crime scene and the victim.

He notices there are two dragons on the Tower Bridge walkway, directly above the victim's head and the two on his torso makes four. Evander frowns, there must be another dragon that is visible and in sight.

There can't be two victims who are fourth on the list. Evander then remembers the note and the dragon on the reverse of the paper. He searches for the photo, finds it. The dragon holds the victim on Tower Bridge in its claw, obviously that makes them connected. Therefore, Tower Bridge is the fifth victim. No wonder this display was so elaborate, this guy must be seriously pissed off over all his work that was missed. The Tower Bridge victim wasn't just an elaborate display, it was the smack in the face he - or she - thinks the police need in order to have their eyes opened.

Evander reads the bio on Murphy, the Leadenhall Market victim.

The victim, Joseph Murphy - or 'Murph' to his mates - a bar man at a nearby public house - had supposedly hung himself, but looking at the evidence, Evander now knows this must be a victim of the *Dragons of Justice Vigilante* (as the press have already labelled him). Attention seeker, murderer, serial killer, whacko, any of the above will just about cover it.

Evander discovers he was wanted for the murder of a young man whom he hanged. He got off because of a calamitous mishandling of the case, various discrepancies and contradictions in the arrest report, which was complicated by technicalities.

The chain of evidence had not been stored correctly, so because the results were corrupted, the judge had no choice but to dismiss the case. When a witness came forward with new evidence, it was too late to try Murphy again, due to the double jeopardy rule of law, so he got away with murder. His hanging was clearly retribution for the crime and that he should die by his own methods, was his just desserts.

Evander walks out of his office, he whistle's loudly, everyone stops and looks towards him. He clears his throat. "Everyone, we're looking for four previous victims…"

"FOUR?!" Eastwood questions loudly, shock and surprise evident in his voice.

"Yes, four. No! Just three more now... It's three." He waves the file in his hand and continues. "I just found number four. Number five is Tower Bridge, so three left to find. It's no wonder he was so pissed off with us for missing the others. To miss one would have been bad enough, but to miss four connected cases is more than atrocious. He must think we're all idiots and he'll be furious we've missed all his previous work. The clues may be subtle, and they may not even look like they are connected but, anywhere you can find a dragon in any way shape or form. Either on the victim, connected to the victim, near the victim, above, below, beside or behind the victim. Anything at all with a dragon in the SOCO photos or reports, put on the pile to be considered and we will review them in more detail once we have narrowed the field down. We need something solid to add to the Major Incident Room. We have our work cut out people, so get back to it."

Everyone returns to their tasks, but then Evander remembers something and calls. "Oh, and if you have already eliminated something, please review it again, because now with this information, we may well have missed something we didn't think was relevant on previously discounted cases."

An audible groan elicits from some team members.

Evander chastises them. "Suck it up and get to it people."

CHAPTER THREE

Evander drinks his second cup of Americano and sits at his Scotland Yard desk, while he reads Violet Jackson's report on the autopsy of the Tower Bridge victim.

Evander is appalled to find that the I.D. of the victim is none other than notorious London gangland boss, Freddie 'Shreddie' Corvus. Quite ironic - or maybe cleverly planned - that a guy with the Latin name for raven, should be put on display within spitting distance to the Tower of London, where the legend of the raven became global knowledge. He can't help but wonder... Will Freddie's death start a war on a scale that gangland London has not previously witnessed? Scotland Yard will have to conduct a press conference by tomorrow at the latest, to avoid a retaliation attack from rival gangs. That hopefully will avoid any proportion of blame, as this is not a message of war from one side to another. This is something else entirely.

Evander dreads the press conference every time. It is with good reason he has a hate-hate relationship with the 'Papanasty', as he refers to them these days. He also needs to decide who from his team will join him. Maybe the trusted Eastwood, he knows how to handle the press, something to ponder on later.

Evander sips his coffee as he reads through the extensive notes that Jackson has written. He tries to understand the big fancy words. There are parts, especially about the carving of the dragons into Freddie's torso and the cables in his hands and feet that are disturbing. It is cold, calculating and risky too.

Evander has some unanswered questions that seem to be lost

in translation somewhere in the pages of science that is Jackson's report.

He needs to speak to her, and he plans on doing so as soon as he has read the rest of her report. He jots notes down on a pad as he reads, which he will remember for later.

Once he finishes reading, he will confer with his colleague, but first - more coffee.

~~~~~~

Evander sits by a coffee table in one of two comfy chairs in a corner of Jackson's small office. The office comprises a desk and two chairs, one on either side - one for Jackson and a guest chair opposite. There are also two filing cabinets, which partly obscure the comfy seating area Evander is sitting in. Behind her desk hang framed diplomas, certificates and two black and white photos of a man and a woman – both of whom Evander doesn't know, but assumes they are family or friends of Jackson's.

Lost in his own thoughts, he initially doesn't hear the door open. Wearing a white lab coat, Violet has an armful of files, which she drops on her desk with a heavy 'whack'. She turns, pushes the door shut with force, then turns back towards her desk. She puts her hands on the guest chair in front of her and lowers her head. She squeezes the back of the chair tightly. A few strands of her blonde hair fall in front of her eyes.

She blows out her breath as she curses. "Fucking idiot!"

Evander raises an eyebrow and wonders who she is talking about - she's obviously unaware she has company in her office - he hopes it is not him she curses.

About to say 'hello' to let her know he is there; he is suddenly
~~~~~~

struck mute when she moves the hair that had fallen in front of her eyes. It pierces his heart like a blade as she briefly reminds him of his wife Jasmine. Dear, sweet, adorable, lost Jasmine.

It's been two years now - three this November that he lost his wife in a road traffic accident at Holborn Viaduct. Jasmine had a sweet habit of brushing her hair away from her eyes with her fingers when she was nervous, or shy about something. Even if her hair had not actually fallen in front of her eyes, she would find some to move from somewhere. He missed those moments when she made him smile.

He misses her beautiful eyes, the feel of her, the smell of her hair, her stunning smile. God, he just misses *her*. Her birthday is fast approaching, and his heart feels like it is about to break when he thinks of the lonely pilgrimage he will have to make.

Jackson turns around to see Evander and she jumps, then curses him. "God damn it, Evander, you scared the shit out of me. What the hell are you doing in here?"

A small smile curls Evander's lips - he is thankful to her for distracting him from his thoughts that run too deep. He waves her report in the air. "I have some questions."

"When do you never have questions!" she exclaims.

"Who's pissed you off?"

Jackson avoids the question, she retorts. "What do you want to know?"

"The part about the carving of the dragons, the wounds to the hands and feet and the Fedora secured to his head. Can you answer some questions for me?"

"Gee, there was me thinking it was already in there." Jackson says sarcastically as she points to the file in Evander's hand.

"Well, I need to know…"

"I told you - it's all in the report - didn't you read it?"
"Of course, but there are questions I have that you do not answer, which is why I'm here."
"You do know I have answered them, my reports are detailed."
"Too detailed I have to say. If you do answer them, I don't understand enough of the science to know they are answers. Or you've blinded me with so much science and as I don't know what the big, long fancy words mean, well..."
"Really - you mean I missed something?"
"That's not what I said."
"Okay, so what exactly do you mean?" Jackson asks, folding her arms defensively.
"Assuming I understand correctly, your report says that the victim was awake while the dragons were carved into his torso, but he was immobilised so he couldn't move. Correct so far?"
"That's correct."
"Okay, so explain to me, if he couldn't move, why didn't he just call out for help?"
"Because he was administered a Neuromuscular…"
Evander holds a hand up to stop Jackson mid-sentence. "I've no idea what the long fancy names mean, or what they can do to a human body. Not unless you tell me. So, please can you explain, in humble English without blinding me with science?"
"There was me thinking you were blessed with the smarts." Jackson quips.
"For understanding thingy majigy science geek speak mmmm, not so much." Evander retorts.
"Okay, basic English for the simple human?" Violet smirks,

unable to hide her amusement.
"Simple human - I really hope not, but simple English, yes please."
"He was given a neuro - a muscle relaxant to bring on physical paralysis, but it also paralyses the vocal cords, so it would have been impossible for him to move or call out to anyone. He probably needed some sort of ventilation support while the procedure was being carried out too, as it also relaxes the diaphragm which, if that doesn't work - means you don't breathe."
"Seriously, there are drugs that can actually incapacitate you like that?"
"How do you think they perform operations daily? It's even listed in the tox report. Small traces of Chondrodendron Tomentosum were found, or did you miss that too?"
"I'm not even going to attempt repeating that name, but that's a drug?"
"Yes, in fact, a lot of people have it in their homes and don't realise it."
"Wow, really?"
"Yes, it's more commonly known as the rubber plant. The drug is an extract of it."
"I have a rubber plant in my house! Holy shit, I never knew that!" Amusement evident in his soft Scottish brogue.
"Glad to be of service as a teacher, you can pay me later."
"It's your job, you already get paid for this!"
"Well, maybe you can…"
Evander interrupts her mid-sentence and asks. "Wait, if he was going to kill him, why would he need him to breathe?"
"He wanted to torture him. The victim would have been aware of pain even after being paralysed. The pain from the

slicing and dicing would have been excruciating. It possibly may have caused him to pass out at some point, but I'm just guessing that part, so..."

"My God, so he kept him alive and awake on purpose?"

"Yes. He only gave a drug to paralyse him; he didn't give any general anaesthetics or analgesics to prevent pain. None were present in the tox report. He wanted him alert while he worked, he wanted to inflict pain, while the victim watched and felt everything. He was helpless to do anything about it to stop him. I think that was the point of the exercise. He wanted him to know how it felt to be helpless. Quite a clever, but sadistic bastard if you ask me."

"Anything unusual come up?"

"A murder victim hung out to dry on Tower Bridge isn't unusual enough then?"

"You know what I mean!" Evander responds with a quickness that gives a lilt to his accent.

"Well, the Fedora was interesting."

"Ah yes. This was something I wanted to ask you about, but what did you find interesting?"

"Well, it could have been just put on his head as you would if you were wearing it yourself. Yet this was secured in place with pins."

"What type of pins?"

"Lapel and tie pins."

"When you say... 'secured in place', you mean secured to his head, literally?" Evander asks.

"Yes. The pins were driven into his head through the edge of the hat where it meets the brim, hence all the congealed blood flowing down his face when we found him. I guess the killer didn't want the hat to come off in any potential winds."

"There was only a gentle breeze when we found him though. Nothing that was gusty enough to dislodge a hat."
"We know that now, but unpredictable British weather and the risk of the breeze off the river, I guess there were no chances being taken of the display being ruined."
"That, or more likely it was just to inflict more pain, or something else altogether." Evander ponders. "How many pins were used?" He asks.
"Mr Corvus must have had a vast collection of pins I believe. We withdrew over 100 of varying designs, shapes and sizes. Some with longer needle points than others, but all equally sharp. What is the 'something else altogether' angle you're thinking of?" Violet inquires.
"A modern-day version of a crown of thorns, innovative usage of lapel and tie pins for symbology. That's really clever, don't you think?" Evander muses out loud.
"What, seriously? You sound like you admire him."
"Not at all, but even you must admit that as far as metaphors go, that's a clever one without going back to the days of Jesus and actually making a crown of thorns. C.O.D. you said was eventually cardiac arrest?"
"Correct."
"So, it wasn't all the injuries, being carved up, or the crucifixion?"
"No. As we suspected, he was already dead when he was put on display. The other injuries contributed to physical trauma, but death was cardiac arrest brought on by tachycardia, due to the drugs administered to produce paralysis. I'd say he possibly took him off the ventilation system he was using - and I'm conjecturing he will have had some equipment, even a crude improvisation, but something for sure - and watched

him suffer. Then after he was dead, he did all his arranging for the big finale on Tower Bridge."

"What about the wounds on his hands and feet, pre or post-mortem?"

"Pre-mortem I'm afraid. The connections were driven into his hands and feet with great force, breaking bone, severing cartilage, sinew and tendons, while tearing muscle apart as they were inserted. It would have been extremely painful, because they were driven in slowly and precisely to ensure the holes did not rip flesh or tissue; to the point of rendering them useless for the big reveal when he dropped from the walk-ways on Tower Bridge."

"That's sadistic."

"Yes, but the killer probably enjoyed it, having that much control over someone apparently so powerful, yet seeing him so helpless. I'm not sure why, but I have this image of the vic pleading with his eyes for mercy. He could do little else to be honest and the killer just watched him die a painful death, but that's just my imagination - hopefully."

"Why do you think they did it, apart from the obviousness of being insane?"

"Attention. Given that we missed his previous attempts and the note left, I'd say the murderer wanted the attention - or is it glory? - so badly that they went to great lengths to ensure it this time. I'd say that was attention grabbing enough, wouldn't you?"

"It would be hard to ignore, and he has our attention now that's for sure."

CHAPTER FOUR

In the conference room, the Chief Super starts to wrap up the staff meeting in preparation for the press conference. An unusual move for the Chief to lead the staff meeting. Ordinarily as Senior Investigating Officer, Evander would be in charge of team meetings, but this case has ruffled feathers much higher up the chain and stretches to ranks beyond the Chief Super. Understandable that, as he is likely being asked some difficult questions, that he currently has no answers for, he would want to be a bit more hands on with this case.
Evander sips coffee, while he leans against a wall at the back of the room and watches his team from a distance. He observes them and their attitude towards what the Chief says. The newest member of his team looks the most engaged. He is eager and interested in what is being said and takes notes too by the look of it. The more senior and more experienced team members have heard and done it all before and no doubt will be running on auto pilot during some parts of the meeting.
Done with his briefing, the Chief directs Evander and his team to remain behind for further instruction. Everyone else is dismissed to carry on with their duties.
Chief Super Walter 'Walt' Ferguson looks every inch a man of the Force. A man of many years in standing. Dressed in full uniform, he stands almost as if to attention as people leave the room.
Evander watches the Chief intently. He is aware of some of the stories about the man, of course. He is curious as to how he got where he is, but not interested enough to ask, for fear of giving the wrong impression; that Evander may have designs on the Chief's job when he decides to retire.

The Chief is shorter than Evander, with a portly frame, his hair is as white as snow, short and spiky and he sports a matching white beard. He holds his hat gently under his arm.

"Close the doors please Kincaid and come up front." Walt says authoritatively.

Evander pushes himself from against the wall, closes the doors and joins his team. He stands behind them, while they remain seated.

Clearing his throat, Walt says. "Kincaid, for this case, given how dramatically, hopelessly and publicly wrong this has gone from the start, I want you to report directly to me and only to me on this one. Clear?"

"Yes Chief, understood."

"You will still report to your reporting officer Detective Super Jenkins for everything else except this, although you will keep him appraised on findings on this case, everything comes to me first. Am I absolutely clear on that?"

"Crystal clear." Evander confirms.

"Right then. Kincaid, you and one of your team will attend the press conference, fielding any questions from them. I'll leave you to choose who gets to join you. However, you need to keep a lid on your attitude with them."

Evander rolls his eyes to the ceiling, when he looks back at the Chief, his cheeks have turned a subtle shade of red and he reminds Evander of a not so jolly Father Christmas.

Almost spitting his words out, Walt fumes. "Don't you dare roll those eyes at me. That's exactly the attitude I'm talking about. You're really skating on thin ice with the press, especially after the last outing and the roasting you gave that young reporter. He was just inexperienced; everyone must start somewhere, even the likes of you. In case you've

forgotten, I'm your Superior and I can pull rank if I want to, and I also have the power to give this case to someone else if you don't watch your arse. Clear?"
"Crystal." Evander confirms, raising an eyebrow, resisting the urge to roll his eyes to the ceiling again.
"You know the rules around this one Kincaid, if we don't know the answer, make sure you don't tell them that we don't know - the usual line of while we are still conducting enquiries and the case is still under investigation, you can't comment any further blah, blah blah… you know the drill. While I understand your loathing of the media, we still need them onside. Don't make life any more difficult for us by ostracising them further with your contempt. Understand?"
"I do indeed." Evander says in a sing-song sarcastic tone, that Walt either ignores or misses.
"Tell them what we discussed during the meeting, that is alright to tell them, but the finer details, keep under your hat and no, that wasn't a pun. Now, any questions?"
"Not from me." Evander says.
Walter looks to the rest of his team and waits to see if anyone takes up the reigns. They remain silent.
"Right then." Walt begins as he takes his hat from under his arm and puts it on his head. "I've got things to do, so will leave you to get your team together. Don't keep the press waiting too much longer, you're already 15 minutes late."
Walt makes his way out the room and closes the door behind him.
Adam Eastwood stands and turns to face Evander, he asks.
"Are we ready Boss?"
Evander drains the last of his coffee and moves in front of Eastwood and the team, so his back is to them as he drops the

cup in a wastebasket, before asking. “Ready for what?”

“The Papanasty, Boss!” Eastwood proclaims with a note of boyish excitement in his voice as he moves in front of Evander to face him.

Isabella 'Izzy' Johnson protests as she chimes in. “Awww Boss, come on let me go.”

“You?” Eastwood snorts disapprovingly, while he looks over Evander’s shoulder at her.

“Yes me. There needs to be a feminine touch on this one.” Izzy reasons, as she pushes her long brunette hair over to one side of her face, which tumbles in wild unruly waves down her left side. Eventually, she rises from her seat and joins Eastwood at his side.

“You’re not the only female on this team you know.” Grace Murphy protests, as she rises from her seat and joins Eastwood and Johnson. Grace pushes the fringe of her short red hair behind her right ear, she chews on her lower left lip and tries to look vulnerable, so the Boss will want to protectively choose her.

“But Boss, Grace went to the last one and Izzy the one before. Got to be my turn now, right?” Eastwood counteracts.

In sync, Izzy and Grace say, “Got to be a girl!”

Eastwood pulls rank. “But I’m your senior detective Boss, should be me. Gotta be me.”

James Reeves, the newest team member is the only one not to voice his opinion on why it should be him. He is also the only one that now remains seated behind Evander.

James watches intently as the members of the team bicker with each other and talk over one another, over who should share the table with Evander.

Adam... “Got to be my turn, I outrank you all. The seat's so

hot for me right now…"
Izzy... "No way, not a guy, got to be a girl Boss and I am that girl! It makes sense…"
Grace... "With my green eyes and red hair, I can flirt and be a distraction to divert attention…"
Evander sighs and leaves them to it for all of 10 seconds before he whistles loudly to call a halt to their childish behaviour. They stop, look to Evander and eagerly wait for him to choose one of them. Instead, to their surprise, Evander turns around to face James, the rest of the team now to his back. James, who is still in his seat but leaning forward engrossed, watches quietly and attentively.
Evander points the index finger of his right hand to the newbie. "You're up." He confirms.
"Me?" James asks, his eyes wide with surprise, excitement and fear flicker across his fresh face all at once.
In unison, the rest of the team say questioningly. "Jimmy?"
James stands, fumbles with his note pad and pen and corrects the team. "It's James. Not Jay, not Jim nor Jimmy - but James. J.A.M.E.S. Please stop calling me everything *but* James!"
James is not your typical member of the force, he's small in stature and frame and his fresh face is almost baby faced. He looks more like a teenager rather than the 25 plus something he really is, yet his intelligence belies his tender age.
He looks back to Evander, smooths his short dark hair in place and asks. "Me, really?"
"You have done press conferences before, have you not?"
"Yes - two or three, but nothing like this. I mean nothing this big."
"Well, you have to learn sometime, may as well begin now. Just follow my lead, you'll be fine." Evander assures him, the

disarming, calm part of his gentle accent coming forth.
James gulps audibly, drops his pen, bends quickly to pick it up, then confirms. "Yes, Sir." James glances over Evander's shoulder at the team, their expressions disapprove of the 'Sir' title he has given in response.
"Boss. I mean Boss."
Thumbs up, the OK sign and smiles from the team confirm 'Boss' is the right word.
Evander walks past James and heads towards the doors at the back of the room. "Keep up" he calls to James.
Evander can't help but smile to himself as he walks ahead, all the team now to his back. Hearing his team all vying to be up front with him, it's good to know they want to be involved with the job and all aspects of it too. They may have been running on auto pilot while the Chief was talking, but they were still listening and now they are all eager to get in on the action at his side, although he kind of guesses that they just want to be there to see him devour the press. They all know he has a loathing for the press, and they know why, James however, is still relatively wet behind the ears with his press handling experience on Evander's team, and even more so of Evander's contempt for the media. However, he needs to break his duck at some point, and this is as good a starting place as any, even if he is in at the deep end on his first meet and greet with the Papanasty sharks and vultures.

~~~~~~

Seated at the Press conference, Evander introduces himself and James before he reads out the carefully prepared police statement. He then announces that he and Detective Inspector
~~~~~~

Reeves will field any questions there may be and the onslaught begins. Evander was ready to wrap things up after the first idiotic question, but he must play nice - at least as best he can - he hates that.
Evander allows James to answer a few questions and the kid does alright mostly. He's far too nice to them for his liking, but that will change the more he deals with them and learns what snakes they are and of course the more he is mentored by Evander and no doubt the rest of his team too.
Never trust the Papanasty. Ever.
After a series of questions and answers, Evander announces they can take one more question and then they must wrap things up.
A voice at the back of the room calls out. "Detective Chief Inspector Kincaid, Detective Inspector Reeves - Persephone Cruise for The Evening National News Standard. Can you tell us how many victims there have been? I mean if this is a serial killer as you say, well I don't think the number of victims has been made clear so far. If it has, I have no note of it and I'm sure I would have noted down something that important."
Murmuring fills the room from the rest of the press, all in agreement apparently.
James takes the lead and starts to answer. "Well, we are still investigating…"
'Good'. Evander thinks - James must remember what the Chief said, but instantly, intuitively he realises James is about to commit a mortal sin and be too forthcoming with the media hacks. Thinking quickly, Evander snatches his mobile up off the desk in front of him and pretends to read a text.
James continues with his reply "… this case and at this stage we…"

Evander gets to his feet and leans over to James, covers the microphone in front of him as he does so and whispers to him. "Don't say it, stop talking, now."

Having interrupted James, Evander announces. "Ladies and gentlemen of the press, we have to leave. I apologise, but duty calls." He picks up his notebook and pen off the table, pockets his phone. "But like my colleague was saying, we are still investigating this case and at this stage, while we are still conducting our enquiries, we can't comment any further right now. Thank you for coming, have a good day." He switches the microphones off on both consoles in front of him, which mutes himself and James.

Evander leans down to James and whispers to him. "Take that look off your face right now, get up and let's go. Don't speak to anyone."

Once safely out of the press room and they have walked down hallways where there are no eaves dropping reporters, Evander demands angrily. "What the hell were you thinking?" His accent broader now and more robust, an inflection to it that instills purpose, urgency while having an air of disbelief.

"You didn't get any text message and I was just answering the question." James protests.

"No, you were going to tell them that we don't know how many victims there are, because we have not collated all our facts and research yet. While you're at it you may as well have told them that we have actually missed the first four and there may even be more; oh, and by the way, even we don't have a fucking clue what's going on. That would be a bloody stupid thing to tell them, that we don't know exactly how many victims there are."

"How the hell did you know I was going to tell them that?"

"Because I know you were trying to build a rapport with them, and you can't."

"We have to give them something to go on, we have to be honest with them. Like the Chief said. We need to keep them on board."

"No, we must tell them only what we need them to know, so that we can gain assistance from them and, to make the public aware of the situation so they can try to keep themselves safe. We don't have to be and can't be buddies with them lot, ever. The press are not your friends, they're parasites. Persephone Cruise, who you were answering, it pains me to say it, but she is good at her job, clever bastard that one and smarter than all of the others combined. She'll wrap you up in knots if you give her an inch, I'm telling you. She's still not to be trusted you hear me?"

"Why do you hate them so much?" James asks innocently, unaware of Evander's past with the media.

"Why do you like them so much?" Evander shoots back.

"I asked first."

"You seriously did not just say that! Oh my God, don't be so fucking childish man."

"They're not bad people, they're just doing a job like you and I." James protests.

"Didn't you learn anything from going to the zoo?" Evander snaps.

At the end of their walk down the hallways, they stop at a bank of lifts, Evander pushes the 'Call' button, and they wait for a cab to arrive.

"What's the zoo got to do with the press?" James asks perplexed.

"There are signs everywhere at the zoo that tell you. *'Do not feed the animals'* and there you are ready to hand feed them, un-bloody-believable. School boy error. Don't do that again. No, you *won't* do that again, certainly not on my watch."

"But…" James begins before Evander stops him abruptly.

Evander speaks rapidly, his accent fluid, clean, crisp, sharp and clear. He explains in greater detail. "Look, the press doesn't care about me or you, or the police. They don't even care about the victim, not even the killer. What really matters is the tale. It's the story that matters and nothing else. All they are interested in is getting the next big news story, which is really their scoop for their paper, a headline so sensational it will help sell their tabloid rag and make them a name. The people they write about are just a jumble of letters that make up words to them. They lose sight of the fact that the jumble of letters, when jumbled together in the correct order form a name and they are real people. They lose sight far too easily that behind that name is a person. It doesn't matter whether that person is good or bad, what matters is that it is a real human being, with family, friends and others who love them, regardless of what they have or have not done, that is reported by them in the media. Have you any idea how it tears people's hearts out to see their loved ones being sensationalized as a headline and some of it born of lies, just to sell a paper and to make a name as a hard-hitting journo? They don't stop to think of anything else other than the story, it's all about getting juicy gossip, dirt, muck, scandalous photos, and intrusive stories with a headline that will get them click bait and hard copies sold, and screw anyone else it may affect along the way; even if it could and does ruin the lives of those people connected to that person. They'll do just

about *anything* to get the damn story - have you *any* idea?" Evander inquires finally taking a breath.
Evander pauses exasperated, places his hands on his hips, waits for James to reply, but wisely James keeps quiet. He must see something in Evander's face or maybe hear something in his tone that he knows he is best to remain silent. Evander continues and tells James. "You see today you are the paper selling headline but, tomorrow you are yesterday's news and will be getting thrown in the recycle bin, which those media hacks won't give a shit about. For them it's impersonal, they'll move on to the next big thing, but for that person in their story, the things written about them stick like glitter to glue and like glue to paper and everywhere they go, they have people judging them without knowing a single thing about them, just because they read it in the paper, so it must be true. Also, glitter gets everywhere, and you can't get rid of it. They pretend they are sympathetic and how they just want to report the facts, but that's all bullshit. You give them one paragraph and they'll dissect it like a piece of meat, looking for the tastiest part of it and that one line will be the headline, it's this they will twist to put a spin on the story. It is just a story to them, another bloody sensationalist headline just to sell their crappy papers, as they ruin another life in the process. Twisting quotes to suit their agenda and editing paragraphs down to a single sentence that doesn't tell the whole story. I have no idea how the celebrities deal with them in their face all the time, printing lies and misquoting them." Evander finally stops his ranting when the lift arrives with a long, deep dinggggg.
The doors slide open slowly.
James is unsure what to do, so he waits for Evander to make a

move.
Evander points to the open cab of the lift and tells James. "Go on in, I'll be up shortly. I need coffee. I'll get some for the team, maybe some muffins too, with all the file reviews we'll need a sugar rush at some point, but just remember the press are not your friends and not to be trusted. You hear me?"
James nods his head but says nothing.
"Good." Evander confirms.
Evander is annoyed with James, but more so with himself for not giving the kid a heads-up first on the manipulative media. He'll make sure he is alright later, though he guesses James won't make the same media mistake again.
The doors slide shut. The lift whines and whirs as pulley cables kick in and starts its ascent. Frustration gets the better of Evander, he stretches his arms out and splays his fingers in frustration, then he curses out loud. "Fuck!"

CHAPTER FIVE

With coffee and muffins distributed to the team to help with their search for more victims. He has files to peruse too so his team are not alone in reviewing cases, he sighs audibly as he is aware it's going to be a long day. He heads into his office, places his coffee and muffin on his desk, removes his jacket, hangs it on the back of his chair, pulling the chair out, he sits down.

He takes a drink of coffee and returns his cup to a coaster on the desk.

He logs into his computer and accesses the HOLMES database. He unlocks his drawers and takes out the notepad he had written down case numbers on that Adam had received from the I.C. team. Noting the file number, he picks up the first file he had previously dismissed and begins revising.

Halfway through, Evander stops reading. He picks his coffee up and takes a drink, returns it to the desk. He picks up the lemon and poppy seed muffin, peels the paper back from it and takes a bite, just as he looks through the window of the office to see James, rising quickly from his seat and grabbing his notepad as he moves.

He turns to walk away from his desk, forgets something, runs back to the printer behind his desk and grabs something off it. He then walks hurriedly towards Evander's office. He's got something, Evander knows it. In anticipation of James' arrival, he puts the muffin down and brushes crumbs from his hands into the bin beside him.

James enters Evander's office "Boss, look at this." He says, handing Evander a list of documented evidence, which

catalogues the victim's personal belongings.
"What am I looking for?" Evander inquires through a mouthful of muffin he is still chewing on.
"It says that the victim was wearing a badge with three lions on it."
Evander finds the item listed and points to it. "Right, I see it. So?"
James passes two crime scene photos to Evander. "Look at the badge, do they look like three lions to you?" James asks.
Evander looks at the first photo and then the second, which is in close up on said badge. "No, I don't think they are." Evander responds.
"They're dragons, right? Well, I think they are. Boss?"
Evander looks closely at the photo. He can't say under this lighting what is on the badge. He gets up from his chair, walks to the window to get natural day light and looks at both photos again, paying particular attention to the close up.
He agrees with James. Three dragons - the third victim.
Evander turns back to face James, he says. "I agree. This is great work James, well spotted."
A smile spreads across James' face. He looks like a little boy on Christmas day, who gets the best present ever. He fiddles with the notepad in his hand, unsure what his next move should be.
"What is he guilty of?" Evander asks softly, relieving him of the worry.
"You're not going to believe this." James begins, referring to notes in his notepad. "His name is Clive Argyll, a media hack who was renowned for his hard-hitting interviewing techniques. He got in trouble on more than one occasion with the crap he was writing.

"A few stories got out of hand, turned out that he made them up. His publication printed his lies and two cases - spread over nine years - caused the death of two of his targets, who both turned out to be innocent of the accusations the journo had printed. The two dead committed suicide."
Evander interrupts him. "You see, I told you - parasites the lot of them."
"Well, the last one he wrote about; the guy was hounded so much by people who read the article, that he had to leave the country for a while."
"I can't say that surprises me. I take it he returned to England?"
"Eventually he did, yes."
"What happened with the story?"
"Well, Argyll ended up withdrawing everything that had been said in connection to one of the victims of his lies, but it was too late, the guy was found dead. Argyll got sacked by his newspaper and he never wrote again after that. But at the scene of the first suicide, they found a note where he named Argyll as the reason for ending his life. The police investigation into the death, lead to the discovery of the other guy who also committed suicide as a result of Argyll's lies."
"So, he had gotten away with it all?"
"No, not exactly, one of the families decided to press charges against Argyll, citing the suicide note as evidence of Argyll contributing to his death, they wanted him tried for murder."
"Jesus H Christ!" Evander exclaims.
"I know, but the courts didn't want to know, said legally there was nothing to support it, as Argyll didn't put a gun to his head and pull the trigger, so he wasn't legally accountable or responsible. So, the family decided to sue him instead,

wrongful death - that went to trial, but he got off with that too. It was during the police investigation however, that research dug up the lies around Argyll and his stories."
"Now you see why at the press conference, that we don't give the media too much information and we certainly don't tell them what we don't know." Evander waves the photo in his hand and continues. "That's why we make sure we get all our facts together before we tell them anything. We were not being evasive, I cut you off because we didn't have all our evidence, didn't have all the information and currently don't know for sure how many victims there are. To tell them that we don't know exactly, would have made us look incompetent and we're not. We just needed more time to gather our evidence and conduct investigations. But this is great work, great. Well done James."
"Thanks Boss and erm, I won't make that mistake again, with the press I mean."
"I know James. Look, I'm sorry if I came across as a bit of a prick and I'm sorry if you were angry with me, but I know how they operate. You have to trust me when I tell you to not get too close to them, they just want to use you as a 'source' and that's how they'll quote anything you give them in their reports. They'll quote you and you will know it's come from you, but they won't credit you and if you question why, they'll say they were 'protecting' you, which is bollocks. You see what I'm saying?" Evander asks sighing.
"It's okay Boss, I understand now. Eastwood told me erm, he explained about well, I mean, you know, he told me what happened with Jasmine, what they said about her. Why you dislike them so much..." James stops himself from saying anything more. He looks down at the floor.

Evander thinks he catches a flicker of understanding and regret evident in James' face, or is it pity. He hopes it's not the latter. The look is gone as soon as it appeared.
Evander pats James on his back as he walks past him out of his office.
He calls out to everyone. "We're now looking for two more victims. Two more thanks to James, get to it people."
Evander goes back into the room he hands James the photo.
"I'm gonna get back to it Boss." James says as he slots the photo into his notebook and heads towards his desk.
Evander watches him as he interacts with the team. He gets high fives, low fives and slaps on the back from everyone.
Right choice taking him on board, 'he'll be a great addition to the team'. Evander thinks.

CHAPTER SIX

As he stands over the body of the murdered man, Detective Chief Inspector Evander Kincaid squints as he tries to focus on the victim's face from his standing position, he bends slightly to take a closer look. He sighs, stands up straight, looks quickly around the room, then back to the body.

"Are forensics done?" He asks in his distinctive, melodious baritone.

"All clear, you can examine, Sir." A reply comes from whom, he's not sure.

Evander squats down to inspect the smartly dressed body. On the lapel of the victim's jacket, is a badge adorned with six dragons - the sixth victim. So, this is definitely the work of the serial killer and he's repeating himself tut, tut.

Evander looks closely at the victim's head. There are deep ligature marks around his neck from multiple strands of something that had been wrapped around his neck as he was strangled. Though it is not the ligature marks that interest Evander, he notices something much more interesting on the victim's face, on his nose in fact.

On closer inspection he confirms the marks he thought he saw from his lofty six-foot standing position looking down at the body.

With gloved hand, he pats the pockets on the jacket of the victim and then, the trousers. Nothing there. How curious. He has a thought and pats the breast pocket, also empty.

He stands and places his hands on his slender hips. He looks around the room, his eyes scan a coffee table, end tables, mantle piece, bookshelves, display case.

"Where are his glasses?" Evander eventually inquires.

Nobody replies to him. He turns away from the victim and walks out of the room into a hallway to look for someone to ask questions. He looks to his left, then up some stairs directly in front of him. As he turns to his right, he sees Evans, one of the assistant SOCO's, who watches him curiously from the front gate of the pathway to the house. He must be about to leave as he isn't in full SOCO get up any longer.

Evans has his hands held in front of him and it looks like he plays with something string like held between his fingers, but if he is, it is an imaginary string, as there is nothing in his hands but his own fingers. He must be in his early 40s but tries to look like a teenager. He is a short, squirrely looking type of man, with shocking blonde hair with equally shocking streaks of varied colours from black to brunette, to green to blue, to red to yellow, to orange, dotted through the spiky parts of his short hair. The spiky peaks of colour look like cones on his head. His unbuttoned lab coat reveals an anime T-Shirt.

Evander imagines he got called squirrely type names at school. Evander points an index finger towards him, he wiggles it for him to come over to him and Evans follows his command but, stops about halfway up the pathway - obviously conscious of contaminating the scene without protection from his SOCO suit.

He asks Evander, "Sorry, can't come any closer, can you hear me?"

"Yes, I can. Where are his glasses?" Evander asks as he points to the room he has just left, indicating he is referring to the victim.

"He wasn't wearing any." Evans replies.

"Yes, I know I can see that - so, where are they?"

"We don't know that he wore glasses, so why would we look for them?"

Evander rolls his eyes in exasperation and tries not to be curt in his reply but fails. "Any idiot could see he wore glasses just by looking at his nose. You're a forensic scientist, are you not? You did examine the body as part of your job, yes?"

"His nose?" Evans asks. Perplexed, he ignores the condescending tone in Evander's question.

"Did you examine him?"

"Briefly, just to assist but Jackson took charge on this one, because it's another dragon victim. What about his nose?" Evans asks.

"Is Jackson still here?"

"In the van - writing notes, I think. What about his damn nose?" Evans asks puzzled, agitation marks his voice at what should be obvious, yet eludes him completely.

Evander ignores the question and walks away. He starts taking his gloves off as he is leaving the scene of the crime.

In the back of the van, Jackson is indeed writing notes for her report, she is startled as the door opens abruptly.

Before she can say anything, Evander speaks "The victim's glasses, where are they?" He asks as he begins to disrobe out of the SOCO suit.

"What glasses?"

Evander tuts. "Not you as well! His glasses he wears to see, to read, to write, to pretty much live a life with vision - where are they?"

"We didn't find any. No indication that the Vic wore them."

"Well, he did - it's evident from his nose."

"What?"

"The bridge of his nose, on both sides there are little

indentations from years of wearing glasses. Has the house been searched?"

Jackson opens her mouth to reply, but Evander raises a hand to stop her and speaks quickly before she can respond. "No, of course you didn't because you didn't know he wore glasses, even though it's obvious he did. We need to search the house. If the victim doesn't have the glasses and they are not in the house, where are they? Did you look for them? No, of course you didn't look, because you missed what was right under *your* nose, but glaringly obvious from *his*." Evander states, grit in his tone.

"Evander, what are you talking about?" Jackson asks baffled as she watches him step out of SOCO all in one get up, to reveal a steel silver/grey suit that when it catches the light shimmers like liquid silver and accentuates his complexion.

Evander replies rapidly, his words seem to run into one another. "If you are of a certain age and wear glasses you always have them with you. Sometimes, people of a certain age have a spare pair in case they can't remember where they left the main ones. What if you leave them at a relatives or a friends, or the Doctors or on the bus, or they break, or something just happens to them, there are usually always spare glasses in the house of a spectacle wearer of a certain age, always, even if they're not prescription glasses. If they are missing too, that means he took them, but why? The killer has never taken a trophy before so why now? Unless we overlooked the missing items at the other crime scenes. We haven't even identified them all yet, weeks after we found Mr Corvus and we are still knee-deep wading through all those unsolved cases, still looking for another link in the chain. But if no trophy was taken from the others, what was different about this one? Why now? Why glasses? What was so special about this one?"

"You really got all that from his nose?" Jackson replies astounded.

"Yes, his nose. Now, do we know who he is? Has our victim got a name?" Evander asks as he rolls the SOCO suit up and places it in the disposal box inside the van.

"House is registered to Harry Shaw originally from Halifax. He moved to London after meeting his wife on holiday. His wife was recently deceased, and he wasn't going out much, became a bit of recluse according to the neighbours, so it wasn't unusual not to see him for days on end. He was sick too and only had six months…"

"Oh my God, I don't believe it." Evander interrupts.

"What?"

"The name of the victim - and the fact the killer took his glasses. Do you see it?"

"See what, exactly?"

"Connection!"

"Connection to his name from glasses - no. What should I see?"

"Shaw is the surname of Percy Shaw who came from Halifax."

"What's that got to do with the victim's glasses? Percy who?"

"Our victim is Harry Shaw from Halifax, and his glasses were taken as a message, not a trophy, that's important. Percy Shaw came from Halifax. He invented cat's eyes because people couldn't see the road in the - OH! Maybe that's why he took his glasses; because he believes we can't see him, because he's surrounded by fog, and we can't find him. The bastard thinks we are blind to him and his identity, he thinks he is invincible, undetectable, immune, safe - at least from capture and discovery, but not from threat like, illness for example, but in terms of us and our man hunt, he thinks he has power over us."

"Really? You got all that from missing glasses. Wow!" Violet responds.

"The killer took the glasses possibly as his way of saying we are blind to him. Or, in a symbolic capacity."

"There could be another meaning to taking the glasses."

"Really? Like what?" Evander asks.

"Well, I don't know exactly, but I'm not the Detective am I? I don't think it is to taunt the police. Trophies are not his thing."

Evander mulls over the idea for a few moments and decides if - no when - they capture this guy, it will be one thing he will be sure to ask him and he will break him.

"What are you thinking about?" Jackson asks.

"That he's underestimated something."

"He did? What's that?"

"He forgot about something. Something he has not counted on and that's his first mistake."

"What?"

"He hadn't expected anyone to get inside his head."

"Oh, and you have?" Jackson asks, incredulous.

"I know him better now and I'm beginning to learn how he thinks and when we find him, I'll be the one to break him down and get a confession, as I have a feeling that isn't going to come easy."

"You're confident of that just because you think you understand the hidden meaning behind missing glasses?"

"Ask the team to search for those glasses. Although, I'm sure you won't find any." Evander says as he turns away, leaving the van door open.

"What didn't he count on?" Jackson calls out to him.

"Me."

CHAPTER SEVEN

Adam Eastwood sits with his feet up on the end of his desk, his chair tipped back slightly. Eight weeks after the crucifixion of Freddie Corvus and the team continue to look through unsolved files. 1,000 plus files have been reviewed as they hunt for victims one and two on the dragons of justice killer's hit list. The I.C. team have bumped the most promising of those unsolved cases up to Evander's team for closer inspection.

Adam has been studying the history of London and the transatlantic crossing of the Mayflower to America and in the process has been dealing with hard copy source material. It's given him a yearning for the feel of proper files in his hand. With the case he is currently reviewing, he has gone old school and actually printed some items out, including the autopsy report, crime scene report and numerous photos. He's collated them in a file and now has that file on his lap. He turns the pages of it with his right hand, while in his left, he holds the coffee cup that the Boss brought in, one for everyone on the team; a daily custom he has maintained even when it was just the two of them who formed the team.

Adam takes sips of coffee as he looks through the file on his lap. An individual, but generous cherry Bakewell tart in a silver foil tray sits on his desk.

Having read the autopsy report, coincidentally written by Violet Jackson, he moves on to the crime scene report. Firstly, a synopsis, followed by photos and then a more detailed read of the crime scene.

The victim - a Catholic priest named Father Jameson - was found in his quarters, poisoned. There were plenty of suspects brought in for questioning, but all had solid alibis that were easily corroborated with witness testimony, or work commitments, which confirmed whereabouts.

One firm still employed a 'clocking in' punch-card and stamp machine print system, the more technical firms employed an electronic entry key system whereby codes were used to gain entry with numbers that only staff knew. Some had key fobs or cards of some description, which would have been swiped to get into the buildings and access to their respective offices. All of these were backed by the respective company management and work colleagues, who confirmed that the potential suspects, were in fact at their various workstations, or on the factory floors going about their daily duties.

For those with no entry system, the IT departments were brought in to provide evidence of the employees logs on their company systems. For those people who surfed the internet looking at things they shouldn't on company devices, or doing things they shouldn't with company systems, this may have been a bad day for them, for everything is documented - every action taken, every website visited, and every system accessed, is all catalogued by the IT departments.

Anyone stupid enough to think they won't get caught will inevitably be exposed by the IT department. Those that think they can commit company treason (in whatever capacity) should not be stupid enough to think they can get away with it, or cover their tracks, because Big Brother always watches.

In cases where none of those sources were viable, C.C.T.V. footage was used and exonerated the most likely suspect of the murder. He claimed he was at the cinema, but went alone, had no ticket stub and paid in cash, so no credit card receipt; but C.C.T.V. footage of him getting off a train, enabled them to

track him.
An A.T.M. camera across the street from the cinema caught him going in and exiting three hours later. He had also been clearly identified buying a large coke and popcorn at the snack's kiosk, all of which covered the time of death. He couldn't be in two places at once and they were also 20 miles apart, so definitely not him.
The police were at a loss to find the culprit, so the case remained unsolved and open.
Father Jameson had been revealed as a child molester, having his pick of children from the choir and the congregation, as well as the adjoining school connected to the church.
His acts ranged from the improper touch of fingers brushing against flesh, while lingering a bit too long, to the more intimate touching of children, too innocent to know it was wrong, right down to the lecherous acts that Adam decides to skip reading about. The man was evil in a dress, professing God's love and abusing it in the worst ways imaginable.
Adam's stomach flips at the mere thought alone of what Father Jameson may have done to those children. Adam has no children of his own yet - maybe someday, just need the right girl - but he has plenty of nieces and nephews and is Godfather to a few of them, so the picture is clear enough for him to imagine how a parent would feel knowing their child was abused in a place of worship, where they should be protected, always.
Adam drinks the last of his coffee, not because he needs the caffeine rush, but to try to take away the nasty taste in his mouth that this case provides.
Cup drained, without looking what he is doing, he extends his arm and drops the cup in the waste basket at the side of his

desk. He glances at the cherry Bakewell tart and decides not to attempt eating that yet, for likelihood that this case may give cause to the cake making a rather unceremonious return if consumed now.

He cannot help but feel that in this case, justice was served to this reprobate and part of him wants to shake the hand of the killer for getting this low life off the street, out of the church and away from innocent children; though he feels poison was too quick and merciful a retribution for his crimes.

Adam is sure Father Jameson would have had more than his fair share of justice, that would have been metered out from the inmates he would have ended up living with, had he been tried for his crimes and of course convicted, because he confessed to his sins. He crumbled like a wall with the first accusation from a child brave enough to tell their parents what had happened and then came the flood.

Adam reviews crime scene photos, he had done enough reading, which left that terrible taste still lingering at the back of his throat. Adam looks at the photos of the quarters that belonged to Father Jameson and he studies the room he was found in. The room, while neat and tidy is minimal in furnishings; a two-seat sofa although it is oversized and could easily accommodate three people, a table with a portable radio on top, two chairs on opposite sides of the table, a writing desk and a solitary chair. There is also a crucifix, correctly positioned on an East facing wall.

On the table is an almost empty bottle of wine, a cork that is covered in a broken old-fashioned wax seal, which sits in a saucer.

The wax seal peaks Adam's interest. He notes how unusual it is now to have an old-fashioned method that secures the cork.

Most manufacturers opt for cheaper screw top bottles, but in cases where wax is used, there is usually only a dollop of it, which covers just the exposed cork at the top of the bottle. Rarely now do you see the whole neck of the wine bottle covered in wax, obscuring the cork completely from view through the bottle. Adam wonders if it is an expensive bottle of wine, given the fanciful seal of the cork with today's modern methods.

He hunts through photos and looks specifically for pictures of the bottle. He finds a series of photos and takes his time to look at them in more detail. The cogs in his mind whirl and formulate a few ideas about the bottle of wine and why the wax seal was so important. He looks at pictures of the bottle, he looks at the label, a 2001 merlot from the central valley in Chile - okay, so not an old bottle as he initially thought, so that explodes that theory about the bottle being so old it had become poisonous.

Adam quickly runs a Google search and finds that wine will not turn to poison due to the alcohol content being a preservative, so no bacteria can develop in an old bottle. Sure, it may taste like vinegar, but it won't kill you.

Back to the drawing board then on theories.

Rare! Ah, maybe it is a rare bottle. Adam notes the brand and the year, then runs another Google search with negative results for this being a rare bottle. This debunks that theory too. Crap!

Adam clicks on 'images' from the search results for the bottle of wine.

He is surprised to find some results, but more so, because the bottles do not have the wax seal on any of them. The cork is visible and exposed and there is not a hint of wax in sight.

Now Adam knows how the poison was administered to the wine; injected through the cork and the offending puncture hole in the cork was cleverly disguised with the wax seal.
No receipt was found for the purchase, so this was what - an impulse purchase, paid for with cash and Father Jameson got the wrong bottle? Unlikely.
A gift. Ah yes, a gift, that is more likely and makes more sense, but who would still be friends with Father Jameson knowing what he had done and that he would be facing criminal charges? He wouldn't have had very many friends once his secret was revealed, so possibly a family member, a close friend, or a member of the church, or the congregation. Or a vengeful parent of an abused child offering forgiveness and a bottle of wine. Possibly all of them, although, according to the notes, all persons of interest had been exonerated of the crime.
He looks through more crime scene photos, there is a close-up on the table contents. The saucer with cork and wax, the almost empty bottle of wine, the glass and underneath that a note.
Adam finds a photo of the note, which has a wine stain in the top right-hand corner in the shape of a semi-circle that covers the last word. This indicates that, at some point, the glass was placed on the note, possibly as more wine was poured, and traces of the wine must have caught the rim of the glass and ran down the outside of it to the base. The stained note reads:
'For he is a minister of God for you unto good. But if you do what is evil, be afraid. For it is not without reason that he carries a sword. For he is a minister of God; an avenger to execute wrath upon whoever does evil.'
Some type of note that is and it is no suicide note that's for

sure. Another Google search reveals this to be a passage from the Bible, specifically from Romans 13:4. What if this is a suicide note? Adam ponders, but then dismisses it, because it is not addressed to anyone and not signed by Father Jameson either. As far as 'goodbye' notes go, this is not of the same ilk. So, what then? Observation? Possibly. Adam reads the note again. No, this is more of a promise than an observation, but, by whom?

Adam thumbs through more crime scene photos. He notes that the glass is not actually a glass, but more of a goblet that Father Jameson drank the wine from. The glass, or goblet is elaborate in decoration and was assumed by the officer who catalogued it, to be part of the Church and listed as a chalice. Fine - glass, goblet, chalice - whatever. He looks at the chalice. Adam knows from his time in Catholic Church that this is not something the Catholic Church would use as part of their official ceremonial cups. It is more akin to Wiccan practice rather than Catholic.

The chalice is half metal and half glass. At its base is the tail of a beast that coils around and slithers up the length of the stem of the glass and splits in two at the base of the bowl and emerges on the sides of the glass as two dragons.

Shit.

Dragons.

Adam sits upright in his chair now. He rummages through photos and looks specifically for pictures that include the glass, or chalice as it is listed. He takes the most useful of the 10 shots that include it, he stands up and places them on his desk, side by side. He eliminates three pictures, because they do not give enough detail. He reviews the remaining photos, removes another one and reviews them again. He moves the remaining six photos closer together.

It was thought that the wine was poisoned by Father Jameson himself and was his way of committing suicide, but that theory was easily dispelled. No suicide note was found, and it is doubtful that any Catholic man, certainly a practicing clergy man, would commit suicide and risk eternal damnation in hell, or is it purgatory?

Adam always struggled with those concepts but settles on hell. This Catholic man, however, would want to be cleansed for his crimes against humanity. His soul would crave redemption, forgiveness for his sins and salvation at the eleventh hour, before he went to meet his maker. So maybe purgatory may have been a choice Father Jameson would want after all. For here, he would get to purge his soul of his earthly sins, before his purified soul could ascend to God, ready for acceptance into eternal life.

Assuming God would allow a soul to be purged of something so heinous as the crimes he was guilty of, but given that he was murdered, he may catch God on a generous day, and He may even reduce the time he spent in purgatory.

According to Violet Jackson's autopsy report, the poison was cyanide, made from ground peach, apricot and cherry stones. Exact quantities of each are not precise in Jackson's report, but there was enough of all of them to gradually asphyxiate the victim upon ingestion of the wine. She likens the initial effect of the wine being akin to the natural feelings of intoxication that alcohol produces and that it would have been apparent that something was off when it was too late.

Back to the glass. Chalice. Adam looks at the detail on the dragons. They face opposite to each other on the glass, which gives the illusion that one chases after the other. Upon closer inspection, Adam notes that each dragon holds a shield in the left claw. He looks at the detail and it is unmistakably the shield of the city of London, with the distinct Saint George's cross and the inset sword in the top left corner of the shield. Adam is 99 percent certain he has found victim number two. He gathers the file content together and heads into Evander's office to conclude the discovery.

Later, Adam will devour that cherry Bakewell tart on his desk.

CHAPTER EIGHT

Unable to sleep, Evander drives into H.Q. early. It has taken them just over ten weeks to find the victims prior to Freddie Corvus and number one is still missing in action. They still have a lot of work and there are still some unsolved files to review as the search for the first victim continues.

Evander arrives at his section of office space and is surprised to find Adam sat at his desk, he has his hand under his chin as he reads something on the computer screen before him, he has a cup in his other hand, poised ready to take a drink. Evander heads over to him.

"Is there any more coffee?" Evander asks.

Adam flinches and replies. "Jesus H, Boss! Don't do that." He gains his composure and sits up in his chair, then he continues. "Yes, I brewed a pot as the coffee shop wasn't open when I arrived."

"How long have you been here?"

"About an hour, maybe two, give or take."

"Have you made any more progress with the files?"

"Not yet. What are you doing here anyway?"

"I might ask you the same question." Evander replies.

"I'm working! You know I do most of my best work when the office is my own. So, I'm not the only one who couldn't sleep huh?" Adam says knowingly.

"Yup." Evander replies, trying not to give anything away and apparently failing.

"Another nightmare, or you really just couldn't sleep, Boss?" Adam inquires.

"No flies on you right!" Evander notes sardonically.

"Did you remember any of it this time?" Adam asks, curiosity

marking his voice.
"No, but then I never do, I'm not sure I'm meant to remember them either." Evander ponders more than answers, with a tone that demands sympathy but not pity, in his soothing accent.
"Have you noticed you tend to have the nightmares when cases get under your skin?"
"Yeah, I had joined the dots." Evander changes the subject. "I think we have more than enough now to finish the set up in the major incident room and have something with substance. I need to map the cases."
"I was wondering when that would happen. We haven't really been able to do that before, especially with the missing victims, the picture has been too dotty, but after my second victim finding, now we're down to one, I think it will work. It will work now, right Boss?" Adam asks.
"I think so. Going to give it a try, anyway. See what the string web of colours looks like!" "Need any help with that Boss?" Adam asks, hopefully.
"Maybe but I'll work on my own initially. I need you to carry on with the search." Evander says, as he gestures to the file on Adam's computer screen. He continues. "Also, to guide and help the team, when they get in here, to keep digging looking for the first victim."
"No problem, Boss. I'll keep them busy, and we haven't got many files left from the I.C. team, so we should be done with them today. Another reason I'm in early, I want them done and dusted and out of our hair."
"We all do I know. I'm going to get coffee. I'll be in M.I.R. if you need me."

~~~~~~

Evander collects a folder from his office. It lists them from the second to most recent murders.

There are six victims, though they are still yet to identify the first victim, as they still have no details on that. While they can't really include it, they also know it exists somewhere, so technically there is a tally of six, but actual accounted for are five. The figures become confusing at times.

In the staff kitchen, Evander opens a cupboard and retrieves his cup, which is adorned with The Who bullseye target logo on both sides, a gift from the team - Evander grabs a teaspoon, puts sugar in first and then fills the cup with some coffee. The steaming brew has a rich aroma, he breathes it in, as he stirs the hot liquid to help dissolve the sugar. He places the used teaspoon in the dishwasher.

Cup in hand, he wanders down the nearest suite of rooms in the corridor adjacent to his office. He walks along the empty hallway in silence, there is no noise except the sound of his own feet on the carpeted floor. H.Q. can be an eerie place in the early hours of the morning when devoid of the hustle and bustle of people. Amazing the difference that the presence of people can make to the atmosphere of a building.

At room 17/6 - denoting the room number and the floor number – he opens the door to what is the investigation's Major Investigation Room - M.I.R. He leaves his coffee cup on a coaster on the table, places the file on the table, opening it to begin work.

~~~~~~

From a supply desk in the room, Evander takes out drawing pins and balls of string of various colours, puts them on top of the draw to leave the table free. He opens the file and spreads photos across the large desk.
A photo representation of the killer - which is currently just a black question mark on a white image of a featureless person - already adorns the large cork board on the wall.
Evander takes his jacket off and hangs it on the back of a chair, unbuttons the sleeves on his shirt and rolls them up, ready to work.
From the file, he selects a one-page synopsis relating to each victim, he works clockwise and places each of them in front of a chair around the table, leaving the head of the table near the window free, as that will belong to victim number one - when they find them.
Starting with victim number two, Father Jameson - Evander pins a 5X7 photo of the victim to the cork board at the two o'clock position, indicating victim number two. He repeats the process for victims three, four, five and six. Then, using one colour string - red - he links them all to what he knows is a definite connection - each victim to the killer.
Any new discoveries that forge connections can then be added later with different string colours, but first he needs to dig deeper into the case files they already have.
While Evander is sure that the investigating officers did their work correctly first time around, he likes to reach his own conclusions, rather than rely on someone else's interpretation to tell him how to view a case. One at a time, starting with victim number two, he spreads the documents out in their respective order, gleaning information from the synopsis sheets to bullet point and annotate on paper, which he will

then attach to the board beside the photo of the victim. He documents brief information like the victims name, age, their home, where they found the body and COD.

Evander spends most of the day in M.I.R. as he reads notes, periodically returning to his office to check on the team, and access HOLMES and read through forensic reports. In the M.I.R. he moves from chair to floor, the edge of the table to the notice board, to which he pins things occasionally, but finds he still has no use for any of the different coloured string to try to form more connections.

He must have used every part of the room over the last four or five hours going over SOCO photos, autopsy reports, victim backgrounds, work and private lives, friends, mutual acquaintances, places of interest that the victims may have frequented; hobbies, internet history, social media activity, phone calls, mobile phone contacts, where they went shopping, if they owned a car, where they got it serviced, where they filled up with petrol, if they shared a train or bus route, other interests like movies, music, theatre, sport, politics, religion - literally anything that could join the dots. The lives of these people have all had a deep delve with no stone left unturned. In terms of connection, all draw a blank. Evander has photos of all the victims apart from number one who remains anonymous and a mystery. He cannot find anything to connect the victims together personally, but collectively, the only connection between them all is marked on the cork board on the wall and all strings are red and all lead to the question marked killer.

Evander stands before the board and looks at the photo of the question mark. He folds his arms and sighs heavily. All five strings lead to that one thing they have in common, this is where the connections begin and end: The Killer. Just the Killer.

He stares at the board and tries to look for something, anything, just a tiny morsel that he may have missed. Apart from Harry Shaw - victim number six, because they are still investigating his background, but so far found nothing on him - all the victims are guilty of a crime, so they are all accountable in some way of something the killer thinks they went unpunished for, until they met their demise at his hand. The killer, in his mind believes he meters out justice for the innocent by taking the lives of these people. There is no M.O. and the styles of the killings are all different. There is no consistency, except for meticulous attention to detail. The only thing that identifies the same killer is the dragons he leaves as his calling card.

This serial killer is organized and methodical, yet at the same time inconsistent, but only in respects of the victim that he chooses. They don't all look similar, they're not all blue eyed, or dark haired, or tall, or small, or thin, or overweight. Their only connection to the killer is the crimes they are guilty of getting away with.

How the killer knows this and even before the police in some cases, is a mystery. What did number six do? Something to ponder for sure.

While he looks at case number five, Evander is reminded of the killer's anger when the police miss something that he had gone to a lot of trouble presenting to them in the first cases. His calling card was missed on the first four murders and they were not linked, so, maybe due to the subtle use of the dragons, especially in the case of the fourth victim, the dragons would not have even been noted as part of the crime

committed, because the pillars housing the dragons were part of the fixtures and fittings of the crime scene, not an addition to it like on the chalice for the second victim, or the badge for the third with three dragons wrongly identified as lions.
The dragons on the fifth victim however, two were carved into his chest and he was put on display on the most famous bridge in London, the most famous bridge in England, maybe even Great Britain, no - the world and the killer made sure he was seen and heard.
He was meticulous about the carving and didn't want the victim to move during any incision, which is why he medically paralyzed him. He wanted him conscious and alert at the time to see what was happening yet, be helpless to stop it. He is cruel, calculating, lacking in empathy and yet capable of compassion only when it suits him. He demands attention from the police force and boy how he got it with number five.
In defense of the police investigations into the previous murders, the clues he left where obviously there, but they were so subtle that they went undetected and therefore not linked till now. Given the subtlety of the calling card for victim two, three and four, he would hope that they could be forgiven for overlooking the connection.
The killer is a contradiction: angel and devil, saint yet sinner. He's not a schizophrenic but driven by something powerful to unleash his psychopathic tendencies, both in his detachment from human emotion and in his apparent need of appreciation for his work, hence the world stage he presented Freddie Corvus on, with Tower Bridge.
You can't get much bigger than that.
While he reviews the evidence, Evander gets the feeling that the killer believes to a degree, not so much that he is a

vigilante, but more of a fixer of wrongs. A messenger for sure given that victim two had a note quoting Romans 13:4 about being a messenger of God and number five was displayed in a state of crucifixion.

Evander is sure he would be devoutly religious in some way. Or perhaps at least he was - maybe he has lost his way with religion and is trying to regain that faith. Or perhaps he's driven by it and believes he actually *is* God's avenger.

He leans back against a wall now and puts one leg up and rests his foot against it. He unfolds his arms and places his hands in his trouser pockets. He looks at the web spread out before him that makes no sense whatsoever.

Number six is a mystery. Here is where the pattern falls apart, not that there was a pattern of any distinction, but it is the only pattern identified that these victims have in common. They are guilty of a crime. With number six however, they can't find anything that this man has done wrong, even after digging around - and they are still digging, but they have found nothing, yet there must be something he has done, something he is guilty of, but what? What? WHAT? Why did he take the victim's glasses? He can't see that anything that was missing, or trophies taken from the previous victims, just this one. Is it even a trophy? That seems doubtful. Unlikely that our serial killer is driven by sentiment.

It's so out of character, given the consistency of the other murders, that he never keeps anything, so that means… this… is… a…. message? Perhaps.

It means something, but it is not a trophy.

Maybe his message means that he thinks the police are blind to him and they can't see him, yet he can't shake the feeling that there is another reason the glasses were taken, which

Evander hasn't figured out yet, but it is there, gnawing away at him, almost as if it should be obvious to him, but it continues to elude and mock him.

He hates to admit it, but the killer is currently right. The police can't see him and can't find anything to proportion this man's death to, other than savagery and because he could get away with it. The killer is smart; and you must respect that. If you don't respect it then you have zero chance of trying to figure him out and capturing him.

Adam arrives with coffee. "Thought you could use this, Boss." He looks for a place on the table to leave the mug, but he hands it to Evander instead.

Evander removes his right hand from his pocket and takes the cup off Adam. He drinks some coffee. "MMMM, That's good, thanks Adam. Maybe this will help." He waves his hand to the display set before them. "Sort this out, as it makes no sense on its own. But together, the only thing to connect the victims is that they are guilty of a crime, and they got away with it, all except the last victim, so it still makes no sense. Why, in some cases are *we* only finding out when we dig around into their lives that they did something wrong… Yet somehow, *he* knows. Apart from Freddie Corvus, because everyone knows him as a gangland Boss - the victims, or more so, their crimes are not known to us like number six. That complicates matters even more, like this isn't complicated enough!"

Adam leans against the wall by Evander and folds his arms. He looks at the mounds of paper set out before him. "I know you said you'd do this alone, but do you want some company? I can help filtering through it. Fresh perspective on what you've found so far. What do you think?"

Sipping coffee at the time of asking, Evander nods his head.
"Mmmm. How are the reviews of the files coming along?"
"Only 10 left to review now, I've got one left and I've split the rest between the team."
"Okay, then yes please, when you have reviewed your remaining file, then you can come and dig in. Another set of eyes may help. I'm getting bored of asking myself questions out loud and only hearing my own voice answering back."
"What are you thinking?"
"It's all so bizarre, there's no pattern, no M.O. and it's unpredictable, random even. I can't figure out how, or where he finds these people, or how he knows of their crimes and that they got away with it all. But I will find him, I'm getting to know him more, beginning to understand him and I will get him, just a matter of time."
"I know you will, Boss. I was wondering, why kill an old man when he only has six months left to live himself?"
"I know, right?! I've re-checked the files a dozen times and can't see it, not yet anyway."
"I take it you did go over everything - scrap that, I know you did." Adam says.
"Yes, double checked, triple checked. The whole team has gone over them before I got everything together in here. I know I'm being a pain in the arse and obsessive with it all. I must be driving you all mad."
"Well, we're certainly not bored. We've got no time for anything else however."
"You're right, there is literally no reason to kill the old man. Well, none that any of us can find. It's there somewhere though. Or perhaps we need to look at it from a different perspective." Evander ponders.

"Maybe if I stand on my head, close my right eye and squint through the left I might see something we missed, it might make more sense." Adam says, trying to lighten the mood. Evander laughs. "If I thought for one second it would work, I'd tell you to get to it."
"The old man, he must have done something wrong. How can we have missed it?" Adam reaffirms.
"The same way we missed the four victims before Freddie Corvus. One of which we still can't find, so that means we have six victims, but only five accounted for. I ask myself you know, what would Jack Regan and George Carter do? You know, they'd have had this wrapped up in 60 minutes."
"Yeah, but that was a TV show, this is real life, and we need more than 60 minutes."
"Maybe Regan and Carter would need two episodes, a double header that says at the end of the first one... 'to be continued…' the good old Flying Squad to the rescue!"
"Even Regan and Carter would be perplexed by this one Boss."
"I'm surprised you even knew what I was talking about."
"How could anyone not know about The Sweeney? Regan and Carter were T.V. legends; it'd be absolute sacrilege not to know them."
"I knew there was a bloody good reason I picked you as my Senior Detective."
A smile as broad as the river Thames spreads across Adam's face.
"Right then." Evander begins as he drains the last of the coffee from his cup. He pushes himself away from the wall. "Shall we crack on with this?"
"Sure, Boss. Where do you want me to start?"

Evander looks at his empty cup, hands it to Adam. "A refill is a good one. But don't bring it to me until you've reviewed your remaining file."
Adam laughs and takes the cup off Evander and heads to the door, as he opens it, Evander calls out to him. "Ad's, get the rest of the team in here too when they are done with their files. I want my immediate team on the case with me."
"Sure Boss." Adam replies as he leaves the room.
Evander looks at the paper strewn room before him. He knows exactly where everything is, so it is organized chaos at this point. He needs to tidy stuff up before Adam and the team get here to help. He puts his right hand through his hair and sighs.
'*We may be here some time*'. He thinks to himself.

CHAPTER NINE

Six weeks have passed since the last murder, victim number six. The media have not reported on the case for a while either on T.V., radio, online, nor in the papers. There have been no more developments, no new leads, no new witnesses, no new evidence and no latest victim either.

Evander becomes more unsettled with each passing day, each week the recurring nightmare troubles him, sometimes more than once a week. They never used to be this frequent, but this case is different, for it has gotten under Evander's skin far more than any other case and he is not sure why.

They say silence is golden, but that is not necessarily true. In the case of serial killers, the longer the lull, the more chance that another victim is likely to show up sometime.

Probably soon too. Evander has an overwhelming feeling that another one is due imminently.

Evander sits at his desk in his office at the Yard, while he fiddles absent mindedly with the cuff link on his left shirt sleeve. He rubs his fingers over the raised surface of the cuff link that forms the St Andrew's Flag. He feels patriotic today, for no reason, just because.

He unlocks and opens the draw of his desk and takes out the folder that contains a manila envelope his adoptive parents left him.

He puts it on his desk, laces his fingers in front of him and stares at it for a while, as though it has some unknown magical power. If that was all he had to contemplate, he may have opened it sooner. Yet it remains intact, despite the fact he has had it since the passing of his adoptive parents several years ago now.

In all this time, he has managed only to have played with the edge of the flap that forms the seal, succeeding only in raising the corner and nothing more. He picks the file up off his desk and swivels his chair around, so his back is to the door and the rest of the office.

He opens the folder and looks at the envelope, brushes his long fingers over the raised part of the envelope where he has played with the idea of opening it. He wants to be brave enough to just open it and get it over with, but he fails.

There are far reaching implications to opening the envelope to find things out about yourself that, once you know about, you can't un-know. He wishes he could stop procrastinating because he hates indecisiveness. It is not an easy decision to make though - opening the envelope. It could be life changing. Or perhaps even a complete let down. Or it could be that there are revelations in it that even he does not expect, nor is currently prepared for.

What if his adoptive parents reveal information about his biological Mother that he didn't know? What if it contains information about her murder, that he witnessed as a child and has blocked from memory, which he thinks is the likely cause behind the nightmares he has; nightmares that he can never remember.

How can he know what to be prepared for, if he doesn't open the envelope and, can only just lift the corner and never progress it any further? He is not even sure why he brought it to work, when something this personal should really be done in private, at home. Though he has tried to open it at home and only managed to raise one corner.

Maybe he will take it home again at some point. Then, a realization why he brought it to work. He feels safe here being with his team, surrounded by what he knows, who he knows, something that is familiar and supportive, something grounding that brings a sense of security. At home however he would be alone, at risk and vulnerable, but at least his reaction, if there is to be one, would be private. He sighs. Suddenly, he is aware he is being watched. If Evander were Spiderman, his Spidey senses would tingle right now. Evander closes the file and covers the manila envelope, although he is sure that it has already been noticed by the person who hovers over his shoulder. The person is in close proximity now too, for he can smell the distinct cologne that is worn by only one member of his team.

Without turning around, Evander asks. "Can I help you with something, Adam?"

"Whoa, Boss! How did you know I was here?"

"Spidey senses." Evander replies.

"No, I mean, how did you know it was me?"

"Told you, Spidey senses." Evander jokes, as he swivels around in his chair. "Now, what is it?"

"Think we may have another murder, possibly…"

"Where is it? Who is it?" Evander interrupts. He opens the draw from where he took the file and returns it back to its dark hiding place. He locks the draw as Adam watches him, his curiosity obviously peaked.

"Well, this one is a little… bizarre." Adam notes, while he watches Evander's every move.

"Are any of his murders ordinary by definition?"

"Well, this one is a bit, as we have two bodies. Well, one body and one head actually."

Evander is surprised, Adam is right, this one is bizarre. He has not done this type of thing before.

'Why two?' he wonders. Were they planned to coincide, to be discovered together, or a coincidence? If there is such a thing? No, there are no coincidences, everything happens for a reason whether we like to admit it or not.

Evander is very much a believer in cause and effect, law of attraction, karma; quite simply there are no accidents. Too many questions, not enough answers - need to get to the crime scene, oh, crime *scenes,* but which to go to first. Now his mind free falls, his thoughts come to him so fast that he doesn't have time to complete a thought before another one pushes the previous thought out of the way and makes room for another one and another one.

His mind churns furiously, he plays with the scar on the left side of his lips. He rubs his fingers across it one way and then his thumb across it in the other direction. Wait, does Adam mean two victims, or one body and one head comprising one person, or two?

Evander looks up, about to ask him that question, but Adam stands quietly watching him. He realises he hasn't asked Adam any questions in all the time he was there, nor has he given any directions on what he wants Adam to do. Suddenly Evander realises that Adam isn't quiet because he is waiting for instructions, he knows exactly what he's doing, Evander does it himself, so he knows the signs of study when he sees them.

"Stop it, Adam."

"What?"

"Don't try to read between the lines."

"What makes you think I'm trying?"

"In addition to Spidey senses, I have eyes; I can see you trying to read me."

"You got me, Boss. I'm just trying to develop my ability at reading people, always looking to improve my skills as a Detective."

"That's great, but don't try to read me."

"Why?"

"I don't want you inside my head, it's crowded enough already."

"I just want to learn."

"No, you want to see the subtext, to try to understand the things I leave unspoken."

"Got me again!" Adam laughs.

"There are some things I leave unspoken for good reason, like maybe I haven't figured things out myself yet." Evander says, as he glances at the draw in which he has placed the envelope, which Adam notices.

Evander contemplates asking Adam what he would do, but now is not the right time to ask. The job takes priority.

"I have to try to work it out, to figure out what you're thinking." Adam replies, genuine curiosity in his voice.

"Why would you want to do that? What do you need to figure out about me?"

"How you did it?"

"Did it? Did what exactly?" Evander asks, unclear what he means, doubt evident in his voice.

"How you nail them, time after time."

"Oh." Relief marks his voice, followed by regret as he continues. "Well not every time. The Crow Man didn't yield." Evander has never forgotten he did not break Aloysius De'Ath.

"That was a long time ago and he's behind bars, but you've nailed them since."

“Well, even so, still not quite every time. Anyway, stay out of my head, I’ve got enough baggage to carry around, I don’t have room for passengers.”

“There are things I don’t know how you know, what you know and that you know, I need to learn how you know what you know, y’know?”

“Huh?” Evander asks.

“I still have much to learn from you.”

“You will and you are. Why do you think you’re my senior Detective on the team?”

Adam remains quiet.

“No, it’s not because you’ve been with me the longest either.”

“You see!” Adam exclaims in a high-pitched voice, his hands splayed out before him to exaggerate the point. “That was my first thought, and you knew! You *knew*!”

“You’re my senior Detective, because you’re good at your job and you have more experience than you give yourself credit for. Yes, you still have much to learn, but don’t we all, me included. This job of ours offers no chance of complacency, we are always learning. I’m sure even the Chief Super is still learning too. However, you wouldn’t want to know what goes on in my head. Trust me. Now, back to work - what have we got? Is it one body, but two crime scenes or two bodies and two crime scenes?”

"Two bodies and two crime scenes, Boss. One body is still in situ. SOCO are working the scene as we talk, so I think you'll want to see that one first before they take it away too."

"What? Take it away too? You mean the other one has been removed already?"

"They had to."

"Why?"

"You know Traitors Gate?"
"I don't have time for one of your history lessons, Adam." Evander replies impatiently.
"It's not a history lesson Boss, it's a murder location. Yet another spectacular display. Although I could give you a low down on the history of Traitors Gate if you needed it?"
"Adam!" Evander says in a tone that Adam knows to mean he just wants details of the crime.
"Have you gathered the team together?"
"Yes, they're downstairs awaiting your instruction."
"Send them to Traitors Gate and we'll take the other one. Let's go."
Evander stands up, retrieves his jacket off the back of his chair, puts it on. He slips his fingers beneath the arms of the jacket and pulls the cuffs on his shirt down from under the sleeve. He fiddles with the raised flag on the left cuff link again as they head out of Evander's office and make their way to the hallway and to the lifts.
"They had to remove the corpse no, the erm, body, no, the erm, the victim, well what there was left of him from Traitors Gate."
"What do you mean, 'what there was left of him'?"
"Well not really even a body as such."
"What is that supposed to mean?"
"The victim at Traitors Gate, it was just his head stuck on a spike, so they had to remove it quickly - although it was a clean decapitation, there are some not so nice things to see, so you have to consider the tourists. Jackson wanted it out of the water A.S.A.P. to try to preserve evidence, though it is likely gone, as the head was revealed with the tide going out, so they're not sure how long it was there and what degradation

there has been to any evidence."
"Delightful!" Evander says mockingly with a raised eyebrow.
They arrive at the bank of lifts and Adam pushes the call button.
"You're not going to believe who it is. I don't think the choice of location was an accident either, we know he plans things out, but this must have taken some work. Quite poetic actually where he was left."
"Who is it?"
"Do you know anyone from MI6?"
Evander thinks about it. He knows a few people who work there, but not anyone of significance. "Hmmm, not really, why?"
The lift arrives, Evander and Adam get in. The lift descends to the car park where the team wait.
"The victim at Traitors Gate is - was - Jeremy Stone." Adam replies.
"WOW! So, the dragon man knew. Of course, he bloody knew."
That is a name Evander does know. He was an MI6 operative who went missing for a while and turned up after four months of being AWOL with no explanation. He claimed he could not remember anything about where he had been. He woke up in a hotel room and did not recall how he got there. He also did not realise that he had been gone for months when he re-emerged, yet he remembered everything else about his life; his family, who he was, that he was allergic to nuts, that he loved opera, but hated pop music, that he liked cricket, but hated football, knew what he did, where he worked.
Something did not add up to Evander when he heard about it.

He trusted his gut on it, but the case was not in Scotland Yard's jurisdiction, so they had no reason to get involved and Evander did not pursue the case.
Evander and Adam arrive in the car park and join the team. Evander decides there is no point in splitting the team up, because one crime scene has been cleared already, so they take two cars and head to the intact crime scene. Adam rides shotgun with Evander, while Izzy drives James and Grace.
As they drive, Evander ponders out loud. "I wonder how he knew?"
"How who knew?" Adam inquires.
"That our not so friendly neighbourhood killer knew the truth."
"Knew what truth, Boss?"
"That Jeremy Stone was a traitor."

~~~~~~

At the second crime scene, Evander is surprised that the location is Bank Tube station, in the heart of the city. Evander and the team are initially kept at a respectable distance at the end of platform eight, while they suit up to be SOCO compliant. A scene guard stands watching them, making sure they are suited and booted. Once they are all ready, the scene guard radios in asking for Jackson and her clearance for the team to cross the threshold and be let in. Initially, he gets no response and has to radio in again before there is a response. Further down the platform, a petite figure that Kincaid recognizes to be Jackson heads towards them. She pulls her gloves off as she walks towards them, a sure indication that she has done as much inspection here as possible, and
~~~~~~

anything further will be done at the morg.
"Finally! What have we got?" Evander asks pointedly, impatience evident in his voice.
"Not a pretty one, not that any of them are." Jackson replies. She folds her left glove into the right one, then starts to roll them into a neat ball ready to place in her pocket.
Evander has never known her to leave gloves at a crime scene, never in a bin, nor in something to be taken back to whichever morg is nearest, always wrapped in a ball and placed in her pocket to dispose of herself. He finds it anal but wonders why she does it. One day he'll have to ask her what the obsession is and how she disposes of them. Waiting has made him take note of her habit and it's annoying him for no reason other than impatience.
"Who is it, do we know? What about C.O.D.? Or do I have to wait till you get him back for dissection as usual?" Evander asks curtly.
"Jeez, someone got out of bed the wrong side this morning didn't they!" Jackson replies sarcastically, while she still works on the gloves.
"Nope, just don't like being dragged down here with my team, only to be kept hanging around. So, can you answer my questions or not?"
Jackson replies, but initially keeps her answers clipped and to the point. "Male, early 40s. No I.D. yet. He's beaten to pulp. C.O.D. I'd guess blunt force trauma of some sort judging by the state of his body, but you know how I feel about guessing."
"Any idea how long he's been here?"
"Given that it's a working tube station and that they were open yesterday, it will have been after close of business

yesterday evening, so less than eight hours. Rigor is just starting to set in, so he hasn't been dead for long."
"Who found him?"
"Station manager discovered him this morning, thought he was a vagrant apparently. Realized he wasn't when he got closer, scared the life out of him I'm told."
"Did he touch anything?"
"No."
"OK, so can we go in for a closer look?"
Violet Jackson stands to one side and holds her hand out to invite them over the threshold of the crime scene. The team follow Evander and Jackson follows, their SOCO suits rustle as they walk. The sound of a train approaching a neighbouring platform filters through the tunnel. The familiar rush of warm London underground air buffets them gently as they make their way along the platform to the victim.
Evander and the team approach the victim, who resides on a platform bench made of metal. He is in the centre seat and has been secured by restraints to both his hands and feet, the bench used to secure the shackles that bind him to the spot. His head is tilted back, and it rests against the wall, but lists heavily to the left. He is dressed in what looks like underwear and only that - white boxer shorts and a plain white vest, however he is blood soaked, so there are very few patches of white clothing visible.
His face is bloody, the right eye swollen shut, nose broken, jaw dislocated for sure. The lips are cut, and white fragments are embedded in the lower lip, which Evander realises are shards of his teeth, his hands have been savagely beaten. Evander is sure every bone in both hands likely shattered as opposed to broken. If he had survived his injuries, he would

no doubt never have recovered full use of his badly disfigured hands again. A compound fracture of the right collar bone protrudes through the vest, the body is covered in bruises, although Evander is not sure if they are pre or postmortem; some of them look a bit strange in shape and colour. The right leg has clearly been dislocated at the knee as the kneecap is not where it should be and the leg kicks out at an obtuse angle, his ankles have been beaten with the intent of hobbling. Gruesome.

"Oh my God, I feel sick!" Grace exclaims as she covers her masked mouth with a cupped, gloved hand.

"Why did he bring him down here?" James wonders.

"Because he could scream all he wanted and no one would hear his cries for help, or the pain of his torture, so no hope of rescue." Evander replies.

"That's quite twisted." Grace says, her voice muffled.

"It's cleverly planned, meticulously planned in fact. Have security any idea how he got in?" Evander asks.

"They think he hid somewhere with the victim till everyone had gone." Violet begins. "They found chloroform-soaked rags in one section of the tunnels. Looks like he over-powered the victim and that's as much as we know for now."

"What about security footage?" Adam inquires.

"You expect me a mere Forensic Scientist to know such things how?" She inquires.

"We both know you get the skinny through the grapevine via the scene guard. Spill it." Evander commands.

Jackson raises an eyebrow, which tells the team there is no footage.

"Figures. How does he do it?" Adam wonders.

"Formulates the idea, reviews requirements. Acquires the

right environment and location, strategic planning carried out before implementation. Conspiracy or assistance in some limited capacity I think, not sure how he gets them onside yet." Evander replies.
"You think he has a partner, Boss?" Adam asks, an obvious note of disbelief that marks his voice.
"No. I think he has people who give him assistance somehow, but not an accomplice. He likes the wet work too much to share - no, wait that's not it, I think he's too much of a control freak to allow anyone else to share in the booty. He wants all that glory for himself. Either that or…"
"Or what?" Izzy inquires.
"Or he doesn't want anyone else to be guilty of *the* actual crime."
"I wonder what he did to deserve such a torturous end." James ponders.
"I think he got what he deserved." Evander replies.
Everyone looks at Evander in amazement.
"I mean as far as the killer is concerned, going by past form obviously." Evander clarifies.
"Any more questions for me, or can I go and start on my notes?" Jackson inquires.
Evander asks. "Is there anything we should be aware of that is unusual?"
"You know I can't answer that till I get to, oh what was it you called it…. 'dissect' him, yeah that was it. Once I've got him to the morg, I'll know more. There are two autopsies to be performed and two Forensic Pathologists fighting for first dibs on a table, so the morg maybe busy."
"One is only a head, so it won't take long to deal with that, it's not even half a job." Evander replies curtly.

Jackson laughs as she lowers her head, she mutters under her breath and through gritted teeth, "God give me fucking strength."

"I'm sorry, what did you say?" Evander inquires.

"I see. *'Just a head'*. So that means you only have half a job to do as part of your investigation into the murder victim at Traitors Gate then, yes?"

Evander laughs himself now and realises his mistake that offended Jackson's work ethic. He doesn't say anything but holds his hands up apologetically.

Jackson continues and addresses Evander and the team. "I like to be thorough, just like you all are, and you have no idea what I can do with a human head and what it can tell me about C.O.D. Now, let me know when you're done here, so I can send the guys in to remove the corpse. Rigor mortis is starting to set in, and it will make moving the body more problematic." Jackson says, as she finally pockets the gloves after rolling them into a ridiculously small, tight ball.

"Wait, where are the dragons?" James asks.

Jackson points to the wall behind the victim and everyone looks to where she points.

Adorned on the wall are the *Dragons of Bank station*, immortalized in tile as part of the ornamentation on the platform, ready made almost as if prepared for this purpose.

"How many are there?" Izzy asks.

Jackson says. "12 I think, or is it 14? I'm not sure now."

"That's too many, it can't be right." James replies.

"This is platform eight, so I think we are on track if you'll pardon the pun." Jackson replies as she walks away.

The eighth victim, therefore Traitors Gate will be the seventh.

The team now in silence as they watch and listen to Violet

Jackson walk away, her SOCO suit crumples noisily as she walks away from the team in the otherwise unusually quiet tube tunnel.

CHAPTER TEN

At the hospital, Evander makes his way to autopsy with Adam.

They make small talk about the football on T.V. last night, but Evander is not really listening and as Adam is doing most of the talking, Evander doesn't interrupt his flow.

What he really wants is to ask Adam what he would do about that un-opened envelope he has hiding in his office drawer. What would Adam do - open it, or not? Should he give it to someone else to open for him and let them decide whether he should be aware of the contents? Should that someone be Adam? Oh, so many thoughts, but not enough logic. Not enough analytics. Not enough sense in the rationale. Not enough bravery from Evander and his own self-doubt, his own fear. Fear of what, he is not sure – fear none-the-less. Now is not the right time to discuss a personal dilemma either, yet he is somehow distracted by the presence of it and the fact it is still un-opened. Something is gnawing at him; but he can't quite put his finger on what it is about the envelope. Why is he toying with the idea of opening it again after it being shoved in a draw unthought of for so long. Why now? He feels compelled to open it but is afraid to do so. He has felt the need to open that envelope in the past, but this time, his feelings are different, but he can't pinpoint the reason why. Now, it seems like it is urgent, almost as if it is his duty to do so, but he cannot afford distractions on this case. Will there ever be a right time given the current workload. What, with all the whack jobs out there in addition to a serial killer running amok around London. Serial killer... Yes. Now he is in a conundrum if ever there was one. Just when you think you

have his M.O. figured, he throws two bodies at you at once.
"You alright Boss?" Adam asks.
"Hmmmm? What?" Evander replies, as he comes back to his surroundings and realises, he has not listened to all the conversation.
"You seem distracted, are you alright?" Adam asks.
Split second decision not to mention the envelope to Adam - yet - work takes priority as always, rather than his own demons. Evander replies. "I'm just trying to get inside his head. To see if I can figure out what his motives are, what his next move may be, how he thinks. Why he gave us two bodies this time? Just, well wondering - you know?"
"Righttttt." Adam replies, in exaggeration, obvious notes of disbelief in his voice. He knows the Boss well enough by now to know when he isn't telling him everything and there is something he is hiding, but what? Adam wonders if it has anything to do with that file the Boss has in his desk that he has never found out the contents of.
Adam formulates an idea how to ask him what is in the manila envelope but, doesn't get time to ask as they reach the doors of the hospital morgue.
Violet Jackson has a file in her hand which she drops into a tray just as they enter the morgue, the door opening catches her attention, she turns to greet them. "Good morning boys. So, who do you want first? The wife beater, or the wife beater?"
Adam laughs asking. "Is that a trick question?"
"She means she hasn't done the head of Jeremy Stone yet." Evander interjects.
"Why didn't you just say that?" Adam asks perplexed.
"Because she likes to talk in riddles, see if we are paying

attention."
"I like to keep you on your toes." Violet corrects.
"Whatever." Adam quips. "What can you tell us, is there anything to connect them?"
"Still to conduct Jeremy Stone's autopsy, so couldn't say yet."
"Isn't the Forensic Scientist who was called to Traitors Gate conducting the medical examination on that?" Adam asks.
"Chief Super asked for the autopsy to be passed to me due to it being part of our ongoing investigation as he is another dragon victim." Violet confirms.
"OK so, you're done with the Bank Station victim, what have we got?" Evander inquires.
"Report on Stanley Grimes is gruesome. I hope you took your strong stomach pills this morning."
"C.O.D. blunt force trauma?" Evander guesses.
"Yes, B.F.T. was the cause. Are you ready for this?"
"I am, but not sure about my senior Detective?"
"Always ready Boss." Adam replies confidently.
Jackson walks towards the autopsy table, and a body covered by a sheet. Jackson wiggles her index finger for them to follow her.
At the table, Jackson pulls the sheet back to waist level, to reveal the savagely beaten corpse of Mister Grimes, his head propped up on a black mortuary brick. His right eye is still badly swollen, as are both his upper and lower lip.
Suture marks in the shape of a Y on the chest are signs of the autopsy being completed and the gaping wounds stitched up. The compound fracture also taken care of, so no exposed bone through flesh, which Adam is secretly pleased about.
Jackson begins her tour of the body. "Can you believe this piece of shit left instructions to be an organ donor!"

"What's wrong, Violet?" Evander asks, aware that something is wrong - she never normally refers to a murder victim in such a derogatory way.
"After what he did, I'm surprised he had any capacity to think about humanity."
"What have you found out" Adam begins, and Evander finishes the question, "And what about the organ donor, has his death saved someone?"
"The organs were badly damaged during the beating he took and his liver was so badly diseased from alcohol abuse, that he'd have probably only survived another seven to nine months even without being beaten to death."
"So, he wasn't in any pain?" Evander asks.
"What makes you think he wasn't?"
"What?"
"How would you know he wasn't in pain? He may have been for all you know. Unless you knew the victim and his condition?" Jackson ponders.
"Well given your prognosis I... Well, I assumed there would be something wrong physically to tell him he wasn't well, but by all accounts, he was still wandering around unaware."
Adam and Violet remain quiet, but both of them look at Evander questioningly, although Evander isn't sure why they would doubt his train of thought.
"Sooooo?" Evander asks impatiently, exaggerating the word, waving his hand in the air in a forward motion encouraging the conversation to move along.
"Well, you can function quite unaware of any physical illness with a liver problem, obviously dependent upon the type of illness, but he was constantly drunk and never gave his liver time to recover to a normal state for him to feel if anything

was wrong. Not that he'd have known what normal felt like going by the state of his liver."
"Quite the pop man then?" Adam snorts.
"Yes." Violet replies.
"So, I was right then?" Evander confirms his own theory.
"About?"
"That he wasn't in pain?"
"Most likely not, no. He may have got the shakes, but he'd have probably put that down to needing another drink, rather than his liver collapsing under the strain he was putting it under."
"Why couldn't he be an organ donor for the other organs?"
"Exclusions in place on the cornea, pancreas and bowel, but he said they could take the heart, liver, lungs and kidneys. Acute cirrhosis ruled out the liver, the kidneys were also affected as a result. The heart and lungs may have been alright, except broken ribs punctured the lung and pierced the heart, ruling them out."
"So, what's the story with the full extent of his injuries? Why so many and why do you think he is a piece of shit?" Evander asks.
"My car is off the road at the moment, getting repairs done..." Jackson begins.
"With all due respect, I don't have time for your car's service history Violet." Evander says.
"With all due respect," Violet retorts. "This will lead to why I think he is a piece of shit. Still interested in the service history on my car now?" She asks sarcastically.
"Alright, what is the point?" Evander asks, his response clipped so she will hopefully return the clipped response in return.

"As I was saying, my car is undergoing repairs, so I got a lift to the mortuary from one of the police officers attending the crime scene En-route, we are talking, and it turns out the young officer knew the family due to previous call out requests to the house where the Grimes' family live. He brought me up to speed with the call outs and the injuries sustained by family members. So, imagine my surprise to find some of those same injuries inflicted by this sack of shit, on the dead body of Stanley Grimes. These injuries were not just part of a random beating, they're quite specific and they seemed to be replication of something that has previously happened. The wife called the police a few times and on the last occasion, she was taken into A&E by the police. You know she didn't press charges?"

"Yeah, we read that." Evander notes.

"She'd been kicked in the lower back, badly bruised. I imagine she was in a fetal position trying to protect herself. She was lucky he didn't damage her spine and cripple her. Additionally, from this one visit to A&E, she also had a dislocated jaw, a broken nose, her right eye was swollen shut too. Sound familiar?"

"Stanley Grimes was given his wife's injuries?" Adam conjectures.

"Yes. And the children's too."

"What?" Evander asks sharply. Anger rises from his feet at the thought of Stanley Grimes beating his children.

"The eldest son was brought into A&E, the parent's told the staff that he had fallen off his bike, head over handlebars. Guess what his injury was?"

Evander and Adam remain quiet.

"Compound fracture of the clavicle, although it is more

commonly known as the collar bone." Jackson says as she points to Grimes mirrored wound.
"How did the kid really get the injury?" Evander asks.
"A few possibilities and without talking to the child, I'd be guessing."
"What are your guesses?"
"You know how I feel about guessing."
"Humour me for once!" Evander pleads.
"He could have been slammed into a wall, or fallen against something, or maybe pushed downstairs. It would need something with great force to make it a compound break."
"Didn't they question it at A&E?"
"I'm not sure. But I wouldn't know for sure as I don't have records access, but I don't believe so"
"What? Why?"
"Probably because the injury can occur from falling off a bike in the manner they described."
"Didn't they know the history of the family?" Adam asks.
"I doubt they'd have looked into their background in such detail, they had no cause to with the explanation given, so why would they?"
"And you know all of this how?" Evander asks.
"Car trouble." Violet responds with a smirk.
"Just as well the bastard is dead, because I'd have gladly beaten the crap out of him too." Adam says, Scouse accent prominent - he's angry too.
"I was thinking the same thing." Evander replies. "Now I know why you think he is a piece of shit, Violet. You're not wrong either."
"What was he beaten with?" Adam asks.
"Everything but the kitchen sink, I think. Punched, but the

punches are rather unusual. Weapons were used too. When we did a search for weapons match analysis, we found distinct impressions from a crowbar on some of the fractures and the jaw dislocation. We got other weapon match likelihoods' too for other inflicted wounds."

Adam winces at the thought of the pain that the crowbar must have caused when it connected.

Violet continues. "I think a baseball bat, possibly a cricket bat, the wood samples taken from the flesh are used to make both types of bat, but more likely the baseball bat given the pattern and indentation formation, it's more consistent with a curved weapon, rather than the flat surface of a cricket bat. Obvious that other injuries sustained are replications."

"So, who else was beaten at home?"

"No idea but, given what little I do know I'd say the injuries he'd inflicted on his family were being given to him in return; I'm guessing that there are some that were never reported to the hospital or doctor. I'd say this was retribution for all the beatings he subjected his family to."

"How did the serial killer know what injuries he'd inflicted on his family?" Adam ponders.

"Curious isn't it?" Violet notes.

"The crowbar, I guess some poor sod got hit with that too. What a bastard. Oh, perhaps Stanley Grimes knew the serial killer. Maybe he was bragging about beating his family and maybe the serial killer decided to give him a taste of his own medicine." Adam's mind free falls at the implications on that one.

"Like I said earlier, he got what he deserved." Evander says.

"For once, I agree with you over a murder victim and their violent death." Jackson replies.

"What was unusual about the punch marks you found?" Evander asks.
"Punching someone leaves a distinct bruising pattern in the flesh, which will help us if the clenched fist has a distinct identifier, like for example a missing digit or a ring worn on a finger. They can leave an indentation or an impression in the flesh of the recipient and sometimes they help to identify the punch thrower."
"Okay, so why was this unusual?" Evander asks.
"We can identify it is a punch, but it does not have any distinct patterns showing in the punch mark, so we can't see knuckles in the bruising and there is no distinct hand shape."
"So, he wore something to cover his hands?"
"Yes, most likely boxing gloves."
"WOW! Boxing gloves. Didn't see that one coming!"
"I bet the victim didn't either."
"Is that the only reason he would have worn boxing gloves?"
"No, it's also about having maximum impact in the punch too. You can hit hard with a gloved hand and afford some protection without breaking your own hand. With the force delivered in these punches, if he'd have delivered them with bare hands, there is an element of risk that he may have injured his own hands in the process of delivering the blows. The gloved hands afforded some sort of barrier in that respect. Also, they protect the killer's hands from showing he has been in a fist fight."
"He? You're quite sure it was a man who inflicted these injuries and not a woman, or a young adolescent?" Evander asks.
"Definitely a man. The impact of these blows is something that are masculine in the impact and the force with which they

were delivered. A woman wouldn't be able to generate that much physical power and a young boy hasn't got the strength of a fully grown man. So, I'm confident the killer is a man. You can stop looking for a woman." Violet explains.
"So where did he centre the boxing glove blows?"
"Mostly, all around the head, just like a real boxer would do, likelihood for concussion is from this type of injury. Initially I thought it may have been a brain bleed that was C.O.D. but I'm leaning more towards the piercing of the heart from the broken rib. I do think this is how the teeth ended up being embedded in his lips - they likely broke during the beating, but then they got smashed into his lips from follow up punches."
Changing the subject Adam asks excitedly. "So, when are you gonna start working on Jeremy Stone?" Not giving Violet a chance to reply, Adam continues. "When are you going to slice and dice?" He makes a whirring noise that imitates a saw and raises his hand as if he has the saw in hand and he wields the tool.
"When we're done here, I'm going for my lunch and when I get back, I'll begin then." Violet replies.
"Can I watch you do it?" Adam asks.
Jackson laughs at the innuendo in his choice of words.
"What's funny?" Adam asks.
Jackson does not engage in any innuendo in this sombre autopsy room but replies. "Sure."
Not the answer he was expecting, Adam asks surprised.
"Really?"
"You'll have to scrub up."
"I can do that."
"And put the gear on."

"I can do that too." He says eagerly.
"I take it you know how to use a Stryker saw for cranium exposure and you can safely remove grey matter?"
"What?"
"I thought as much."
Evander interrupts their conversation. "I need a copy of the file to review the notes you've made on Grimes."
The phone in the morgue rings twice. Violet heads towards it, but it stops ringing before she gets anywhere near it. A few seconds later, her mobile buzzes in her pocket, she fishes it out of her lab coat and notes the caller I.D. She raises a finger in a 'wait' action. She answers the call, listens and says just seven words in reply. "Thanks, I'll get to it right away." She ends the call.
Finally, Jackson replies and tells them. "I sent the file up to your team already. Now, get out of here, I have another autopsy to conduct. I need to do it now, so scoot."

CHAPTER ELEVEN

Evander sits perched on the end of Izzy's desk, he thumbs through the autopsy report on the tube station victim, Stanley Grimes. 'Stan the Man', as he was known to all his drinking buddies down at the local pub.

His wife and children were the victims of his drunken rages when he rolled home from a late one with the boys, which was a regular occurrence. He would find something when he got home - literally anything - as a reason to beat the crap out of the wife and if she did not satisfy his rage, then the children caught the fall out of his drunken rage.

The Police interviewed the wife on two occasions after Mrs. Grimes had called the police, because she thought he was going to beat her to death, but she would never press charges against him.

Police Officers had visited the family earlier in the day to give them the terrible news. They were confident that none of them had anything to do with the murder, although the eldest son expressed joy that his father was dead, and he got what he deserved. He said he would like to shake the hand of his Father's murderer.

While disconcerting to see such a lack of emotion and empathy on the death of a family member, it is also a rational reaction to an irrational situation. Given the beatings he must have endured as the eldest of the children, Evander can't say he is surprised by the reaction either. The boy no doubt had grown to hate his Father and probably wished he were dead on many an occasion.

Evander is just about to turn the page when his mobile rings, he fishes it out of his jacket pocket. It's the Chief.

Evander answers on the third ring. "Kincaid."
"Kincaid, we may be losing jurisdiction over the dragon murders. I know you're not going to be happy about it, but..."
"Say that again, I think I misheard you." Evander says.
"MI6 want jurisdiction on..."
Evander stands and turns to face the team, who now know something is wrong from the expression on his face. They fall quiet and pay attention to Evander's side of the conversation. Evander stalls for time, dropping the file on Izzy's desk, he asks, "What? You can't be serious."
"Look Kincaid I'm just..."
Evander remedies their one-sided communication by putting his phone on speaker, he motions for the team to come closer, placing his phone on Izzy's desk in the spot he had previously been perched upon, he places his left hand on his hip. "Repeat that for me Chief. I want to be clear I got that right."
"Don't put me on speaker Kincaid." The Chief instructs him, pre-empting his move too late.
"I haven't." Evander says, as he puts his index finger of his right hand up to his mouth to form a 'shush' to his team.
"Now, what do you mean we have to give MI6 jurisdiction? We don't have to do anything on *our* own case. Besides, last time I checked MI6 don't investigate murders on home soil."
"When I say they want jurisdiction, they just want Stone. At the very least, we have to let the Jeremy Stone case be a joint investigation with MI6."
"No." Evander spits out the word, as though he has tasted something nasty. He can feel anger rise from his feet about to explode through his skull any second, dread briefly flickers in his sapphire blue eyes.
"They're pulling rank because it's one of their own. They

want jurisdiction over that, but insist they are going to assist in the investigation, so they're sending a team over to collect everything we have. Be sure to have it ready for them. I want you to be *prepared*, I'm sure you know what they will want and need. I'm equally sure you'll have everything *prepared* and *covered* too."

"No." Evander says vehemently.

"I'm sorry, what?"

"You heard me. I said 'no'. This is my case. It's part of an ongoing investigation and they are not taking it from us."

"They don't want the whole case…"

Evander Interrupts and replies sarcastically. "Oh well, that's comforting. Not. It's still a 'no'."

"They just want to assist with Stone. It's one of their own, which I can understand."

"I told you 'no' and I'll tell them bloody desk jockeys 'no', too. Who is it in charge over there?"

"Kincaid, you're not to have any contact with them. Don't go riding in gung-ho with this, you hear me? Just make sure everything is re-produced for them when they come calling."

"I hear you Walt, but they are not taking this case. I'll make sure of it. Who is in charge?"

Walter replies, but avoids the question. "Kincaid you're not listening to me, they don't want all of it. They just want to assist with Stone. I think we can accommodate a joint investigation, at least on Stone. They'll need everything we have on him."

"They don't own anything. It's integral to our ongoing investigation that we retain jurisdiction over every one of the victims on this case. I don't give a crap if it's one of their own. This is the seventh victim in a chain of evidence that currently

consists of eight cases."
"I appreciate that, but how would you feel if it were one of our own? Wouldn't you want to deal with the case? Deal with it yourself? I know you would. I'd want copies of everything given to me and I'd want my team to be involved."
"That's not the point, they can't just come waltzing in and take over because it's one of theirs. They may have a bigger stick, but we investigate murders – not MI6."
"You're still not listening to me. I told you they want *'joint'* investigation on Stone, not sole. They want *'copies'* of everything we have." Walter says, exaggerating certain words.
"They've not been involved with anything else we've done on our investigations on this serial killer, not one offer of help, or anything they can do to assist, blah, blah, blah. It's not happening Chief."
"I have my orders. Like it or not we have to…"
Evander cuts him off part way through his reasoning. "Look Chief, if we let them have joint investigation on one case, we won't be privy to any of their findings, you know they'll be redacted to hell and back, erasing anything of value we do get given back from them."
"I know."
"Which will of course take months to get from them and the information they obscure could be crucial to the progression of our investigation. We don't have months to wait around."
"Kincaid, listen to me…"
Evander ends the call.
"Whoa Boss, the Chief will be seriously pissed off you hung up on him." Adam says, unable to hide a note of excitement in his voice at Evander's act of defiance.
Evander's phone rings, it's the Chief calling back, he declines

the call.
Evander wonders if Jackson has completed her autopsy on the head of Jeremy Stone yet. Over four hours have passed since they last spoke, but she said she was going for lunch after they left, so she may have started it, but he doubts she will be complete on it. He needs to get to her fast and make sure she conducts the autopsy before MI6 roll up.
If they do take this away, he will at least be able to secure a copy of Jackson's autopsy notes and know it was done by someone he works with and has a working relationship with, and with full notes on the findings and no blackouts on the report. If MI6 take over and he must request copies, they will be prone to excessive censorship.
Evander's phone rings. It's the Chief, he declines the call again. He realises time is short and he must act quickly. He turns his phone off and pockets it. He can't be tracked now with what he plans as his next course of action. Digitally, he needs to disappear, just while he conducts some covert operations of his own.
"Adam, Izzy find everything we have on Stone - copy it and hide them somewhere that MI6 won't think to look for it. Obviously don't tell them we have copies. Let them think they have the original documents and that this is all there is. Keep them out of the M.I.R. In fact, don't even reference it in any way, shape or form unless they ask."
"But Boss…" James begins.
Evander raises a hand to stop his protests and interrupts. "I don't wanna hear it James. Do whatever Adam tells you to do."
Adam looks surprised. "Me?"
"While I'm not here, you're in charge. Keep them out of

M.I.R."
Adam protests with a half laugh. "But Boss..."
Evander cuts him short and replies. "You're fond of pulling rank when it suits you, now I am. So, as you are my senior Detective, be my '*senior Detective*' and delegate. Just copy everything we have, if MI6 take it away and then give it back to us, you and I both know they will redact the versions they give back to us. If you need me call Jackson as I'll be with her for maybe 15 minutes or so when I get there and after that, I've got to be somewhere else. Don't tell the Chief where I am when he comes down here, which he will. Actually, you can tell him I've gone to see Jackson, and I've gone to cool off. If those clowns from MI6 show up, stall them by whatever means necessary. Be aloof, be clumsy, act dumb if needs be, flirt if you need to Grace, faint if it will help, but tell them nothing, especially about where I am!"
"I thought you were going to see Jackson, Boss?" Izzy says.
"I am, but it's after that."
"Where are you going afterwards, Boss?" Grace asks.
"Best you don't know – plausible deniability but if anyone asks - I've gone to see Jackson, then I'm going for a walk and then coffee and cake."
Evander heads to his office and grabs his jacket off the back of his chair. After seeing Jackson, he needs to stop by his buddy, Timothy Little's office. He is in charge of the N.C.A. and he has the power to award jurisdiction to certain departments. He aims to ensure that jurisdiction remains with Evander and his team on all the cases that link his victims together. Even if he has to agree to a joint investigation, he will ensure that his team take point. He has a strong case to present to him too, all off the record of course, just two buddies having a drink.

First Evander needs to see Jackson.

CHAPTER TWELVE

Evander hurries to the hospital mortuary and upon his arrival is surprised to find no sign of Jackson. All autopsy tables are clear of cadavers, so they all must be stored in the cabinets at the end of the room. Evander walks over and opens the cabinet doors to look for Jeremy Stone - well, his head any way – to check if he is still in their possession. He is on his third door when Jackson startles him, he whips around to face her.

"This isn't Parkland!" She affirms.

"Oh my God, you scared the what the fuck out of me." Evander says, composing himself.

"You don't walk into my domain and tell me you're taking a victim and expect me to roll over and die - no pun intended - and I just let you... Let them."

"Oh God, have they been here already? Did they threaten you?"

"Pleaaaaase!" Violet says laughing. "I'm far more scary calm with a scalpel than any of them MI6 hacks with a Walter PPK. You don't fuck with my work, or the visitors who end up in autopsy in need of my help solving their murders and I ain't wearing any of that jurisdictional crap either, because they can cram it where the sun don't shine. They may have been here, but I haven't seen them, yet."

"So, what's all the Parkland talk about?"

"It's all very Kennedy like, don't you think?"

"Conspiratorial?"

"Yep."

"What makes you say that?"

"Evidence."

"You've already done the autopsy?"
"Of course." Jackson smiles as she walks forward towards Evander. She produces a file from behind her back, that she waves under Evander's nose.
"But how did you know they'd be coming?"
"I got a tip off from a friend."
"A tip off? You?" Evander says surprise in his voice. "You got a tip off?" Evander recalls the phone call she received when he and Adam were there earlier, and the penny drops for him.
"Ah, so that's why you hurried us out of here earlier." Enlightenment in his voice now. "Who told you?" He asks curiously.
"You're not the only one with friends in high places." She smiles.
"Do I know the 'friend' in a high place?"
"On pain of death, I swear I'll never tell. Had I known sooner they were coming, I'd have done his autopsy first, but either way, it's done now. I hate to say it, but you were right about only having the head to inspect. Four hours gave me ample time to conduct a thorough examination. If it would have been a full body however, I may have been rushing the job somewhat."
"If they're not here already, when are they coming - did your 'friend' give any timescale?"
"The tip off gave me enough time to conduct the autopsy and document the findings. If anyone asks where that file is, well it is currently sitting on my desk waiting to go up to your team. That's my story and I'm sticking to it." She says as she hands the file to Evander, which he duly takes from her.
"You know you could get in trouble for this?" He holds the file up, waves it.

"How can I be in trouble for doing my job? Anyway, I don't have to tell them I made a copy."
"Not telling them is also known as withholding evidence."
"Not if they don't ask me if there are more copies when I have to give them what I do have. I don't need to tell them an answer to a question that hasn't been asked, I mean why would I, right?" She smiles sweetly and flutters her eyelashes innocently.
"Wow, look at you and that smile - butter wouldn't melt." Evander quips.
"Anyway, I haven't seen you or anyone else for that matter, you couldn't find me, you're not really here and we're not really having this conversation. I went on a late lunch oh, 10 minutes ago and you couldn't find me. But when I come back, if they are here asking for the autopsy report, I can give them it. But should they ask if you have seen it, well I've not seen you since discussing the eighth victim's autopsy results this morning."
"So, I couldn't find you this afternoon?"
"That's right, you didn't find me!"
"Really, I couldn't find you in autopsy? So, where were you exactly if not here?"
"I wasn't in the morgue. I went to a colleague for assistance as my assistant left early. You didn't know where I was and I was just doing my job, blissfully unaware of the jurisdiction." She says smiling sweetly again.
"You're the devil in disguise Violet Jackson." Evander says as he turns to head out the door.
"That's a great Elvis song." Violet calls after him.
Evander makes his way onto the streets of London. He hails a black cab and gets in. He heads to the office of Timothy Little

across the river Thames.

CHAPTER THIRTEEN

Evander sits in one of two art deco style leather armchairs and sips Jack Daniels, which Timothy 'Tim' Little insisted on pouring for them, as Evander knew he would.

They became best friends having attended the same junior and senior school and remained good buddies outside of it too. They instantly got along as they had interests in common and Evander also stopped 'Tiny Tim' getting his butt kicked all over the school playground one day.

Tim failed to run after he hit a home run that would have won a game of rounders. This, in turn would have gained a prize for the team he was reluctantly chosen for.

After he hit the ball and knocked it out field, Tim just stood and watched the ball sail over a fence. He did not expect to hit it at all, let alone belt it out the playing field, so he stood there and gawped at the ball. His teammates yelled for him to run, which eventually he did, but not before he was beaten by the third base player with the returned ball.

Evander and Tim were always the last ones to be chosen for a team. They hated this ritual, because they both knew no one really wanted either of them on their teams. Tim was the posh kid with a well-off family, while Evander was the adopted kid no one wanted. Kids are petty and mean when it comes to who is cool and who is not - neither Tim nor Evander made the grade and it obviously made them a good fit to become friends.

Now, they laugh as they reminisce and look back at sports selection, especially sports day and what a fiasco that always was.

When they left school, they lost touch with each other for

several years, but a chance meeting at a police function rekindled their friendship. This time, they exchanged numbers and though they kept in touch, they were not in contact as much as they ought to have been, but they were always good friends and could pick up where they left off whenever they bumped into each other.

Now, Evander feels closer to Adam as a best friend, which is why Adam was best man at his and Jasmine's wedding, rather than Tim, who admittedly was out of the country at the time of the wedding anyway.

Reminiscing over, Evander still has most of his Jack Daniels in his glass. Tim has drained his already and replenishes his glass, before getting down to business.

Tim takes his seat again, runs his hand through his thinning hair, then fixes his tie and smooths his shirt. "This is about the Jeremy Stone case isn't it?" He asks.

"You can still read me like a book." Evander replies.

"I know you." Tim smirks and points his index finger out at him, while the remainder of his fingers stay wrapped around the glass. He takes a mouthful of Jack Daniels. "You want me to award you sole jurisdiction, don't you?"

Evander smiles and looks down at his glass and the face inside his drink, which stares back at him; he lifts the glass and takes a sip but remains quiet.

"Okay, maybe that's not what you're here for?" Tim asks when Evander doesn't reply.

Evander takes a sip of Jack Daniels and finally replies with a carefully worded response. "Well, it's like this - the team at MI6 want jurisdiction. We, at the very least want a joint investigation and I want to lead and have point on it, not MI6. As it is one of their own, I respect that they want to fully

investigate it. I understand their logic for it."
"But?" Tim interjects.
"But there is a whole lot more at stake than Jeremy Stone and the secrets he leaked."
Tim's eyes open wide. The fact that Evander knows of this obviously closely guarded information about the treachery of Jeremy Stone is a surprise to Tim.
"How on earth do you know he revealed secrets?"
"Well, he had his head skewered on a stake at Traitors Gate and given our killer's disposition for exacting revenge on those who escaped justice, I did the math. I know enough about my country's history without any assistance from my Senior Detective, to know that this was punishment served for high treason in centuries gone by. Our serial killer likes old fashioned traditions it seems. Although admittedly beheading was for nobility and as far as I can tell there was nothing noble about Jeremy Stone. Though there was nothing noble about his beheading either. Nor his treachery for that matter."
"Well, that's part of our country's history, so how did you know about Jeremy Stone's indiscretions? It hasn't been revealed anywhere, at least not as far as I know."
"Coupled with his disappearance some time back and the unanswered questions about his reappearance months later, you don't have to be Einstein to figure out the connection. That plus the fact that our serial killer is always informed of the sins of his victims, that's how he chooses them, you see. A person he believes deserves justice for a crime that has gone unpunished, so like I said doing the math, it is quite an easy leap to make on the reason he was a victim. To be honest, beheading was kinder."
"Kinder, how do you come to that conclusion?"

"He could have been hanged, drawn and quartered and dragged through the streets of London so, small mercies, you know."

"I doubt he'd get away with dragging a body through the streets of London now."

"Who would have thought he'd get away with a crucifixion on Tower Bridge, but he did."

"Right, of course, I see. So how will it help you to investigate what should be retained in the strictest confidence, on such a publicly catalogued case? Jeremy Stone is a national security risk, you do appreciate the seriousness of his victimology, don't you?"

Evander laughs ironically and replies. "Well, I think we're beyond national security risk now. He's already done the damage and he's dead, so at least he can't betray the country any further. Besides, not all of information on the victims has been made public. We have kept a lot of information from public disclosure, last thing we need is a copycat. We could have vital evidence in the chain that may be broken if we must award MI6 jurisdiction over the Stone case. We're up to eight murders already. There is nothing to join the dots, nothing to connect the victims other than they are guilty of a crime themselves and they are all victims of the same serial killer. But if we lose the lead on one case that is connected and we get documents - eventually - relating to the case of Jeremy Stone that have been subject to censorship before being passed along to us, well we won't have a hell of a lot left to go on."

"If there is nothing to connect the victims, then how will losing jurisdiction on just one of those victims hamper your investigation?"

"Because we may never know which of the cases could be the

one that closes the net on the killer. What if he made a mistake that leaves us vital evidence that my team may find, but MI6 may miss? All because we are missing that one victim and all the detail contained in the evidence therein."

"How will that assist you and your team?"

"Because my team knows the full history of the victims and where they fit in the jigsaw we have. We are not focused on just one piece of the puzzle here, there isn't just one victim we are looking at; we can see the bigger picture that relates to the whole investigation. MI6 would just look at what is important to them because he was an employee and a traitor, they don't investigate murders - we do. All MI6 would focus on is Jeremy Stone, they'd lose sight of that bigger picture that encompasses all the victims collectively. We would be closer to nailing the bastard if we retained ownership of all the information on all the victims across the board. So, if we must share jurisdiction, I want my team to have access to all documentation and it be free of censorship. If you lose one piece out of the puzzle, you'll never have a complete picture; we'll always have a missing link and that link just maybe the one thing that solves things quicker."

"That's a lot of 'ifs' you have in there."

"I know, but what if - sorry, there's another 'if' to add to the list - it may save someone else from a grizzly death. We can't afford to lose this just because a victim worked for a top government body. It doesn't serve the public as a whole and that's what we're meant to do."

"You know there's a process for this don't you." Tim confirms, more than asks.

"I do. However, if MI6 are to be involved, they... well, like I said, they don't investigate murders they won't have a clue

and will need some…" Evander pauses as he tries to think of the right adjectives. "Shall we call it assisted guidance." He concludes.
"You mean you want to be in charge."
"I need to… they need to be told how a murder investigation works" Evander affirms.
"You mean you want to boss them about." Tim snorts.
"I didn't say that, but same horse - different jockey." Evander quips, as he raises an eyebrow, a hint of a coy smile curls his lips.
Tim sits quietly and weighs up the options he has available and though he says nothing, Evander can be sure he will not decide until he hears the argument from MI6. Tim drains the last of his Jack Daniels, puts the glass on the table before him, then sucks air over his teeth and advises. "You know I can't…"
"I know." Evander replies quickly.
"Because I…"
"Yes, I know why." Evander interjects.
"Besides, there needs…"
"To be an approach via the proper channels, I know."
"I will however…"
"Give due consideration to both sides to be fair."
"Once…"
"Once you've heard from the other side, officially."
"Finally..."
"This conversation never happened as it's unofficial, off the record. I'm not even here. I know, I know! I know the drill."
"You're still…"
"Finishing your sentences for you, my brain still works quicker than yours."

Tim laughs and flicks the glass before him with his finger, the glass chimes the way only crystal chimes. "Maybe I shouldn't drink this stuff when in your company."
Evander rises from his seat, places his glass on the desk with most of the Jack Daniels still in it. He fastens the buttons on his jacket.
Tim eyes the glass and asks. "Are you going to drink that?"
"I'm on duty." Evander replies.
Tim picks Evander's glass up and drains the glass in one mouthful. He winces at the burning sensation at the back of his nose. "So am I, but I never let a good glass of Jack go to waste." He puts the glass down.
Evander holds his hand out across the desk, rising from his seat, Tim takes Evander's outstretched hand in both of his and they shake hands, like old friends do.
"Don't call me for any updates; it will all have to be above board now."
"Why do you think I came to your office without an appointment and unannounced?"
"You always were the smart one in class."
"You weren't so bad yourself."
"You know I can't let you know what the outcome will be in advance either."
"I know. Thanks for seeing me. I'll wait to hear from you Tim. I don't expect you to show any favours, but I'd hope that you'd make the right ruling and not be influenced, or should I say bullied by MI6 and their single-minded vision. While this may indirectly be a case of betrayal and of national security, any secrets revealed will already have been passed on. The death of Jeremy Stone won't prevent the knowledge he shared with the enemy become unshared. However, this is now a

murder investigation, and that job belongs to me and my team. I'll see myself out." He turns and heads to the door.

"Evander?" Tim says as Evander reaches the door, his hand on the handle, which he doesn't open.

Evander turns to face Tim. "Yes?"

"Be careful, this guy is dangerous."

"I will. Thanks." Evander replies, as he opens the door and exits Tim's office.

Evander turns and leaves the office the way he came - the back entrances in order to dodge cameras as he goes.

CHAPTER FOURTEEN

Back in Westminster, Evander stands outside Scotland Yard. He takes his phone out of his pocket and switches it back on. The phone searches for a network connection and locates the one he uses. Four out of five bars show the signal strength in a corner of the screen. A text message comes in from Adam, then another one from Izzy, another from the network provider advising he has voice mail and five missed calls from the Chief. He will no doubt have steam coming out of his ears when he gets in the office.

Evander takes a detour and heads across the road to Starbucks. He orders coffee and cakes for the team; they're going to need a sugar rush during the next few hours and he's happy to provide the supplies for the spoils it will hopefully provide.

While he waits for his order, Evander listens to his voice mail - an irate message from Walter, telling him to get back to the office sharply. Then he reads his texts from Adam and Izzy, then he calls Adam who answers on the second ring.

"Hey Sis, now isn't really a good time. Can I call you back later?"

Adam's way of telling Evander the Chief is there.

"I'm at Starbucks. I'll bring coffee and cakes in oh, 10 minutes maybe. I take it the Chief is waiting for me?"

"Yep, that's right it's quite busy here. Heard there are some unexpected bees nesting." Adam continues with the cryptic analogy that he knows Evander will be able to interpret.

"Ah, I see so he's steaming mad then? Oh, and MI6 are there too?"

"Oh yes, he sure seems that way. It's a quiet hive for now that

nests in the roof, loitering."
"I'll see you soon, better batten down the hatches. Have you told him anything?"
"No of course not."
"Okay, will be back shortly."
"I'll call you later for a proper catch up. I have to go, got to get back to work."
"Be in there shortly." Evander replies and ends the call.

~~~~~~

Evander heads into the corner of the office he and his team occupy and glimpses the Chief waiting in Evander's office, his hat under his arm, while he paces the floor. Evander decides to play it cool and walks into the office like it is any other day and the Chief is just passing through.
Evander places coffee cups and a bag, which contains cakes on the end of James's desk, then advises the newest recruit.
"Don't ask questions, just go with the flow. Follow the lead of your colleagues."
Evander looks up and calls out. "Damn fine coffee and great cakes for everyone. Come dig in guys."
The team gather around, Grace opens the bag of cakes and feigns a hard choice over which cake to choose, even though they all have a favourite the Boss always gets each member.
"What's the game plan Boss?" Izzy asks.
"I think it's time for ignorance and innocence, both of them blissful." Evander replies.
"Got it, we can do that."
"Did you copy everything?" Evander inquires.
"All taken care of and filed discreetly Boss." Adam confirms.
~~~~~~

The Chief appears in the doorway of Evander's office.

"Kincaid! Get in here, now."

"Oh, hey Chief, if I'd known you were going to drop in, I'd have brought you coffee and a cake too."

"Office. Now!" The Chief bellows.

Evander grabs his coffee and heads to the office. He turns and calls out to the team. "Lemon poppy seed muffin has my name on it, keep your hands off that one!"

The team assume blissful ignorance and innocence.

Evander walks past the Chief into his office and places the coffee cup on a coaster - which is the Marvel logo - on his desk, which he then walks around, taking his jacket off as he goes; he hangs the jacket on the back of his chair.

"You come to give us a hand Chief?"

Walter's face flushes red, his cheeks ruddy with anger, he looks the proper Christmas card Santa Claus right now. "You hung up on me and switched your God damn phone off. Why? Where have you been?"

"Walking; then went for coffee and cakes. I needed time to calm down and think."

"There is nothing to think about Kincaid…"

Evander interrupts. "You mean they said 'jump' and you said, 'how high?'"

"Kincaid don't test my patience. Your ice is as thin as it gets right now. One more smart-arse comment from you and I'll suspend you for insubordination and don't think I won't, because I am seriously hacked off with you right now." He slams the office door shut and turns to face Evander, his back now to the rest of the office so the team can't see his face. He throws his hat on the edge of Evander's desk and puts his hands on his portly hips.

"I'm going to contest jurisdiction if they ask for it." Evander informs Walter.
"I'm counting on it."
This was not the reply Evander was expecting from the Chief. His demeanour has changed too. His tone is softer, which shows in his face. Evander isn't sure what's going on here, but something is shifting and changing.
"You are?" Evander asks amazed, certain that the tone is notable in his question.
"I was trying to tell you when you were on the phone, but I had MI6 for company in my office. You probably didn't notice he is in your office at this very moment either."
Evander is surprised, he wasn't expecting this play from the Chief. "So, you're not annoyed with me for wanting to retain the case, to hold jurisdiction?"
"Of course not, I was telling you things I knew would piss you off and make you dig your heels in to keep the case."
"But you said…"
"I know what I said, but I also know you Kincaid. I learned long ago if I tell you not to do something, you take it as if I'm giving you a dare, a bloody challenge to see if you can do it and without breaking any rules. I swear sometimes you do it either just to prove a point, or to piss me off, probably both. But I knew if I told you not to do something and stressed the right words, you'd go ahead and do it anyway."
"Holy shit Walter. I wasn't expecting that one. Wait, MI6 are here now, where?"
"Don't make it too obvious, but over my left shoulder, sitting at the empty bank of desks on the other side of the room, if he still has it in his hands, he is playing with a hat."
Evander walks around the desk and goes to a filing cabinet,

opens it and takes a random file out of the draw. He notes the MI6 agent, who sits drinking water, his hat on a desk now. He turns around and waves the file in the air for effect.
"I see him. Who is he and why is he still here?"
"That's the MI6 Chief. I was trying to give you some sort of hint that I was on your side, but you missed the hints and then you bloody hung up on me."
"Ah, so that's why you're pissed off, because I hung up on you?"
"You made me look like a tit in front of the MI6 Chief, while he was sat in my bloody office grilling my arse. The smug look on the bastards face, I just wanted to punch his lights out while he sat there smirking at me, thinking he had one up on me, but he didn't account for something hidden in my locker."
"Oh, and what was your ace card?"
"You!"
"Oh, I see. I think." Evander responds, unsure whether to be offended, or happy at the compliment that his reputation precedes him.
"No, you don't. There is no love lost between me and the MI6 Chief and we meet out of necessity, not because we're best buddies. Not like you and Tim Little."
Evander tries not to blanch at the mention of Tim's name, but wonders if the Chief knows this is where Evander went. "You don't want them to take the case?"
"Of course not. I hope you've got your team to make copies of everything, just in case. That sniveling little shit outside is waiting for me to give him everything we have."
Evander smiles and looks down at the floor but says nothing.
"I see you already have."
"I didn't say that Chief." Evander replies as he picks up his

coffee, takes a drink.
"You don't have to. I don't want them taking this case either. I know how vital a link can be in the chain of evidence. Now where are the files? I need to give them to MI6."
Evander walks around the table, opens the door and calls out to Adam. "Eastwood, can you bring me the Jeremy Stone file please."
Adam grabs the file off his desk and heads into Evander's office, he gives Evander the file, turns and heads back to his desk.
Evander closes the door, and hands the file to Walter asking. "What do you want me to do?"
"What you do best."
"Be a pain in the arse?" Evander asks sarcastically.
"Create an unassailable case, you have my support behind closed doors and off the record, but right now my balls are yet again in another vice, and I can't do anything to protest. But as lead D.C.I. you can. I have to look like I'm complying."
"Why didn't you tell me this on the phone?"
"I told you, I had that sniveling little shit sitting in my office. My hands were tied to a degree, but I knew you'd defy me if I pushed the right buttons."
"WOW. I feel used. I may need to change my approach in future."
"Don't change a thing, you're one of my best Detectives, Kincaid. I wish there were more like you. But you must make this a priority to find the bastard who did this. It's not just Stone he's responsible for, there are others as you and I well know."
"I know Chief, we're working on it."
"If they get their hands on him first, before we do well, it

won't reflect very well on our division. That's another reason it's so important to retain jurisdiction, we must be the ones to capture this lunatic, so we run the questioning. If they get him, it'll be like a CIA covert operation, where they deny they have him, but meanwhile, he's in a black site somewhere being water-boarded or worse, to find out what he knows and if he is working for the Russians or the Chinese. They'll want to know how our serial killer knew Stone had leaked information, how much did he know of the leakage and where did he get the intel from that he was a security risk. They'll think he was tasked with taking Stone out and used the serial killer angle as cover for one murder."

"Holy shit Chief, you think that's their angle and that's why they want to take over?"

"I'm not sure but I wouldn't be surprised. Thank God we don't have Feds in the UK like they do in America, or they'd be crawling up our backsides right now complete with industrial sized flashlights just in case we squirreled anything away up there."

"Oh, I don't know". Evander counters. "I think our own intelligence service can be just as intrusive as our American counterparts, or the Russians, or Chinese for that matter. Only difference between theirs and ours is we've been doing it longer."

"Despite what the public think that we are all one and all work together to battle crime. We may be different departments dealing with different levels of security, or criminality, but we all have the same agenda - to protect the people of this country and defend the country against enemies both foreign and domestic. The public don't see behind the curtain and the competition there is between departments to be the best. But it's not just competition, we owe it to the victims and their families, to those who we look after. They will only be interested in capturing him because of Stone, we have more at stake as we are responsible for justice for all those people on your cork board in M.I.R. We must find him in order to get justice. We must get him first. We have to."

"I know, and we will." Kincaid reassures the Chief.

"Now, don't forget to pretend I'm annoyed with you." Walter picks his hat up off Evander's desk, puts it under his arm and assumes his steaming mad face as he turns to exit Evander's office.

CHAPTER FIFTEEN

Almost a week has gone by since the jurisdiction papers were submitted via the proper channels. Evander is not sure why it takes so bloody long to award it.

He sits at his desk in his office and reads through Violet's report again on the autopsy of Jeremy Stone, which is stored on the HOLMES database.

It is yet more gruesome reading: Beheaded post-mortem - mercifully.

As the tide ebbed away and his head became exposed, a member of the public alerted local security that there was a 'body' in the water. When the police arrived by boat to inspect and remove said body, further inspection revealed a sign had been draped around what was eventually discovered to be a severed head, it was at this point they realised it wasn't a suicide as they suspected, but a homicide. The area was then quickly cleared of tourists trying to peer over the railings down to the dock where Traitors Gate had been bricked up some years ago.

The laminated sign in sync with the laminated piece which secured the mouth had a note, etched in the neat, typed calligraphy our serial killer is so fond of, which reads:

"Here lies Jeremy Stone – where Traitors belong."

At this point, the area was closed off and a makeshift 'tent' constructed over the head to hide it from public view. This was complicated however due to the ebbing tide and a stiff breeze, which continually buffeted the tarpaulin. It didn't help with evidence preservation either and the Forensic Pathologist called to attend the site wanted the head out of the water as soon as possible to prevent evidence degradation. The frog team were brought in too in order to conduct a search for the body, which was clearly missing in action.

The first indication this was the work of their not so friendly neighbourhood serial killer was a now familiar London dragon, drawn on a small square of laminated paper, just big enough to cover the average human mouth. This was secured over Stone's mouth with sutures, which was the first clue as to who this was a victim of.

His lips were sewn shut to keep in place a double sealed, handwritten confessional letter, which was hidden in his mouth. The confessional letter was written in waterproof ink on homemade waterproof paper, adorned with London dragons, six of them to be precise.

The letter was then placed in what looks like an airtight sandwich bag, only better quality. This was then placed inside yet another sandwich bag of similar quality, his mouth then sewn shut with the laminated last dragon, ergo - the seventh victim.

The killer had a triple use for the sutures that had sewn his mouth closed. They kept the letter secure, as that was entwined to the stitches in his lips, which also secured the laminated dragon over his mouth, which in turn kept his mouth shut. Maybe that was the point of stitching his mouth up - not so much to keep the confessional letter in place and secure, but to send his own message about loose lips sinking ships and that Jeremy Stone should have kept his mouth shut. For now, he is dead at the hands of the most notorious serial killer in Britain, who kills not for kicks, or for fun, nor out of necessity like hunger, but because he has a purpose, a role to play, a duty to fulfill, to whomever he is a servant of. Evander realises the killer sees his purpose is to deliver justice to those who escaped punishment. For Jeremy Stone, his death is the just rewards for his betrayal of Queen, country and the people of this nation. Beheading. At least this is how the killer will view it.

Evander looks through SOCO photos from Traitors Gate. There are also autopsy photos that follow the stages of the sutures being removed - which was, by all accounts a neat job according to Violet - from inside the mouth and externally, to the lips, to the reveal of the small waterproof parcel, which contained the letter within the victim's mouth.

Great care and attention had been given to the placement of these items, so that they not only stayed in place, but were double protected against the rigors the Thames would levy as a test of security.

The endurance of the plastic envelope that contained the letter was worthy of the secondary insurance of the plastic sandwich bags, the outer one especially, as this leaked a little water, due to the bag being pierced by the stitches that kept it in place. Meticulous attention to detail to ensure the evidence of Jeremy Stone's treachery, and his admission by way of written confession of these acts was retained intact and unsoiled.

The letter of confession once written, had been waterproofed by way of candle wax, commonly available at many stores, supermarkets and online retailers. The paper itself was found to be a one-off design, quite possibly killer specific, for it is inscribed with six dragons by his own design and something not readily available online or mass produced.

The contents of the letter in which Mr. Stone lays out the facts of his betrayal of the country he was supposed to be protecting, are quite atrocious. He details how he gave people information in order for them to infiltrate companies tasked with the security of the country, by way of job application trickery in high profile companies.

Once they were within respective departments of importance, they could source highly confidential information. Some of the information went all the way up to the Prime Minster and the deeper roots of the Government that are entirely anonymous, and all knowledge of their existence denied, as something only used in movies - spooks. It is sickening to think someone could harbor such hatred towards their own country and ultimately, its people.

What type of information Stone was privy to, Evander is not sure, but given that he had gone AWOL for months with no accountability of where he had been and what he had been doing, he should never have been above suspicion, surely? Why was he allowed to return to work at MI6 and what exactly was he doing in his new day to day duties? Better the devil you know. Perhaps. Keep your friends close and your enemies closer? Possible. Let him go about his business and think all is forgiven and his explanation accepted, but really 'they' are monitoring everything he does to try to track the sources he gave secrets away to? Maybe.

Evander is not sure which is the best fit. Even so, if he was given basic desk duties, rather than anything more responsible, he was still back in the fold and that was dangerous. The dragons of justice killer may have spared the country, and MI6 more embarrassment by killing Stone, for God knows what else he'd have gotten up to as part of his betrayal.

Stone had declared memory loss, but Evander knew in his gut that there was something wrong with that.

If Evander had been called in to investigate it, he would have freed the mind of Stone to the point that his memory went into free fall on what he had given away, to whatever nation or group of idiots claiming to be free radicals, acting in the interests of the people, or the freedom fighters that claim so many innocent lives in that quest for freedom.

Evander finishes reading thc lctter Stone had written before his demise. It is nauseating to read the crimes of which he was guilty. Though even more interesting is the fact that our serial killer knew of the treachery committed and he found the leverage needed in order to glean a confession, in writing, which is something all those hacks at MI6 failed to do.

While reading the letter, he can see why MI6 want jurisdiction, but they need to be content to share the booty on the findings of the investigation.

It is also clear, they need to try to contain the information that is released out there in the public domain, because if the press got hold of this information, it would likely lead to mass hysteria over the safety of the people, the country, the monarchy, the constitution, democracy and the way of British life, as well as the land itself. Britain would look like sitting ducks with targets and big signs pointing in one direction for take over of a nation, which would lead the way in for the potential enemy to infiltrate the right organisations right to the top.

It opens the floodgates for all sorts of revolutionists and activists and all other types of weirdoes and whack jobs. Once they were in situ in high profile roles in high-risk environments, with access to all the information needed to start an uprising, well the consequences would be fatal, not just to the organisations involved, but to the functionality of a

nation and the lives of the people living here on this island of nations that is the British Isles.
The lives affected would include Evander and all of those of his team.
He looks up from the letter and surveys his team. He watches them going about their daily duties; they investigate, gather data and evidence, chat with each other, share details, compare notes.
Adam and Izzy laugh out loud, they high five each other, they must have found something amusing, or a joke that only they get, as none of the other team members share the laughter.
Evander tries to imagine a world in which they are not safe, under threat and possible attack, because of the revolution that may come, based on the secrets leaked by Jeremy Stone.
It could be seen to represent an establishment, which cannot be trusted by the people. Their safety would be integral to Evander, he is fiercely protective of his team, and he would do anything to look out for them and keep them safe.
The world he imagines in which they are under threat because of one man and his treason if his plan were successful in infiltration sickens him even more. He would sooner be-friend the Papanasty, rather than his people be put at risk.
Would he be able to protect his team from harm? Possibly. But could he watch them 24/7? No. There would be times when they could be vulnerable and open to attack and maybe unprepared for it if - or when - it came upon one of them.
Evander watches Grace and James, they seem to get along well, though he notes they sit awfully close to each other.
Their body language is suggestive of a situation in which they could be more than work colleagues, perhaps dating each other. That would be nice, but also cause conflict of interest

too. One of them possibly may end up having to be moved to a different team to avoid that situation. Unless they kept it quiet, which Evander thinks would be impossible for them to do, as he has noticed it already and he is sure it is very much early stages at this point, but the signs are there.

For now, however, they are just work colleagues. Evander guesses they may try to maintain that façade so they can continue to work on the same team. That may not be it at all, it could be that Grace has just taken him under her wing, because she is no longer the newbie on the team, and she knows how James will be feeling.

She is great at integration and making sure everyone is involved, she is great at pinpointing people's strengths, although Adam usually pulls rank on her as his methods of investigating are somewhat unusual, but he normally gets the job done with resounding results. Therefore, Evander lets it slide when Adam pulls rank in order to pick and choose his job for research in an investigation, but Evander is also quick to remind him of his rank when he tries to shirk responsibility to someone else.

It is not clear at this point if any of the information that Jeremy Stone leaked remains un-utilized, nor who it was given to.

It is also not clear what has been done with that information, nor whether it has been put to good use already and whoever received it may have been able to pass it along in order to infiltrate one or more of the organizations listed, to the point that they were compromised. Evander is sure that there will need to be a complete review of new employees hired with the last 12 months, although if Evander were in charge, he would probably go back on staff records for the last five years. You just never know what reviewing the candidate, their background and their job application will reveal if put under a microscope.

At this point it is not clear how far their career may have progressed or how deep their integration has gone. Because Stone's indiscretions have only recently surfaced, does not mean that his treachery is a recent occurrence.

Therefore, Evander thinks a five-year review is enough scope to review staff files, responsibilities and promotion within those years, so, if asked, that is the time frame he will recommend for reviewing job applicants in positions and places of high risk and security.

Fast tracking the gifted is always an advantage, but sometimes there may be underlying reasons why their fast progression should come under scrutiny and this scenario is one such situation. Reviewing that idea, it may even be more effective to review staff files from the start of Jeremy Stone's successful application.

Plotting his course of career progression may assist in identifying other potential leaks and surely, he had other brothers in arms who were in support of his betrayal, this level of infiltration is not something he has done alone.

Traitors are usually recruited from within the organization they work for.

Betrayal, as far as Evander is concerned, is one of the most hateful things to be guilty of. To betray one person is unforgiveable, but to betray a nation - unthinkable. The consequences of that are not for the feint hearted. The beneficiary of such information would wield power untold. It is worrying, but if they act quickly, they can control and extricate those under suspicion and no doubt they will be carted off to a secure facility for their own safety, in order to question them with the intent on containment.

Protection of the nation must be paramount, and they need to act quickly.

Evander's phone rings, which disturbs him from his deeply worrying thoughts. He doesn't recognise the caller I.D. on the display, but he answers the call on the fourth ring. "Detective Chief Inspector Kincaid speaking."

"Ah, Detective, good, got the right number."

"Who is this?"

"My name is Richard Smith. I'm the Chief of MI6, I'd like to arrange a meeting with you to discuss Jeremy Stone. Are you free this afternoon?"

"What do you want to discuss?"

"Well, the case of course."

"I'm not sure I can share information with you yet."

Silence at the end of the phone. Five seconds. Ten seconds. Evander wonders if he has lost connection. He, takes the phone away from his ear and looks at the display, seconds count up, good signal strength, so still connected.

He puts the phone back to his ear. Kincaid asks. "Are you still there, Chief?"

"Yes. I, well... I think we may need to come to some sort of agreement to meet and discuss your findings. This whole Stone thing has far reaching implications. The safety of the nation may be at risk if we don't act quickly."

Evander smirks and wonders if Big Brother is at work, because similar thoughts ran through his head only a few moments ago. The 'thought police' in action. "Like I said Sir, I don't know if we can discuss things yet - we're still waiting on the jurisdiction decision to be made and if my understanding is correct, as this is an unusual and unprecedented situation that we find ourselves in, we are not supposed to discuss anything until that has been awarded."

"Look, I understand how determined you are to retain this case, but there are far bigger fish to fry than a stubborn determination to keep what you think is yours. Jurisdictionally speaking, we must work together for the good of the country. I hope you're ready to work with us and take direction from me, or a senior member of my team?"

"I'll call you back." Evander replies and terminates the call before Richard Smith can protest.

Evander goes through his phone contacts. He finds Walter's number and calls it. Walter answers on the second ring.

"Kincaid, what is it?"

"I just had a call from Richard Smith at MI6."

"What the bloody hell is he calling you for? Really, the damn cheek of him! What did he want?" The Chief snorts disapprovingly.

"Are you still at the Yard?" Evander asks.

"Yes."

"Are you free?"

"Yes."

"Good. We need to talk. I'm coming to your office." Evander hangs up.

Evander puts the phone on his desk and stands up, retrieves his jacket off the back of his chair, he puts it on, picks up his phone and pockets it.

As he pushes his chair in to fit snuggly under his desk, a well of anger rises, volcano like from his feet, all the way up through his legs, torso, arms and by the time it reaches his head, he is so full of rage that he is not even sure what is fuelling this anger, which frustrates him even more.

He punches the back of the chair, which jerks forward and pops back towards him as it recoils from the force of his punch. The chair quivers for a few seconds, as though out of control and its structure is about to collapse before it suddenly settles and becomes calm.

Evander is suddenly aware that the source of his anger is control - or the current lack of it - he doesn't like not being in control of situations and even more so when it comes to case investigation.

He closes his eyes, takes in a long deep breath and tries to calm himself before he leaves his office. He opens the door and heads towards Adam's desk, Adam is not there.

"Izzy, Where's Adam?" Evander asks.

"Not sure Boss, toilet break maybe, he never said."

"I'll be with The Chief Super if you need me. As Adam isn't here, you have point, when Adam comes back, if he tries pulling rank on something that needs doing, tell him I said you're in charge. If he has a problem with that, tell him to call me."

"Oh, I got it Boss." Izzy replies with glee in her voice. A smile spreads across her face.

"That doesn't give you license to order him around doing all the crappy jobs that no one wants to do, he's not your errand boy. Share the load."

Her smile falls away and she replies. "Awww Boss, you gotta let me play with him, please?"

"Really, Izzy?"

"Well, you know how he delights in pulling rank, so may be just a little bit?" She smiles pleadingly, puts her index finger and thumb in proximity, which mimics what 'a little bit' may look like.

"Maybe just a little bit." Evander smiles. "Now, if you need me, I'm with Walter."

CHAPTER SIXTEEN

In the Chief's office, this time it is Evander who paces the floor. He tries to run off excess energy, make that excess anger. Walter tries unsuccessfully to calm him down.

"I don't like this at all, they are still deliberating jurisdiction and already he is trying to stamp his authority over the case, over me, over my team, our department. Why are we still waiting around for red tape to be sorted out? Why can't things move quicker I mean, for God's sake this isn't the eighteenth century, we don't use telegrams and horses anymore, we have fast moving computers and cars and a more streamlined process, so why are we still stuck in the dark ages when it comes to jurisdiction? Fuck!"

"Kincaid, you're not going to get there any faster by being frustrated and angry."

"I know that. Fuck!"

"Putting additional pressure on yourself isn't going to help."

"I know that too, but fuck!" Evander says, as he kicks the back of a chair.

"Kincaid, really you need to calm down."

"It's either the chair, or the MI6 Chief, which even I know won't go down very well and besides, I really like my job. He was such a smarmy bastard, Chief."

"I told you that when I came to see you when he was here last week. I also told you that we had our show downs, so yeah I'm aware of what a dick he can be."

"Dick by name - dick by nature."

Walter can't help but smile at Kincaid's observation, which he whole heartedly agrees with. He rises from his seat, goes to a cabinet, opens it, takes two glasses out and a bottle of Remy

Martin VSOP. He pours out two glasses and returns the bottle to the cabinet, which he closes.

He turns to Kincaid and hands Evander a glass. "Here, drink this and for God's sake sit down."

"I'm not sure that's a good idea."

"Take it and sit down."

"Chief, I'm…"

Walter interrupts him and commands. "Kincaid, take the damn glass and sit down. Now."

Evander takes the glass from Walter, pulls out the chair which bore the brunt of his anger and sits down still wearing his jacket, something he never usually does.

"Drink, but make sure you sip it, don't gulp or swallow it in one shot, that's not how you treat this drink." Walter advises as he moves around to his seat.

Evander sighs and takes a sip as instructed. He looks at the glass as the taste pleases him. "What is that Chief?" Evander inquires.

"Cognac."

"Nice, I like it. I like it a lot."

"Look, pressure is something you can't control by being angry, you have to manage it in a different way. It's a lot like gravity actually."

"Gravity? What are you talking about Chief?"

"Gravity isn't something you can control, so there is no point in fighting it. There is no point in getting angry about something you can't control either. Think of your anger and frustration like a type of gravity but make it a positive and productive type of pressure. You know it's there, yet you can't feel or control it, so you ignore its existence; you're only aware gravity exists when someone mentions it and brings it to your attention. Treat pressure like gravity and it will work for you. If you channel that energy well, then it can be good if it is something that you use well, you have to embrace and make it your friend."

"Make pressure a friend? Jesus Chief, what's in this Cognac?"

"Yes, let the pressure give steel to your will and determination and don't bow to anger."

"Why would I want to do that?"

"Because it will consume you and eat you alive if you mishandle it. But channel that energy and you have something you can use to make your case stronger. It aids the gut when making a choice and feeling your way around the underbelly that is the murky waters of the criminal network, or in our case a serial killer, though in this instance, the MI6 Chief. Sometimes you need to detach yourself from it, being too involved can work against you. Therefore, you need to channel that energy in the right direction and then it can be a positive negative."

"Okay, so how do you do it? How do you channel that energy? No, more so, how do you harness it?"

"Think of it like brandy and cognac, they're both pretty much the same thing, but one is more refined than the other and more expensive too, so the drinking experience is a whole lot more satisfying. With brandy and cognac, I always buy more expensive bottles, rather than cheaper versions. If you intoxicate yourself with a cheap imitation, while the results you'll get will be pretty much the same outcome with a hangover from hell, but the experience of drinking such fine spirits won't be as rewarding. Pace yourself, use it in the right context and at the right time and in moderation and the benefits will be warming and rewarding. It will help you with your judgment calls. Keeping control of jurisdiction is currently not in your purview, but when it does come, if it does come, then you can assert yourself more. For now, you must be patient and drink slowly, savouring the process; you need to play the game by the rules. You understand what I'm trying to say?"

"Okay Confucius, what do I do - what do we do?"

"About what?" Walter asks, finishing the last of the cognac in his glass.

"About a type of gravity called Richard?"

"Nothing."

"Really?"

"Not yet, no."

"Why?"

"Because he hasn't broken any rules by phoning you, so if he wants to come down here and poke around, let him."

"What are you thinking?"

"If he is intent on getting ahead by digging a hole, let him dig his hole."

"Wait, you want him to poke around while we await jurisdiction?"

"Pretty much yes. If he gets too involved it will give me some wiggle room to complain that he is harassing my staff, phoning them, coming down to the office un-invited, throwing his weight around and getting in the way of the team conducting their investigations. Then I can lodge a complaint with the team of staff deciding on jurisdictional ownership. If we must work together with MI6, you can be sure Kincaid, that it is you who will oversee the investigation. But you must play the game. Gravity can work for you if you let it."

Evander sits back in his chair and relaxes for the first time since he ended the call with the MI6 Chief. He raises his glass to take a drink and is surprised to find his glass empty. He doesn't remember draining it, but he must have needed it. He holds the empty glass in front of him and asks. "Do you mind, Chief?"

The Chief takes the glass from Evander and goes to the cabinet, pours another two glasses of cognac, then returns to his desk and hands Evander a glass before sitting in his chair.

"Okay, so, what happens now?"

"Next time he calls, and he will, tell him he shouldn't really come down till jurisdiction is settled. If you word it right, he'll kick back at you and start asserting his authority, throwing his seniority around like a child throwing marbles in a playground. Then tell him if he wants to come here, he can, but you advise against it as MI6 already have everything on file and there is nothing more for them to have, though if he feels the need to check up on the team and the investigation he can do, but he would just be getting in the way and you advise restraint until a decision has been made on jurisdiction, so you and your team can work with what you do have right now."

"Right, got it - give him a shovel to help him dig his hole, right?"

"Pretty much, yes."

"Let him come along and then complain about his presence."

"Yes. Of course, you can't do so straight away, you may need to let him order the team about a little bit, before you step in and tell him to stop and that you're going to complain to me about it, but don't do that right away, let him get comfy first, get his feet under the table and get used to making demands of your team and him expecting them to jump every time he snaps his fingers."

"I tell you now, Adam and Izzy will take umbrage to that, I don't like it. Although I can see the logic in it. None of the team will like it."

"Good, you'll need to give them no indication that this is all part of the plan, if you tip them off about it, then their reaction and anger at the injustice won't be as convincing. Who is likely to pop their cork first?"

"Adam. He's not the most patient of people. He'll put up with shit for the shortest amount of time before he speaks up. Gobby Scouser, you know kind of goes with the territory."

"Good. Assign him to liaise with the MI6 Chief when he gets here, so anything he needs goes through him and if he is not around, then Izzy can help him."

"I've got my reservations on Adam, as he is especially not going to like this and his angry little Scouser will come out full force. He'll take orders from me and you and to some degree my team, but outside forces don't survive his wrath. He'll likely disappear to calm down like I've done here, and the Chief isn't even here yet."

"How will you know when he's had enough? Will there be a point where you know you have to step in?"

"He's a Scouser and though he's been down in London for a long time, well when he's pissed off, the angry Scouser is there full force, and you can hear it in his voice. He drops letters off his words and talks a lot faster than usual. In normal circumstances, he deliberately slows down his speech for people, but piss him off… his speech is over a hundred miles per hour. You can take the Scouser out of Liverpool, but not Liverpool out of the Scouser. Actually, I don't think he'd allow that to be taken away from him, he's proud of his roots."

"Good, good. Next time Richard calls, allow him to visit, but be clear you don't approve."

"Actually, I kind of told him I'd call him back."

"Don't. It will piss him off no end and he'll end up calling you, though he'll try to use his position to stamp his authority on his visit. That's all well and good, because it can be used to our advantage, in that he was demanding even before he got here. You follow me?"

"Oh yes, most definitely. I'm now actually looking forward to seeing him squirm, let him come on down here, throwing his weight around. Just let him." Evander drains the last of his Cognac and places the glass on the desk in front of him.

"You see Kincaid, I told you, didn't I?"

"Told me what?" Evander asks as he rises from his seat.

"Gravity."

Evander thinks about their discussion and realises the Chief is right. Pressure made positive, makes gravity work. He laughs a knowing laugh. He buttons his jacket and turns to exit the office "Thanks for the drink and advice Walter. Now I know why you're the wise Chief."

CHAPTER SEVENTEEN

Two days later, Evander gets a phone call. He answers on the second ring. “D.C.I. Kincaid”.

“Ah, Kincaid good, got you. Richard Smith, MI6 Chief here.”

“Good morning Chief, how are you?” Evander inquires and almost kicks himself for asking.

“I’m good thank you, the odd ache in these old bones now and again, but otherwise, very good indeed.”

After a short pause, Evander notices there is no reciprocation, so Evander decides to get straight down to business. “Did you want something Chief? Only I’m extremely busy, and don’t have time for pleasantries.”

“Right, yes of course, you have a murderer to find.” Smith replies condescendingly.

“Yes, we do, so what do you want?”

“You didn’t phone me back after we spoke the other day, so I’m following up. When can I come and meet your team and do a gestalt?”

“Excuse me, a what?”

“I need the whole picture of what your team has managed to discover so far. A gestalt pretty much covers what I want, what I expect.”

Evander can’t help but shake his head. who speaks like that when asking for everything you have? What a pompous dick he is.

“Did you hear me Detective?” The Chief inquires.

“Oh yes, I did. So basically, you want an overview of where we are up to?”

“Well, if you want to put it so crudely and in a somewhat simplistic yet ugly way, then yes an overview.”

"Oh, so you mean you've been awarded jurisdiction and we have not been told?"
"What? No, I didn't say that D.I. Kincaid."
Irked at his now obvious deliberate dropping of a letter in the title of his role, Evander decides to correct him. "It's D.C.I. Kincaid and until jurisdiction has been awarded, I don't think it is wise for you to come and interfere in what we do, or do not have as an overview. Your team had already taken everything we had on Stone. What more could you possibly expect to get from us apart from what you already have?"
"Oh, so you mean you don't have copies of everything?"
"You took everything we had, and it wasn't something we had a say in." Evander replies, side stepping the question about copies somewhat wisely.
Richard brings the conversation back to visitation and asks. "So, you haven't answered the question. When is a good time for me to visit?"
"As I said, we are still awaiting the verdict on who has been awarded jurisdiction."
"How does this afternoon sound?"
"We're busy this afternoon."
"Oh, it's quite Okay, I think I can navigate my way around a filing cabinet and a cork board."
"But can you follow the strings?" Evander retorts as he thinks about the M.I.R. and the corkboard with just one colour string, all of them leading to the killer.
"Follow what?" Richard asks, puzzled.
"Never mind, you'll figure it out. Look, I don't think it is a wise idea to come over here till the N.C.A. has made a decision."
"Look, D.I. Kincaid…"

Evander cuts him short. "I told you it's D.C.I. Kincaid."
"Right, yes whatever. Look if we are going to work together, then we need to start somewhere and if we can build a working relationship before any decisions are made, it will make the whole process a lot more streamlined and effortless."
"I see. So, you want to bypass protocol, is that right?"
The Chief raises his voice in response and replies abruptly. "That isn't what I said. Stop trying to put words in my mouth or... " He stops. The threat caught in his throat before he can voice it.
"Or what, Richard?"
"It's Chief to you."
A knowing smile curls Evander's lips - got him. He doesn't like it when his authority is undermined, so it is obvious that titles are important to him, especially his own. He will likely see a D.C.I. ranking as way down the pecking order now he has Chief Super as his title, so he likes to undermine the title by dropping a letter, purely to imply you are beneath him, no matter how many letters follow your name.
"Or what?" Evander presses.
After a moments silence, Smith replies. "Or it's going to make a working relationship more difficult later down the line. Now, I'm coming to visit this afternoon."
"I told you, we're all busy, I can't afford any of my team to be taken away from their daily duties while we investigate this case."
"Ah, but I was under the impression that you thought we should wait until jurisdiction was awarded?" Smith answers smugly, thinking he has caught Evander out.
"Well, that is only for your Agent Stone and the claim on

authority for jurisdiction."
Smith replies dismissively. "So. What does that have to do with it?
"The rest of the case is not open to petition for authority."
"Again, so what?"
"So, therefore my team has their work to do as they conduct their investigations."
"Investigations for what exactly?"
"You may be contesting jurisdiction on one aspect of the case, but that does not give you leeway on the rest of it. There are eight murders so far, my team and I are currently working on the other seven, so your MI6 traitor is just another casualty of my serial killer. We may not be looking into Stone now, but believe me, we have plenty of work to be getting on with." Evander states deliberately trying to provoke a reaction.
"Got an answer for everything haven't you, Kincaid?"
"Just doing my job to the best of my abilities within the boundaries in which they are set."
"I see. Well, you can expect me to come visiting soon, it won't be this afternoon as I was planning, but it will be when you least expect it and it'll be sooner rather than later."
Before Evander can respond, Chief Super Richard Smith terminates the call.
Phase one complete, now they just need to wait for him to toddle down and start throwing his weight around.

CHAPTER EIGHTEEN

Evander sits and stares out the window of his apartment, which overlooks a section of the river. He watches life drift by on the banks of the Thames, as he drinks his morning coffee before he heads to the office.

He puts the cup down, still half full and picks up the manila envelope that his adoptive parents left him. He plays with the edge of the envelope, toys with the idea of opening it, but is reluctant to do so.

He feels as though he is being watched and when he glances out of the window, he sees a crow perched on the ledge of the rail of the balcony outside his apartment, it watches him intently. The crow hops around so that its back is to Evander, it turns its head to watch him from the corner of its eye, then it cocks its head and seems to study him.

Evander notices it's tail and he realises it is not a crow at all, but a raven. Should have known really from the size of it, it's too big to be a crow.

"Morning, Raven." Evander greets the bird.

"Cawwww, cawwww, cawwwww." The Raven responds.

Evander laughs nervously and he is suddenly disconcerted by its presence and just wants it to go away. He feels as though it is not the bird that watches him, but Freddie Corvus judging him, waiting for him to find his murderer. He stands up just as the bird spreads its wings and flies off.

Evander still has the manila envelope in his hand. He opens the draw of his desk, drops it in and closes the draw. So much information that his adoptive parents collated for him. He knew of course that he was adopted after he witnessed his Mother's murder at the age of four. What he didn't know, was

background and family history of who he was before the murder. It is, however, all contained in the envelope. So, if he felt the need to know more it was available to him. All he had to do was find the courage to open the envelope.
His phone rings, caller display shows it's the Chief.
"Kincaid, you're needed in theatre land."
"Did you say theatre land Chief?"
"Yes. There's been another one called in."
"Oh my God and so soon after the last one."
"That's what I thought too."
"Where is it?"
"The West End - at the Theatre Royal on Drury Lane."
"It's outside the theatre?"
"No, it's inside. It's an absolute bloody farce. Not only is it in the theatre, but the victim is a politician."
"Oh my God, who is it?"
"Peter Noble."
"Holy shit, really? What happened, I mean how do we know it's our guy?"
"The dragon is present, definitely him. I've been given orders from upon high to try to keep this low key, so when you arrive at the theatre, no blues flashing you hear me?"
"Sure Chief. What did Noble do to warrant the wrath of the dragon's killer I wonder?"
"He's a politician, so the field is wide open on his misgivings and potential crimes. Clearly the killer holds no counsel for the wicked that people do, regardless of their position in the world. If they're bad, they're bad. But it seems he left us a clue with the 'why' in this case, in respects of how he was put on display."
"What do you mean 'display'? Is it another Tower Bridge

presentation?"
"Almost yes. Just grateful this one isn't public viewing; the press would have a bloody field day. Anyway, you'll see when you get there. Get your team together and get there A.S.A.P."
"Yes, will do Chief."
"And no 'blues' you hear?"
"Yes, no flashing lights."
"Keep me informed." The Chief hangs up, without saying goodbye.
Evander calls the team and tells them where to meet.
He needs to pick Adam up en route first while his car is off the road undergoing repairs for an M.O.T. to be passed. He grabs his jacket off the hanger on the back of the door in his study, he goes to head out the door, but stops and returns to his desk. After a brief hesitation he opens the draw and takes out the manila envelope, places it in a buff folder that they use at work to disguise it and heads out the door with it.
He may open it later.
Then again, he may not.

CHAPTER NNETEEN

Evander pulls up slowly in front of the Georgian terrace where Adam lives. He looks up at the top floor and spots Adam in the window looking out for Evander's car. Evander honks the horn twice, so he is sure that Adam knows it is him, then he turns the music down - The Who are playing, of course - the front door to the terrace opens and Adam comes out, half a piece of toast hangs out of his mouth.

One arm is already in his jacket, but he puts his other arm in the jacket as well, then closes the door behind him. The multi-tasking detective.

Adam runs down the steps to the car, opens the passenger door and gets in.

Through a mouthful of toast, he greets Evander with a muffled... "Mornin' Boss. What we got?"

"Another dragon victim in a London theatre."

"No shit, really? A theatre! WOW!" Adam exclaims like an over excited schoolboy. "Where is it, which theatre?" He asks, as he munches on the toast.

"Theatre Royal."

"What, as in Drury Lane Theatre Royal?" Adam mumbles with a mouthful of toast.

"Yup."

"How the hell did he do that?" Adam wonders.

"Wondering the same thing too. He definitely likes putting on a show."

"I know, quite the dramatist isn't he."

"I think he almost belongs on the stage himself."

"It'll be the dogs bollocks this one Boss. I've never had a crime scene in a theatre before, it's quite exciting."

Evander looks at Adam with a note of disbelief on his face.
"That was inappropriate wasn't it?"
"You think, Einstein!"
"Sorry."
"When do you get your car back?" Evander asks, changing the subject.
"Monday. Costing me a small fortune to get it fixed, but you know I love my little Trixie"
"What's the problem with it?"
"Failed on the brakes and two tyres. Be glad to get her back, you know I love my Mini. She's my version of Rule Britannia. Thanks for picking me up Boss." Adam says.
"No problem. Just hope the traffic starts moving quick. Want to get this one back to the Yard, so we can start investigating and try to piece more clues together."
"Did the Chief give you any idea what we're looking at?" Adam asks, finishing the last of the toast.
"Nope and your guess is as good as mine."
"So, no clue what we're walking into."
"Apart from it being the dragon killer and it's a theatrical crime scene like Tower Bridge was - only not so public - no. Feeling my way in the dark with the rest of my team I'm afraid. No heads up on anything till we get there. Oh, and the Chief said no 'blues', so don't switch them on, got it?"
They stop at a pelican crossing. A woman pushes a pram across the road. She smiles at Evander as she crosses, Evander nods his head in return. They wait for the lights to change.
"No problem Boss, got it." Adam confirms as he reaches to an inside pocket.
"Don't even think about it."
Adam looks at Evander with a 'What?' Expression.

Evander glances at him quickly, before turning his eyes back to the lights, waiting for them to change. "I've told you, no smoking in my car and I mean it. I don't give a shit if your own car smells like an ashtray, but don't stink my car up with your cancer sticks."

"Blimey! Cancer sticks, that's a bit harsh."

"True though." Evander states with conviction.

"I was going for my phone." Adam protests.

"Bollocks, you keep your phone in your right jacket pocket, not the inside breast pocket."

"How do you do it?"

"What can I say, I'm blessed with X-ray vision, just like Superman." Evander jokes.

The lights change and Evander drives off.

"They say an ex-smoker is the worst and it's certainly true with you!" Adam reminds him.

"Yeah, but I quit, you should too."

"How did you do it? I mean, what motivated you?"

"Izzy asked me to."

"What, that was it? Just because someone asked you?"

"Yeah. Now I'm asking you. Give them up."

"Wasn't there more incentive than being asked?" Adam challenges.

"I caught a glimpse of how upset she'd be if I died as a result of smoking."

"Hate to break it you, Boss, but we all have to die of something." Adam quips.

"I know, but Adam, the pain in her eyes ripped a hole in my heart. In that split second, I saw what it would do to her. It was like looking into her soul and seeing the wound forming, wrapping itself around her heart and strangling her emotions like barbed wire. It was then that I realized I had to give it up. I didn't want to be the cause of that pain, not when it was all in my control to stop it happening."

"So, what if you die doing your job?"

"That's different, it goes with the territory, and we all face the same risks, not just me. Hell, just opening your front door has a risk, crossing the roads has a risk, it's a chance we all take, but some risks we can control. I just had to do something about it, so she didn't have to live with the pain of watching me die from a smoking related illness. Quitting, with her in my mind helped. I caught sight of that pain and if that happened, knowing that I had the power to do something about it to stop that being an outcome in her life, well it was an easy choice."

They sit in silence for a while. Adam ponders over the information.

"Wow. I wanted profound and I guess that just about hits the mark."

"How profound?"

Adam reaches inside his pocket and pulls out the pack of cigarettes, he opens it, takes a cigarette out and raises it in front of him. He waves it in the air. "My last cigarette, which I'll have later." He offers Evander the pack with the remainder of the cigarettes in them. "Can you discard them for me?"

Evander takes the packet off him and puts them in the recess in the side of his door. "I'll get rid of them later, don't want to leave them on the street for kids to find." He turns his head briefly to see Adam looking at the cigarette like it had mystical magic contained within.

"What's wrong?" Evander asks.

"I never knew such insight could be so life changing. I know this will be my last one. I know my family won't have the burden of my death from smoking. I don't know if I should be thanking you, or Izzy."

"You're really going to quit?"

"If that isn't motivation enough, what you saw in Izzy's eyes, well I don't know what is. Besides, if it means I'll also get to spend an extra10 years nailing bad guys with you, well I'll take it. I'll be the Carter to your Regan."

Imitating Jack Regan, Evander exclaims. "We're the fucking Sweeney son, and you're nicked you bastard!"

"The Flying Squad!" Adam laughs. A smile as broad as the river Mersey spreads across his face.

CHAPTER TWENTY

Evander walks into the theatre with his team following him. Evander stops in his tracks when he sees the display before him. Adam and Izzy walk on ahead of him to get a closer look. Grace and James remain with Evander.

"Oh my God, is that Peter Noble, the politician?" Grace asks.

"I thought it was him too." James replies. "Quite a come-uppance for him, never did like him. Horrible little racist."

"What did he do?" Grace asks.

"Money mad, control mad, lying and cheating you know, basic politician training they receive for brain washing the unsuspecting public."

"How?" Grace wonders out loud.

"Don't you know anything about politics?" James asks in dismay.

"Not really, not enough room in my pretty head for politics when there is so much police work to do, real work."

"You're quiet Boss. You alright?" James asks, changing the subject.

Evander doesn't answer but nods his head.

"You sure Boss, you look like you've seen a ghost." Grace notes.

After a few seconds pause Evander replies. "Yeah, I'm good. Go on ahead with Adam and Izzy. I'll follow you. I just need a minute."

Without saying anything, but giving surreptitious looks to each other, Grace and James walk towards the front of the stage, to where Adam and Izzy stand in front of the body of Peter Noble.

Evander watches them as they talk to each other. Evander

knows Grace and James have said something to Izzy and Adam, because they both look at the Boss, but try to disguise it. Izzy furtively looks around the theatre, while Adam peers over Grace's shoulder, but he knows they are watching him. Evander needs to get it together, but this scene, this crime has got to him so much and he can't figure out why. Yet.

When Evander first saw Peter Noble hanging on stage, held by wires like a puppet... No, like a marionette, that's it... A marionette.

It stirred something so deep in his psyche, that he felt like hands made of ice had caressed his body, giving him a chill, which caused the hairs on the back of his neck to rise and goose flesh to claim his skin, while an almost arctic winter frost climbed his vertebrae, like ice that forms on water-soaked stairs.

Evander wants to just turn around, walk out and pretend he had never walked in, never witnessed the display on stage, but there is no denying it and you can't un-see something once you've seen it. He's on the border of what psychologists call 'fight or flight'.

Evander takes deep breaths and tries to clear his mind in order to conduct his job. As distraction, he tries to recall the last time he went to the theatre, probably with Jasmine he imagines. It was such a long time ago now, a musical he vaguely recollects, but he can't recall what they saw, probably Phantom of The Opera as it was her favourite.

The theatre has a different feel to it when people are not there to see a show.

Evander wonders what it must be like for the actors who work in theatre and take to the stage each night. How they cope with the rehearsal in front of an empty theatre and then the shock on opening night, to be confronted with a full house of people sat in the seats watching them. He can understand why people would get stage fright, but when it works, to watch them weave their magic of make believe, it is quite an amazing skill to have. It gives people a means of escape, even just for a few hours. To escape, by being someone else for a while. Evander needs to escape himself, which probably explains his train of thought right now. Stage fright - fight or flight; it makes sense why his thoughts are making connections like that, at least it does to him.

However, the scene before Evander is anything but make believe. It's very real and too close for comfort for him for a reason he hasn't put his finger on yet. Acting, that could work, pretend it's just a movie set and it's not real.

Evander takes a deep breath and steels himself as he moves forward to join his team. They all stand at the foot of the stage in the gap between the stage and the front row of seats.

They are all looking up at Peter Noble, who is suspended by wires and pulleys, similar by the look of it to the ones used on Freddie Corvus on Tower Bridge. Only difference here is that the wires, pulleys and cables are connected to Peter's body in a different manner, for a different purpose. They pierce his feet, his lower legs, knees and upper leg. His arms, torso and even his head. It maybe would not be so bad if he were not in such a strange position.

He is at an obtuse angle, bent in half. His legs are splayed, so you can see his head, which peaks between his legs. He looks like he's been snapped in half and it's quite sickening.

Crime scenes have disturbed him before. The most sickening of sights to discover and just when you think you've seen it all, a psychopath will have a more imaginative way of plummeting to new depths of depravity, that will keep you shocked. Evander felt the blood drain from his face as he looks upon the sorry state of the politician.

Many people won't be sorry to see him gone. He was extremely far right wing in his policies, most distinctly a racist and his somewhat provocative, bordering on extreme speeches, incited all sorts or retaliation on his home, his office, car and the party headquarters.

Maybe he had been vocal once too often. Although the dragons killer is not a hit man, he will be thanked for this one by many people, because he generated a lot of hate crimes in the extreme against many groups and not necessarily minority groups either. It could be as simple as, if you spoke out against him on the news, or in the press and opposed his political views and aspirations. He had a way of encouraging people to do his bidding in order to keep those opposing tongues from wagging again.

"Do you want to see how he moves?" A voice asks from behind them.

Jumping, the whole team turn around to find Violet Jackson behind them.

"Oh my God, Violet, you scared the bejesus out of me." Izzy tells her.

"Me too." James confirms.

"Me three." Grace concurs.

A loud bang makes everyone jump again. They look around for the cause of the noise. A small bump can sound like a loud bang in an empty theatre, because its echo in the auditorium is a sound distorted and displaced.

"Sorry, that was my fault". Adam calls out, as he holds his hands up in the air apologetically.

"Jesus H, Adam." James curses.
Finally, with a grip on his emotions, Evander asks Violet "How he moves? You mean he can be operated like a real marionette?"
"Yes."
"Why would you want to show us that?"
"Because he has a message, and I knew you'd want to see it."
"Am I going to regret this?"
"Possibly, but you need to watch it."
"Right. Get it over with. The sooner we are out of here the better." Evander says rapidly, his words almost running into one another, his accent hard and edgy on this occasion.
"You don't like it in the theatre?" Violet asks.
"It's not the theatre that's the problem, it's the play that's on." Evander says, sweeping his hand towards the stage.
"Right. I'll get on with it then."
Violet walks away and pulls out a walkie talkie and asks someone if they are there. She gets a reply and gives instructions that Evander can't hear. A few seconds later she returns to Evander.
"Hey guys?" Violet calls out to Evander's team, "You may want to move back from the front of the stage. This is one front row centre seat you don't want to be in, trust me."
They all walk to the aisle and stand together with Violet and Evander.
Violet speaks into the walkie talkie and says one word.
"Now."
On stage the wires and pulleys move, they make Peter Noble's legs go above his head, so it looks like he is standing on his head. His arms come up and try to reach up to his feet, he tilts his head, his mouth opens in a look of shock, then his hands

come to his mouth like he's going 'OH!'
His right arm moves towards the ceiling, he looks like he is stretching, reaching for something, but can't grasp it and as his arms falls back, a cable comes loose from high above and whips across the front seats of the stalls. It crashes into them with a whip like crack, as the cable hits the chairs. Evander's team look at each other and then to Violet, who gives an *'I know'* smile.
From above the body of Peter Noble, a banner unfurls, and Peter's hands point up to the banner, a message is revealed in that neat calligraphy the dragon killer likes.
"I've been a bad boy Detective Kincaid. I wanted to be a real puppet rather than a greased one. Now I have my wish."
Adam laughs nervously, "What the fuck is that supposed to mean?"
"Well part of it is self-explanatory, but the rest of it, I think your killer is inviting you to dig around and find out what is going on in the seedy world of our politician. I guess nothing is ever what it seems in the life of a politician." Violet observes.
"Looks that way." Evander concurs. "I guess there's no point in asking you what the cause of death was?"
"I'll know more…" Violet begins but doesn't finish.
"… When you get him back to autopsy. Yeah, yeah - I get it."
"If you know what I'm going to say, why do you even ask?"
"I live in hope that you may tell me straight out one day what the exact cause of death was without the need for an autopsy." Evander forces a smile.
"I'd hazard a guess at this one, but I could be wrong, and you

know I don't like to guess till I have all my facts and tox reports back. I'll be dealing with this as soon as we get him back to the mortuary."

"Great, so we're done here?" Evander asks.

"Not much else to see, unless you want to see the show again?" Violet smirks.

"Once is quite enough. Now, can you take him down please?"

"No problem."

"Let's get back to the Yard team." Evander calls out to his team.

He walks away with wider strides than usual in his hurry to get out in the fresh air, away from the display in the theatre, away from death, away from deep seated hidden memories. Away from the 'marionette man'.

CHAPTER TWENTY-ONE

Walking over to Evander's office, Adam Eastwood stops as he reaches the open door and watches his Boss, who is at the window, with his back to the door. His arms are folded, his left hand rubs his right bicep, kind of looks like he's hugging himself, while he tries to ward off a chill.

"You okay Boss?"

Evander turns around to face him. "No. I want to know how the hell this killer got into the home of Peter Noble to play with his dolls."

"What dolls?"

Evander goes to his desk, picks up a file, opens it and takes out a set of photos. "I was just checking HOLMES for an update and found these."

He hands them to Adam who becomes more uncomfortable with each photo he looks at. The photos were taken in a bedroom.

A weird looking doll is on a bed in the exact same position as Peter Noble's body was found on the stage, bent in half, the head peering through the legs, the same clothes on the doll are the clothes that Peter Noble was found in. Adam glances up at Evander, the expression on his face shows he is clearly disturbed by the images before him.

"I know. I thought the same thing too." Evander reassures Adam of his reaction.

Returning his attention to the photos now, Adam continues working though the set of photos. The marionette wires are also in place in the same positions as they were on Noble, and the doll looks like him as well. Adam looks up. Evander knows what he is thinking because he was thinking the same

thing too. Adam hands the photos back.
"What the hell?"
"I know quite bizarre don't you think, or is it just me?"
"Not just you, Boss. They were in his house? Why would a grown man have those type of dolls? Are they dolls, or ornaments?"
"Yes, they are dolls. I had to research them, didn't know what type it was, but found they are B.J.Ds."
"B.J.Ds? Sounds like a sex act! What the hell does that mean?" Adam inquires.
"It's an abbreviation for 'ball jointed dolls.' It seems Peter Noble was quite opposed to a lot of things in public, but he was quite a strange man where his private life was concerned."
"Most single men have different types of erm, 'dolls' in their bedrooms to the one he had in his. Kinda creepy looking if you ask me." Adam notes.
"Yes, well it seems the public persona of a straight man wasn't quite the same behind closed doors. All the dolls he has are all male, not one female in his collection. Some of them are dressed in normal attire, while others as you can see from the photos, are dressed more exotically and that's without all the B.D.S.M. stuff."
"Okay, so what, he was in the closet and was punishing himself?"
"Perhaps. Guess we'll never know, as it is all conjecture now that he is dead."
"How did this all come to light?"
"His housekeeper found a door open that she wasn't ever allowed to go in. So, when it was ajar, she couldn't resist taking a peek inside through the gap. She said it freaked her

out but decided to pretend she had not come across it. Then she got to the bedroom and saw B.J.D. Peter Noble on the bed and it being in his likeness, it got her worried that something was wrong.

The housekeeper knew he had not been home all weekend, because she made the bed every day during the week, but when she came in on Monday, it was exactly how she had left it on the Friday before, with the exception of the doll.

She said he was messy at the weekend and liked to party, so she had to stay longer to do her housework on a Monday. Quite a shock for her to get there and find that the place was clean and tidy, but when she went in the bedroom, she found that. She tried to call him, but his mobile was in the house, and he never went anywhere without it.

She then called his P.A. who came over and when he saw the display, well he tried everywhere that he knew, or places he thought he might go and when he couldn't get hold of him, that's when he called the police to report him missing."

"So, when he was found at the theatre, who found him?"

"The manager when he arrived. No shows in theatre-land on a Monday, so after the show on Sunday, when everyone had gone, our friendly neighbourhood serial killer got in and had plenty of time to set the stage out - no pun intended. There's a new show starting next week, so the place had been stripped back to bare stage for the new set to be rigged up. The manager had gotten in early and found him."

"It must be him, mustn't it? The dragons killer I mean." Adam wonders.

"Oh no doubt, I agree definitely our dragons guy. Not sure how he knew, what he knew about Noble, but none the less, he did."

"I mean in the house, not at the theatre, that's pretty clear it is him." Adam confirms.
"Oh, I see. Yes, absolutely him at the house". Evander ponders. "He's never done anything like this before. I know he took the glasses from the last crime scene, but that was different. He took them to cause confusion more than anything else. I've still not wrapped my head around why he took them and the more I think about it, the less likely it seems now that he took them as a trophy, or a message to us that we are blind to him. Anyway, that doesn't really matter, as it doesn't count, because they are not the same thing, taking the glasses and leaving the doll staged at the house. I know a trophy isn't why he took the glasses anyway, but this is quite personal. He took a risk going into his home in order to position the doll the same. He's getting bolder."
"How did he know that the doll was there, so he could set it out like how his body was found?"
"That's what I'm wondering too. Thinking that maybe he knew the killer, or someone who knew him told him of the doll. The housekeeper had never seen it before, and she's been with him for six years now. She said if it had been there, she'd have noticed it, because the doll is too creepy to be kept on display, so he must have kept it in the locked room, somewhere she wasn't allowed to go in and clean, which explains the door being left open to said room."
"How does that explain it?"
"Because Noble would never be so careless to leave a door open to a room that the housekeeper was forbidden from going in, which he kept under lock and key. That's how she saw his collection."
"Did forensics find anything in the house, or the theatre?"

Adam asks.
"No, same, zero as usual."
"How the hell does he do it? He never leaves any evidence at all, not even a trace, not even so much as a skin cell."
"I know. We just have to hope he slips up at some point, leaves something behind, that he contaminates the crime scene in some way." Evander says.
"Have a feeling he's not that stupid, he's too organised."
"Exactly". Evander agrees. "His type usually always is. Makes it that much harder to catch them, but it's not impossible.
"We will get him, eventually. I'm beginning to understand him more. That doesn't mean I sympathize with him, I don't, but it will help me catch him the more I understand him, so the more absurd the crime scene, the more information there is about him to learn and understand the type of animal he is, all the better to capture him, but we are getting closer, just hope that we get him soon."
"Sooner, or later we will, yes."
"Preferably sooner rather than later."

CHAPTER TWENTY-TWO

In the M.I.R. room, Evander explains to the team the details of the crimes that Peter Noble was guilty of in the eyes of the 'Dragons of Justice killer'.

Upon looking through his financial affairs, it is obvious that Peter Noble was not as noble as his name suggests. He would take back-handers of substantial amounts of money to *'ease business procedures'*, so they moved along much more fluidly, without any long protracting *'red tape'*. He greased the wheels for highly lucrative contracts to be awarded to certain companies, said companies had made a 'donation' to his party. He was seen at expensive restaurants, stayed in hotel suites that cost three months of his salary for two nights stay, wore only Rolex watches, dressed only in Versace suits and lived way beyond his means. The corruption he was involved in was neck deep. but no one could prove it, and he always had an answer for everything when pressured by the media, although that usually involved deflection by changing the subject to something more pressing than his personal expenses. He always got away with it and was never found guilty of any crime. However, he was no match for the dragons of justice killer, and he clearly wasn't one to be bargained with, for this time, he lost.

There are other counts of money laundering and tax evasion, even blackmail, albeit that the evidence for that is circumstantial. Now the clue about being a *'greased puppet'* makes perfect sense. Finally, Evander gets to the point on what happens next.

"There's a pub Noble used to frequent, The Mayflower in SE16. Adam, I want you and Izzy to go and check it out. See if

you find anything, if he met anyone there, was he a regular? Did he leave with anyone? You know the usual stuff."
"Oh sweet!" Adam exclaims.
"What?" Evander asks, perplexed at his obvious excitement.
"Well," Adam begins excitedly. "It's one of the oldest pubs in London, the oldest pub on the river Thames, I think. Oh, and you know it's named after the Mayflower ship that sailed to America, taking early settlers to the new land? Though it had many names before.
"Think it was fire damaged at some point and had to be part rebuilt…" Adam stops himself when he sees the rest of the team look at him incredulously.
"WOW! I didn't know that, but thanks for the history lesson. Geek!" Izzy says sarcastically and gives Adam a congratulatory slap on the back.
"History is cool." Adam says assuredly.
"Anyway, talk to the bar staff and the regulars." Evander continues. "See if they noticed him talking to anyone last time he was in. Doesn't matter whether he knew them or not, I want to know who he spoke to, see if they have any C.C.T.V. in situ and if so, if they have any footage from his last visit. Also, anything unusual, any strangers in the pub hanging around or acting suspicious. Anything out the ordinary they may have noticed. It may seem unimportant, but it could be vital to help us progress our investigation. Any questions?"
"When do we go?" Adam inquires, looking at his watch.
"After this meeting is over. And no pub lunch."
Adam can't hide his disappointment, which causes giggles from Grace and James.
"Grace, head on over to the party headquarters, see if they have received any hate mail…"

"What, apart from the usual hate mail he gets. Got?" Grace asks sarcastically.

"Well, you just never know what type of things there could be and possibly something the people at the H.Q. may have hidden from Noble. Take James with you. Show him the rocky road. I expect you all back here by sixteen hundred hours to brief me."

"What are you gonna do Boss?" Adam asks.

"Think I may get me a pub lunch." He says jokingly, looking at Adam. Everyone laughs. "Alright people, get to work."

"Seriously though Boss." Adam asks. "What *are* you gonna do?"

Evander raises an eyebrow, questioningly.

"Well." Adam continues. "I was just wondering if you were gonna tag along with me and Izzy?"

"Nope, I got work to do here, need to review the files again and update the board. There has be something else that can be gained from reviewing the evidence we have. Now, go on get to it." Evander tells them. All the team grab their gear and head out the office leaving Evander alone in the M.I.R. room, with nothing but a cup of mint tea for company.

CHAPTER TWENTY-THREE

Adam and Izzy arrive at The Mayflower pub and Adam is like an over excited schoolboy. He is amazed at all the history in the pub and the artifacts they have on display. Even the floorboards creak 'historically' as they approach the bar.

It thrills him when he thinks of the people who have trodden on these boards before him. If only floorboards could speak, the things they could tell of the people and the stories they know, all that history!

A barman spots Izzy and makes a beeline for her. He instantly flirts with her, in front of Adam with no apparent thought that they could be together, as in a couple as opposed to police partners.

Adam initially stays with Izzy as she starts to talk to the staff member, but Adam's got his number. Fancies himself as a bit of a ladies' man this one, he can tell. When Izzy flashes her badge to the barman and introduces herself and Adam as Detectives and tells him that they hope he'll be able to help with inquiries, the barman can't help himself but flirt even more shamelessly. He wants a policewoman as a babe he's bedded, that's apparent.

Adam sighs wearily rolling his eyes to the ceiling. Amazing how the badge can have different effects on different people. This man knows no shame in flirting. However, Izzy reciprocates and flirts back. Adam knows it is only to get information, nothing to do with her being even remotely interested in him. She is not that easy, or that cheap and he's not her type. Izzy does all the talking to start with, the barman drinking in her beauty, and it's obvious he's undressing her in his mind.

Adam has seen enough and finds himself looking around the pub, initially so he doesn't have to watch this creep drooling over Izzy, but then he finds himself wanting so much to go and look at all the memorabilia on the walls. He's barely listening to Izzy, or the barman and the few words he speaks, and it's not long before he wanders off, leaving Izzy at the bar talking to the ladies' man. Izzy seems to have this, so he decides to let them get on with it. Adam looks at the framed photos and the writing on the seat backs, lanterns, candelabras and old documents framed on the wall. He absorbs the information to hand, little bits of history on display before him. Adam is genuinely interested in history, always has been, especially British history. Fascinating stuff, especially when it's about your own country and how it helped in the creation of other, younger countries and helped give birth to their dreams.

~~~~~~

As the barman likes to flirt, Izzy plays along, so long as it will get her a head start in obtaining information.
Izzy tries to confirm the last time Peter Noble was in the pub. After the barman checks with a colleague, they establish the last time he was seen in the pub was last Tuesday, three days before he was murdered. The barman is starting to annoy her now, she would never date him, and Evander wouldn't approve anyway, he would dislike him - a lot.
"So, about Peter Noble. Anything unusual during his last visit here?"
"Not sure". The barman replies. "I don't really know him or the locals that well. I've not been here long enough, so I'm not
~~~~~~

familiar with what his normal activity would be."
"You're new to the area, or to the job?"
"Both. I'm a work butterfly, that's why I'm a temp. I get bored easily and like to flit from one job to another to broaden my horizons."
"Bar work broadens your horizons. How?"
"Oh, you'd be surprised at the people who come through the doors. The interesting men and the gorgeous girls, such babes!" He exclaims as he winks at her.
"How long have you been here?"
"Only a few weeks. I'm only filling in for a sick permanent staff member. My agency will probably be moving me on to something else by the end of the month. My feet are getting itchy already anyway. I want to try something new, but not sure what yet. How is police work?"
"Nothing you can do on a temp basis that's for sure. We require more loyalty on the force, it's not for work butterflies, or the faint hearted."
"Hmmm, really not sure what I want to do next." He ponders.
"Is there anything you are sure of?"
"Oh yes, one thing I am sure of, baby... Is how much fun we could have together. How about you and I ditch this place and go make some of our own entertainment?" The barman licks his lips suggestively.
Izzy giggles like a little girl, puts her head down pretending to be shy, but she's really thinking how she wants to vomit. The man is so vile and slimy, she'd like to put his arse on the floor. Sexist pig. She sees now he thinks women are playthings. What a moron, stuck in the dark ages like Captain Caveman. Getting back to the job, she asks. "Can you remember if Noble looked uncomfortable, or uneasy, did he leave in his usual

manner, or was he in a hurry?"
"Can't say to be honest. There were only a few people here, a priest and two girls, Noble and I think one of the regulars."
"Did you notice him leaving? Did he leave alone? Did he leave with someone?"
"You know, if I was leaving with you on my arm, I'd be in a hurry." He winks.
"He left with someone?" Izzy asks interested now in what he has to say.
"I have no idea, but what I'm saying is, I'd like to leave with *you*. You get my drift?"
Izzy ignores him this time and asks. "I'm sorry, I didn't get your name?"
"Friends call me 'The Stallion'. You can guess why!" He exclaims, winking. Again.
"Your real name?" Izzy asks, trying to keep calm, she resists the urge to smack him, which he would thoroughly deserve.
"Oh, it's Johnny, but you can call me annnnnnnnything you like, sweet cheeks."
'Urgh, sickening vile man, does he really believe any woman would fall for that crap? Sweet cheeks? What the fuck type of talk is that? No one talks like that anymore to chat people up, or do they? Does that even work?' Izzy thinks to herself. She looks around and spots Adam, who is absorbed in the history on the walls.
She looks back to Johnny, who leans on the bar with his left hand propped under his face, cupping his chin. A brown stain runs down the side of his hand, extending to his little finger - fake tan.
He leans towards her. He's opened a button on his shirt and leaned on the bar so she could take a glimpse at his chest, and

she's annoyed with herself because she falls for the ploy and takes a peek. Izzy rolls her eyes to the ceiling, she asks. "Did he seem okay to you, or distracted?"
"Who?"
"Peter Noble. The man I'm asking you questions about, the last night he was in here."
"Oh him… erm, I don't know." Johnny stands up, not flirting any more, buttons his shirt. Apparently, he's offended that she's not impressed with his excessively hairy chest. Whatever.
"So, do you know or not, can you remember anything that may help our inquiries?"
"Tuesday was supposed to be my night off, so I shouldn't have been here. I had a date, and I was distracted as all I could think about was the fun we were going to have when I finished the shift."
Izzy imagines herself as a cartoon character with steam coming out of her ears. She is so annoyed with this idiot. He has just wasted all that time trying to chat her up when really, he knew Jack shit and couldn't organise a piss up in a brewery, even if he had diagrams.
All she wants to do is punch his lights out, but she has to restrain herself and remember her training on self-control. It might help if she could just punch something, anything at all, even a cushion would do.
Just then a loud crash of glasses smashing makes her jump. She turns around to see Adam sprawled across a table with his hand up to his face. A large man with a clenched fist and arms that have muscles upon muscles walks towards him and grabs hold of him. He pulls his arms back, clenching his fist, he is ready to take another pop at Adam.

~~~~~~

Adam is fascinated with all the information he takes in. He fishes his phone out of his jacket pocket and takes some photos of the really interesting stuff. He is quite amused to find stuffed rats on display in a small cage next to a bust, of whom he was not sure, but they nestle quite well together in a window alcove.

He looks up and finds a winch with a large hook and a ship's wheel on the wall. He turns around, away from the bar and walks further into the pub, past Izzy and the barman, who stands at the far end of the bar, just on the curve where it tapers off and meets the wall.

The floorboards squeak under Adam's feet as he moves.

He spends time looking at photos and reading printed matter and writing on some of the seating backrests. All the history and little quirks made for interesting knowledge of the building.

Done with pictures, Adam pockets his phone and turns around to head back to Izzy. As he turns, he bumps into someone by accident, unaware someone is in close proximity behind him.

"Oh, I'm sorry." Adams says as he holds his hands up apologetically.

Beer sloshes out of the pint glass the man holds. He is a large man, built like a bear with a human head. His biceps bulge like Arnold Schwarzenegger on a good day. He looks at Adam, scowls, then looks to his pint of beer and the floor where the spilt beverage landed, then he looks back up to Adam, the message on his face is clear.
~~~~~~

Not wanting trouble Adam says. "Can I put one in the pump for you?" Pointing to his glass. "I didn't know anyone was behind me, sorry mate."
The man's expression changes from a scowl to one of hate. Adam isn't sure why, but then when the man replies, it becomes clear why. He is an English regionalist.
"Bloody stupid fucking Scouse git. Get back up north where you belong. You have no place being among Londoners, *mate*." The man says *'mate'* sarcastically.
"I've lived in London for around ten years now and I pay my London taxes like you or anyone else living in London. I have a right to live anywhere I want in my own country and London is not exclusive to Londoners."
"Get out of my sight you Scouse cretin. You're best leaving while you still have the use of your legs."
"Are you threatening me because I spilt your beer."
"Think again. Nothing to do with beer."
"Because I'm a Scouser?"
"You're quick for a Northern sissy. Well done. Only took you two attempts to work that out. Now, leave, or I'll make you. If you're lucky it will probably be in an ambulance."
"An ambulance? As opposed to?" Adam asks.
"A body-bag. Now fuck off."
"You and whose army?" Adam asks, his Scouse accent becoming more prominent.
The man puts his beer down on the table behind him, then says. "Let me introduce you to my friends." He raises his hands one at a time, forming fists as he does so. "Meet *'pain'*" He says as he raises his left hand. *"'and more pain'"*. As he raises his right hand. "They're here to teach you a lesson."
Before Adam can reply, the man throws a punch, which sends

Adam backwards into a table that is behind him, which sends glasses and cutlery crashing to the floor. Adam tries to get up, but the bear with a human head grabs him by his jacket, lifts him up with both hands. He is ready to punch him, and no doubt punch him again and again and again.

~~~~~~

Izzy knee jerks into action when she sees Adam down. She runs towards him just as the big man grabs hold of Adam and pulls him up off the table, which is in her way.

She jumps on the table next to it and slides across it, throwing her foot in the big man's stomach. The momentum forces him backwards, but he remains on his feet. She slides off the other side of the table, lands on her feet and is stood before the man who has assaulted Adam. She lands a punch - an upper cut – hard and squarely on the end of his chin and he goes down like a sack of potatoes.

"Holy shit!" Adam exclaims from behind her.

The man looks up and can see Izzy looking down at him.

A look of anger washes over his face. He looks like he wants to crush her in his big arms.

He pushes himself up, gets to his knees, but Izzy can't let him get up, or he'll gain the advantage with his formidable size. Izzy smacks him again hard.

The punch connects solidly with the man's face. Izzy thinks she caught him in the mouth, which he would not have expected. He stumbles backwards into tables and chairs and crash lands on his backside. He bumps his head on a chair that has been knocked over.

Izzy reaches to her back pocket, grabs her hand cuffs and
~~~~~~

reads the man his rights, but the bear with the human head tries to get up. He is not listening to Izzy.
Izzy warns him. "Stay down, or I'll put you down."
He gets up, ignoring Izzy, spits blood from his mouth and continues to rise.
"I said '*stay down*', or did you miss that part?"
"The Scouser's bitch doesn't get to tell me what to do. You're going to regret touching me." He says, still trying to get to his feet.
"The Scouser doesn't have a bitch, he has a partner." While she is still speaking, he won't be expecting an assault while she is still talking. She hits him as hard as she can, the element of surprise giving her an advantage over his formidable size, he goes down again. "That last warning wasn't a challenge, it was a promise."
Izzy quickly slaps the hand cuffs on him and arrests him for assaulting an officer of the law.
"Come on, I didn't know he was an officer of the law. He didn't say he was a policeman."
"I don't give a shit what you thought he was or wasn't. You hit him and no one hits him except me and maybe my Boss. But most definitely not you. Now get up." Izzy says pulling him by cuffed hands up onto his feet.
Adam rubs his jaw and watches Izzy man handle the guy towards the door.
"Hey, Izzy?" Adam calls out to her.
She turns around to Adam. "What?" Izzy asks sternly.
"Thanks."
"No problem."
"Izzy?"
"What?" She asks impatiently.

"Remind me never to piss you off."
Izzy smiles as she pushes the guy towards the door to take him for booking.

CHAPTER TWENTY-FOUR

Evander is with his team in M.I.R. They all have coffee and cake. Evander picks at a lemon poppy seed muffin, which he isn't really enjoying at all, but continues to pick at anyway. He thinks about the phone call earlier that week from the MI6 Chief and replays it in his mind. He wondered at the time if there was enough bait in his responses to lure Richard Smith into his den. After the phone call earlier this morning however, Evander is clear he baited him enough.

Smith left it just three days before following up with a call to advise he was going to visit and today is the day. Evander grows more impatient for him to just turn up and get the party started.

While they wait for the mighty MI6 to arrive - whenever that may be - Evander and his team trawl through paperwork, which everyone has double checked.

They are fully aware they need to be careful not to have anything about Jeremy Stone on display. It just wouldn't reflect well if Smith found paperwork scattered around desks or on screens, while jurisdiction was being contested and MI6 were supposed to be holding everything on him.

All that there is on show, is a photo of Stone at the seven o'clock position on the notice board. Evander wants MI6 to believe they hold all the cards and all the evidence on him. The other evidence however is in Evander's arsenal. Anything that is required on those cases means Richard will have to ask for it, thus giving rise to team irritation.

"Are you okay Boss?" Adam asks.

"Hmmmm?" Evander replies, only half listening.

"You're quiet, distracted and only picking at your muffin - not

like you at all. What's wrong?"
Evander smiles at how well Adam knows his moods, he replies. "Oh, well, you know, just want the case wrapped up and put to bed and the murderer behind bars."
"No, that's not it all, there's something else bugging you. What is it?"
Evander decides to tell the team that MI6 are coming to visit, but he won't tell them about the baiting. Evander replies.
"Adam, everyone... we may have a visitor today from MI6 - Chief Super Richard Smith and we should, to the best of our capacity attend his every need."
"Boss, you can't be serious?" Grace asks surprised.
"As serious as John McEnroe contesting a bad call, I'm afraid."
"Who?" Grace replies, puzzlement marking her voice.
"Never mind, it's a tennis joke. It's only funny if you remember him playing tennis and screaming at the umpire, obviously you're too young." Evander replies, unimpressed that his quick retort did not gain the response he hoped for.
"Oh figures, I was never that much into sport." Grace replies with an element of redemption in her voice.
"When is he coming over Boss?" James asks.
"John McEnroe?" Grace jokes.
"No, the MI6 Chief of course." James clarifies.
"He called me again earlier this morning. Said that he'd be here sometime this afternoon, but he hung up before I could get a time from him."
"You mean you pissed him off?" Adam guesses.
"No!" Evander protests softly, innocently, his accent at it's most disarming.
"What? So, he hung up on you for no reason at all; he does know who you are, right?" Adam says, disdain in his voice.

Evander smiles and replies. "Well, okay, I may have pissed him off just a little bit during the call. And I may or may not have baited him. He tried to take control as best he could." Evander says mockingly. "Bless him." He scrunches his face up in mock compassion.

"You mean he threw his toys out of his pram." Adam says.

"I hang up on people too. I did that with our very own Chief Super not so long ago." Evander replies.

"Yeah, but Boss it's different when you do it, I mean you're you, you're D.C.I. Evander fucking Kincaid, so you're allowed to be petulant, to make a statement and prove a point." Adam says.

Raising an eyebrow questioningly, Kincaid asks. "Petulant? Really?"

Back peddling, Adam laughs nervously as he tries to make petulance sound cool. "Well, I mean, I just mean that you know it's different when you do it, as it's with good reason and it sends a message that you're not happy and it makes people want to work harder to keep you on side. So you're not throwing your toys out of your pram when you do it, you're making a statement, you're putting things in perspective for people, so they see that you are pissed off and it will make them think and re-evaluate their position and I think I'll stop digging now."

"I see, well I think I see. That was meant to be a compliment, right?"

"Well of course Boss." Adam smiles his cheekiest smile.

"So, what is the plan when he arrives?" Izzy inquires.

"Give him what he wants, he may be a pain in the arse, but let him be one."

"How is that going to help?" Adam asks puzzled.

"You'll see when the cork pops."
"When the cork pops? Are you cracking open the champagne for his visit, Boss?"
"Good God no, not at all, but you'll see. All will become clear. For now, be prepared. Oh, and obviously if he asks for anything on Jeremy Stone, what is the answer you give him?"
In unison all the team collectively answer. "MI6 have it."
"Good, yes. Correct. Right answer."

~~~~~~

Later that afternoon, when the team are all back at their desks, Richard Smith arrives. It's three forty-five pm, and a buzz of activity sweeps through the floor space occupied by Evander and his team. Initially, Evander is not sure what all the fuss is about at the other end of the office.
A text from Walter alerts him that Richard Smith has arrived at the Yard and he is wandering around the office, taking time to stop by to check in on people he knows. Obviously, this is a tactic Smith is using to put the team on edge but keep them waiting with bated breath. He knows that word of his arrival at the Yard will spread like wildfire.
Fifteen minutes later, Chief Super Richard Smith rounds the corner and enters Evander's office.
"Kincaid. Good to see you, hoping we can work on this together. I hope all is well in the land of Scotland Yard?" Smith says, as he stands in front of the team.
"We're busy, always busy." Evander responds.
"So, are you going to introduce me to your team?"
"Yes of course." Evander confirms and proceeds to introduce each team member.
~~~~~~

Smith nods his head as a greeting but offers nothing more than that.

Introductions over, Smith gets straight to business. "Okay, so I need to commandeer a desk while I'm here. Which one can I use?"

Adam points to the other side of the room and responds before anyone else can. "There are plenty of empty desks over there you can use, one of the teams are on location at a stake out and won't be back all day, so you won't be disturbed over there."

Smith turns around to look at the desks and decides to be difficult. "Oh no, I couldn't possibly sit over there; it's all-in shade and I need some natural daylight to work in. Besides, I don't want to be isolated way over there."

James offers his desk as a solution. "Sir, you can use mine here."

Smith smiles and wanders over to James. He stands in front of the desk and inspects the workstation. Once his decision is made, he replies. "Thanks, but no, this won't do. The sunlight shines on your screen and my poor old eyes would struggle with that."

Smith wanders around the bank of desks in search of the right one. He stops at Adam's desk, reviews the position and light and makes his choice. He pulls out the chair and sits down without asking. He takes a good look around the desk before asking. "Who sits here?"

"I do." Adam replies.

Smiling smugly, Smith says with chagrin. "You got the monopoly on desks, for this is the Goldilocks position. I like it, this will do."

"Yes, so do I and there are plenty of desks empty over there

you can use."
"No, no, this one will do just fine, thank you Andy."
"It's Adam and I need my desk. You can sit over there and flick on the lighting."
"No, I'm quite content here thanks Son." Smith replies condescendingly.
Before he can reply, Evander cuts Adam short. "Adam you can sit with me in my office, I'm happy to share a desk with you."
"Oh, I never thought about your office, Kincaid." Smith responds. He gets up from the chair and looks through the office window at Evander's workspace before he changes his mind. "Second thoughts, this one is simply fine, I'll stay here. Goldilocks."
Adam heads over to his desk, gathers some files together ready to take into Evander's office, while in the process, Smith lowers the chair, which stops Adam mid file collection.
"Excuse me, did you just adjust my chair?"
"Yes, too damn high for my liking, this is much better, more in line with the computer height."
"It's not your desk, nor your chair, both are mine and they are perfect for me."
"Don't worry Son, you can always adjust it later." Smith replies as he tucks himself under the desk.
"Adam, can you help me with something please." Evander asks, trying to distract Adam as he is obviously irked and already about to pop his cork. Evander doesn't want him to blow a gasket too early.
"Gladly *Boss*." Adam replies exaggerating the word 'Boss' with an obvious tone of who the real Chief is in this office space.

Evander and Adam head into the office and Evander closes the door behind them. "Keep calm for now Adam, I know you are ready to pop, but not now, he's only just got here, give him a chance to…"
"A chance! A chance for what? For me to punch his lights out, may be?" Adam interrupts.
"I know he's a tosser and he will do his best to piss the team off as much as he possibly can, and I think that is the purpose of his visit. We need to appear to be accommodating as best as possible, respecting his ranking. At least until it becomes disruptive."
"He kicked me off me desk. I think we're already beyond being disrupted Boss!" Adam exclaims, his voice high pitched and angry, his Scouse accent on display in full force.
"Well, we have to give him what he wants. He is the Chief Super of MI6 after all."
"Desk jockey." Adam retorts.
"Yeah, he is now and a jobs worth at that too. I am sure he is here to test us, to be a thorn in our side."
"Is that a polite way of saying he's a prick?" Adam inquires, to which Evander smiles, but says nothing in response.
"What did you want anyway Boss?" Adam asks, trying to calm down.
"To get you out of his way, before you gave him a Liverpool kiss."
Adam laughs out loud. "Ah of course, I should have saw that one being lined up."
"Pull up a chair." Evander says, gesturing to the selection of chairs at Adam's disposal.
Adam pulls out one chair on the opposite side of Evander's desk and sits down.

Evander walks around to his chair, takes the chair out and sits down.
"Now, did you find anything new in your review of files early hours?"
"How did you know I was here early hours?"
"Coffee pot. Always a giveaway when you're here before Starbucks opens." Evander replies.
"Maybe I should clean that up to try to hide evidence in the future."
"I'd still know."
"Yeah, I'm pretty sure you would." Adam laughs.
"So, did you find anything?"
"I was wondering about something actually…" Adam stops talking when it dawns on him that he didn't bring the files with him that he was collecting from his desk. He looks over his shoulder as he realises he will have to go back out there.
"Fuck!" He exclaims.
"Did you leave the files on your desk?"
"Yes, I did. Shit man! I've got to go back out there, and I was just getting off my horse."
"Don't speak to him unless he speaks to you."
Adam gets up and replies. "Yeah, on it, Boss."
As Adam approaches his desk, he is annoyed to find that the Chief is sat with his feet up on the desk and is browsing through one of the files that Adam had gathered to take away. Now he has no choice but to ask him for the file.
Being polite, Adam asks. "Excuse me Sir, can I have that file you're reading?"
"What for?"
"I want to show the Boss something and it just happens to be in the file you are reading."

"Exactly on the money."
"I'm sorry, what?"
"You said it yourself, I'm *reading* it." Smith replies, exaggerating the word 'reading'. He un-crosses his ankles and places both feet firmly on Adam's desk.
"Well, it is needed right now. You can review it later, but I have a job to do and you're delaying me going about my business." Adam replies, resisting the urge to knock the chief's feet of his desk.
The chief laughs out loud. "Listen to you, busy boy! Anyone would think you were close to catching this twisted little shit. Fact is you're not. My having this file is not going to speed up your capture of him either. I don't think giving you this file that I am reading is going to miraculously give you an arrest, in whatever little shift hours you have left."
Adam's fists clench at his side. He realises he can't chin the Chief; he retrieves the remaining files from the desk and turns to walk away.
The Chief calls out to him. "Oh, Andy wait, I'll be wanting those files, so leave them be."
Adam turns back to face Smith and replies. "Well, you can't read them all at once now can you. When you're done with the file I want, you can have one of these. I'll be in the office with my Boss. And the name is Adam."
He turns back quickly, but not before he spots the chief pursing his lips together angrily. Good Adam thinks, got under his skin.
Back in Evander's office, he closes the door and drops the files on the edge of Evander's desk. He thumbs through files for no reason other than he needs the one Richard Smith is taking his sweet time over reading.

Adam sits in the chair opposite Evander and props his elbows on the edge of Evander's desk, then puts his hands in his hair, ruffles it and flicks his fingers through and then out of his hair and into empty air before him. His fingers splayed stiffly. He sighs and closes his eyes.

Intuitively Adam asks. "Okay, I get it. Something needs to happen here doesn't it and tick, I'm it, right?"

"Wow! That was quicker than I had anticipated."

"So that's a yes. Now I know something needs to be handled in a certain way and I need to allow this prick to be as disruptive, rude and arrogant as he can possibly get, is there any reward for me landing one on him?" He leans back in his chair, eyes still closed and puts his hands to his head, he weaves his fingers through his hair grabbing some of it tightly in frustration.

"Now Adam, you know that's not what we're aiming for."

"Okay, let me rephrase that - so is there any reward for me *not* landing one on him?"

"Possibly." Evander ponders, more than assures.

"It had better be bloody good. What do we get?"

"Hopefully, running point over the inevitable decision of a joint investigation."

Adam's eyes open wide. He takes his hands out of his hair and leans forward in his chair now, a gleeful smile spreads across his face. "We get jurisdiction?"

"Possibly. I think it will be a joint operation, but we may be able to lead the op."

"So, like MI6 would have to give us copies of everything?"

"Yup."

"And they can't redact information?"

"Nope."

"And they'll have to bring us copies, no, no, no, wait we'll have to go and get copies of everything from MI6 H.Q.?"
"Most likely."
"Oh, Boss, if that's the case, you have to let me go and collect the evidence. James can come with me, can't let the ladies suffer that fool again, He's a misogynist and I'm not letting the ladies go through that in his house. Please promise me you'll let me go and take James with me. Please, please, please?"
"Sure. You're my senior agent and you can choose who you want to go with you. I may just come along with you. But Adam, you're unlikely to get into Smith's office, so unfortunately you won't be able to fuck his chair up and scuff his desk and disrupt his files."
"Ha, you know me too well." Adam laughs in response.
"Oh, here we go, Smith's done with the file, and can you believe this; he's actually bringing it here to my office!"
Resisting the urge to turn around, Adam picks up a file and thumbs through it.
He looks through photos and talks randomly about the first photo he comes across. "So, in this photo we can clearly see the message the killer is trying to send and..."
Adam is interrupted by the door swinging open. Smith enters the room and, in a demanding tone states; "Files, I need more files to review. Here you can have this one back."
Evander is annoyed and he lets it be known. He rises from his chair, walks around his desk and stands beside Adam. He snatches the file out of the Chief's hand and irately tells him.
"Next time you want to come in my office, do me the courtesy of knocking on my door before just barging in. Would you like it if I just waltzed into your office without being invited?

No, you wouldn't. I don't care what division you're in, or how high your clout reaches, or how many stars you have on your shoulder, but know this; you will give me *and* my team respect when you're in *my* house. Got it?"

Smith stands silent and weighs up Evander's assault and whether he should be outraged at the defiance or impressed that Kincaid has the balls to call him out. There are not many men - or women - who stand up to him, so he decides to accept the confrontation, not so much as a challenge to his authority, but as one of protection of office. Something he himself has done in the past when his office has come under assault, even from an internal, friendly foe.

He decides not to rock the boat and replies with three words only. "Noted. File please?"

Adam hands the Chief a file, which he duly takes and leaves Evander's office, closing the door gently behind him as he goes.

Adam lets out a long-held breath. "Holy shit Boss. I could hug you right now for putting that idiot in his place!"

"Yeah, that probably wasn't a wise move on my part." Kincaid notes.

"Are you shitting me. That was totally epic!"

"Not the way it's supposed to play out. However, he may now actually show some respect."

"Annnnnnd that's a bad thing why?" Adam ponders.

"Wasn't part of the plan. Supposed to let him throw his weight around, be a complete dick and it adds weight to the protestation."

Adam catches on quickly and joins the dots succinctly. "Oh, I see. Game plan is to let him be a pain in the arse, which adds more weight to the protests from our Chief Super that the MI6

Chief Super has been a nuisance and has interfered with our investigation and he's been disruptive, slowed us down, got in the way. I see, I get it, I dig it, I like it and yep, you're probably right. He'll now show some politeness and God forbid he may even be nice. Crap."

Izzy marches towards Kincaid's office. She's not happy about something. Evander gives Adam a heads-up not to give the game away. "We may still have something to play with, keep quiet about the plan, Izzy is here and she's not happy."

Evander wiggles his fingers to her for her to enter his office, so she doesn't need to stand on ceremony and knock on his closed door. She storms into the office and slams the door shut behind her. The frame of the door protests at the force, as it reverberates through the glass in the door.

"Boss, you seriously better send me out on an errand that doesn't exist. I swear I'll poison the old fool. He asked me for coffee, so I got him one, he wants water, I get him a cup. He wants more coffee and he's snapping his fingers at me, unable to remember my name as he says 'Girl, you girl, get me a refill'. I ignore the old toad, so he gets up, slams the cup on my desk and demands a refill. I swear Boss, I don't have time to be his little milk maid. He's disrupting my day to the point that I can't get anything done, he's rude and demanding and stopping me from doing my job. You need to do something or the next refill he asks for, he may end up wearing it."

Evander and Adam exchange a knowing look. "Game on." Adam notes.

Evander fishes his phone out of his jacket and calls Walter, who answers before the beginning of the second ring.

"Kincaid, you have news I assume?"

"I do. Need to lodge a complaint against Smith, he's

disruptive, rude, inconsiderate, demanding. He's taken over the office, ejected one of my team from their workstation, treated another like a maid. He's stopping the work flowing and causing disruption to the point of distraction. Is it enough to get his ass hauled back to his plush office back at MI6 so we can be left alone?"

Although he can't see him, Evander can hear the Chief smiling in his response.

"I believe it is elegant sufficient. I'll get back to you." Walter ends the call.

~~~~~~

Three and a half hours after his arrival, MI6 Chief Richard Smith departs the office to head back to his own HQ, or his home, or whatever rock he dwells beneath.

After he sends his team home for the night, Evander stops by Walter's office for a night cap before heading home himself. The Chief pours some of the fine tasting cognac he keeps in his office to share with Kincaid.

"You look tired Evander. You should head home and get some rest."

"I will do. Just wondered if you've heard anything yet about the complaint you lodged over the intrusion by MI6?"

"No. Way too early for that to come back to me. Probably be a few days before we get anything on that one."

"But we will hear something about it, right?"

"Hopefully yes we will. May not be in detail, but yes we should get some feedback, it is a complaint after all."

Evander sips the cognac to savour its warm, lingering taste. He delights in the tingle it leaves in his mouth after he has
~~~~~~

swallowed some of the amber-coloured liquid. "Is this stuff expensive Chief?"
"They can be, some bottles of Remy Martin can go for over two thousand pounds, but this, you can get at most supermarkets, or off-license, but this one I like a lot for it's consistently smooth taste."
"Holy crap, two K huh?"
"I know, insane isn't it - you can buy a secondhand car for that and still get change too."
He drains the last of the liquid in his glass, stands up and takes his jacket off the back of the chair. He slips his arms into it and buttons it up. He takes his phone out of the pocket and checks for messages before pocketing the phone again.
"Chief, I bid you a goodnight" Evander said. "I'm going home to my bed, I'm so tired, but I'll be back, bright eyed and bushy tailed tomorrow for a hopefully event free day in which we can work on resolving this case."
The Chief raises his glass and replies. "Goodnight Kincaid - to victory in battle."

CHAPTER TWENTY-FIVE

Evander Kincaid wakes in a sweat. His breathing ragged, tears run down his face. He looks around his bedroom and in the gloomy light from the window, he can make out the shapes of objects in the room that are familiar to him; yet they are somewhat distorted by the tears that flow involuntarily and copiously from his eyes. He sits up.

It's the same recurring nightmare he has had since he was a young boy. A nightmare he had not had for many years. The last time was the death of his wife in fact. God, how he missed her. Prior to that, it was only when a case was getting under his skin. As is the case now.

He tries to calm his breathing and realises that it was the subconscious trauma of the deeply disturbing crime scene at the theatre, that has brought this nightmare home to roost. He is certain it was this that triggered something in his psyche to bring the visions to him in his sleep. With his left hand he wipes away the tears from his eyes and with his right hand, he brushes the touch lamp on his bedside cabinet once and a dim light bathes the room, chasing the darkness away as it recoils into the far corners of the room, casting away the gloom.

Evander looks towards the window. He can see and hear heavy raindrops beating down against the glass. The night sky looks ominous, threatening, dark and moody - the clouds heavily laden.

He throws the covers back, slides his legs out of the bed, sits on the edge. His fingers dig into the mattress. He takes deep breaths, sniffs occasionally; beads of sweat trickle down his perfectly formed pectoral muscles.

He raises his hands and runs his fingers through his dark

wavy hair, which is damp with sweat. He holds his face in his hands. His trailing fingers wipe tears away from his eyes and stop by his cheekbones, which are clearly defined under his fingers. He has what Hollywood would call 'chiselled features' with a strong jaw line.

He gets up, strips the bed, leaves the mattress and quilt to air before he heads to the bathroom. He brushes his teeth, then pees, then runs the shower. He holds his long fingers under the spray to check the temperature before he gets in.

Once in the shower cubicle, he stands with his back to the shower, tilts his head back and lets the spray run on his head before he runs his fingers through his hair, brushing it back from his face, sloshing excess water away. He dispenses shampoo, washes and rinses his hair before changing dispensers and using shower gel to wash away the dying embers of the nightmare he can't remember.

Once washed and rinsed, he stands with his back to the shower again, closes his eyes and lets the water wash away the final cobwebs of said nightmare, but not before a brief memory of it flickers through his mind's eye.

Something made its way through.

That something that he remembers is fear.

Suddenly, he is not in his nightmare anymore.

Eyes closed, he stands with his back still to the shower, water runs over his body. He places his hands against the shower wall in front of him as he remembers when he was held hostage at gun point at a bank raid. It was the perfect 'wrong place at the right time' scenario that you hope you never stumble into, yet there he was.

He was a young officer sent to investigate a tip off from a member of the public about someone acting suspiciously

outside the bank.
When he arrived, he walked right into an armed raid and found himself with a sawn-off shot gun thrust into in his face upon entering the building. He was sure he was going to die and the fear he felt in that moment is akin to the type of fear his nightmare imparts on him.
He catches his breath at the flashback of the memory, he snaps his eyes open quickly to stop the scene playing out on the back of his eyelids. It is something he tries not to think about anymore and he thought he had successfully trapped the memory and locked it in a room at the back of his mind somewhere, but it seems the memory picked the lock and now wanders freely around his conscious thoughts again.
He tries not to think about it, but now it is there it is all he can think about, the memory of it sets his jaw into a tight grip, which makes his jaw ache.
He is not sure which is worse: the nightmare he barely remembers when awoken by it, or the memory of being held at gunpoint and a sawn-off shotgun in the face. He really thought his time was up that day, the guy with the gun was high on crack and had already shot one victim dead, had wounded another and he was the next target. Evander was able to talk him down and it was that ability to make a connection that saved his life, to get into the head of someone with nothing but destruction as their motivation isn't an easy task, but he did it.
He gets out of the shower, dries himself off and wraps a towel around his waist, with another he towel-dries his hair and heads into the bedroom. From a draw he grabs some clothes, boxer shorts, a T-Shirt and jogging bottoms. He removes the towel around his waist and steps into boxer shorts and then

the jog pants. He remains bare chested for now.

He picks up the laundry from the stripped bed, plus the towels from showering, heads to the kitchen and snaps the light on. He loads laundry into the washing machine, adds detergent and switches it on.

He needs coffee and plenty of it. He prepares a pot. Once it starts to gurgle, he looks at the clock on the microwave - 03:31. He has managed four hours sleep, which will have to last him now until it is once again time for bed and the battle of trying to find slumber.

Evander goes to his study, flicks the light on and switches on the computer.

Once loaded, he accesses his account at Scotland Yard and opens files on the serial killings of *'The Dragons of Justice Killer'* as the press have labelled him. Why must they always sensationalize crimes with nick names? It drives him crazy having to work with the media, but unfortunately, he must tolerate them.

When it comes to toleration, there is only one journo that he does tolerate enough to engage in conversation with and that is Persephone Cruise. Sure, she pushes his buttons as all journalists do, but she seems different to the rest of the pack and it's not just her appearance. It hasn't escaped Evander's attention that she is a beautiful looking woman, at least he thinks she is. She is quite the conundrum when it comes to the media too. It must have been a difficult journey for her to get to the respected position that she is in as journalist, in what is a largely male dominated profession. But this little lamb is always one step ahead of the wolves she dances with in her industry, always the smartest one in the room out of them all, always asking questions the others don't see, and that gives her an edge of respectability. Evander is not even sure why he is thinking about her, or how this train of thought led to images of her.

Refocusing his thoughts, Evander reads forensic notes and cross references them to S.O.C.O. photos. He flicks through them all and stops at the one that chilled him to the bone when he first saw it at the crime scene itself.

He wasn't sure at the time why it should affect him so much and looking at it again, he is not sure why it still resonates deep inside him, but he knows there is something about this one, something - something, but what, something?

Why should a marionette disturb him so much?

Whatever it is, this is what caused the recurrence of his childhood nightmare he is sure of it. He is brought back to the room by the faint sounds of the coffee machine gurgling in such a way, that he knows it is almost finished. He should have enough time to put freshly laundered linen on his bed. He leaves the computer and heads to the bedroom. As he walks along the hallway, the aroma of the distinctive Colombian blend coffee he selected drifts towards him, the aroma comforts him somehow, it smells great and makes him feel that everything is calm and normal - or at least as normal as it gets in his line of work - but in fact, he knows right now, life is anything but normal.

He has the distinct feeling that something is eluding him and yet again, he is not sure what, only that he is missing it. Or maybe 'it' is missing him.

Once in the bedroom, Evander opens draws and removes matching pillowcases, a duvet cover and an Egyptian cotton fitted sheet and sets about redressing the bed.

Once done, he picks the T-Shirt up and puts it on as he heads back into the kitchen. He grabs a breakfast muffin, slices it in half and toasts it, grabs a cup and teaspoon, adds one teaspoon of sugar and pours coffee in, stirring as he pours. Then, he takes a knife from a draw and butter from the fridge while he waits.

The toaster pops and lightly toasted muffins jump up to greet his waiting fingers. He butters both slices, returns the butter to the fridge and puts the knife and teaspoon in the dishwasher. He takes the muffin and coffee back to his study.

He sets the cup on a plain black leather effect coaster and takes a bite of muffin. The screen saver on his P.C. has kicked in and little dots that resemble falling stars tumble like rain down the screen of the monitor. He remembers his phone and while eating the muffin, he heads back to the bedroom and goes to the docking station where his phone has been charging.

He checks it - no messages and no missed calls. Good.

He takes the phone with him back to the study, then he devours the other half of muffin. Once finished, he rubs his hands together to free his fingers of flour from the muffin, picks up his cup and sips coffee. He returns the cup to the coaster, takes a deep breath and expels it with a slight whistle.

"Back to work" he tells himself out loud as he settles down.

He wiggles the mouse the screen saver disappears and the SOCO photos reappear. Evander examines the photos in detail, zooming in on some slides and cross references with forensic notes for some of them. He lifts his cup to take a drink and is surprised to find his cup drained.

He doesn't remember finishing the coffee. He heads to the kitchen for a refill, checks the microwave when he enters and notices the time is now 04:45am. He decides not to head into

the office just yet. Cup replenished and back in the study, he goes from SOCO photos to forensic notes and analysis.
He refers to his own notes now too, he likes to be thorough when searching for things, but right now, he's not sure what he is looking for, hence his obsession with reviewing the photos and forensic reports. He is sure there is something here that he has missed, something is nagging at him, gnawing away at a thread in his mind. He is also sure that they triggered his nightmare, yet he has got a job to do, so needs must.
Second cup of coffee drained and already onto his third, his mobile rings.
Evander answers the call, it's Eastwood. "Hey Boss, are you at home?"
"Yeah, why?"
"Coming to the Yard any time soon?"
"Why, where should I be? And don't say the Yard"
"How do you know you need to be somewhere else?"
"Why else would you be calling me at O five thirty?"
"We got another 'dragon killing', but this one is a bit different."
"Different how?"
"Its, erm…" Eastwood hesitates and then concludes "… it's been personalised."
"What? He left something behind. What? A fingerprint, or D.N.A., or something else? Did he get sloppy?" Evander inquires, curious, almost excited he leans forward in his chair in anticipation of the reply.
"No, nothing like that. This one has been personalised…"
"Yes, yes, I got that, just get to the point Adam. Personalised how?" he says impatiently.

"It was personalised - for you Boss."
Evander kind of saw this coming after the press conference. Another reason he hates the Papanasty. It puts him out there as a target for the killer to play with. Some of them like to play with the police, like a cat plays with a mouse.
The fact that this has been personalised intrigues him and if he's honest, even only to himself, it excites him a little too, even though he knows it shouldn't, there is no denying it does.
"How has it been personalised?" Evander inquires.
"On my way there now, so not sure yet."
"Where?" Evander sighs. He closes his eyes as he partly listens to Adam tell him about location and where to meet the team.

CHAPTER TWENTY-SIX

Evander arrives at the crime scene, gets out of the car, closes the driver's door and opens the back door. He takes his jacket off a hook above the window and puts it on.

He closes the door and engages the lock, force of habit - a crime scene that is surrounded by police vehicles and police officers, yet he still locks the car. He buttons his jacket as he walks towards the hive of activity.

The atmosphere feels strange to him at this one. Maybe it's because this one has been personalised. From what he has been told so far, which is not a lot, he knows that another note has been left.

Though Eastwood didn't know when he called him what the note said, or how it had been personalised, nor who the victim was, because he was en-route to the crime scene when he called him, so didn't have a lot of information to hand.

Arriving here, this one feels different. It carries a different quality. Somehow. A gut feeling. Or maybe his imagination is just running too far ahead of him and yet, it is palpable.

Eastwood sees Evander approaching. He runs towards him. His face is a mixture of emotions, his eyes are red. Evander is surprised to see an emotional Eastwood, he's normally stoical at crime scenes, but this one has obviously upset him.

"What is it?" Evander asks.

"It's James…" he begins, emotion cracking his voice, unable to continue.

"What about him?" Evander asks, but he already knows what he's going to say, he just doesn't want to hear it coming from Eastwood, who for the first time has called his colleague by his preferred name - James.

"He..."

"He's what?" Evander asks, concern and dread marking his voice.

"He's the victim." Eastwood forces the words through his mouth, anger evident in his tone as the words tumble across his lips, his voice quavers with emotion.

Eastwood's words hit Evander like a ton of bricks. He repeats the words out loud to be sure he heard them correctly, "Did you say he's the victim?"

Eastwood nods, but doesn't say anything. He turns and walks ahead, knowing that his Boss will follow him. Adam leads Evander to the scene - now, they walk side by side in silence.

A million thoughts run through Evander's mind. All of them clamour for his attention at once. He doesn't know which one to listen to first and wishes they would all shut up. This was his gut feeling, the reason it felt different. Not the note after all.

They turn into the car park at the rear of the tube station on Acacia Road. Evander approaches Jackson and Evans who are standing with their backs to them. He stops and calls out to her to avoid contaminating the crime scene. "Jackson?"

She turns to face him. She holds it together, better than Eastwood. She waves a hand, beckoning at him to head over.

As he approaches, he asks "Is it safe? I mean I don't want to contaminate the scene. Is it bad?"

Jackson beckons him over to her "We've cordoned off the area and the perimeter is over there so you're safe up to here. 'Is it bad' you ask? Well, a man has been murdered Detective; how much worse can it be?"

"You know exactly what I mean." he scolds and regrets it right away. "Sorry."

"Me too. This was left for you." Jackson hands him a note in a sealed evidence bag. He takes it from her and reads the typed note:

'This one was regrettable Kincaid - he'd have made an excellent addition to the team. D.O.J.' "What the hell is that supposed to mean?" Evander asks. "What team?"

"I think it means your team." Jackson says.

"My team? How would he know who was on my team? Evander says. "Ah, press conference. Bloody Papanasty." Evander assumes, answering his own question.

"Can I see him?"

"We're still investigating, gathering evidence and..."

"Please." Evander pleads.

Jackson stops talking at the pained expression on Evander's face. She sighs. "Don't touch anything. And I mean anything. Stop when I tell you to, oh, and put these on and these too". She says as she bends down to take a pair of gloves and shoe covers from a forensic kit bag.

Evander takes them from her and puts them on. She walks over to where James' body is. Her coveralls crinkle as she walks. She leads Evander behind some grey bins. He begins to feel angry, even without seeing James, he feels it rising in him, he must force it down.

He is surprised to find that James has been positioned as if he is laid out like an Egyptian King. His arms are folded across his heart, his hands rest on his shoulders. He looks peaceful, which surprises Evander. Resting between his folded arms is a single white rose. There is little to no blood and the surrounding area does not look like a struggle took place here. He is not even sure why he would think of a struggle taking place - possibly because he knows James would have put up a

fight.
Evander asks. "Is this the primary, or secondary crime scene?"
"We think it's a secondary, no primary evidence so far and what there is of the secondary may be contaminated."
"What, how?"
"We're in the middle of a car park at the back of an underground tube station. The body is surrounded by rubbish bins and god knows what other unmentionables. A couple of the rubbish bags look like they've been ripped open by animals, a fox or feral cats possibly. Some of the rubbish has been dragged across the Vi…" Jackson stops herself abruptly. She was about to say 'Victim' but she changes it "… the area, so I wouldn't hold out much hope of finding anything useful here. He never leaves any trace evidence anyway, he's too smart for that, but you already know that."
"Is there anything unusual about this one and don't give me any more sarcasm. I'm really not in the mood." he warns her.
"Well, there's the note, which doesn't happen often, although the note is missing his usual neat, typed calligraphy so it may have been unplanned, rushed even. Also, there isn't a dragon anywhere in sight."
Evander turns the note over, the reverse side is blank. No dragon. "So, no dragon. What makes you think this is one of his killings? He always takes ownership for his work."
Jackson continues. "I'm sure it's him, but he isn't claiming this one as a justice killing, hence no dragon just a signature."
"Signature, where?" Kincaid asks.
"Look at the note, he signed it D.O.J."
"And?"
"D.O.J. - Dragons of Justice. I think this one wasn't planned. James wasn't supposed to be on his list. This one is, as he says,

regrettable."
"So, what! He was in the wrong place at the right time?"
"I think more like the right place, but the wrong time. I think James stumbled across something and there was only one option available to make sure that his silence was maintained. Also, unless it's under his body, his mobile may be missing, but we won't know till we move him."
"How do you know it's missing? He may have left it somewhere"
"Really?" Jackson snorts somewhat amused, raising a questioning eyebrow.
"What?" Evander asks with wonder.
"A Detective on *your* team leaving his mobile somewhere other than on his person, or within arms-length reach? Surely no member of your team is stupid enough to leave it just anywhere when they know you may need to get hold of them right away. 'Never be unreachable.' You're always telling them that. It's one of your obvious rules. Remember? You should draw up a list of rules you know, just to make it easier for the newbies to your team. Rule 1 - don't trust the Papanasty. Rule 2 - never be unreachable. Rule 3 – there are no coincidences. They're just what comes to mind as the rules go on. I'm sure you have more to add to the list."
'She's right'. Evander thinks and not just about the rules, some of them unspoken yet understood by the team. None of them would be unreachable, certainly never without their phones. No Detective on the Force would be without their phone, they are practically glued to your hand. It also goes to the loo, the shower, to bed - everywhere you go, it goes.
"Okay, so, if it's not under his body, that means the killer took it." Evander says.

"Yes. Or, more like destroyed it, threw it in the river, did something with it for sure. Why would he take his phone? A trophy maybe?"

"No, he has reason and purpose with this one. Not sure where he's going with it though. Intriguing." Curiosity evident in his voice on the last word. Annoyed with himself and realizing it may sound inappropriate, he clears his throat and asks. "Is there anything else?"

"Well, till we can move him and get him back home, I don't know what I'll find till I conduct the autopsy."

"You want me to call someone else in for that?"

"No!" Jackson says quickly, protectively. "I'll do it. Got to look after our own."

"How long till you are done here?"

"Maybe an hour or so, but it depends how much more time you want to waste standing here, when you could leave and find the bastard."

Evander takes his gloves off and says. "Be thorough, but get it done quick. I want my boy out of there A.S.A.P." Without waiting for a reply Evander walks quickly, with purpose, away from the scene. He looks for Eastwood, can't find him. Maybe he's left the scene.

He leans against a wall, removes the shoe covers and wraps the gloves around them, he pockets both to dispose of them back at the Yard. Violet's habits are rubbing off on him.

Evander heads back to his car. He's angry. He can feel the rage rising in him from the pit of his stomach like bile; churning, whirling, stirring his emotions into a frenzied storm. He feels like he's going to explode in a gamut of emotions and all of them are on fire and enraged.

Back in his car, he removes his jacket and throws it on the

passenger seat, rather than hanging it up. He gets in, closes the door and puts the key in the ignition. His hands grip the steering wheel tightly, he squeezes it tighter and tighter, his knuckles go white. He opens the car door and vomits, then closes the door once done. He feels like shooting something, kicking something, punching something. He is alarmed at all the violence he is feeling towards someone he doesn't know and currently can't find. But he will.

Evander drives away. He knows he is going to have to address his team when he gets back to the office, a task he is not looking forward to.

James' family too will need to be advised and as his Boss, it will be his responsibility to tell them the sad news.

He is not sure he can look any of them squarely in the eye when speaking about the latest victim of the killer. Intentional, accidental, regrettable, or otherwise, still a victim.

Any victim is difficult to deal with, especially as, so far, some of them on this serial killing trail have been brutal. Inventive, but brutal.

But this with James, this is too far over the line, and it is the start of his downfall. Evander is now focused. Intent. Vengeful. Violet is right. Find the bastard.

Bastard. Game changer. *What a bastard.*

This is too painful.

You complete bastard.

This has just got personal.

You utter, complete bastard.

Now, he's made his biggest mistake.

Enraged, he starts the car and screams at the top of his voice as he drives. "*You're mine. You bastard.*" He thumps the steering wheel. "*I'm coming for you. You, BASTARRRRRRD!*"

CHAPTER TWENTY-SEVEN

After a hard day's work, he gets in the shower and lets the water slosh through his mop of wavy dark hair. He slicks it back and wishes it were straight and sleek all the time, like it is when he does his cleansing work as an avenger for God, which he will undertake tonight, but first, he must shower and exfoliate vigorously.

'Don't want to be leaving any trace evidence for the lovely Violet Jackson to find'. He smiles when he thinks of her, she's such a pretty little thing and oh the fun they could have together. A wicked smile plays on the corner of his full lips, he chews on his lower lip as he imagines a vivid daydream that forms in his mind's eye of the acts, all of them, that they could carry out together as partners in crime.

The avenger side of him needs to be unleashed tonight. Just as well he has someone deserving of his skills and the metaphorical sword he will wield on God's behalf. It's time to unleash Jacob, God's servant. He recalls his duty and quotes out loud Romans 13:4 as the water cleanses him, ready for the work ahead in his evening:

"For he is a minister of God for you unto good. But if you do what is evil, be afraid. For it is not without reason that he carries a sword. For he is a minister of God; an avenger to execute wrath upon whomever does evil."

Tears form in his eyes. The words mean so much to him, now he knows what his true vocation is and always has been. Yet he fought it for so long, thinking it was wrong to have these urges outside of his daily life. Especially given his job which has the trust of the public.

His purpose, he sees has always been - not to serve the people and offer them shelter, but to serve the people up to God for their wrong-doing and evil acts that go unpunished by the law.

He resents playing the good guy all day, listening to people whining and moaning about their lot and how they are hard done to and how they don't deserve to be punished by being sent to prison. Some of them are right, they don't deserve to be punished by being sent to prison and Jacob wishes he had the authority to extinguish their light but, they have the protection of prison bars.

He is thankful therefore of the loose tongues. Those who complain about their fellow criminals. Those who have escaped the wrath of the law and it is these people Jacob hears about in his work, people that he decides will have a different type of justice bestowed upon them. How amusing he thinks, that in their final moments, if he were to offer them life in prison, they would no doubt take it, rather than the wrath he delivers to their soul.

A man needs his escape and a way to let his hair down after a hard day's work. Doing God's work this evening will be his release from the constraints that he has to adhere to daily. How he loathes the protocol of his work at times, all those confines and institution rules that he must work within, but oh how thankful he is for the justification in the Bible, that is Romans 13:4, here is his own salvation for sure.

When he is done, he may indulge in some wine. That will be a nice reward and a relaxing way to round off his evening pleasure.

CHAPTER TWENTY-EIGHT

Evander wakes to strong sunlight that streams through a gap in the curtains, which somehow seems to be focused like a light sabre in direct line with his eyes. He blinks, squints and raises his hand to shield his sapphire blue eyes from the piercing light of day.

He is not in bed as he thought but sprawled on the leather sofa in his living room. He is not sure how he got here, but he is sure he went to bed - although, apparently not if he is on the sofa. How did he get to sleep here and why, he ponders as he doesn't remember? He sits up too quickly and oh his head. He promptly puts his hands up and holds his head in sympathy, as he becomes aware of the band parading around his skull.

Out of the line of fire of the light sabre directed sunlight, Evander looks at the coffee table in front of him. There is a wine glass with but a mouthful of red wine at the bottom of it and not one, but two empty bottles of Zinfandel on the table. One bottle is on its side. The other still stands.

Ah, maybe that is why he doesn't remember falling asleep on the sofa. He picks up the glass and drinks the remaining mouthful of wine. '*shame to waste it*' he thinks. No, more like '*hair of the dog*' his conscience chastises him. He winces at the taste of the wine in his mouth this early in the day but swallows it anyway.

Today it is Jasmine's birthday. He sighs, shuts his eyes and tries not to think of the painful day that is ahead. Every day is painful without her if he is honest with himself, but there are times and some days that are more difficult to deal with than others; like Christmas, New Year, his birthday, their wedding anniversary, valentine's day and today... thirty first of August, Jasmine's birthday.

He remembers how much her birthday upset her, because it became known as the day Diana, Princess of Wales died. Evander remembers her telling him how much she cried when the news came in that Diana had been killed.

After that, she couldn't bare her birthday unless she took flowers to Kensington Palace to leave for Diana. It became a ritual for her and now, he carries on this tradition, because he knows her spirit would be restless if he didn't. Jasmine said that she just had to take Diana flowers so her spirit would know she wasn't forgotten about by the people. It was a difficult day for her to deal with.

Evander looks at the photo, the only photo he has still on display of the two of them together - to have more would be too painful - of their wedding photo, which was the happiest day of their lives.

She wanted a romantic wedding and insisted that Evander wore a cream suit, because that would make him look different to every other man in the room. Her husband had to be the one every woman - and no doubt some men - was looking at. He was the most handsome man in the room, and all would be painfully aware that he was taken.

The photographer had told them to talk for a minute while he changed the settings on his camera. That piece of hair of Jasmine's that would fall in front of her eyes broke free and dropped in front of her eyes.

In a tender moment, Evander moved the hair for her, she glanced down to his free hand and held onto it with both of hers as he moved the hair from her eyes, and it is this that the photographer captured. The intimacy between the two of them in that moment was so personal and when the photos came back, Evander was angry that they had been snapped in an unrehearsed photo. It felt like an intrusion to him, but not to Jasmine.

The fact that it was taken without their knowledge, and they were not ready for it, not posing annoyed Evander, but Jasmine loved it. She said it showed what a tender man he is, and she was glad that the photographer took an impromptu photo of them, and it became her favourite. Over time, Evander got to like it too. He loved the intimacy they had together, and it was a painful reminder of an intimacy lost.

"I miss you Jasmine." Evander whispers into the air. A lump in his throat brings unwanted tears into his eyes, which, when he closes them, escape from his eyes down his cheeks. He snaps his eyes open and stands up slowly, a little wobbly on his feet at first but then regains his equilibrium and heads into the shower. He hopes it will sluice away the wine induced headache and the tears of his soul for the loss of the beautiful Jasmine.

He will make the pilgrimage to Jasmine's grave and take her flowers, but from that bouquet he will take one flower, usually a white rose and he will tell Jasmine that he will take it for her to Kensington Palace to leave for Princess Diana from her. Today is going to be a difficult day. How glad he will be when this day is over. He just needs to find a way to get through it. Again.

Technically, he has the day off work. Eastwood is in charge in his absence, but he has been told to call him if anything important crops up, especially another dragon serial killing. For now, he potters around his home until it is time to take flowers to Jasmine.

CHAPTER TWENTY-NINE

Now that jurisdiction is not a hotly contested competition, though it felt like it at times, it was finally awarded to Scotland Yard with Evander running point. This case is without precedent as an MI6 active agent was murdered. However, MI6 don't investigate murders, so for them to contest jurisdiction raised some eyebrows. Now Evander and his team are taking the lead, things are moving along at a more regular pace. Although now he wants things to move along much quicker, because one of his team has become a victim. To a degree, Evander can understand why Richard Smith wanted to take ownership on this one, now it has happened to him, and he's lost one of his team, he can relate to the emotions driving the campaign to investigate something normally outside the bounds of their territory. Now, given the twist on events, Evander is relieved that it sits squarely on his team's shoulders.

Gathering information about James, means Evander has to visit Violet. He has put it off all day and cannot do so any longer. He would normally have one of the team with him, but to spare them he goes alone. There are some journeys you have to take on your own.

~~~~~~~~~~~~

Jackson is on the phone when Evander arrives at the mortuary. She turns when she hears the door open and waves him in, she continues talking on the phone. She may as well be speaking an alien language for all Evander understands of it - all that blinding with science stuff.
~~~~~~~~~~~~

He switches off from the conversation and his eyes wander around the room. They come to rest on a body, covered by a white sheet - he knows it is James and it twists his stomach into knots.

He dreads the prospect of Violet removing the sheet to reveal his deceased colleague. He feels responsible in a lot of ways, guilt clenches in his gut and his psyche plays games with his mind. He puts his hand through his hair and wishes Jackson would hurry up and get off the phone to give him a distraction.

He turns his back to the slab that James lays on and looks at instruments. Samples in jars that he cannot identify and does not even want to hazard a guess as to the contents. Forensic equipment - something that he knows is a mass spectrometer, which purrs gently as he approaches it.

He knows it is an important machine but has no idea how it does what it does, nor how to analyse any of the results it may spit out. He tries desperately to distract himself, anything but be left alone with his own terrifying thoughts here in this room with James. Dead James. His fault.

Jackson calls his name "Evander, did you hear me?"

He hadn't - obviously. He'd switched off from her voice completely.

"Sorry, what?" he asks.

"I asked, how are you?"

"Well… you know."

"I do. Unfortunately."

"You said on the phone before that you have something you wanted to show me?"

"Yes." Jackson says as she walks towards the body under the sheet.

Evander realises she's going to take the sheet off James - he feels sick.
He holds out his hand in a stop motion and asks urgently.
"Wait - do you have to take that off?" he asks pointing to the sheet.
Perplexed how he knew that when she wasn't even close to the table, she asks. "What makes you think I was going to take the sheet off?"
"My gut."
"Well, I'm sorry, but you're going to need to get over your squeamish side and look at this, it's addressed to you and Adam."
"I'm not squeamish." Evander protests. "I just find it hard when it's, when I…" he pauses, choosing his words carefully "… I find it difficult when it's someone I know."
Violet takes pity on him. She leaves taking the cover off James a while longer. She picks up her report and thumbs through some pages and then... "He treated him well…"
"I'm sorry, did I just hear you right? He's dead, but he was treated well?"
"He was not tortured, or beaten, he was fed and watered and though he used chloroform to knock him out and put him in the boot of the car, he didn't hurt him until he shot him. He, well… he was relatively merciful with him."
"How do you know he was in a car boot?"
"Fibres on his socks and shoes, Mass Spec over there gave us a match to car boot carpet that is commonly used on a number of vehicles."
"Right, got it. OK and the meal? Why would he feed him and water him knowing he was going to kill him?"
"I have no idea."

Realisation hits Evander. "Ah, I get it, he gave the condemned man a last meal."

"Oh my God, I think you're right."

"What was the meal, do you know? Well, of course you know. What was it?"

"Roast lamb dinner. Glass of wine."

"So, what was the cause of death?" He asks, saying the words rather than abbreviating them this time.

"Single gunshot, through the heart, which stopped instantly. He wouldn't have had time to register pain, or awareness of being and then not being. It was clean and painless."

"Is that why there was so little blood at the crime scene?"

"Yes and no. It would have stopped his heart, so it wouldn't be pumping blood, so there wouldn't be pints of it everywhere, but that was not where he was shot, that's just where he was left."

"But why there? Why behind the tube station? He didn't even live in the area, he had no reason to be there, no family or friends in the area. No interests that would bring him to the area. It's important that he left him there, but I can't figure out why yet. Wait, are there any London dragons in that area do you know? Have you got the crime scene photos?"

"Nothing like that Evander, there was nothing whatsoever to connect the serial killer to James. All there is that confirms we know it's him, is the signed note. I have no idea why he took him out there and left him there. I don't think he meant for him to be a dragon's victim."

"So, what is he, if he is not his victim?"

"A victim of circumstance maybe." Jackson ponders.

"What, you mean like collateral damage?"

"Possibly. In context with everything else, nothing else would

make sense."
Steeling himself, ready for the reveal, Evander asks. "What did you want to show me that was on the body?"
Jackson walks towards the mortuary slab where James rests, she grabs hold of the sheet and pulls the lower part of it up, she stops just above the knees. Evander is grateful that he doesn't have to see his colleague's face.
"Come look at this." Jackson says, redirecting his attention.
Evander gets closer and looks where Jackson points. "Is that writing?" He asks.
"Yes, it's a message for you and Adam."
Evander reads the message that has been written on the inside of James left leg, just above the kneecap in ink, probably a biro: *'AE - check your mapS. Get EK for me.'*
"What does that even mean?"
"I was hoping you could tell me." Jackson says.
"Damned if I know. Have you shown this to anyone else?"
"No, not yet."
"Okay, so AE is obviously Adam Eastwood and he's telling him to get me, the EK part, but maps? And why has he spelled it like that, with the S as a capital?"
"I have no idea."
"Have you shown Adam this?"
"No, wanted you to see it first."
"Good, don't tell him or show him just yet."
"Why not? It's meant for him too." Jackson asks, curious why he doesn't want Adam to know.
"Well, he was pretty upset at the crime scene. I want some time to investigate it myself first. Give me a day or two, please."
"You have twelve hours, no more. Good enough?" She asks

unconvinced.
"Yes. Now, do you need me for anything else?"
"Not right now."
"Can you cover him up now, please?" Evander asks.
"Why, does he make you uncomfortable for some reason?"
"Take a wild guess." He says evasively and walks towards the door to leave.
"Evander?" Jackson calls.
He stops and looks back to her and waits for her words.
"Are you alright?" She asks, genuine concern in her voice.
"As alright as I can be, given the circumstances."
"If you need to talk, you know I'm here for you."
He smiles but says nothing and turns to leave again.
"Evander?" Jackson calls him again.
Evander rolls his eyes to the ceiling; he just wants to leave autopsy and get out of there now. He needs to get away and be alone for a while. He composes himself and turns back to face Violet. "Yes?" He inquires.
"When you find him, and I know you will - you'll have to interrogate him won't you?"
"I'm pretty sure we will, yes."
"When you do get him, when he is in that room and you're the other side of it looking at him, I want you to remember James, although I know you will, but remember him and ask the questions he would have wanted answered."
"You know my interrogation techniques."
"I do and I know you get more confessions than any other Detective on the Force. However, what I really mean is, beat the shit out the little runt."
Evander raises an eyebrow at her last statement. "You and I both know I can't do that."

"I know, I know, but I wanna kick him in the nuts oh so badly."
"Would that make you feel any better?"
"Probably for a minute yes, but then I'd remember James and a minute wouldn't be enough satisfaction for me."
"There are other ways to hurt a man."
"I know and you're good at it. I want you to make him suffer somehow, mentally will do, it'll have to suffice, but just make him suffer. I know that's not the right thing to do, and I shouldn't be saying it. But this is the hardest day in my work life. I want you to make the bastard squirm and I know you're the best at that, making them sweat, making them feel things they would rather not feel. Make him feel our pain, you hear me?"
"Loud and clear." Evander says, he forces a smile, turns and exits the autopsy lab.
Outside he leans against the wall, he composes himself before he heads out to get coffee and cakes for the team.

CHAPTER THIRTY

Tommy Trent is a reporter. A grubby one that you usually find in the movies, and one that Evander has had run ins with over previous years, he's a bit of blood hound but also an irritating jumped up overconfident shitbag, one who will stoop to any level to get his story, he's relentless and keeps pushing and pushing. Evander listens to him as he badgers Adam.

Adam has stepped outside for a cigarette and here Trent has found him and is pushing for information. Obviously, the loss of James has set Adam back somewhat with his steps out of being a smoker. Trent stands by Adam's side trying to sweet talk and cajole his Senior Detective into giving away some juicy piece of information. Evander can hear every word perfectly from his visual yet hidden position. Adam and the Papanasty, however are unaware of Evander being in close proximity, a concrete pillar affords him some anonymity. Tommy is trying to goad Adam into giving away information about the case, but Adam is experienced enough, and he hopes under his guidance, wise enough not to say anything silly, he certainly does not give anything away while being questioned which is at first, along the usual lines that this idiot begins with:

"Have there been any more developments in the investigation."

"No comment." Adam replies.

"Are there any new leads?"

"I can't comment any further on the case."

"Can't comment any further? All you've told me is no comment! Do you have any suspects?"

"We are still conducting our inquiries. No further comment."
"How many notches does the Dragons of Justice Killer have on his bed post now?"
This one clearly annoys Adam as he spits out a reply, his distinctly unique Liverpudlian accent starting to become more pronounced, "Look mate, I'm not telling you anything and this killer is not a vigilante hero for you to glorify. He's a murderer."
He's conducting himself quite well, Evander thinks.
That is, until James' name is mentioned. Here is where the reporter steps too far over the line not just for Adam, but for Evander too.
"A police Detective was found murdered recently, a Detective James Reeves. Is he a victim too?"
It has not been made public knowledge that James was a victim of the Dragons of Justice Killer, and he technically isn't although he is dead by his hand, so Evander would count it. That brings the tally to 10 people. No parole for this murderer when they find him.
Although the reporter hints that he knows it's true, he doesn't have anything solid to go on, he is just fly fishing, throwing things out there, to see what he can reel in and if he gets any bites with the worms of deceit he throws in the water.
While he doesn't give anything away, Adam stumbles over his words a little. "I have, no thoughts for....I mean, I can't, I mean - no comment."
The reporter notices the hesitation and Adam's lack of composure with the response. Sensing a sensational headline, he verbally pushes and prods, trying to extract information from him, asking a variety of questions in quick succession.
"Why was he targeted? What motive did the killer have for

taking him out? Is Detective Reeves a bad apple in the Yard? Did he get too close to the killer? Or did the Detective know the killer possibly? How do the team feel knowing that one of their own was a victim of the Dragons of Justice Killer?" He's doing anything he can trying to provoke a reaction, an outburst of emotion an admittance that he is on to something. Adam tries to walk away telling the reporter "No comment. I have nothing else to say to you Trent, this conversation is over."

Evander can tell from the tone in Adam's voice and the emergence of the full broadness of his Scouse accent, which is so prominent now, that Adam is extremely pissed off and one step away from reacting badly, and you certainly don't want to make this Liverpudlian angry when he is already guarded. Time for Evander to step in.

As he tries to walk away, the reporter grabs hold of Adam's arm. "Look *mate.*" He says, exaggerating the word 'mate' in what he thinks passes for a Scouse accent. "I'm just doing my job. I'm asking you what the public would want to know."

"I still have no comment." Adam says angrier than before, he snatches his arm loose from the grip of the reporter; but Tommy is having none of it. He won't take 'no' for an answer, he follows Adam as he heads away from Scotland Yard. Evander follows him close enough to be able to hear what is being said.

"If Scotland Yard can't protect one of their own, how can they protect a nation?"

Adam stops in his tracks and turns around to face the reporter, that was the one which would pop the cork on Adam's anger. Except, he now sees Evander over Tommy's shoulder, opens his mouth to say something and stops when

he sees his Boss tapping the reporter on the shoulder.
Trent turns around and Evander punches him hard and square right on his nose, sending the reporter flailing backwards, arms wind milling as he tries to stop himself from falling flat on his backside.

"He said 'no comment' you prick. Now fuck off." Evander spits at him, his own accent flourishing broadly too.

Adam has a mixture of emotions all crossing his handsome face, first shock, then 'wow', and was that a fleeting look of suspicion? Evander thinks so, but that disappears quickly and is then followed by relief, topped by a look that, if they were alone, he is sure Adam would rush over and give him a high five that would flow into a low five, and possibly what would pass for a man hug too.

The reporter moans and groans, raising his hand to his nose touching it and wincing at the pain, he takes his hand away to find it is covered in blood.

Now, he starts groaning loudly "Ohhhhhhhh my nose, you broke my fuckin' nose. Oh help, HELP!" He shouts loudly "HELP! Please someone help, don't let him attack me again. Did anyone see that? I was just assaulted by a Detective."

Adam asks Evander, "Where were you going?"

"Coffee run. Go back upstairs and get your head on right."

Adam knows better than to question him and he follows orders and leaves.

He looks back and sees Evander walking in the direction of the coffee shop, the reporter still on the floor two people, three people now gather around him to see if they can help.

The reporter milks the attention for all he can get.

CHAPTER THIRTY-ONE

Adam arrives late at the office due to traffic congestion. He walks into a hushed office. He heads over to Izzy who, so far, is the only other member of the team in the office. He whispers. "What's going on? Why is it so quiet in here? Where is everyone?"

"Traffic jam and the Chief Super is here waiting for the Boss. The reporter the Boss punched yesterday; he's pressing charges. I think the Chief is here to rip Evander a new one."

"Holy shit." Adam begins. "Where is the Boss anyway?"

"Even more late than you. The Chief has been getting more agitated the longer he waits. There are going to be some serious fireworks when he does get here."

"When who gets here?" A voice from behind them asks.

Both Izzy and Adam jump. They turn to find Kincaid standing there, as he shrugs out of his long coat.

"Boss, erm the Chief Super wants to see you as soon as you get in." Izzy tells him.

"Does he now!" Evander exclaims.

"Yes Boss. He said you're to go right in when you get here."

Evander hooks his fingers around the collar of his coat, throws it over his shoulder and heads towards his office. He stops part way, turns back to Adam and Izzy and says. "Don't worry, I'll leave the door open so you can hear. Where is Grace by the way?"

In unison Izzy and Adam reply. "Traffic."

"You're sure?" Evander asks, concern evident in his voice.

"Yes, she called a few minutes ago, she's fine." Adam reassures him.

Evander makes his way into the office. He takes his coat off

his right shoulder and hangs it on the coat rack in the corner.
"Morning Chief. To what noble cause do I owe the pleasure of your company?" He asks sarcastically.
"Don't be a smart-arse Kincaid, you're in enough trouble as it is without dissent."
"What do you need to know?" Evander asks, exasperated.
"We have work to do."
"I need to know what the hell in God's name were you thinking? Punching a reporter, the slimiest little bastard out there and it had to be him you chose to land one on."
"I didn't choose him, he chose himself." Evander interjects.
"Why didn't you tell him to go away, to leave."
"Adam did, he didn't listen."
"You should have walked away, both of you!"
"Adam did and he still didn't listen. People like him do not understand reason."
"You didn't give him a choice."
"He pushed things too far. He was disrespectful to a lost member of my team and went after another one of my team right in front of me." Evander becomes angry now, even though he tries not to, his voice rises as he tells the Chief why he did what he did. "You don't fuck with my team." He says protectively. "And I don't care who you are, or what piece of trash you may write for. No one fucks with *MY* team."
"You put him on his arse."
"He deserved it."
"You punched him in the face."
"He's lucky he went down first time, or I'd have hit him again till he did go down."
The Chief's jowls glow red as he bellows. "You broke his bloody nose!"

Evander murmurs under his breath. “He's lucky it wasn't his neck.”
“What!?”
“I said he's lucky he ended up on the deck.”
“Look, Kincaid. You may have a member of your team called ‘Eastwood’, but that doesn't give you license to behave like Dirty bloody Harry!”
“Prefer James Bond if I'm honest. And, he has a license to kill. Connery is still the best too by the way before you ask who my favourite Bond is.” Evander quips.
“This is England Kincaid, not America. We don't have serial killers of this ilk…”
“Really? Have you forgotten about Ian Brady, Myra Hindley, Dennis Nilsen, Fred West, Rose West, Harold Shipman, Peter Sutcliffe, Beverley Allitt and all these in the modern era; but we can always go back to John Christie, or before that to Mary Ann Cotton and Jack the Ripper. Shall I go on?”
“I was going to say, before you interrupted, that we don't go gung bloody ho in our quest to bring them to justice and assault innocent people in the process. This is not the movies! Do you have any idea the position I'm in?”
Evander resists the urge to give a smart-arse reply and waits for him to continue.
“I've got to go now, with my balls in my hand and try to talk to this… this, I can't even find the right adjective for him… this reporter and ask him to drop the charges against you.”
“You don't need to do that on my part Walter.”
“It's Chief Super to you today and in this serious a situation. And actually, I do have to do this, and you know why?”
Evander waits for him to continue.
“I have to do this, because this charge needs to disappear,

because God help me, you're my best Detective. I know you bend the rules to within a hairs breadth of breaking point, but you get me results and I need you on this case. It's too late now to bring in another Detective. You need to find this bastard Kincaid and you need to find him fast. You've had months of searching and come up with nothing, meanwhile the bodies are stacking up."

Evander opens his mouth to say something, but Walter cuts him off. "Don't you interrupt me; I'm not finished yet. If I didn't know any better, I'd think you were hiding something, stop dragging your bloody feet and get me this son of a bitch!"

The Chief waits for a reply from Evander that doesn't come.

"What. You have no wise cracking comment to come back with?" The Chief asks.

"I'll find him, my team and I, we will find him. We're getting closer now. I think I understand him better and you're right, I'm much better than any other Detective. I can understand his reasoning to a point."

The Chief's face glows red, his cheeks rosy like someone stacking a furnace behind his jowls and they put the bellows on to warm his face. "For God's sake man."

"What?" Evander asks perplexed. "We must try to understand him because…"

"Oh my God, you admire him!" The Chief spits the words out like something nasty he has just tasted. He walks over to the door and slams it shut. He knows things are going to get heated and he doesn't want the rest of Evander's team to hear every word.

Now Evander is angry. "Don't be stupid, of course I don't admire him. But I do respect him."

"Are you going to start a fan club for him? Respect! Never

heard anything so bloody ridiculous in all my time on the Force. Jesus H Christ, what is wrong with you?" Walter asks. Indignation apparent in his voice, Evander says. "Don't confuse admiration with respect."
"He's not a hero!" the Chief yells.
"I already know that, and I don't need *you* pointing it out to me. I know that. But regardless of what it may mean in the dictionary, we must have respect for him, or we will never find him. How do you think I get the bad apples time after time? I go through phases of understanding no, I mean learning - yes, learning. I learn about them and when I've gotten over the hatred of the crime, of being offended that they hurt people in this great city and got away with it, of being angry with them, that's usually when respect comes. There has to be respect as it helps me get in their heads to work out why they do what they do and you, Chief you're going to have to deal with it, because it's how I catch people. If you don't like it, fire me." Evander grabs his coat, flings the door open and marches out the office.
"Kincaid get back here!" The Chief calls out to him.
Evander walks past Izzy and Adam. "Coffee?" He asks.
They both nod their heads, but say nothing, they watch him walk away.
The Chief is still calling out to him "Kincaid, don't you walk away from me, insubordination does not happen in my house you hear me? KINCAID!" he shouts.
Evander keeps walking, sweeping his coat around him, he puts it on as he heads towards the lifts.
Idiot.
If only you knew.
If only you could understand.

CHAPTER THIRTY-TWO

It is Friday evening, and the weekend is upon them. Evander cannot settle at home, even though his shift at Scotland Yard is technically over for the day. A Detective is never really 'off duty' and can never fully 'switch off' from the job.

He tries to relax and fails miserably. He is like a coiled spring; agitated, unsettled, and ready to explode into action.

He opens a bottle of red wine - a fruity Merlot from the Central Valley in Chile - and pours a large glass of it. He takes it into the living room, sits on the sofa, glass in one hand, he picks up the remote control for the TV with the other.

Evander channel surfs and searches for anything, but nothing specifically, to help him switch off from work. He leaves a channel on for a minute or two and if he has not kept his interest piqued, and he finds himself thinking more than watching, he surfs again.

Nat Geo has a program on about the society that is the Freemasons. The voice over talks about the history of sacred rites, passages, and the secrets they protect. People have a misconception that the society is secret, but this is incorrect. It is the undisclosed information that they protect, which is the secret, not the society, which is, of course known about by humanity, so therefore, not a secret society.

An image of the Freemasons emblem and the items that make up the emblem appear on screen. Evander is just about to surf again when he hears the word 'Acacia' mentioned. He turns the volume up on the T.V. The voice over explains the different meanings and importance of the Acacia tree in the history of the masons and how it symbolizes the soul and immortality.

Evander sits forward in his seat and listens intently about how 'Acacia' derives from the Greek word 'Akakia', which means 'innocence' or 'free of sin'. The program covers other symbolic meanings and details one example of the earliest known affiliations of its usage of Acacia. It is attributed to ancient Egypt and is about Osiris and Isis, who are centered around immortality, but some uses in various cultures and societies agree, that it is a symbol of immortality, a sign of innocence and representative of a soul.

Evander switches the T.V. off, he gets up and goes to his study, taking his wine with him. He switches on the computer and logs into his account at the Yard.

So much for trying to relax.

He takes a few sips of wine, while he waits for the computer to load.

Once logged in, he goes through the file on James.

His last meal was roast lamb. Symbolic of the sacrificial lamb.

He was left with a white rose. White roses symbolize purity and innocence.

The tube station where his body was left is on Acacia Road.

Acacia a symbol of innocence.

He was laid out with his arms folded across his chest. Evander is not quite sure why he was positioned in this way, nor what it means. He initially thought it was to secure the rose from moving, but now he realises that everything the killer does is with reason and purpose, even if only in his own twisted form of reality.

The positioning of the arms will be important, and it will mean something, because everything in this case has been symbolic somehow.

Evander conducts research on 'arm folding during burial' and is surprised to find that this was a ritual used in ancient Egypt and is something that was reserved only for Royal male mummies.

Evander is perplexed and not quite sure on the significance of the arm folding - after all, James was not a member of royalty. He researches Egyptian Royalty and comes across Exodus and the story of Joseph and his brothers. He thinks of the musical 'Joseph And The Amazing Technicolour Dreamcoat'. He's just about to close the page, when he notices it is taken from the King James I bible.

Could the connection really be something that lame and weak? Possibly, yes. Can't rule anything out no matter how subtle. It will, he is sure, have a religious tone to it.

All the messages are subtle and alone they mean nothing, but all pieced together they speak volumes to Evander.

The murderer is telling him in as many ways as he can, that James was an innocent and he was a regrettable addition to his tally, although he was not part of the justice killings he has exacted. That much is evident from the fact that he left a note, which is undoubtedly the dragon killer, but the absence of the dragon is confirmation, like Jackson observed that perhaps, James was in the wrong place at the right time. But what wrong place? What right time?

Evander believes the killer does have regrets over the murder of James and all things considered with the evidence apparent, he has shown a rare empathy on a level that is unprecedented; this is something he has previously not shown towards a victim. His death would have been quick and painless, small mercy.

Evander takes a mouth-full of wine, quickly followed by another, disregarding the etiquette of sipping red wine rather than gulping it. He puts the glass on the desk and runs his fingers through his dark hair, which he pulls tightly away from his face. He sighs and releases his hair from the prison of his fingers.

He opens his email account, nothing new.

Evander swivels his chair around and looks out the window and for a minute, he watches life drift on by along the Thames. The reflection of his computer screen is evident in the window from the darkening sky, which seeps in through the window. He is missing something, he knows it, feels it, can almost touch it, but it is just beyond his grasp and yet so tantalisingly close, just a fingertip touch away from realization. Something he is sure, if he could just grab a hold of that thread it would be the breakthrough that he seeks to catch the Dragons of Justice Killer.

He puts his arms above his head and interlocks his fingers and pushes his hands palm up towards the ceiling. He stretches, arching his back.

He unlocks his fingers and swivels the chair back to the computer. He hovers his fingers over the keys, unsure what they are there for. He clenches his fingers, which form fists of both hands. He feels an anger rising in his stomach.

This case has become so personal to him now, not that he wasn't focused before, he is and was, as is always the case with his work - probably even more so since the loss of Jasmine. If it were not for throwing himself into work, he is not sure where he would have ended up. Work was his salvation and his mistress, almost like family.

Family.

He thinks about James' family and how they will cope. That was painful telling them all. The hurt in their faces, the pain of the loss of a son, an uncle, a brother, a friend and not being able to say goodbye - unbearable. He wonders what it must be like to have family, to have siblings.

For the first time in his life, he wants to know about his Mother. His biological Mother.

His adoptive Mother had prepared an envelope for him that contained details of his life before he went to them, but he was never interested in it, he didn't want to know, but now, something tells him it is important, and he cannot fight the 'need to know' urges.

He opens a draw in his desk and pulls out the faded manila envelope and places it on the desk. He stares at it for a long time.

He drains the last of the wine from his glass - some Dutch courage.

He picks the envelope up and finally opens it.

CHAPTER THIRTY-THREE

It is Friday evening. The weekend has started, and everyone has gone home for the evening, except for Adam Eastwood. He sits at his desk, his right-hand cups his face. His chin rests in the palm of his hand. Absent mindedly, he has a pen in his left hand, which he flicks back and forth in an up-down motion which raps on the table, a steady but furious and impatient rhythm plays out on his desk.

He stares at what was once the desk of his colleague James Reeves. He had only known him as part of the team for around four, maybe five months, or is it six? He is not sure. He was going to be a great member of the team, that is one thing the killer did get right.

Adam is not even sure why he is still at the office. Even the Boss has gone home and yet he lingers for some reason. He is vaguely aware of an annoying rapping sound, which comes from somewhere nearby, and he is surprised to find it is he, himself who is the annoying one with the pen in his fingers. He drops the pen on his desk and sighs, then folds his arms on the desk in front of him. He leans forward and rests his head on his folded arms. He sighs again.

Adam is not really one to be all emotional in his work. You get to a point where you must cut your emotions off, because with the things you see in this job, you need to find, what he calls, 'a coping mechanism', because taking those things home with you is just too much baggage to carry around.

You would feel constantly upset, depressed and in a real emotional state if you didn't switch off. He pretends that the disturbing cases, the deeply disturbing crime scenes and murder victims are from movies and in cases where it is a

serial killer, a T.V. show.
Although he knows they are real and that someone has died, he gets through it all by pretending it is a movie or T.V. set he has walked on to. This way he can cut his emotions off and get through the day, without being affected to ensure his humanity remains intact.
Not on this one though. He couldn't even hide his emotions from Evander. He was relieved he did not have to go with him to tell James' family of the loss. He figured that the Boss took one for the team on this and some pity on him, so he went alone.
He lifts his head up and looks around the office, then to James' desk again. He realises that James is not going to magically appear, just by repeatedly looking at the empty desk. Time to go home. He stands up, takes his jacket off the back of his chair, puts it on and pushes the chair under his desk. He opens a draw and takes a case file out.
The case is James' unsolved murder. He is going to take it home and review the contents again, certain that he has missed something. He also wants to review the new evidence that has been given to him by Jackson, the message that James left for him and Evander. He is not sure why the Boss told Jackson not to tell him, sure he gave her a reason, that Adam was too upset by James' death, which is true.
However, something is gnawing at his conscience. Something won't leave him alone about the secrecy around Evander not wanting Adam to see the message from James. Unfortunately, it all adds weight and credence to his suspicions about his Boss. All this coupled with the other pieces of information that he has strung together has aroused those ideas.
Suspicions that his own Boss is the Dragons of Justice killer.

It is just too bizarre to even contemplate and yet it persists. The thought slithers around his mind like an oily serpent and it is not something he can ignore, yet he has no proof. He can't run gung-ho to the Chief Super with a halfcocked theory that his Boss is the murderer. Yet he knows he will have to do so eventually and before he kills again, but evidence, he needs something more than the flimsy pieces of unsubstantiated evidence he has.

He needs something solid and as soon as he gets that he will be going to the Chief Super to present his evidence and to ask for permission to make an arrest. The arrest of his Boss. That thought makes his stomach somersault.

Adam turns his computer off, locks his draws, picks up his mobile and checks the battery - he will need to charge it when he gets home, he knows he cannot be unreachable. He pockets the phone, grabs his coat from the coat rack, leaves the office and heads home to review the file on James. Again.

~~~~~~

At home, Adam takes a bottle of beer from the fridge, opens it and goes to the dining room table where he opens the file on James. He reviews the evidence, the autopsy results and soon, there are many papers strewn across the table before him. He looks at the photos of the crime scene, while he drinks beer straight from the bottle.

Half a bottle of beer gone he finally looks at the message that James had written on his leg. How smart he was to write a note somewhere that the killer would not think of looking for a message. He reads it:

'AE - check your mapS. Get EK for me.'
~~~~~~

What does that mean? He should know what it means and yet ever since the message was made available to him, it has eluded his puzzle solving skills. Adam doesn't have any maps to check, well certainly not any that he and James had poured over or shared, or even discussed. He finishes the last of his beer and goes to the kitchen, gets another beer from the fridge and opens it.

He returns to the dining room and fires up his laptop, with the intention of researching maps of London. Adam is not sure what he expects to find, it is hardly likely there will be a map with a circle and big arrows pointing to the evidence that would lead him to solve the murder. 'Some Detective I am'. He thinks to himself.

Logged onto his computer, he opens a web page and in the search bar, he types in 'maps of London.' The results are as expected, maps of London! Nothing screams at him... 'Over here Adam, look at me. Here is the clue you've been looking for.'

He is not even sure what he should be looking for in the damn maps, but he should know, because James would be certain that his friend would work it out.

He opens a new browser and logs into his email account. He reads an email from his Mother back home in Liverpool. She asks him when he is going to come back to the 'Pool' to visit her as she misses her son. He replies to her quickly and lets her know that he will call her soon to plan a visit, that he misses her and his sister and of course, the city. He explains that he's busy with a case right now that is really important, and he can't take any leave.

He is just about to log out of the email and close the browser, when he notices that he has one item in junk mail he needs to clear. He clicks on the folder ready to delete the item in there, but when the screen loads, he is shocked to find an email from James.

He looks at the date and time - it was sent the day James died. He puts the bottle of beer down and glances at the file with the message:

'AE - check your mapS. Get EK for me.'

"Son of a bitch! It's not mapS! It's Spam." Adam says aloud to himself. That's why he put the letter S as a capital – it was cryptic to be read backwards. And he missed the clue!

He reads the message again as James wrote it:

'AE - check your mapS. Get EK for me.'

Now he reads it the way it should be read:

'AE - check your Spam. Get EK for me.'

James must have known full well that Evander would be reading the message too and he did not want to give it away to him, so he left the cryptic message for Adam, knowing that eventually, he would figure it out. Or rather, eventually he would check his email, specifically the Spam folder. Adam opens the email. One line has been written:

'The justice guy, it's Evander. Stop him.'

There is an attachment, he downloads it. It is a photo. It loads slowly and reveals someone dressed in blue. It looks like the head-to-toe coveralls that the SOCO team wear at a crime scene. The photo continues to load and reveals someone in profile with a shock of dark hair, that peaks out of the SOCO suit he wears.

The angle is somewhat strange and disorientating. It looks like James may have been on the floor when he somehow managed to take the photo. Adam's stomach twists into knots as he realises this must have been the moment he was attacked by the killer. The photo loads from the bottom of the page up and when both parts meet to reveal the full photo, he is sickened to find that the man in the blue coveralls is Evander, in profile.

Evander has an angry look on his face, no - a murderous look. Adam's stomach churns and flips, fear, anger, betrayal and the sickening realization that his suspicions about his Boss were right.

Now he has enough evidence to go to the Chief Super to tell him his concerns and to make an arrest.

He rushes to the kitchen and just makes it to the sink in time as he vomits.

He will get EK, just like James asked him to do.

Now, Evander will pay.

CHAPTER THIRTY-FOUR

Evander had worked through the night and has lost track of time. He calls Adam but he doesn't answer, so Evander leaves a voice mail. So much for being unreachable. He looks at his watch and realises that it is 03:30 in the morning, so he could be forgiven for being asleep. He did not notice the ungodly hour he was calling Adam, no wonder he doesn't answer. Adam is now the only person he is closest to, if he feels he needs to talk to someone, Adam would be the one he would confide in and right now, he wants to talk. Things like this do not happen to Evander every day. it has rocked his world to the core.

Evander decides not to give Adam details of his discovery, at least not until he can talk to him properly, rather than in some voicemail, which is decidedly one sided as far as input goes. This is not something you tell someone in a voicemail, it is quite a revelation.

The message Evander leaves Adam is quite different to what he really wants to say: "Adam, can you get the rest of the team to the Yard tomorrow. I've got an idea for a new line of investigation and want to make a start A.S.A.P., apologies about cutting into everyone's weekend. I'll brief everyone when I get there. I'll be arriving late at the office, as I need to make an unexpected visit to Belmarsh Prison first. I'll bring coffee and cake when I get back. Oh, and you're in charge till I get there." He hangs up.

When he ends the call, he breathes out heavily and is surprised to find that his breath is shaky. He is normally so together and composed. There is not much that ruffles his feathers these days but this... this more than qualifies in the list of acceptable feather ruffling.

.

~~~~~~

Adam can't sleep he has spent the last two hours tossing and turning, restless, agitated and angry. He sits up in bed, looks at the bedside clock. 3:15am.

He has nervous butterflies that relentlessly stomp around his insides every time he thinks of his Boss, which is every second. Then he has the prospect of presenting his evidence to the Chief Super and to request permission to make an arrest. Not that he needs permission from the Chief, but he feels it is the last line of respect that he can show his Boss, he is after all still his Boss.

Respect matters. Evander was right about that.

He still cannot believe it is him. He feels guilty harbouring all these suspicions with no evidence to support it, other than his skills as a Detective and listening to his gut, which ironically is something Evander instilled in him. The gut is, admittedly the most valuable piece of equipment a Detective can have in the fight for justice, the quest to find the truth, it is the most valuable addition to any Detective's arsenal.

His phone buzzes and lights up the room as the screen glows brightly from a phone call. He looks at the screen to see the words 'The Boss' as the caller I.D. of his silently ringing phone. An insane idea runs through Adam's mind why Evander would be calling him: Evander must know he has figured it out, that Adam knows he *is* the Dragons of Justice killer, and he is calling him to tell him that he will be coming to get him too, just like he got James.

A shiver runs up his spine.
~~~~~~

He doesn't answer it and leaves it to go to voice mail. He knows what he must do in the morning. The last thing he wants to do right now, is listen to Evander's soothing Scottish baritone speaking to him and pretending that everything is alright. He would never be able to pull that off, the Boss just *knows* things and he would know something was wrong. Tomorrow Adam will no doubt oversee the team, Evander's team and he will be in charge of arresting his Boss.

Adam runs through the evidence in his head. The 'exhibits' he has gathered over the last few months, knowing that he will have to present them to the Chief Super tomorrow. He wants to be clear he has everything detailed, although he has already exhausted the 'evidence'.

A... They cannot find the first victim. Though Adam knows it wasn't Evander who killed her, he can't help but wonder if the first victim was Jasmine, Evander's wife.

He has irrefutable evidence that it wasn't Evander; a confession from the driver, multiple witnesses, police accident reports, photos, and C.C.T.V. footage that confirm it was not the Boss. Besides, he was nowhere near Holborn Viaduct that fateful day, he was across town at the time making an arrest and Adam was with him.

Adam had reviewed her case without Evander's knowledge, thinking it would help him understand his Boss more as, despite the years they have worked together, Evander is a man with many layers and there are layers that Adam is yet to unravel, just when he thinks he has understood everything, another layer reveals itself. He is an enigma, even to people who know and are close to him.

He is not sure what made him look at Jasmine's case again, for although he knew Evander didn't kill her, it was evident he adored her, worshipped her even. The Boss never talks about her now, not even to Adam. He followed his gut and reviewed her file again

After she died, Evander took a break for a month and wallowed in understandable grief, but after a chat with Adam, he threw himself into work and now his team are his family. The only people he cares about, and now the only people who he lets his guard down with, the only people he trusts, the only people he has gotten close to. Probably more so with Adam as they had worked together for several years before Jasmine and Evander were married.

Adam was the first Detective assigned to Evander's team when it was newly formed. He will never forget the first case they worked on together, the man with the crows, another serial killer. Equally deranged as the dragons killer, but in different ways. Different mostly in that now his Boss is in the crosshairs as the serial killer. Maybe working with criminals for so long has had an adverse effect on the Boss, some sort of twist on the Stockholm syndrome.

Adam was curious about Jasmine, and he had to satisfy it. However, his curiosity coiled and slithered like a snake in his stomach when he found one vital thing at the crime scene of Jasmine Kincaid. It was here, where her fatal accident took place at Holborn Viaduct, that Adam noted the presence of something he couldn't ignore. In the crime scene photos of the accident that killed Jasmine, Adam found a dragon on the Viaduct. There are many of them in fact all part of the elaborate design of the steel framework, but this one was right in the middle of the photo, just above the car and Jasmine's body. Your eye is automatically drawn to the dragon as you looked upwards and away from Jasmine to the car, and then -

the dragon. You couldn't *not* notice it and the prominence it took in the photo. That is what started Adam's thoughts that Evander could be using the dragon as a symbol, representing her and that every subsequent victim was marked, linked or connected somehow to a London Dragon, as a way of taking revenge for her death. Therefore, they cannot find the first victim, because there wasn't one. He may not have killed her, but he wonders if her death was what tipped Evander over the edge, to then try to seek his own form of justice. The Dragon murders started just three months after Jasmine's death.

That may have been the catalyst for Evander's anger and all the victims afterwards were just collateral damage from the fall out. Technically, even though she may not have been the first victim, Jasmine could be the first casualty of the dragon's killer. What was to follow was merely a play on evidence, using her memory as motivation for revenge on anyone guilty of a crime, who escaped punishment. Some sort of twisted psychology that is.

B... Evander has said more than once that he understands the killer and he has gotten inside his head and knows how he operates. Of course - he would know himself best of all.

C... The time he looked over Evander's shoulder and he became secretive and evasive. He questioned Adam, asked him if he could help him with something. He was looking at some documents that Adam had not seen, and he wondered if they were part of the investigation. Perhaps evidence, or something else entirely. He never found out what those documents were.

D... How overprotective Evander became when Tommy Trent, the reporter quizzed him, to the point that Evander lashed out at the reporter. It made Adam wonder if Tommy had hit a nerve with the mention of James being a victim too and now of course, his reaction makes perfect sense, but at the time it just added a bit more weight to the suspicions Adam harboured.

E... The row Evander had with the Chief Super. Adam had to agree with the Chief Super, that it sounded like Evander admired the killer. A killer of course *would* admire or, as Evander put it, *respect* their own work, thinking that what he was doing was worthy, right and justified.

F... Evander told Jackson not to give Adam the evidence that James had left. Yet it made no sense to him why he would want to hide that. Until now.

That was all superficial in comparison to the most substantial piece of evidence that supports his suspicions. That is his next and final exhibit to present to the Chief. Exhibit G, the proverbial nail in the coffin of any lingering doubt.

G... The message from James and the photographic evidence of an angry and murderous looking Evander, as he towered over James, maybe ready to kill him. James had obviously gotten too close to the truth somehow and he needed to be taken care of. So, Evander had to kill him. Adam wanted James to be the last piece of Evander's collateral damage rampage. The last victim. It had to end here.

So much for the protective speeches that he flouted when he spoke about his team and looking after them. He always made it sound like he was fiercely protective over his team and that if anyone touched them, or harmed them, or threatened them, intimidated them, he would be there to sort you out.

If someone so much as looked at a member of his team the wrong way, he would be there to make you regret it. Yet, he murdered James, a member of his own team. It doesn't make any sense, unless James caught him out which, obviously he did.

Part of Adam hopes he is wrong about his Boss, it makes him feel better to think he may have gotten it wrong, but then, the evidence from James is irrefutable it is as solid as it can be. Plus, he wore the blue coveralls that the SOCO's use at a crime scene. No wonder they never found any evidence, trace or otherwise at any of the crime scenes, because he was able to protect himself from detection by using the very thing that the SOCO's use to protect a crime scene. It is protecting evidence against cross contamination, which helps them solve the crimes and here, he used it against them.

Unbelievable. Or is it clever? The latter he is sure.

Adam realises he will have to listen to his voice mail from Evander at some point and he will do before he goes to the Chief Super tomorrow. Later today now thinking about the time.

~~~~~~

Adam nervously waits for the Chief to come into the library of his home. The Chief has a nice home, but then on his salary he can afford it. He looks out of a window at the perfectly manicured lawn. A blackbird sings a happy song, and all seems normal in the world, except it isn't. Far from it.

The door opens and the Chief walks in. "Eastwood, good morning. Would you like tea or coffee?"

"No, I'm good thanks." Although his mouth is so dry, he can't form any saliva.

"Now, what did you want to see me about that was so urgent
~~~~~~

you got me out of bed at 7a.m. on a Saturday morning?"
"I have a lead on the dragons serial killer, and I want you to review the evidence."
"Me? Why me? Why aren't you giving this to Kincaid?" He asks, sitting down in a wing backed chair.
Clearing his throat, Adam says. "I have some evidence and I think I may know who the killer is. We'll need to make an arrest and I need your permission to do that."
"My permission? Why would you need my permission, that's what arrest warrants are for?"
"Well, the suspect is a member of the Force."
The Chief looks at him, eyes wide - evidently surprised. "Are you sure?"
"I had suspicions, but nothing substantial to go on, until last night when I was reviewing the file on James Reeves' murder. What I found last night is now too much to ignore and I wanted to extend a final courtesy to a member of the Force, by asking not only for your permission, but also your guidance and advice on my compilation of the evidence."
"Do you have it with you? This, evidence?"
"Yes Sir, I do." Adam says handing him a file. "Chief Super, before you look at the file, I… well, you should be prepared. The suspect I want your permission to arrest is my Boss, Detective Chief Inspector Evander Kincaid."
Oh, how it pained Adam to utter those words, like a knife through his heart.
The Chief jolts back in his chair, shock now evident in his face. "You're sure?"
"It's in the file."
The Chief opens the file and looks at the evidence. When he sees the email from James and the photo, his face quickly

reddens. Adam is not sure if that is anger or embarrassment. He looks up at Adam, tries to speak, opens his mouth, but he cannot find the words.

With the file still in hand, he gets up out of his chair and goes to the window. He looks out at the garden. He puts his hands behind his back, his left hand cupped around his right hand which holds the file. He breathes heavily and Adam thinks he's going to keel over. Adam is about to ask him if he is alright when the Chief turns around to face Adam. The look on his face is one of hurt, loss, nausea and anger. He knows those emotions well.

He hands the file back to Adam.

"I feel sick to the pit of my stomach. One of our own. You have my permission Eastwood. He'll be at home I imagine." The Chief says.

"No Sir, he won't be at home. But I do know where he will be." Adam says, as he removes his mobile from his pocket and accesses his voicemail and plays the message Evander left. With his hands still behind his back, the Chief listens to Evander's message.

"Keep this under wraps. Take a team with you, but not your team. I don't want them on this detail. I don't care who you take, will leave that to your discretion, but make sure it is people you trust to keep their mouths shut."

"I trust my team Chief. They'd want to be there. I wouldn't trust anyone else."

"Fine, alright. But take back up. He's obviously more dangerous than we thought. Take people with you who you know can get the job done, but don't know Kincaid like you do. They need to be impartial when making..." he pauses "when making the arrest."

"Understood."
"Call me when you have him. I will call into the Yard myself to conduct the interrogation. I, and only I will interview him. Is that clear?"
"Yes Sir. Understood." Adam confirms.
"I don't care who it is or what the circumstances are - no one but me in that room."
"Yes Chief. Understood."
"Don't wait around any longer Eastwood. Get a team and then head to Belmarsh and arrest Evander Kincaid on sight. Bring me the Dragons of Justice killer."

CHAPTER THIRTY-FIVE

Evander arrives early at Belmarsh Prison. He passes the security gate and parks in the visitor car park. He switches the engine off, but sits in his car listening to The Who, 'Behind Blue Eyes' plays. He has always loved this song and he doesn't want to turn it off halfway through the song, so he sits and listens.

While it plays, he thinks maybe a little too much. He stays there for longer than he had planned, and the next song begins. Evander switches the music off.

He takes his phone out of his pocket and checks it. No messages. He thought Adam would have called him, or at the very least text him, to confirm that he got his message and that he and the team would be waiting back at the Yard for him, no doubt looking forward to their coffee and cakes. He thinks of calling, decides not to.

Evander ponders, no not ponders - procrastinates. He is nervous about this meeting, understandably. Unsure what to say when he finally comes face to face with the man who has eluded him all this time. This man is a stranger to him and unaware that Evander is knowledgeable of his existence. A stranger no more.

He tries to imagine how the conversation will pan out and, he runs through a few scenarios in his head, he can even see some of them in his mind's eye. However, he can't know how this conversation is going to flow, nor the type of response he'll get to his revelatory reason for visiting. He also cannot sit in the car for much longer, he only has a short amount of time before he needs to head back to the Yard. He opens the door, gets out, but leans into the back and retrieves his jacket off the

hook, then slides it over the driver's seat and out of the car. He puts it on, buttons it.
It's cold and there is a sharp frost in the air that nips at his nose and bites at his fingers, his breath clearly visible in the air. He can feel the cold seeping through his jacket and his shirt wrapping its frosty arms around his torso.
He grabs his long coat from the passenger seat and shrugs into that. He slams the car door shut and engages the alarm. As he walks away, he buttons his coat to try and afford some protection against the frost that surrounds him, which claims his gooseflesh. He is not sure however, if it is the frost, or the prospect of the meeting that give him goose bumps.

~~~~~~

Adam, Izzy and Grace ride in silence on their way to Belmarsh prison. Two cars accompany them, the 'back up' to assist in the arrest of Detective Chief Inspector Evander Kincaid. When they arrive at the prison, Adam turns the engine off, they sit in continued silence in the car park. The atmosphere in the car is thick, heavy and syrup like – it's cloyingly overwhelming and you can cut it with a knife, you know something, or rather someone is going to pop any second.
Eventually, Izzy breaks the silence. "This is wrong. I don't like this at all." She says angrily.
No one replies.
"Got it. It's just me who thinks this is wrong?" She states.
Adam replies. "I don't like it either, but we need to do this. All the evidence is apparent."
"No, one piece of the evidence *might* be apparent. That doesn't make him guilty. We don't know what the circumstances
~~~~~~

were."

Adam looks at Izzy in disbelief. "The circumstances whatever they were, cost James his life. We have a suspect to arrest." Adam tells her.

"WOW! Suspect. You've already detached yourself from him, haven't you?" Izzy says.

"Suspect. He is one, yes. We have a job to do. If you don't want to do this, stay in the car." Adam says sharply. He opens the door, gets out, slams it shut. He walks over to the two other vehicles, the first one is to transport Evander when they arrest him, the second is the backup that the Chief insisted he take with him.

The occupants of the second car - the muscle as it turns out, as both are big strapping guys, so if there is trouble, they can handle it - get out to greet him. Adam talks to them and gives orders, then Adam walks back to the car to talk to the team.

He opens the door and leans in. "If you're coming - let's do this. I want this over with."

Grace gets out of the car. Izzy folds her arms in protest.

Obviously staying put Adam thinks.

He asks her. "Are you coming, or not?"

She is about to answer when they hear a direction being yelled out. "Evander Kincaid, stay where you are!"

Adam looks up to see one of the strappingly built officers' jog towards a man, who buttons his coat up as he walks towards the prison entrance.

Shouting again. "Detective Chief Inspector, stop. D.C.I. Kincaid, please stop!"

But he carries on, it looks like his pace has picked up. He walks faster now, defiantly. The officer breaks into a run and heads across the car park, homing in on his quarry. Adam

takes off after him and tries to catch up.
The officer calls out again more urgently this time.
"KINCAID! stop right there!"
But he carries on walking. The officer is now on top of his prey. He reaches out and grabs an arm, but the suspect spins around and snatches his arm out of the officer's grasp.
"Don't you touch me. I don't know who you think I am, but I am not who you say." He spits the words out with venom, turns and walks on.
The officer tells him, "This is your final warning. Stop right now, or I will take you down."
Adam almost there now.
The suspect carries on walking, moving away from the officer. The officer approaches a grass verge and rugby tackles the man before him. He wrestles him to the ground, they struggle. Adam approaches and grabs hold of the officer. He screams at him and pulls him away. "Get off him. Don't hurt him!"
Adam is annoyed that he is being so protective, but he cannot stop himself either. His instinct kicks in that he shouldn't be hurt. "Don't you touch him."
Adam pushes the officer off and away from the suspect, who lays on the ground with his back to Adam. He lays motionless. He does not move an inch.
Adam's heart skips a beat. He thinks that he is hurt, but then he gets angry with himself for feeling compassion, when he showed none to any of his victims, nor to James. Adam grabs the suspect's arm and rolls him over onto his back. he is unconscious, he must have bumped his head when they fell to the ground. He moans. Adam is relieved. His eyes begin to flutter as he comes to. Thank God, Adam thinks.
"Boss? Are you hurt?" He asks and internally chastises

himself. Old habits.

Eyes fully open now, he raises a hand to his head and asks. "What happened?"

"You were knocked out briefly, but you're okay now. Let me help you up, Boss." Damn!

"No, I'm fine. And stop calling me that. I'm not anyone's 'Boss', you hear me?"

Adam looks at the suspect quizzically. There is something odd about his behaviour.

Maybe the bump on his head has done something to his memory. Unless he is pretending, and it is a game to him. 'He is a suspect, not your friend, or Boss.' Adam chastises himself again.

On his feet now, he brushes bits of grass from his clothes. He turns towards the prison entrance and walks towards it.

Adam quickly rushes in front of him.

"Boss. D.C.I. Kincaid. Evander, I'm sorry I can't let you go in there."

"I'm sorry what did you call me?"

"Evander." Adam says slightly bemused.

A smile plays at the corner of his mouth as he says. "Son, I'm not Evander. My name is Jacob. I'm here to work, now leave me be." He goes to walk away again.

Adam puts a hand in front of him, and presses his palm against Evander's torso, which stops him from passing. Then Adam notices his attire, which includes a roman collar. "What are you wearing?" Adam asks, puzzled by his clothing.

"I always wear these to work." The suspect replies.

"Not today, Boss. Today there is no more work for you."

The suspect looks down at the hand on his chest. He looks up at Adam, from under his eyes, not moving his head. It was the

same murderous look he saw in the photo James sent him. Adam removes his hand quickly, almost like he had touched something icy, freezing and was burned. A shiver runs up his spine, which reflected the icy chill he felt.
The suspect moves forward towards Adam and leans close to his ear, he whispers. "Touch me again and you'll regret it."
He tries to walk past Adam again, but Adam puts an arm out, which stops him.
Adam says. "Detective Chief Inspector Evander Kincaid, you're under arrest for the murder of…"
The suspect decides to try to walk off again, and Adam can't get any more words out. This is harder than he thought it was going to be.
This time, the two officers take matters out of Adam's hands. They grab hold of him, put his arms behind his back and cuff him. He does not resist this time. They read him his rights. Adam is relieved he did not have to progress with the arrest and that the impartial back up were around to take matters out of his trembling hands. The Chief's advice about taking back up was good, because he would not have been able to see it through alone.
They march him towards the cars and as they walk, the suspect laughs, a low sinister laugh, one that is full of knowledge, because they have no idea what is coming.
He is placed in the back of the car that will escort him back to the Yard, he still laughs as the car drives away.

CHAPTER THIRTY-SIX

Back at the Yard, the suspect sits in the interrogation room, his hands rest on the table in front of him, fingers laced together, relaxed. He looks calm, in control, even though he is not, certainly not in this room.

Evander's team wait for the Chief to arrive. They are under directives that no one is to go into interrogation until he gets to the Yard. The Chief has made it perfectly clear no one goes in there but him for first point of contact and Adam waits on a phone call from the Chief, to let him know he is on site and ready to take charge.

However, the Chief did not say anything about observation being off limits. The team are all together in the observation side of the interrogation room and they watch their Boss in silence for a while. All of them unsure what to say to each other.

Izzy, who is in front of the glass that separates the interrogation room and the observation room, finally breaks the silence. "Something's wrong with him."

"Nooooo, you think!" Adam exclaims.

"No, I mean *something* is wrong, he doesn't behave like the Boss. He's… different."

Grace moves over to Izzy and stands beside her. She gets close to the glass to get a better view. Grace watches him to see if Izzy is right.

"There is something different about him, somehow." Grace confirms as she turns her back to the glass.

"See!" Izzy shoots back, spinning around. "Not just me who sees it, Adam!"

Adam sighs and gets up off the desk he sits on. He goes closer

to the glass and watches him. "Well, he looks like the Boss to me." He says, heading back to his seat on the desk.
"Well, I'm telling you, there's something wrong with him." Izzy confirms, as she turns back towards the interrogation room, only to find the suspect standing right in front of the glass, staring at her. It shocks and scares her.
She takes in a sharp gasp of breath and steps back quickly from the partition of the two-way mirror. She whispers. "Oh my God, can he hear us? Please don't tell me the sound is on?"
Adam checks the equipment; nothing is switched on. "No, he can't." He confirms.
"What the hell is he doing then? How does he know we're in here?" Grace wonders.
"He's still The Boss." Adam says. "He knows each one of us and he knows us well enough to know that all of us would, at this point be the other side of that glass watching him, talking about him, trying to figure him out." He pauses and watches him for a second or two, before continuing. "He's been on that side of the room a million times before, so he knows full well how to get into the head of the people on the other side of it. Do you really think he doesn't know how to reverse that psychology to get into our heads? Except now, he is the one on the wrong side of the glass. He knows all there is to know about tactics, how to push buttons. He knows what he is doing."
Everyone is quiet as they watch him watching them. He puts his hands up to the glass and cups the side of his face to try to block the light out of the room. He presses closer, tighter and almost has his face pressed against it, his breath plumes in a swirl on the glass. He mouths something they can't hear.
"Oh my God, what is he doing? What did he say?" Izzy asks.

"You don't want to know what he said." Adam says.
"You know?" Grace asks amazed.
"I can lip read a little, bit rusty on it these days, but I know what he said."
"What was it?" Izzy demands.
Adam looks at the team, his team for now. "Really?"
"Yes, really. We all want to know." Izzy confirms.
"All of you?" Adam asks.
All in unison agree. "Yes."
"He said. 'I see you, come and play.' He's trying to intimidate us." Adam observes.
"I'd say it was working." Grace says, stepping further away from the glass now.
"What game does he think we want to play?" Izzy wonders aloud.
"It's not just any game, it's his game. He likes to be in charge, to have control of everything, so the game must be on his terms. Being the other side of the glass with no one there to toy with, means he has no control over the situation." Adam replies.
"Like he has any control, in there." Izzy observes.
"Well actually, he does have some. If he gets someone in that room with him, then he can see you better. All that much easier to play mind games when you're sat in front of him. He'll be able to target your weakness and play with it, hence his invitation. Why else do you think he invited us to 'come and play'? It wasn't to confess I can tell you that much."
"Yes, but we know him, like he knows us." Grace observes.
"No, he knows us better than we know him. Have you not seen him sitting in his office watching us through the open doorway, or the window? He's been observing us for months,

years for those of us with him for a long time.

"He knows how we operate, what our strengths are, what are weaknesses are, what..." he stops talking as he feels his phone vibrate in his pocket. He removes his phone expecting the call to be from the Chief Super as he said he would call when he arrived. He will need to brief the team first before going in to see the suspect.

Adam blanches when he sees the caller I.D. on his phone. The colour loss in his face, evidently visible to the rest of the team, whom he now looks up at and then quickly to the glass, back to the phone, back to the team. His head spins.

Worry marks Izzy's voice when she asks. "Adam, what's wrong?"

Saying nothing, Adam holds his phone out in front of them, they come closer to the phone and read the caller I.D. They look up at Adam and then to the suspect behind the glass, his hands clearly visible resting at the side of his head, still trying to obscure light so he can see into the room in which they stand.

Adam turns the phone back to face him, he deliberates whether to answer it as it buzzes incessantly, menacingly almost. It stops ringing, gone to voice mail.

Missed call now displays on the phone, a missed call from 'The Boss.'

CHAPTER THIRTY-SEVEN

Evander is disappointed that the meeting at Belmarsh prison was not a fruitful one. He did not get to meet the man he had discovered had been hidden all these years. Maybe it wasn't meant to be this time around. Thinking about it, it is hardly a great environment for a first meeting either.

Evander is loaded with coffee and cakes as he promised his team he would be and as he enters the office, he is annoyed to find his section of the office empty. None of his team are around, it's all so quiet. His office door is closed and empty. He puts the coffee and bag of cakes on a table and looks around the office. All the desks are clear to a degree, apart from pens, pencils, stationery items, photo frames with pictures of family, friends, a dog, the team, but no case related work. All the computer screens are blank.

He wiggles a mouse on the nearest desk and the screen does not come to life, so the computers are not switched on. No coats hanging on the rack. None of his team are at the office. He wonders if Adam got his message.

Evander is fuming and wonders where the hell his team are and why Adam has not gathered them all together at the Yard like he told him. He takes his coat off and heads to his office to hang it up. His face stern, becomes angrier with each step he takes.

'Where the hell are my team?' He opens the door to his office, makes his way to the coat rack, hangs his long coat on it.

He checks his watch - 09:53.

They should be here now, they know better than to arrive at the office after him, especially when he is already late himself. Suddenly, a terrible thought crosses his mind. 'what if *he* has

them too'. Panic, can't lose another team member.
He takes his phone out of his jacket pocket and brings the screen to life to see if he had any calls or text messages he may have missed while at Belmarsh, or driving, or getting coffee and cakes. Nothing.
He unlocks his phone and calls Adam. He gets voicemail. Again. He hangs up.
Damn it, should have left a message, or called another team member to see if Adam had relayed the message to them. He decides to call Adam again and if he doesn't answer, he will leave him a message and then call the other team members. He selects Adam's name and presses the call icon again.

~~~~~~

Izzy is the first to speak. "What the fuck just happened? How is that possible?"
"I have no idea." Adam replies.
"Did he leave a message?" Grace asks.
Adam checks to see if any alert has come up. "No." He says shaking his head.
"You should have answered it." Izzy chastises Adam.
"Are you for real! And say what, exactly? 'Oh, hey Boss, how are you, how is it in interrogation?' Yeah, can see that one happening. Not!" Adam exclaims.
They all look at the interrogation room. Evander now stands against a wall, arms folded defiant. He senses them watching - he smiles and waves.
"He's creeping me the fuck out." Grace confesses.
Adam feels his phone buzz. He looks at the screen. 'The Boss' is displayed as the caller I.D. He walks panicked around the
~~~~~~

room and runs his fingers through his hair. "Oh my God. What do I do?" He asks.

"Answer it." Izzy tells him.

"No fucking way!" He snaps back.

Izzy approaches him, snatches his phone out of his hand and answers the call. "Hey Boss, erm where are you?" She asks, a nervousness apparent in her voice, she puts the call on speaker so the whole team can hear.

Static at the other end, a quietness that is disturbing.

They all look through the glass at the suspect, who still leans against the wall, his head now cocked to one side, as though he is listening, trying to understand what is being said.

"Hello?" Izzy asks.

"Is that you, Izzy?" Evander asks, his voice distinct, deep, rich and unmistakable.

Grace clasps her hands over her mouth to stifle any reaction that she does not trust herself to set free.

"Izzy, what are you doing with Adam's phone?" Evander asks.

Trying to sound normal, she says. "He, erm, he wasn't able to get to it so, I... I picked it up, I mean answered it."

"Where is he? Where are you all? Did he not pass my message on? What's wrong with you? You sound… strange. Are you okay?"

"Well, we're here at the Yard." She says nervously, avoiding his last question.

He snaps. "What? You're here? Where? Not in our office. Where is Adam?"

"Right here Boss." Adam confirms. As he gets a grip on his emotions.

"Adam! Good. Did you see my message about the team being

brought in?"
"Yeah Boss, I did."
"Is Grace here?"
"I'm here." She answers quickly. Returning her hand to her mouth to quell any involuntary responses thereafter.
"Okay, great, so where are you all?"
"Interrogation room number two."
"What! You're interrogating someone without me!"
"Well, technically we're not without you…" Adam says as he looks through the glass at the suspect, who still leans against the wall. Phoneless.
Evander cuts him off. "Don't get all smartarse with me Adam. I'm really not in the mood. I'm coming down there. Who are you interrogating?"
The team are silent.
Evander repeats sharply. "Who are you interrogating?"
"The Dragons of Justice Killer." Adam replies.
"WHAT!?" How did you get him? Why wasn't I told? Do we know him? Is it a man, or woman? No, it's a man, I'm sure of it. Who is it? What's his name? Who is it? Why the fuck wasn't I called and told?" He asks, his words all running into each other in quick succession, his sensual Scottish brogue becoming sharper.
The team are silent.
"Who is it?" Evander demands.
"You." Adam replies.
Static at the end of the phone.
Then... "What did you say?"
"The Dragons of Justice killer - it's you, Boss." Adam confirms.
Snorting a dismissive laugh, Evander says. "I thought you

said it was me for a second."

"Where are you Boss?" Izzy asks.

"Our office." He replies.

The team all look at one another and then through the glass at the man leaning against the wall, his arms still folded.

Izzy asks. "Boss can you come down to interrogation? I'll meet you at the lifts."

"Sure. You all have some explaining to do." He says and terminates the call.

Izzy heads towards the door, but senses someone behind her. She turns to find Adam and Grace following her. "NO!" she shouts at them, pushing them all back into the observation room. She closes the door and stands against it. She is fired up, steaming mad.

"What do you think you're doing?" Adam asks.

"You doubted him, you judged him, both of you and decided he was guilty. But the man in that room." She says pointing to interrogation. "He is not our Boss. I knew it all along. Felt it in my gut something was wrong, and I told you all that something was wrong. I don't know who the fuck that man in there is, but he is not Detective Chief Inspector Evander Kincaid. The man on the phone, the one we just spoke to, *that* is our Boss. I'm going to meet him first. Me. Alone. You're not welcome yet. This is my meet and greet, my turn to *'bring the Boss up to speed'* and none of you are invited. Got it?"

Eastwood opens his mouth to say something, but Izzy cuts him off before he can utter a word. She raises her hand, waves a finger to stop him. "Don't you dare try pulling rank on me Eastwood, because the mood I am in right now, I'd walk all up and down your arse so fast you wouldn't know what hit you, don't fight with me on this one because I promise you,

you will lose. Don't fuck with me, I'm warning you. That goes for you too Grace. I'm going now and none of you had better follow me. Got it?"

No one dares to reply to her, so they nod in agreement. She pushes herself off the door, snatches it open and walks out.

The door closes with a soft schhhhhppppp of the latch that clicks into place.

Adam clears his throat as he speaks. "Man, I've never seen her that pissed off before."

CHAPTER THIRTY-EIGHT

Izzy gets to the lifts and chews on her fingernails. She paces back and forth while she waits for the lift to arrive and the Boss to get here.

She has always admired and respected him and has learned all she knows from him. She used to rattle around the Yard, unsure what to do, what direction to go in and was thinking of quitting the Force, when the opportunity arose to go to M.I.T. and a relatively newly formed team. A team of two - Evander and Adam. Izzy was the third member of the team, and she has Evander to thank for saving her career on the Force.

She gets away with things he possibly would not allow the others to get away with. Safe to say, she is his favourite, but the others don't mind the favouritism, because she is the youngest member of the team, even though it is only by a few months on Grace. She gets somewhat looked after, although never spoilt.

He treats the whole team equally and if she fucks up, he will tell her so, the same as he would any other member of his team. She adores him, not from a lover's perspective, but from a family one. He feels like a protective big brother to her. If she knew what it was like to have big brother that is, this is how she imagined it would be to have one.

She is fiercely protective of her Boss and would do anything to look out for him, like he looked out for her, for all the team in fact. She just knew it wasn't him, it couldn't be him, he never killed James. She knew it. Believed it. Felt it. Never doubted it, or him.

Her mind runs riot, and the lift is taking forever, where the

fuck is the Boss?
A voice startles her. "Are you alright Izzy?"
She turns and lays eyes on Evander. 'Where the hell did he come from?' She wonders but doesn't voice the words out loud. Doesn't trust herself to speak yet.
"Took the stairs." Evander tells her. Like he read her mind. This whole thing has upset her far more than she will admit, even to herself, to see her figurative big brother, her mentor, teacher, guru have his integrity brought into doubt. His honour tarnished and his true nature questioned to the point that everyone had him bang to rights guilty.
She does that thing she does when upset and bites her bottom lip to try and stop herself from becoming all emotional. As hard as she tries to fight them, she cannot stop the hot stinging tears from forming in her eyes, nor can she stop them from rolling down her face.
Seeing how upset she is, Evander knows what she needs. Words will not comfort or stop her tears. He opens his arms to her and yet again, she finds herself sobbing in his arms as he tries to comfort her. Being held by him helps, she squeezes him tightly, he hugs her back, strokes her hair and lets her get it out.
Finally, Evander speaks. "You know, this is twice in as many months now that you've been in my arms. Adam will get jealous." He jokes.
Izzy giggles through her tears. The Boss always knows how to make her laugh.
She pulls away from him and wipes her eyes as she does so. She looks up at Evander who produces a handful of tissues and waves them at her. She reaches out, takes them and wipes her eyes. He just knows what she needs. He is always one step

ahead of her.
"Better?" He asks.
"For seeing you - the *real* you, yes."
He looks at her curiously, but then grabs her hand and takes her through the doors that lead to the stairs from where he had descended from their office. Under the first flight of stairs is a recess and in the recess are two chairs. Evander points to the chairs and they both sit down.
"Now." He begins. "Sitting here will keep us away from the others for a while, they don't know about this place. I come here sometimes to get away from it all and think."
"They really don't know?" Izzy asks.
"Well, who do you know, apart from me, who would come and sit under the stairs?"
"Harry Potter?"
"No, he slept under the stairs, not the same thing."
"Why are there chairs here?"
He looks at her with a *'You tell me'* look.
The dawn breaks for her. "Ah, you put them here."
He smiles. Correct.
"Okay, so why are there two if only you know about it?" She inquires.
"Because I knew one day…" He begins, before Izzy interrupts.
"…You'd have company." She finishes the sentence, always in tune with him.
Izzy dabs her eyes, blows her nose and pockets the tissues.
"Being away from the others, you'll have time to get your hard as nails, kick ass ninja persona back being here." He tells her, trying to pick her spirits back up.
She giggles.
"They won't know where we are, so we have time to chat." He

assures her.
She puts her hands together and then on her legs, she turns to look at him, his blue eyes search hers, looking for what, she is not sure, but she lets him search.
Finally, he says. "Right, so you were going to bring me up to speed?"
Izzy relays the story to Evander from the beginning. From Adam's phone call, going to Belmarsh prison, arresting who they thought was Evander, right up to her waiting nervously for him at the lifts and them sitting under the stairs in the stair well, talking. Hiding.
Evander listens intently. At some points in her relaying of the story, she sees lights of recognition going off in his eyes. She falls quiet when up to date and waits for his reaction and any questions he may have. The Boss always has questions. Usually.
When he doesn't offer any insight, Izzy takes the reins. "Boss, who is he? He looks just like you." She tells him. "Well, almost just like you." She corrects herself.
"What do you mean *'almost just like me'*?"
"Well, he looks like you, but he's not like you. He's different somehow, but physically he looks like you, yet there are things about him that are not like you, and I knew it wasn't you. I just *knew* it wasn't you. Do you know who he is, Boss?"
"Actually, yes I do." Evander confirms.
Izzy's eyes open wide. "You do? How do you know him if you've not seen him yet?"
"Because he's my twin brother." Evander tells her with disappointment in his voice.

CHAPTER THIRTY-NINE

Evander and Izzy enter interrogation room number two and are greeted by the rest of the team who all look relieved to see him.

Adam however is remarkably quiet and for this Scouser, that is most unusual. Evander knows he'll need to talk to him to release him from the shackles that his feelings currently have him trapped in.

Feelings that will be wrapped around his heart, ensnaring him like weeds around the roots of a strong tree. Feeling guilty for the accusations and assumption he made that Evander was responsible for the dragon killings and the most odious of crimes with James.

Evander knows Adam is more upset than he would let on. They definitely need to talk.

Evander goes over to the glass partition that separates him from his brother. A twin brother that he has only recently discovered existed.

"His name is Jacob Caine." Evander tells his team. "Quite an illustrious background he has built up both personally, professionally and now, criminally." He concludes. Evander tries to follow his own rules on '*knowing*' your suspect before going into interrogation to question them. To get them to confess, which they all do. Eventually.

Falling silent, he cannot say any more yet as he watches Jacob through the glass.

Suddenly, aware he is being watched, Jacob looks up to the glass, a smile curls the corner of his mouth. he rises out of his seat, walks over to the partition and stands in front of the dividing mirror. He speaks four words, which the team

cannot hear.
Izzy asks Adam. "Did you see that? What did he just say?"
Clearing his throat, Adam replies. "He just asked. 'Brother, is that you?' He knows you're here Boss."
Evander is unsure what to do with his hands, the brother he does not know, initially unnerves him. He knows him and yet he knows nothing about him either. To stop his hands from fidgeting, he places them in his trouser pockets. He tries to appear normal, calm, in control, unruffled. He hopes the charade holds as he tries to get a grip on his emotions.
He steels himself for the prospect of going into the room to talk to his brother. That word feels as alien in his mind, just as it felt escaping his mouth when he told Izzy who Jacob was. Being raised as an only child, it has never been something he has had to deal with and the thought of having a sibling never crossed his mind - until now. Disquieting.
So many thoughts to process, so many emotions he needs to get his head around and not enough time to go away and think. He needs to compose himself, because he is aware that he will be going into the lion's den that is interrogation room number two, to speak to his brother. He needs to get his act together, to get his *Detective* plugged in and get back online and his game head on. That's enough metaphors he decides. The criminals, especially the smart ones, always think they are immune to being interrogated, that they won't break, or bend, or give anything away, but when Evander zeros in on their weakness and exploits it for his own gain, that is when they screw it up and let their guard down and that is when Evander does his best work at breaking them down, all when they least expect it. He has reduced hardened criminals to a glutinous mess, crying and sobbing, wanting their 'Mama'.

A bizarre thought runs through his head - now that he has a murderer as a relation, will he lose his job on the Force? Not being able to be Detective anymore, that twists his insides into knots, and he does not want to contemplate, or entertain the idea that he may lose his badge.

That thought is more nauseating to him, than having a long-lost brother. He cannot imagine being anything other than a Detective.

He wants the thoughts gone, lost, buried never to surface again. He does not want the thoughts in his head any longer than he must endure them being there. He pushes the thoughts away quickly and captures and consigns them to a room in his head that he can lock and throw away the key. The thoughts he hopes will never escape the locked room in his head.

He closes his eyes trying to imagine blocking the memory. Time to think of something else.

Evander thinks back to last night now and he pictures himself opening that manila envelope and reading the contents.

Part of him wishes he had not opened it. Part of him is glad that he did. The biggest part of him knows that he needed to know the truth. Part of him wishes he had opened the envelope sooner, as things could have been different. The memory of it all now plays out like a scene from a movie that runs on the back of his eye lids…

~~~~~~

Having opened the file his adoptive parents prepared for him and having read the documents; Evander feels like his whole world has been turned upside down. How could he not know that he had a
~~~~~~

brother? A twin brother.

How could he feel so alone all these years and be unaware of his presence? Twins are supposed to be able to sense one another and know when something is wrong with the other. Yet he remained completely unaware of his existence, but this discovery now is a revelation.

The memory of the murder of his Mother must have been more traumatic than he had thought if he completely obliterated his knowledge of his twin.

His brother must have witnessed their Mother's murder too. He has questions and wonders how he coped with it? If he has nightmares as well. He is curious if his brother may be married and if he has any nieces or nephews.

Children are something he and Jasmine were never blessed with and how he rues not having them. So many questions buzz around his head, all of them have a child like innocence about them, but that does not last long.

Evander works through the night, forgetting about the wine that he had opened, too busy calling in favours to track down his brother and his whereabouts.

Evander cannot believe his brother is still in London. He has had a variety of different roles and jobs including a butcher, a vet, and a soldier and not just any soldier, but an S.A.S. Commando. Now he is a prison Chaplin at Belmarsh prison, where the Category A prisoners are.

Unexpectedly, he has an idea for the investigation into finding the Dragons of Justice killer and the prison is just the right place to start.

Some information has eluded the police, but when they have come across the victims and their stories, when their backgrounds and histories had been researched. When they had extensively researched the victim and found things out that Evander thinks may possibly

have come from prison chatter. Evander thinks it is a line of inquiry worth pursuing.
He will call Adam in a while and get him to gather the team together tomorrow. They probably won't be best pleased to have their weekend interrupted, but a Detective is always on duty, always on call.
Evander has found out that his brother will make a visit to the prison tomorrow morning, part of the pastoral care offered to inmates.
He is not sure why now is the time to go and see him, maybe it is just fortuitous timing with the new line of inquiry that has motivated him to head to the prison. Kind of killing two birds with one stone. He never expected their first meeting would be like this.
When he thinks of meeting his brother tomorrow, his stomach flip flops at the thought of it. It is going to come as a shock to come face to face with someone who looks exactly like he does and given that they are identical twins, that is going to be disconcerting.
Oddly, Evander wonders if he too will bare a scar on the left side of his upper lip like he has. He finds he subconsciously touches it right now, one of those little quirks he has when he is contemplative, or his mind whirls, or he tries to think three steps ahead of himself. He takes his hand away from his mouth.
He realises how unlikely it is now, that his brother will bare the same scar, he is not even sure how his got there, but it always has been, for as long as he can remember. Obviously, something he must have acquired when he was with his Mother and Brother. Evander calls Adam, who does not answer his phone.
He leaves him a message. Finally, he picks up his glass of wine, sits on the sofa and rather than sip it to savour the palate of the wine, he quaffs it down in three mouthfuls. He puts the glass on the coffee table and lays on the sofa. Tomorrow he has a busy day ahead of him. He will have to brief the team on his discovery, but first the meeting with Jacob at Belmarsh, then back to the office to work.
But now, he needs to rest, he closes his eyes for a minute.

Sleep finds him quicker than he expected.
Evander arrives at Belmarsh and initially puts off going inside until he forces himself to do so. He sits in the waiting room of the Chaplaincy for over 30 minutes and waits for Jacob to arrive, which he never did. He was disappointed that the Chaplain did not keep to his schedule. Disappointed that his brother did not show, but also relieved.

~~~~~~

Opening his eyes, Evander is back in the observation room. On the other side of the glass, Jacob stands also with his eyes closed, hands stuffed in his trouser pockets mimicking his brother. '*How could he possibly know?*' Evander wonders to himself.
Something suddenly clicks in his head, and he is no longer intimidated by the presence of his brother. He distances himself from any emotional attachment because he realises that they never really shared a bond to begin with and if they did, it was all one sided on Jacob's part. Evander realises that Jacob has studied him in the outside world. When he takes away any sibling connection, the man on the other side of the mirrored glass becomes just like every other person who has stood on that side of the room: a criminal about to confess his sins.
Armour now firmly in place, ready to go into battle, Evander takes his hands out of his pockets and heads towards the door.
"Boss, what are you doing? Where are you going?" Adam asks.
"To do my job." Evander replies reaching the door.
"But Boss, the Chief Super said no one was to go in the room
~~~~~~

other than him."

Evander has his hand on the door handle, but doesn't open it yet, he pauses and turns slightly. He looks over his shoulder.

"I bet that was when the Chief thought it was me." He says.

Adam doesn't need to say anything to Evander, his expression confirms he is right. Evander pushes the handle down, opens the door and exits into the corridor.

"Boss, wait." Adam calls out to him as he follows him into the corridor.

Evander is in between doorways - interrogation to his left, observation to the right. He waits for Adam to exit, the door closes softly behind him, no one follows him.

Adam is silent, he looks at Evander, but says nothing.

Evander eventually raises his hands in a *'Well, what did you want?'* gesture.

Clearing his throat for no reason other than nerves, Adam opens his mouth to speak and struggles to free the words trapped in his throat. He closes his mouth.

Evander cocks his head to the left, raises an impatient eyebrow questioningly, an attempt to encourage him to hurry up and spit it out.

Finally, Adam speaks. "The Chief may not be best pleased if anyone goes in there."

"I'm not anyone." Evander replies.

"I know Boss, I know." He pauses, clears his throat again before continuing. "But he was quite adamant you know, he didn't care who it was, or what the circumstances were - no one in that room, but him."

Evander realises that Adam is trying to save him from a roasting from the Chief and what his underlying motives are he tells him. "It's okay Adam, I don't blame you for thinking it was me. Stop beating yourself up over it and move on. We're good."

Adam's face flushes with embarrassment. "Boss, I'm sorry. I... well, the photos and other things that happened, I just...well, I got too involved, too caught up, too...."

"Adam, you were just doing your job, following what your gut was telling you, am I right?"

Adam nods his head in agreement but says nothing.

"I don't blame you for thinking it was me. From what Izzy told me, if it was me looking at the evidence, I'd think it was me too." He offers as comfort.

The look on Adam's face tells him that's not good enough and the guilt he harbours still swims, shark like in the straights of his mind.

"I'm glad to see my processes have rubbed off and you're taking note of what you're seeing, hearing, trusting the gut - your own gut - honing those Detective skills. Adam, I don't blame you. Let it go. Move on, it's OK, we're good." Evander reassures.

He extends a hand to Adam to shake, to show there are no hard feelings. A handshake, such a quaint tradition if ever there was one. A gentleman's agreement, an understanding that things are OK, that trust is in situ, and they can go about their business without need to discuss their *business* again.

Adam looks at Evander's extended hand for a long number of seconds. Evander wonders if he is going to take it. To his surprise Adam ignores the extended hand and bear hugs him, Evander is knocked off balance slightly by the force of the hug, but there is no doubting the sincerity in which it is given.

Evander puts his arms around Adam to reciprocate the hug, Adam hugs him a little tighter. Then as they part, Evander pats Adam on the back, then caringly holds onto the back of his neck.

"Now, I need you to go back in that room and start recording when I go in there". He says, gesturing towards interrogation room number two.

"When people find out what's going on down here, you may have some unexpected visitors wanting to join in and watch the party, try to keep it to a minimum in there if you can. I don't want this turning into a circus, alright?"

"Got it Boss." He says sheepishly, but he lingers in the corridor.

"Well, go on, get in there and be my senior Detective." Evander says, smiling.

A smile warms Adam's face and he opens the door to the observation room.

Evander hears Izzy, sweet protective Izzy yelling at Adam, that he had better not have given the Boss a hard time, hoping he apologised for doubting him. The door closes before Evander hears the rest of her speech. No doubt Grace had to sit on Izzy to keep her in the room and stop her from following Adam out.

Evander turns his attention to interrogation room number two. He closes his eyes, takes a deep breath, controls his breathing, gets it together, calms his heart rate and the butterflies that flutter their wings rapidly in his stomach. Composed now, he opens the door and walks into the interrogation room to face his brother.

CHAPTER FORTY

Back in the observation room, Izzy bombards Adam with questions before the door has even closed.

"Izzy calm down, I'll answer all your questions, but it will be later. Not now."

"Where's Evander?" She demands.

"Ready to go into interrogation, with *him*." He points to Jacob through the glass.

His emphasis on the word '*him*' tells Izzy how annoyed he is, not only for doubting the Boss, but with himself for more underlying reasons she needs time to figure out. Perhaps because he got his Detective skills wrong.

They all look to the interrogation room. Jacob has moved away from the glass, and he now stands at the end of the table, facing the door.

"What's he doing?" Grace asks.

"Waiting." Adam tells her.

"Waiting for what, the next bus?"

"The Boss." Adam and Izzy reply at the same time.

"You're letting him go in there, after what the Chief said?" Grace asks bewildered.

"You want to try stopping him?" Izzy sneers.

"He can handle him. No one gets in their heads the way the Boss does." Adam says.

"Shouldn't we be recording?" Izzy observes.

"When the Boss is in the room, yes." Grace replies.

"Gonna get it ready now." Adam says and rushes over to the system and sets it up, so it is recording now.

Everyone in the observation room holds their breath as they await the entrance of Evander and his coming face to face with

who they now know is Jacob.
The atmosphere in the room becomes more tense, still the door does not open.
Adam wonders what the Boss is doing.
Getting his game face on.
Letting Jacob sweat a bit longer.
Possibly bits of both.
The silence slithers like a serpent of darkness that coils around each member of Evander's team, squeezing them into an explosive air of anticipation that engulfs the observation room. The tension so taut, the pressure that builds in the room is unbearable.
Suddenly, the door opens and Evander walks into the room.
Finally, the team can breathe.

CHAPTER FORTY-ONE

Evander walks into interrogation room number two and finds Jacob standing at the end of the table, hands behind his back, facing the door. Evander closes the door and faces his twin brother. It seems Jacob knew he was going to have company and was waiting for his visitor. Evander wonders if he knew it was going to be his twin brother, the Detective.

It is a little unsettling, seeing someone who looks exactly like you, looking back at you.

No, *almost like you* - Izzy was right - there is something different about him. Obvious evidence of his military training in how he holds himself at ease but alert, ready for action.. His demeanour is different, stronger.

No, not stronger.

Bolder.

No, that's not right.

Confident.

No, that's not it either.

Arrogant. Ah, yes, that's it... arrogant.

He believes he is invincible, that no one can get to him, that he is untouchable and protected. First mistake. No one is ever truly safe, for everyone has a flaw, a weakness. A way in.

They stand at opposite ends of the room sizing each other up. Assessing. Looking for and seeking said weakness. Mentally circling each other, like hunters in stealth, stalking prey, looking for the proverbial chip on the shoulder, a chink in the armour, a defect in the charade of confidence. It is just a question of time before the façade cracks and a way in is found.

Evander makes the first move; he walks to the table and pulls out the chair facing the two-way mirror.

"Sit down." He tells Jacob, who remains standing.

Evander makes his way around to the other side of the table, his back to the two-way mirror. Jacob remains standing.

Evander rolls his eyes to the ceiling.

He repeats. "I said sit down."

Jacob rolls his eyes to the ceiling too, mocking Evander and he defiantly remains standing.

Evander unbuttons his suit jacket, removes it and puts it on the back of the chair, his back to the mirror. He looks up to see Jacob still standing. Sighing, he bends over, puts his hands on the back of the chair and rumples the jacket, after he had placed it so neatly on the back of the chair too.

Without lifting his head, he raises just his eyes, so he has Jacob in his line of sight and in a low, deep voice he tells him. "Sit down. This is my last invitation for you to *sit down.*"

Evander's emphasis on the last 'sit down' is said through gritted teeth. His voice has a deeper, darker timbre to it than his natural speaking voice, menace and promise are laced through it. He is quite serious.

This is his last chance to sit when invited. If he does not take up the offer, he will make him sit. "Next time, I won't be asking you to sit down." Evander promises.

Jacob stands still for one second, two, then he moves towards the chair and sits down. He puts his hands on the table flat in front of him, but then laces his fingers together. Dressed all in black, he sports a roman collar - a dog collar is it is better known. Obviously, he was ready to conduct his Chaplaincy duties when he arrived at Belmarsh. So, he did turn up to work.

Evander stands up straight now and takes his hand off the

back of the chair. For the benefit of the tape, Evander confirms his name, the date and time and that he is conducting an interview with Jacob Caine, while he straightens the shoulders of the jacket, so that it sits perfectly on the back of the chair. Finally, he pulls the chair out and sits down across the table from Jacob.

Evander tries to remain silent now, although he doubts it will work. He knows it wouldn't work on him if he was in this position and unfortunately, as they are related and cut from the same cloth, though technically not alike in anyway, he imagines Jacob will not yield to this method of intimidation, but he has got to try it anyway, start with the simple, easy stuff first he figures, weed out the easy methods first and then move onto the more psychological ones.

They sit in silence for five minutes, ten minutes, fifteen minutes. They just stare at each other, trying to read the weakness in the opposition.

To Evander's delight, it is Jacob who takes the bait and speaks first. "Do you think I could have a glass of water?"

Well, that was a bit of an anti-climax Evander thinks. All that waiting and he asks for water. Not very fruitful at all, but at least he is talking. Evander turns towards the two-way mirror, nods his head for them to bring water.

A few minutes later the door opens, Izzy places a plastic cup of water on the table, her focus is just on Evander. She glances only briefly at Jacob as she turns to leave. She tries not to give anything away with her eyes, although she fails, because Evander can read her like a book. He hopes Jacob is not so good at reading her like he is, and he does not see her face, or the message in her eyes as she leaves, closing the door softly behind her.

To Evander's surprise, Jacob pours some water into his hands and promptly puts it on his hair. He repeats the process until it is suitably wet enough for him to run his fingers through it to slick it all back from his face, every trace of a wavy curl banished.

Finally, Jacob takes a few sips of water and puts the cup back on the table. He pats his damp hands on his trouser legs.

"Now I feel more like myself and less like you with those ridiculous curls, which are just waves upon waves of hair. How do you keep them like that all day? Especially when they look so terribly silly."

Evander remains quiet, he does not rise to the bait of personal insults, although a split second later, he knows exactly why he changed his hair. Evander is not stupid; he knows the games people play. He waits to see if he will talk any more. He does. Good.

"Now, you may begin the conversation. So, what would you like to ask me *Big Brother*?" He says, emphasising the last two words for Evander's benefit.

Curious, Evander thinks that he would refer to him as 'Big Brother' when they are twins. Is that a reference to the novel '1984' by George Orwell and how he feels about the work they do on the Force, or did he mean it in some other context? Very curious indeed. Maybe he wants him to ask him what he means. Ahhhhh yes that could be it. Perhaps. He won't be asking.

"Surely you do have questions? You're not going to continue with this monotonous silence all day, are you? You have questions, I can tell, so let's talk. Let's have a conflab."

"How many people have you murdered?"

"None." Jacob says in all seriousness.

"Really? None? You're sure?"
"Absolutely." Jacob confirms.
"How many people have you killed?"
"None."
"Quite sure?"
"Of course."
Evander rethinks his question. He needs to find the right word, the right phrase to get a confession. Suddenly he realises how he needs to ask him. He tries again.
"How many people have you avenged with your sword as God's minister?"
"That Detective, is the right question. It's still a work in progress. Hmmm, seven or is it eight now? Perhaps nine or ten. I'll have to check." He says mischievously.
Evander is enraged. He wants to reach across the table and beat the crap out of him but beating a confession from a suspect does not sit well in a court of law.
"Why did they deserve to die?"
"Wrong question Brother." Jacob says smiling, waiting for him to play the game.
"Why did they deserve your wrath?"
"Correct question." He smiles and nods his head in approval.
Evander realises that he is going to have to play this Bible game with his line of questioning, but if Jacob spills his guts and confesses then he'll use it.
"I'm waiting?" Evander says.
"Because they were all guilty of evil that had gone un-punished by *your* laws." Jacob says, emphasising the word 'your', for effect.
"Oh. I see, so God gave you permission to exact revenge?"
"No, God gave me guidance on the evil that is committed by

people who think they can do whatever they like in this world with no accountability. But there is always retribution in some way. They felt the wrath of God and their punishment was that which they used against others to gain for themselves. It was justified." Jacob stops himself abruptly. He realises he has said too much. He composes himself again, rests his hands on the table before him and laces his fingers between each other again.

Evander wonders if he uses it as a watered-down version of holding his hands in the prayer position, so it affords him some comfort and control for his emotions, or perhaps a feeling of being close to God. Some sort of assurance and justification to his actions.

Maybe he is over thinking that one, could be that he just finds that a comfortable resting position for the hands, or to stop them fidgeting.

"So, all of them, every victim deserved what they got?"

Jacob smiles, looks down at his hands, then glances back up to Evander with a *'wrong question'* expression on his face.

He really is going to have to play the game all the way through Evander thinks. Rephrasing his question, he says.

"So, all of them, every person you avenged deserved what wrath they got?"

"But of course. God's wrath upon evil is unwavering and indiscriminate."

Evander places his hands flat on the table, to avoid them forming any shape when he asks his next question. He breathes slowly, measured as he composes himself. He does not want there to be any trace of emotion in his question. He takes his time, slows his breathing more, till he feels as calm as possible. He can't show any emotion.

"What was James Reeves' reason for deserving God's wrath?" After a pause of thought as he remembers James, a pained expression initially crosses Jacob's face and then, one of excitement, then regret. Regret is the one that remains. Long lost brother or not, Evander wants to get up and beat him to within an inch of his life.

CHAPTER FORTY-TWO

Back in the observation room, Kincaid's team watch, while their Boss and the Chaplain play a silent game of cat and mouse, although they are not sure yet who is the cat and who is the mouse, they are both adept at holding their silence.

The team of course have seen Evander do this before. He is in a room with a suspect and not uttered a word and they have confessed because they are somehow compelled to talk.

Evander has this gift of not saying anything to invite people to talk. He just watches them.

Eventually Jacob speaks and asks for water. Evander nods approval to them through the glass to bring water.

Before anyone else has a chance to react, Izzy grabs a cup from the water cooler and fills it, prepared to take it into interrogation.

"Don't look at him." Adam warns her.

She asks. "What? At whom?"

"The Chaplain. He'll be looking for eye contact, he'll be trying to read you, looking for something he'd be able to use against the Boss, to get into his head. Don't look at him. If you make eye contact with anyone, make it with the Boss and the Boss only. Hear me?"

For once, Izzy takes instructions and does not argue back. She nods her head in agreement and makes her way to the door just as it opens.

The Chief Super stands in the doorway, he looks through the glass and sees who he thinks is Kincaid looking back at him. He shoots a questioning look towards Adam. "What the hell did I tell you? No one in that room but me! Who the hell is that in there?" He bellows.

Adam realises that he did not tell the Chief of the developments, only that they had, who they thought was Kincaid in custody and was awaiting the Chief's arrival at the Yard for questioning to begin.
"Chief, I…" Adam tries to explain.
Walter cuts him off. "Don't give me any half-baked excuses. There is no good reason why anyone other than me should be in that room… and I don't even do that anymore."
Adam takes a leaf out of Evander's book and cuts the Chief off before he can continue his ranting. He will be unaware of the twist this case has taken. He speaks quickly, sharply, the hard edge of his Scouse accent prominent. "Chief! Detective Kincaid is conducting the interrogation. The suspect is his twin brother, Jacob Caine."
The Chief falls silent, he walks over to the glass partition to take a closer look.
"Izzy take that water in there now. Remember what I told you." Adam tells her.
She takes the water to Jacob. When back in the room, she shudders. "Jesus, he gives me the creeps. The atmosphere in there is so thick and heavy, it's like wading through syrup."
No one replies to Izzy. She is initially perturbed that there are no questions, but then she looks through the glass and sees why everyone is quiet.
They watch in silence as Jacob pours water into his cupped hand and then onto his hair, repeating the process until his hair is wet enough for him to run his fingers through it.
He slicks it back away from his face and smooths it out tightly. Izzy blushes and is glad that everyone else is in front of her. She finds his actions incredibly sexy, and it stirs feelings in her that she knows she should not be entertaining. She is

enormously embarrassed about her feelings and the thoughts that run through her head. She has no sexual feelings towards Evander at all, he is literally like a big brother to her, but yet, here is his evil twin brother turning her on. '*No, stop this!*' she internally chastises herself.

Finally, Jacob says something that is substantial. '*Now I feel more like myself and less like you with those ridiculous curls, which are just waves upon waves of hair. How do you keep them like that all day? Especially when they look so terribly silly.*'

The first dialogue between the two of them. Adam realises why he slicked his hair back and wonders if his colleagues have caught his act too. Now 'Jacob' is fully present in the room and in character. This is the real Jacob Caine, not the one with the soft curly hair, that is part of his work attire that he hides behind during the day, his costume to go to work if you will. This is his real persona, the slick, smooth looking man, the murderous one.

For the first time, Adam is worried about his Boss and fear clenches his gut. He knows the Boss has a fiery temper and usually if he is pissed off, he walks away from the situation rather than argue about it.

Adam has always wondered why he walks away rather than stay and carry on the with the battle of words. Perhaps it is because he does not trust himself to stay in the room with a suspect when he is angry enough to turn green and change into a cartoon Hulk. Maybe it is because he is being the better person and walking away before things are said that are regretful and not retractable once out there. Or perhaps it is something that he hasn't figured out yet about the Boss.

So many layers yet to still unravel about him.

Grace shivers visibly and hugs herself. She tries to rub away the goose flesh that covers her bare arms. She watches Evander to try to get into the mind of the Chaplain. She has much to learn on the road to being a hardened Detective. Evander is a pro. Adam and Izzy seasoned. With James gone, Grace is now back to being the newbie, she feels she is still wet behind the ears. She imagines it maybe a while before the Boss will think about bringing in a new team member. He knows they need someone, because the workload they have is growing and things need to be more evenly distributed.

In the short time that James was with them, the workload became more manageable. Now, they all work extra hours again.

She watches Evander's mannerisms and tries to see how he interacts with Jacob. She watches Jacob and tries to find if he has any 'tells' that give away what he is really thinking. Either he is bloody good, or she is terrible at understanding body language.

Adam loves watching a suspect go from a confident, complacent son of a bitch to a snivelling, squirming mass that they all eventually become. As the team have grown in their experience, Evander has taken members of the team into interrogation several times, so they can cut their investigative teeth on the lesser criminals, and he has done well with some of them. He has broken a few into confession as well, all of which he learned from observing the master that is Evander Kincaid.

Adam is not normally a nail chewer, not a habit he wants to have, something he has not done since he was a kid but now, he finds himself feeling like a little child again, insecure, despite being 'safe' on the opposite side of the glass, but he knows that is not the source of his discomfort. He is sure it is because he has not quite forgiven himself yet for accusing Evander of being a murderer. He still feels vulnerable. He watches the Boss question one of the most dangerous men he has seen in interrogation. He listens to the questions that the Boss asks Jacob and how he must play a game and be smart in the wording of the questions in order to get an answer.

The Chief cannot believe his eyes or his ears. He is unusually silent and still, as he watches his best Detective doing what he does best - breaking down the walls of suspects to get them to talk, feel comfortable and eventually to confess to their crimes. They all crack in the end, except for one and oh, who was that now... erm the Bird Man, oh no, the Crow Man that's it. Always thought that was the strangest case he had watched Kincaid deal with, although he was at the time relatively new to the world of interrogation and had not been able to break that suspect.

They still got him of course, evidence gathered was enough, so a confession was not vital to conviction. You can plead 'not guilty', but these days, forensic science can convict you regardless of what comes out of your mouth, but it bothered Evander that he did not break him, did not get behind the façade and bring the walls tumbling down.

He learned from it though and studied many interrogations thereafter. He watched, learned and formed his own techniques, which enabled him to get result after result, once he felt he had learned enough to work the skill himself.

Now, Walter watches him try to unsettle the Dragons of Justice Killer, to unravel the web of lies and deceit. He cannot help but admire Kincaid's self control and how he handles himself in what must be a bit of a mind job for him too. He is completely professional and conducts himself with aplomb. It

would be a pleasure to watch, were the case not so nauseating.
Back in the interrogation room, Evander places his hands flat on the table. This causes the first physical and verbal reaction in the observation room which, up to this point had remained so quiet, you could have heard a pin drop.

Adam puts his hands up to his head, grasps his hair tightly and tries to relieve tension. He swears involuntarily and talks quickly, his Scouse accent stressed with a note of anger, concern and anticipation in his voice. "Oh fuck, here we go. This is it, fuck me. This is the one. Fuck. Fuck!"

Everyone turns to look at him. "This is what one?" The Chief asks.

"He's going to ask him about James." Adam tells them.

"How could you possibly know that?" Grace asks.

"Because I know his moves. I know the Boss. Fuck me man!" Adam answers, with quivers of emotion that mark his voice, his hands still in his hair.

In the interrogation room, Evander asks the carefully phrased question that Adam knew was coming. They all shoot a look at Adam in amazement that he was so in tune with Evander's body language, that he knew before anyone else what the next question was going to be. Turning back to the interrogation room, they watch through the glass and wait for Jacob to reply to Evander.

Adam listens, but he cannot take his eyes off Evander's hands, his long fingers splayed out flat on the table. He waits for the response, which has not come.

Noting a subtle movement in Evander's right hand, Adam knows something has happened. He looks away from Evander's hand and up to Jacob. The gleeful expression on his face sickens him. Bastard.

The tension now between Jacob and Evander has seeped through the glass partition and flows into the observation room. The atmosphere is tense, taut. Ready for a volatile reaction from Evander, everyone seems to hold their breath again.

Adam hopes the Boss does not do anything stupid.

CHAPTER FORTY-THREE

Evander keeps his hands as still as he can and says. "Answer the question." His tone is low, almost a whisper, menacing and veiled, unspoken threats in his deep, rich voice. His accent carries a hard edge to it that leaves you in no doubt he will stop at nothing to get an answer.

"He was most regrettable." Jacob replies, mimicking Evander's low tone.

"He wasn't left with a dragon. Why?"

"Most unfortunate that he disturbed me, he wasn't meant to be part of the design for Justice, he was after all someone acting out Humanity's form of justice. He wasn't left with a dragon because he was not an evil man. While he did not deserve the wrath wielded by the sword of the minister of God, he could not get in the way of my duty to God. He did not warrant a violent, painful passing. I gave him a merciful passage. God would have wanted that." He says with sincerity, as though he has regular conversations with God to discuss the next murder over a nice cup of tea.

Jacob shifts slightly in his seat. He leans forward, closer to Evander and continues. "You see, unfortunately he got in my way and was interfering with my carrying out God's work. He wanted to stop me, and I couldn't let that happen. I still had - *still have* - work to do. God is not finished with me yet, there is still much to do, there are more souls to be visited to feel the wrath of God." Jacob says with conviction.

Evander realises that Jacob thinks he is going to walk out of here and carry on where he left off and obviously that is not going to happen.

"He really thought I was you. I tried to tell him I wasn't you and I was me, I tried to clear your name. Right up to when I shot him, he still believed I was you. That was most amusing to me because he didn't believe me, he thought I was you, but I was in alter-ego state, like a Jekyll and Hyde thing I guess. This is why the smile as I know you were going to ask." Jacob concludes.

A slight, but almost undetectable smile curves Evander's lips. At this juncture, the 'almost smile' is not because he is amused at the demise of James, but because he knows he has got him now, right where he wants him.

He has just confessed to shooting an officer of the Force. So, he will be going back to Belmarsh, but as a prisoner, not a Chaplain. Evander knows now that he has nailed this bastard to the mast, and he has not even realised his mistake yet. First mistake.

As Evander and Jackson discussed, James was in the wrong place at the right time. Not meant to be on his list. He wants to ask him more questions about James, but decides not to push it just yet, he will return to that later. Perhaps. For now, he has got a confession to the killing of a member of his team. That is good enough to see him put away. Now to work on getting information for the other victims.

He needs to understand how he knew which victims to choose but, he needs to think on how to ask the question correctly, or he won't answer.

After a pause, formulating the question correctly, Evander asks. "How did you find them? I mean, those who warranted justice from an avenger wielding the sword of the minister of God. How did you decide on the wrath that you metered out? How did you decide what the nature of their punishment should be?"

Jacob answers right away. He sounds thrilled to finally have an audience to present his work to, someone who will appreciate the details of the important work he conducted in God's name. "Well, the problem with prison is that everyone complains how they are hard done to. How they don't deserve to be sent to prison, that there has been a gross miscarriage of justice and the system is all screwed. Some of the criminals in there, they feel their crimes are not as atrocious as some of those who are still walking the streets as a free man, with no retribution for the violations they have carried out." Jacob pauses.

Evander thinks that is it, but he isn't done yet.

Jacob continues. "They see me with my dog collar and this ridiculously fluffy hair, and my puppy dog eyes with the sweet understanding smile, as I sit listening, nodding my head." He assumes the smile and nods his head in imaginary understanding for effect. "They hear the sympathetic and comforting words of the Lord, and they trust me. It loosens their lips when they hear things amongst the prison chatter of who is doing what to whom and how so and so has done this and gotten away with it. The resentment they feel for the injustice of them being locked away spreads like a cancer amongst the inmates. They hear of people on the outside who have committed much worse crimes, at least as far as they are concerned, than what they have done and oh how it pains them that they are still wandering around as free men. When they are incarcerated for a lesser sin, it lingers and festers till they just need to talk about it. They admit their feelings to me in confession, they wish them harm and hope that there will be some sort of justice for..." Jacob stops himself. He sits back in his chair, breathes out deeply, folds his arms. He realises too late he has said too much. Not as smart as he thinks he is after all.

"Why do you do it?" Evander asks, genuinely curious, wanting to understand.

Jacob laughs dismissively and asks with amusement. "Do '*it*'. Do what?"

Evander chooses his words carefully. "Why do you do it? I mean what compels you to do what you do, in your… to conduct your job as God's messenger?"

"I'm a messenger of God sent forth from His house to do His work." Jacob announces with a genuine note of belief in his voice.

"Well, you're not in His house now, you're in mine. God has no jurisdiction here. There are a different set of rules we play by in this place, it's called the law."

"I wear the armour of God and wield the sword on His behalf."

"That doesn't place you above the jurisdiction of law."

"God's law is the only law. Every other law is made by people in parliament. They don't count. They are not true laws. God's law is the only valid law."

"The law of the land exists to keep people safe."

"To keep them blind. Bound. Slaves to humanity, to a corrupt system. They are not servants of God." Jacob says with conviction.

"The law exists to stop ordinary people taking God's law and making it fit their own design."

"No, God's law is the only way, but you must understand it, know it and how to read and interpret it, then how to know and own it, but most people remain ignorant of the facts in the Bible, in the teachings of God. They misinterpret them.

Misunderstand His guidance, His word, His law. The only real, true law."
"That doesn't give you freedom to kill people."
"Are you really that stupid, to think that your law is above God?" Jacob laughs..
"Are you really that stupid to think you're above the law and God will protect you from the punishment that the law of the land deems fit for your crimes?"
Jacob stops laughing. This isn't funny now. How dare he question God's wrath and the messenger He has sent to do his work.
Evander knows that look. He has seen it a thousand times before on the faces of a hundred or more criminals who have sat across this table from him. The look that says, 'he's hit a nerve'. There is the chink in his armour, that is the way in to break him down, the weapon he will use as a tool against Jacob. God is his weakness.
Every criminal has a flaw in their psyche, a seat hidden in the back of their head that they never see Evander making himself at home in until it is too late. Then he plays with their emotions like a cat would toy with a mouse.
This is the part Evander likes the best, as he gets to walk about inside their head and push and prod and poke his way around.
Recognising his mistake, trying to close the door shut on Evander, Jacob tries to turn the tables to his advantage, he tries to make him fearful of getting inside his head. "Ohhhh careful Brother, putting yourself in my mind is swimming in un-chartered waters and trust me, you don't want to get lost in the water ways that form the corridors of my mind that lead you, who knows where. I know from not taking my

medication that you wouldn't want to find yourself trapped in any of my rooms and you should definitely stay out of the basement as that will lead you into the bowels and deep running chambers of my mind and once I have you there, you're mine for an eternity and I will never let you go. I found myself trapped there once, for a long time, but with help I was able to navigate my way back to the surface, but it took me practice and time and medication. You can visit the basement if you must but, beware if you do as you will then you belong to me. and no amount of help or medication can save you if I have you trapped there." He says gleefully.

That is a reveal that Evander was not expecting. Jacob was trying to warn him of the dangers of his psyche, but has in fact, revealed that he is trapped there himself, because he no longer takes his medication.

Medication he thinks, probably keeps him on the straight and narrow. Evander keeps his understanding close to his chest and takes air over his teeth, which creates a slight whistle, which then changes to a hiss. "You have to ask yourself. Before you draw up a chair and put your feet on the table, could you make yourself as comfortable in my head as you have in my house?" Evander asks, raising his hands to indicate the room they are in.

Jacob cocks his head to the left and raises an eyebrow. He looks quizzical, he does not completely understand the riddle. Evander leans forward and puts his hands together, lacing his fingers into each other, which mimics his brother, then he smiles wickedly. "You don't know my mind."

"I know how you think." Jacob is quick to reply.

"No, you know your own mind best, everything else is second guessing. I may not want to go to the cellars of your mind, but there are rooms in my mind that even I don't know exist, let alone what is in them, so trust me when I tell you this... Get caught in my mind and you will never be free to wander your own."

Evander pushes his chair back he stands up and pushes his chair in. He takes a few steps and leans with his back to the glass of the two-way mirror.

A look of dismay crosses Jacob's face. "I thought for a second you were ready to leave, and I was going to have to implore you to stay. I mean we've only just met, so much to discuss and learn about each other. Although I've known you for some years now."

Curious, Evander asks. "What do you mean *'you've known me for some years'*, how?"

Jacob looks up at Evander, raises an eyebrow, which is both telling and inviting at the same time, an indication that he should know how, and Evander should tell him the answer. Evander wonders how he could possibly know him when this is his first meeting. Ahhhhh... realisation hits him.

"There we go, there's the lightbulb moment - now you know." Jacob says congratulatory, as he recognises acknowledgement in Evander's eyes.

"You've been following my investigation in the media." Evander concludes.

"Oh, much longer and well before that. Ever since the incident."

Evander wonders if he is talking about their Mother.

"Incident. Or accident. Both work but are either the correct description?" Jacob says in wonderment. "The accident. Was it? An accident? What do you think, Brother?"

It is not their Mother he is referring to it is Jasmine.

Evander has his hand up to his mouth, he unconsciously rubs his fingers one way and then his thumb in reverse across the scar on his upper left lip.

Jacob watches him and smiles as he remembers how he got the scar. The thought of it thrills him, although part of him knows it shouldn't yet he cannot help the euphoria either. He enjoys watching him play with the scar of death.

He wonders if he should enlighten his brother on how he acquired it. Not yet, may save that one for later. May save Jasmine for later too and change the subject.

There are other things to play with right now.

Delicious things to play with and oh, the joy.

CHAPTER FORTY-FOUR

Jacob changes the subject and direction of the conversation. He decides Evander has had enough questions answered for now.

Now it is time to have a little bit of fun with his older brother before he gets out of here, and back to work to the normal boring day job, and then to the evening when he is free to do God's real work. He has an appointment to keep, where he will gather his next target, yet another worthy cause to tend to tonight and he is eager to take care of business, but first, some defiant fun.

"So, here we are!" Jacob says, as he claps his hands together, then folds his arms.

He sits back in his chair and puts his feet defiantly up on the table.

Evander looks at his feet, then up at Jacob, back to his feet.

'Good'. Jacob thinks, he got that.

Unsure where he is going with this, Evander remains quiet and allows Jacob to play his game a while longer, see if he slips up. Again.

"Brothers in arms, brothers separated, brothers reunited, but brothers divided."

Evander remains quiet, he must have sadness that is evident in his eyes, for Jacob gives a sad expression and asks. "Awww, what's the matter Brother? Someone took your marionettes away?"

A chill, cold enough to freeze the marrow in his bones runs up the length of Evander's spine. He hopes it does not reveal itself in the shiver that runs slowly, subtly through his body.

This is important somehow and it is not in relation to the

murder that was staged in that style. This is something else, something personal, something from their childhood, a memory shared that Evander has blocked out, but what is it he wonders? *'No! I don't want to know, stop searching!'* He protests to his memory.

He has suppressed the ability of total recall for a reason, and he is quite happy to retain ignorant bliss.

Jacob has apparently missed the subtle shiver and the struggle in Evander's eyes as he battles to squash down any memories that may bubble to the surface of his mind, for Jacob changes tack with his little game.

"How cloyingly sweet I imagine you are with your team. I know you're the protective Big Brother to the little one that brought me water, but she's a fiery one she is, best not get on her wrong side, or she'll take you out like a ninja. I bet she was the one that protested your innocence while the rest of the team thought I was you. Now, who was the guy who arrested me? East-something? Whatever. A Scouser, salt of the earth he is, you know he loves you right? I don't mean in terms of lovers, but he loves you as in totally hero-worships you. You do know he wants to be you when he grows up? You have no idea how it messed with his head when he thought I was you. The pedestal he has you on, and his image of you, kind of imploded, thinking you were capable of such atrocities, but don't worry, he's carrying enough guilt now that should keep him wallowing in self-loathing for a good while yet. You may want to milk that as he'll do anything for you now to make it up to you, unless you free him from the enormous guilt he has chained around his heart. But how are you with the other remaining team members, well, one now poor James is no longer here. So what relation are they to you, I'm curious.

When do I get to meet the red head? Didn't catch her name, but she's pretty, nice eyes too and not the airhead people assume. With that gorgeous hair and those big eyes, I bet she's a flirt, isn't she, isn't she? I could have fun with her." Jacob taunts.

Evander's jaw cinches, his teeth clench so tight he could grind wheat between them. Jacob notes the reaction and removes his feet from the table, unfolds his arms and leans forward in his chair. He wants to get closer to the reaction he sees in Evander.

Evander realises that he has let Jacob get under his skin. He is annoyed with himself and tries to shake off the protective feelings he has towards his team, so he can do his job.

Jacob however knows what he is doing. "Oh good, now you're trying to pretend that you don't care but it's too late. *I know*. I know now, what your weakness is. Your team."

Evander places his hands flat on the table, pushes his chair back and begins to rise from his seated position. He stands up slowly, almost as if in slow motion.

Deliberate, measured and with purpose.

CHAPTER FORTY-FIVE

In the observation room, Izzy is angry with herself. She did as Adam had instructed and did not make eye contact with Jacob. It was just a glance from the corner of her eye, mostly she kept her eyes firmly on the Boss. She thought she had not given anything away, but apparently Jacob has the same gifts as his brother in being able to read her.

When she took the water in, she told Evander, without saying a word, that the team were all together in the next room; that she was glad he was there and that she always knew the Boss... her 'Big Brother' was innocent. She actually said the words in her head 'Big Brother'.

She knows the Boss got it, but so did Jacob. She feels mentally violated he was not invited to read the messages in her eyes that were meant for her Boss. It is like he read her diary and then used it against her. Against Evander. Against them all.

Adam is first to react to Jacob's mind games. "Chief you have to get him out of there." He says, before Jacob has even finished his first sentence about Izzy.

"What? He's doing his job!" The Chief exclaims.

"Seriously, you have to get him out. He's going after the team."

"Eastwood, let Kincaid do his job, time to put your feelings of guilt aside."

"Chief, you don't understand. Listen to what Jacob is saying. Can't you see what he's doing?"

The Chief listens to Jacob more closely now but says nothing in return to Adam.

Jacob now talks about Eastwood and his hero worship of Evander. Walter is silent... watching, listening.

"Chief, please? Pull him out. Now. If you don't do it, I will, but it will have more power and less suspicion if it's you, rather than me excusing him."
Thankfully, Jacob side-steps James, but now Jacob is talks about flirtatious Grace.
"What do you see Eastwood, that I don't?" The Chief asks.
In Interrogation, Evander Kincaid places his hands on the table and pushes his chair back, he begins to stand up, rising slowly from his seat, hands still firmly planted on the table.
The Chief realises now.
He picks his hat up off the table by the door, leaves the room and heads next door.

~~~~~~

Hands flat on the table, standing slowly, Evander wants so badly to reach across the table for Jacob.
Instead, he stands and puts his hands in his trouser pockets.
He walks slowly around the table, circling Jacob with menace and malice afore thought. Evander stops behind him. He has un-nerved him, the hairs on the back of Jacob's neck bristle.
The door opens. The Chief stands in the doorway, his hat under his arm. "Detective, we have a development. We need you for a few minutes."
Kincaid leans close to Jacob and whispers to him. "When I return, you're going to tell me everything I need to know. You'll answer all my questions, and it would be wise for you not to play games with me. You. Will. Lose."
Evander notes the hairs on the back of his neck still raised but are now accompanied by gooseflesh. Evander confirms for the tape. "Interview suspended."
~~~~~~

He keeps it short, not mentioning the date and time.
Evander is angry. Ready to put his fist down Jacob's throat and rip his heart and lungs out. He knows that was a veiled threat against his team.
Evander goes to his chair, takes his jacket from the back of it puts it on. He buttons it as he walks to the door, which he closes softly behind him.

CHAPTER FORTY-SIX

In the observation room, Evander opens the door and walks in.

All the team greet him in unified stereo. "Boss!" Relief evident in their voices.

He forces a smile.

The Chief is right behind him. He throws his hat on the table from where he picked it up to go and rescue his Detective from self-destruct mode and closes the door behind him.

"You need to get a grip on your emotions Kincaid." He says vehemently.

"With all due respect Chief…" Evander begins, but the Chief interrupts him. Kincaid hates it when he does that. Especially in front of his team.

"Cut the bullshit Kincaid. I don't know what you had in mind, but you need to wind your neck in on this one. You're letting him get under your skin. You're bloody lucky that your team know you so well." He says, shooting a glance to Adam.

Evander looks towards Adam, who shrugs his shoulders and stuffs his hands into his pockets, obviously embarrassed at the acknowledgement from the Chief.

Adam, reliable, dependable, always looking out for him, making sure he has his back. Salt of the earth - Jacob got that right for sure.

A hard edge to his voice, Evander shoots back. "I got you a confession. He's going to prison for the rest of his life for the murder of a police officer. I've still got work to do to gain a confession for the other murders. Get off my back."

Before the Chief can reply, Evander opens the door and storms off.

~~~~~~

Evander sits under the stairs in the stair well, where he and Izzy had been just a few short hours before. He needs to get his head on right, still more work to be done.

Concentrating on work, he reviews his mental notes of the interrogation. Evander thinks of the 'marionettes' comment. Like a lover's first kiss left on lips full of anticipation, the thought of the marionettes and the chill that came from their mention still lingers in his memory, it crawls over his flesh and seeps into his bones. Now, he has some understanding why that crime scene of the Marionette murder disturbed him so much and why the nightmare eventually resurfaced to haunt his sleep.

He is grateful that he never remembers the details of the nightmare and only the remnants that wake him remain. They, however, are soon taken back down to the depths, by the unseen hands that protect his apparently fragile psyche from remembering anything about it. They spare him the pain of the memory but, afford him the most disturbing way to wake from slumber. There are some toys that belong in the attic, never to be removed or spoken of again and marionettes are such things. He is not sure why he used that analogy to describe his feelings to himself, but it just seemed fitting.

They need to know who the first victim was and why they have never found them. Evander thinks back over the interrogation. When he asked Jacob how many he had given the wrath of God to, Jacob said numerous numbers but landed at nine.

They only know of eight, so where does the extra one come
~~~~~~

from? Evander can use this to cover his departure from the room by the Chief.

Time to head back to interrogation room number two.

CHAPTER FORTY-SEVEN

Back in the room, Evander walks around the table to his chair, removes his jacket and hangs it on the back of his chair before continuing his little journey. He stops at the back of Jacob again. This seemed to un-nerve Jacob, and Evander wants him unsettled and uncomfortable. His equilibrium disturbed and off kilter.

"Have you calmed down Brother dearest?" Jacob scoffs.

"What are you talking about?" Evander asks.

"I know a murderous look when I see one. You had death in your eyes for me before your Commander in Chief rescued you from yourself."

"My acting abilities must be as good as yours. Although my maths is notably better."

Not the answer he expected. Jacob is quiet. Then…"Acting and maths? What?"

"Well, you go about your day job being all fluffy haired, smiley, trusting and understanding, but by night, you're quite a master of disguise. A real-life Dr Jekyll by day, turning into nightmare Mr Hyde at night. Quite a performance. But it seems you were inflating your tally of victims. We only have eight people accountable to your sword. That's why I was called away from our... interview." Evander says, choosing his last word thoughtfully.

Jacob is quiet, contemplating. Evander wonders what he is thinking, one disadvantage of being behind him, he can't see his face to try to read him.

Hedging his bets, he takes a risk on the reaction he thinks he may be getting. Evander asks. "So, which is it - how many have you killed, eight or

nine? We know it's not ten."
"Where did you get that number?" Jacob asks.
"The body count we have is from the victims we have found with your mark."
Jacob puts his head down and makes a muffled noise, his shoulders shake. Evander thinks he is crying. He looks in the two-way mirror; but Jacob has his head down, and he can't see his face, he pushes himself off the wall and moves around the table, pulls his chair out and sits down. When Jacob looks up, he is laughing. No, he is sniggering.
Evander is confused. "I'm sorry, is something funny?" He asks.
"You and your Detectives. Pathetic. You don't have eight nor nine. You have a much different number, and you know it."
"So, you know how many there are?"
"Do bears shit in the woods?"
"If it's not eight or nine how many is it? How many notches do you have on your vestments, Chaplain?" Evander says as a throw away comment.
Jacob's eyes give away a secret at that last statement. Evander used it as a metaphorical notation, just as a womaniser would have notches on his bed post for each sexual conquest, but he didn't for one second think he would be right on the mark.
"Ohhhhhhh" Evander says realisation marking his voice. "You actually do keep a tally, I see. So, you shouldn't have any problem confirming the correct number. Eight or Nine? Answer the question."
Jacob looks up to his brother and replies in a whisper.
"Neither is correct."
Evander whispers loudly for the benefit of the tape. "If neither is correct, why are you whispering? If we're so bad at maths,

enlighten us! Eight or Nine?" He repeats.
"Neither. My answer is going to be the same every time. It doesn't matter how many times you ask, or how many ways you rephrase the question. Neither is right."
"How many do you think we should have? Eight or Nine. Eight? No, wait is it nine, or wait, perhaps it's Eight?"
"Tut, tut, trick questions, Detective. Tut, tut." Jacob chastises.
Kincaid says simply. "How many?"
"Eight is what you have, as you are still yet to find the first one, so you cannot include that one, but that is one you never will discover. It will always be hidden from you, and I'll never tell a soul about that one. So that makes my tally different to yours. It always will be different."
"Why would you not want to add another act of justice to your vestments? Why would you do yourself out of a notch? Why would you not include one to add to your list?"
"No, that's not what I said. I didn't say it wasn't on my list."
Evander wonders out loud. "Why would one be special and all the others not? Why would you keep one for yourself?"
Jacob smiles, but sadly, says nothing.
"Was it your first kill that gave you a taste for murder? Or maybe it was someone you cared about and you..." Evander stops himself when he sees the look on Jacob's face.
"Don't stop brother, I was having such fun watching you try to work it out."
Evander changes the subject and asks. "Why did the old man deserve to die?"
"I'm sorry, who?"
"Harry Shaw. Number six. Why did the old man deserve to die?"
"You mean, you don't know?"

"We couldn't find anything in his life. No criminal records, his connections to other people, nothing to indicate that he was guilty of any crimes, that warranted a cleansing from the minister of God and his sword. Why him?"

"I have my reasons."

"But everyone you murdered had a history, something they did that they got away with. We couldn't find anything on him. You killed an old man already dying for what reason? You had nothing better to do at the time? You were bored? What was it?"

"You said it yourself, they all got away with something. He had committed his crime many years ago and he lived a happy life, marrying his sweetheart, having children, grandchildren. However, it seems the apple didn't fall too far from the tree with his son as he ended up in prison."

"So, that's how you knew of him?"

"It's how I found all except one of my avenger jobs."

Evander resists the urge to laugh at his 'Avenger' comment. It sounded like he was making himself into some sort of superhero and maybe he felt he was.

Evander asks. "What did he do? If you hadn't left us your dragon calling card, we possibly wouldn't have accounted him to you. Why did he deserve to die?"

"Are you actually going to do your job Detective, or do I have to do everything for you?"

"Why did you take his glasses?"

"Oh, you noticed that? Good."

"Was that your message, with that? Was it to say we couldn't see you?"

"You worked that out all on your own, goody, goody. But that wasn't the reason I kept his glasses."

"So, what was the reason?"
"I could really do with a cup of tea, couldn't you? A nice cup of tea."
"Stop changing the subject. What did Harry Shaw do that deserved your wrath? Why did you take his glasses?"
"Not my wrath, Detective. God's wrath. I'm just his avenger, the minister."
"Why did you minister death to him?"
"Check your files."
"We did. Came up with nothing. He did nothing wrong."
"Check again, you missed something."
"Why did he deserve God's wrath from you acting as minister?"
"You didn't do the job right, well not you, but whoever worked the case. They failed."
"Failed at what?" Evander asks impatiently.
"Failed at everything. They didn't investigate properly. Didn't collect evidence."
"Remember I told you that you were going to answer all my questions and you shouldn't play games with me?"
"It's not a game. Your lot missed it. They failed her. He could roam about a free man and after what he did." Jacob stops abruptly, emotion evident in his quavering voice.
Evander realises that now is the right time to push those emotional buttons. Evander asks, "Why did he deserve to die?"
Jacob tries to reply "He…" But doesn't complete the sentence, emotion clearly overloading him.
Evander slaps the table and is demanding now. He shouts.
"Tell me! What did he get away with?"
"Murder."

Speaking rapidly, tinges of anger that stop just short of desperation in his voice, Evander asks. "There's nothing on file about him doing that. Nothing we picked up, by all accounts he was clean. We never figured out why he was on your hit list. Who is he supposed to have murdered?" Evander demands.

"Our Mother."

CHAPTER FORTY-EIGHT

The words that come from Jacob's mouth sound muffled to Evander, as though someone had dunked his head under water, his words were diluted, distorted and unclear.

"Did you say. 'Our Mother'?"

"Yes."

"How did you find him? How did you know it was him? I mean how did you find out?"

"His son."

"How?"

"His father came to see him in prison after his wife died, found he was dying and had six months to live. Couldn't keep his secret any longer and confessed to his son, who confessed to me as he couldn't cope with the burden his father had given him. Prison had given the son to me, so, you see God put the son's Father in my path. If ever you needed evidence of divine intervention, I think that constitutes it. There is always retribution." Jacob says.

"You really believe that?" Evander asks.

"You don't have to believe in the bible, or God for that matter to believe in divine intervention. I mean think about it, what are the chances that the son of the murderer of our Mother was there before me, in my prison? Out of all the others, it just happened to be mine? Him being put in my path, to hear his confession via his son. You've surely got more chance of hitting a jackpot win on the lottery *and* being struck by lightning all on the same day. I mean think about it, what are the odds? Like a gazillion to one, right?"

Evander ponders the odds and must admit the chances of the stars aligning and, making the murderer of their Mother fall

right into the lap of his murderous twin brother at the exact time he is on a killing spree, seem somewhat slim, remote, impossible; But divine intervention does push the envelope.
"They are pretty narrow." Evander confirms.
Jacob appreciates the confirmation. He leans forward towards Evander and replies with conviction. "You see! I'm not crazy. Of all people, even you see it. You see it. *You* get it." The way in which he says... 'you' has an underlying tone to it that Jacob is happy, purely because his brother agrees with him. Evander sees he needed his approval, which for reasons unknown, tug at his heart strings.
"Why did the son confess to you?" Evander asks.
"Well, being in prison there is a lot of time on your hands. You don't have work to go to, a movie to enjoy, a football match to attend, a concert to get lost in music. Prison forces you to make different choices with your life as you are behind bars. Some of them educate themselves, some tend to plants and some commune with their higher self through meditation and yoga, while others find God. The son, he found God. He was repenting for his sins involving drug trafficking. He was working his way towards being what he thought would be redemption for his soul. He believed fervently in the commandments so, 'thou shall not kill', when his Father confessed to him, it brought his family life crumbling down around him. It tortured his soul. He felt that his Father deserved God's wrath for taking a life. When he said that, he was unaware that I *am* God's servant. How could I refuse his request for justice?"
"I doubt he was asking you to carry out a hit on his terminally ill Father." Evander tells him.
"He said he deserved to be punished."

"His wife dying and having six months left to live himself wasn't punishment enough?"

"I said that to him, trying to offer salvation, but he didn't believe it was justice enough. I have to say I agreed with him, although I couldn't tell him that. Not for what he did. No. Not for… not for what he did to her. What he did to us. He tore our family apart." Jacob puts his head down and sighs.

That sounded like genuine emotion, Evander thinks before asking. "How do you know it was him, that you got the right man? That he even knew our Mother?"

"He was the puppet man."

"Puppet man? What puppets?"

"Well, we were four years old at the time and they weren't really puppets, I guess they thought we wouldn't be able to say the real word, so they called them puppets, but when I got older, I realised they were not puppets at all, but marionettes."

Muffled. The last words were muffled, again.

Evander acquires partial deafness again, his mind trying to protect him, shutting out the words so they don't free his memories that terrorize him in his nightmares. He's not sure he can keep them buried. He struggles to keep his head above the incoming tide of emotions he has buried deep in the vaults of his mind, which seem to have sprung a leak and flood his mind with emotions he would prefer did remain sunk in the depths.

His mind still tries to protect him from the horrifying events of that fateful day, which is why words are distorted and distant, muffled and unclear.

He is like a duck on water, calm and serene on top, but kicking furiously beneath the surface, trying to stay afloat. He hopes he does not dissolve into a puddle and become water

before his murderous brother.
"Sorry, what?" Evander asks, unaware he is speaking, still on his autopilot function.
"The puppets, well the marionettes. Don't you remember them?"
Evander, not trusting himself to say a word, shakes his head.
"You loved them as a child. They were your thing made you laugh to see them dance. Me, I loved the toy cars and I always wanted to go fast in the Brum Brums, especially the police cars, rather odd don't you think?" he says seeing the ironic side.
"So, how did that work? I mean, how… I mean what did they have to do with our Mother?"
"The cars?"
Evander has to pull himself together, Jacob is not making any sense. Evander pushes his inner demons down to the depths from which they try to surface.
If he is to conduct this interrogation, he needs to get a grip, get his head on straight. He clears his throat, takes a deep breath and disassociates himself from what Jacob tells him and what he is about to tell him. Thank God, that he will be able to watch the interrogation tapes back, so he can get up to speed on what has happened before he got it together again.
"How did the puppet man… the marionette man know our Mother?" Evander asks the question just as a sickening thought runs through his mind - what if he was their Father?
Jacob sees the unspoken question in Evander's face and answers for him "Don't worry, he wasn't our Father."
Relief must be etched on Evander's face. "Glad I was able to ease your burden with that worry. I felt the same way too."
"How do you know he wasn't?"

Smiling, looking remarkably like himself when he looks in the mirror, Jacob says. "I asked him nicely and he told me he wasn't."
"You believed him?"
"Oh yes, he was in a somewhat compromising position at the time, so one false move and it was good night Vienna."
"Maybe he just told you what you wanted to hear?"
"Well, that's just the thing. I didn't make it clear to him what answer was the right one to tell me. He had no clue if 'Yes I'm your Father,' or 'No, I'm not your Dad,' was the right choice. I didn't give him any indication that I wanted one or the other, but he knew that there would be pain associated with a wrong answer and I fibbed a little. I told him he must be honest with me, as I already knew the correct answer and this was a test, to see if he would tell me the truth. So, he had no choice but to be honest. I may have also implied that I could just as easily get to his son inside and once presented with the evidence of who I am and how I knew of his gross misconduct, he knew I wasn't bull shitting. He wasn't our Father."
"How did he know our Mother?"
"You really don't remember do you?"
"Would I be asking if I did? I was four years old."
"Funnily enough I was four years old too. But I remember. I remember it well. I'll never forget the marionette man. That's how you got this." Jacob says, pointing to the right side of his own lower right lip before saying. "How you got that scar." He gestures to Evander's mouth.
Evander subconsciously plays with the scar at times, which strangely helps him to focus, to think, but he does not want to remember how it happened and does not want to be enlightened any time soon, or any time during the

interrogation. He changes the direction of questioning.
"Why did you dress him afterwards? I mean, we know he wasn't wearing those clothes when he was... sent to the next life. We found the items he was wearing in the washing machine. They had been washed, but there was still evidence on the clothes. Why did you go to all that trouble of dressing him, was that a message for us too?"

"Can I have some water?"

"Answer the question."

"Or tea? Please."

"Answer the question." Evander says demandingly.

"Because I wanted him to know what compassion felt like, even though he showed none to me, or you and definitely none to our Mother."

"Why would you show him compassion when he committed a crime? You didn't show any of the others compassion, why him?"

"Because none of the others were diagnosed as terminally ill, this man was."

"He murdered our Mother and you felt compassion for him?" Evander asks with notes of anger and disbelief in his voice, which he doesn't even try to hide.

"He'd soiled himself and that's no way to go to the gates of hell. Hence the washing in the machine. It was an act of dignity before he crossed the bridge."

"If he was alive at the time that happened, why bother? Because you killed him anyway. Why did you go to all that trouble?"

"I'm an avenger for God, not a heartless animal."

"You murdered people, how does that not make you an animal?"

"I'm not incapable of emotion, I can feel things, many emotions in fact. Did you know there can be great beauty in death Detective? Especially with the right setting, in some cases it is almost like painting and creating something new, different and everlasting."

"Why did you take his glasses? Was that a message for us that we couldn't see you?"

"Not everything is about you!" Jacob says angrily.

Evander prods further. "So, enlighten me. Why did you take his glasses when they served no purpose to you?"

"He didn't deserve them either."

"I hate to break this to you, but they were no use to him anymore, not after your murdered him."

"Do you believe in the afterlife? More specifically, the soul Detective?"

Evander pauses before answering. "I never thought about it. Why?"

"You know, in the bible, it says that the soul will either ascend to heaven, get cast into purgatory, or be exiled to hell. But to me, in whichever realm he was going to end up – I believe it was hell, just an F.Y.I. – I felt that he didn't deserve to see anything, be it good or bad, in whichever said realm his soul would reside. I took his glasses, not because I was having a dig at the incompetence of the police investigation, but because that piece of shit shouldn't be allowed to see well enough in any afterlife, so he can do no more harm and hurt to no one else."

Emotion evident in his voice, Jacob stops himself from talking any further about Harry Shaw. He looks down and clasps his hands together, squeezes them.

Evander is not sure why this one upset him. Why would a

murderer get emotional about killing someone whom, at least to him, he felt needed justice to be served?

Regaining his composure, game face back on, Jacob asks. "Are you thirsty?"

"Tell me, why would he have glasses in the afterlife?"

"Some people believe that when you pass, whatever is on your body at the time, this is all that you take with you as you pass into the next life; shoes, underwear, trousers, a shirt a jacket, a hat, glasses, they go with you. Wearable possessions. He didn't deserve to have any and certainly not something that would afford him the gift of sight in the afterlife. I made sure he wouldn't be able to see the beauty of that world given by God, nor the horrors of hell run by Lucifer and, as a man blessed with vision, not having glasses to see in the afterlife would have caused him more terror, than being able to see what was coming for him. The unknown is a different beast altogether and creates a fear unparalleled for anything that's gone before."

"You strangled him with wire, was that poetic?"

"I made him suffer like he made Mother suffer while we watched, helpless to stop him. Even bought the wire that they use on the marionettes, so it was all authentic."

"I thought you weren't an animal?" Evander says quickly, fearing he may say more about the marionettes. Damn the marionettes.

"I wanted him to know what it felt like to feel his life force slowly ebbing out of his body and be helpless to stop it happening, like it would have been for him with our Mother. For us, in our play pen, watching on helpless as he slowly choked the life out of her before the wire snapped and sprung back. That's where you got your scar Brother. He deserved

the same fate.
However, I also did not want to touch him for longer than I had to. I was sympathetic to his condition, yet angry at his crime. How could I not be angry? He took my... he took our Mother from us; he took you away from me. He murdered her and got away with it for all this time. All this time. I wanted to do much worse to him than the death I granted him."
"You strangled him and that was supposed to be sympathetic?"
"God's guidance told me I was to show him compassion, so he would know what it would feel like, even in death to be shown mercy."
"You strangled him, how exactly is that merciful?"
"I spared him from the consequences that his illness would have put his body through. He'd have died a long and slow painful death had he succumbed to his illness. But his passing by my hand, meant he was shown mercy, a mercy for not having to endure those death throes. And yet I so wanted him to feel all the pain of that illness torturing his body. However, I had a duty to attend to, a purpose to serve and an act of evil to avenge in God's name."
Abruptly, suddenly, a feeling of nausea washes over Evander in great big waves. He needs to get out of this claustrophobic room for a while and quickly.
"Would you like some tea, coffee or water?" Evander asks.
Jacob is evidently surprised and initially struck dumb.
"Yes? No? Any? All? None? You've asked for it." Evander prompts with a sense of urgency.
"Tea, white and strong, no sugar, please and some water. Thank you."
Evander states the time date, his name, Jacob's name and that

the interview is suspended. He grabs his jacket off the back of the chair, carries it over his arm out the room. Once the door is closed, he walks quickly to the men's room.

He goes to a cubicle, hurriedly hangs his jacket on the hook on the back of the door. Turning towards the toilet, he lifts the lid, and the seat together and promptly throws up, purging himself of the various nauseating thoughts that have plagued him since discovering that his Brother solved the murder of their Mother from all those years ago and exacted a revenge most appalling. And most fitting.

Evander is even more disturbed by the fact that he is glad that his brother found their Mother's murderer and he punished him and made the bastard suffer.

He throws up again.

CHAPTER FORTY-NINE

Evander washes his hands, splashes water on his face and grabs three or four paper towels from the dispenser and pats his face dry. He throws the towels in the bin when done.
He leans on the edge of the sink and looks at himself in the mirror, the tap still running. He looks at the scar on his lip and closes his eyes. He feels nauseous again and tries to squash the feeling down. He takes in deep breaths *'mind over matter, mind over matter, mind over matter'* he repeats to himself, while he focuses on the running water and his breathing, while he tries to think of it as soothing and calming.
The feeling passes and he washes his hands again. The door opens.
"You alright Boss?" Adam asks, keeping the door ajar.
"Yeah, sure. Just needed to pee and wash up." He says, not wanting to tell Adam the real reason he had to come in here.
"You want a break? Want me to take over for a bit?" He asks.
"No!" Evander replies urgently, protectively. "I'm good."
Evander rinses the soap off, then shakes excess water off his hands. He takes paper towels from the dispenser and dries his hands.
"You're sure? You don't want me to take a pop at this?"
"Absolutely. I got *this*." Evander says stressing the word 'this' for effect.
"I don't mind Boss, if you want a break." Adam offers again.
"Did the Chief put you up to this? Or Izzy?"
"Wasn't me Boss! I know you can nail his arse to the mast." Izzy shouts through the open door, over Adam's shoulder.
Evander can't help but smile at Izzy's comment and her unwavering faith in him.

"Something you can do though, is bring two mugs of tea and some water for me and the suspect." Evander requests.
"I can do that, yep. How long do you want me to wait?"
"Do it now. I'll meet you outside the room and take them off you."
"I'll bring them in Boss."
"NO!" Evander snaps.
Adam looks surprised at the sharpness with which Evander delivers the '*No!*'.
"Sorry. I didn't mean to snap. I just… I don't want him seeing anyone else from my team. He's not going to use any of you again, like he did before. He's already got the measure of you Adam, so I won't allow him to profile you, or any of my team anymore. I won't allow him to do that again. No one else from my team is to come in the room. He's too good at reading people, I don't want him to… none of you are to come in the room okay? He's got an attraction to Grace, so make sure she stays out of his line of fire. The only person allowed in that room is the Chief Super. Understand?"
"Sure Boss, I get it."
"Tea. Oh, and in proper mugs not them shitty polystyrene things, you hear?"
"We can't give him a proper cup."
"It'll be fine, trust me. If he wanted to physically hurt me, he'd have done so already. He's S.A.S trained, so he wouldn't require a cup to do that. Tea. Proper cups, it's important."
"Okay. Yeah, no problem. Will go do it now." Adam says and lets the door close.
With Adam gone, Evander is alone again in the toilets. Finished with the paper towels, he throws them in the bin. He looks at himself in the mirror and at the scar on his upper left

lip. sometimes it is more visible, though he is not sure why. He thinks about what Jacob said about the marionettes and that they caused his scar. Now the theatre murder makes sense as to why it disturbed him so much. Suppressed childhood memories.

He hopes Jacob will leave that alone now. He doesn't want to know in any more detail how he got the scar, nor hear any more about it. He stands up straight, feels like he has forgotten something. Jacket! He retrieves it from the hook in the cubicle, puts it on, buttons it up.

Sunlight comes in through the window and dapples the jacket in different shades of grey/silver/gun metal from the shiny fabric of the jacket. It reminds him of mercury, and it feels appropriate given his changing mood, while conducting the interview - interrogation - with his twin brother.

He is glad Jacob found their Mother's killer, but even more glad that he avenged her murder. He will never tell that to anyone, it takes all his courage to admit it to himself, let alone mention it to another person.

Then he remembers James and Evander is reminded of his heartlessness. He knows why James was taken away now, but he does not need to understand, or accept it, because he can't. He feels anger rise from his feet over James.

Mercurial feelings. Appropriate for the colour of his suit.

Time to head back to interrogation.

CHAPTER FIFTY

In interrogation room number two, Adam knocks on the door. He has brought tea and water on a tray, but at Evander's instruction, he does not enter the room, but leaves the door slightly ajar. Adam passes him the plastic cups of water, which Evander places on the table in the room, one for himself and one for Jacob, then returns to Adam for the mugs of tea. Adam closes the door, stays out of the line of sight.

Evander puts both cups on the table, turns the handle of the cup that is Jacob's towards him, then moves his own cup to his side of the desk. He goes around the table, removes his jacket and places it neatly on the back of the chair, then sits down.

He confirms for the tape that the interview has resumed.

Jacob picks the plastic cup of water up, pours some in his hand and applies it to his hair. "I can't even see it, but I can feel that curl coming back, and it needs to be banished." He slicks his hair back tightly to his head and pats his damp hands on his trousers again.

Evander picks his mug up off the table to drink tea. Jacob does at the same time.

Evander drinks his tea quietly, Jacob slurps it. 'Annoying', Evander thinks to himself.

Breaking the silence, Jacob says. "Well, isn't this nice" As he slurps more tea. "Two long lost brothers having a catch up over a nice cup of tea, how typically British." He screws his face up in mock joy.

Evander places his cup on the desk and lets his fingers trail down the cup. He plays with a nodule of clay that protrudes on the handle and he tries to pick it off, unsuccessfully of course, but plays with it anyway. When he looks up at Jacob, he watches Evander over the rim of his cup. He smirks and slurps tea.

Evander removes his hand from the cup and gets back to the business at hand.

Interrogation.

Interview.

Catch up over tea.

Whatever.

"How did you stage some of the murders?"

Jacob cocks his head to one side not sure he understands the question.

Evander rolls his eyes to the ceiling at the need to explain, he rephrases the question. "Tower Bridge and the Theatre, Traitors Gate. How did you do it? Avoiding detection? How did you do it? Did you plan it all out?"

"Well, of course I did. Had to. I planned all my work for God meticulously. You wouldn't believe - actually, maybe *you* would - the trouble I had to go to in order to pull some of them off, the little favours I was afforded, allowed me to stage some of the most dramatic backdrops. Quite the spectacle, don't you think? Which one was your favourite?"

He slurps more tea.

Evander asks avoiding the question. "How did you avoid detection on Tower Bridge?"

"Tower Bridge took months of preparation but, look how it worked out. Made the front page of almost every newspaper around the world that one. I hope you're proud of your little brother's ingenuity. So, was that your favourite?"

Jacob slurps tea, which Evander tries to ignore and not show that it irritates him, otherwise he will do it more.

"So, how did you avoid detection?" Evander asks again.
"It's not what you know, it's who you know if you know what I mean." Jacob replies, with a wink, sipping his tea this time. So, he was doing it to try to annoy Evander, he is glad he masked his dislike of the slurping well enough.
"You had people on the inside helping you?"
"Like I said, it's not what you know, it's who you know!"
"That would make them accessories to murder."
"They had nothing to do with murder and it wasn't that at all. I've told you, I'm God's avenger. None of them bore any part on any of it. That was all my work, they fell by my sword and mine alone."
"So how did it work?"
"They arranged things just so… well, you know…" Jacob drinks tea and doesn't finish his sentence, he expects his brother to fill in the blanks. He puts his cup down.
"Actually no, I don't know. Enlighten me."
"Oh, you know; doors were *accidently* left unlocked, cameras were broken and not reported till the day after, or they were just not recording, memory discs were not replaced, people went on lunch breaks and left offices unattended, a back door wedged open while a sneaky cigarette break was taken and of course, people fall asleep on the job on the night shift all the time. It gets so boring you know... all sorts of unfortunate, but timely events happen to allow access, but none of them are guilty."
"How? Did you bribe them?"
Jacob puts his head down and laughs.
"Something funny?" Evander asks.
"Detective. You know I did not pay them to do anything, so you can't arrest them for accepting a bribe as they did not

accept any payment for services rendered."
"You blackmailed them?"
"To what end, gain or purpose? I'm but a humble Chaplain, a servant of God. I have no need for material things, I live a simple life."
"You threatened them?"
"Nothing so crass." Jacob retorts, his face reflecting the distaste.
"So, what did you offer them that secured their services?"
"Safe passage to the next life." He smirks.
"You threatened to kill them?"
"That's not what I said. You need to pay attention to what I said."
"You're going to conduct their funerals?"
"Oh, come on now, you can do better than that, surely!"
Evander replays the words in his head. "Explain what you mean by 'safe passage'?"
"Well, we will all be in need of the services of the Ferryman one day, each and every one of us, including you and me."
"What, you know Charon personally then?"
"Oh, you know him too!" Jacob exclaims, as he claps his hands together in mock excitement.
"What, you're going to pay for their journey into the next realm? That's the deal? How many silver coins will you deposit for them? Or will the coins be gold?"
"Ensuring safe passage is not an easy task, but I have connections." He looks upwards.
"Connections? Ohhhhhhh, because you're God's servant?"
Jacob smiles. "You're learning quickly Detective." He sips tea.
"You really expect me to believe that?"
"It's the truth. I cannot lie."

"Seriously, that was all you offered them?"
"Why would you doubt it?" Jacob asks, genuine notes of indignation in his voice.
"Nothing of monetary value?"
"No."
"No bonds, or shares or stocks?"
"No."
"No silver or gold coins for passage, nor holidays every year?"
Exasperated Jacob sighs. "No, No, Nooooo Detective and the answer is 'No' to every other scenario you can make up. It seems you don't have any imagination to play the game, so why should I continue. You're going to have to accept it and move on to your next question as I'm tired of this game now."
Then, Evander realises what he missed. He smiles, confident he has it.
"What, did you work it out finally?" Jacob asks, a note of sarcasm in his voice.
"It's not anything you promised them and definitely not for safe passage. That's not it all, it's not even close to the mark is it?"
"I don't know Detective, what did you have in mind as a bargaining chip?"
"It's something more personal isn't it?"
"Keep going."
"It's not that you are paying them, or blackmailing them, or offering safe passage anywhere in this life or the next. It's something much simpler."
"Ohhh, it sounds like you're getting warmer Detective." Jacob notes with amusement.
"It's not safe passage. No, this is something they owed you

and you called in your little favour, didn't you?"
"Now, that sounds much more believable doesn't it than safe passage to the next life. Or wait..." Jacob pauses and puts his hand up to his chin and scratches it, as though trying to remember something, a puzzled look on his face "... *did* I assure them of that journey with the Ferryman after all. Just never know with me, I like to make shit up and as God's Avenger, I'll never ever tell the truth Detective. Well, only in exceptional circumstances of course and perhaps to you once we get to know each other better. But they cannot be held accountable. You don't even know who *'They'* are!"
Evander realises that whether he did or did not blackmail, or threaten the people involved, or if they did owe him one, he realises that Jacob will not give them up and his elaborate explanation is one to deflect any retribution for the people who helped him.
Ah, maybe that's the pay off, they will be unaccountable and untraceable. He has guaranteed their anonymity by weaving a web of lies so outrageous, you don't know which one to believe, or if any are even true, even if the truth is in there.
"So, these people who helped you by leaving doors unlocked or going on cigarette breaks... they knew what you were doing? And you told them, trusted them enough to know they wouldn't go against you, or drop you in it. So, they believe in your... your 'work' and they really do believe you are doing God's work. They're your partisans!"
"You see, you worked that out all on your own. Well done, Detective. Bravo! Go to the top of the class and give the pencils out!" Jacob says sarcastically.
"Did they help you with the murders?"
"I told you already, I have not murdered anyone."

Evander smiles, plays with his words and rephrases the question. "Did they help you secure safe passage into the next life for the victims?"

"They are not victims, Detective."

"Did they help you secure safe passage into the next life for the wrong doers."

"That's better. But, no, they did not. I told you, they had nothing to do with the wielding of the sword. That was all my work. I took care of that business on God's behalf. Now, are we nearly done here? I've got work to do and an appointment to keep this evening and I mustn't be late for my appointment."

"Done? We've barely scratched the surface. I have a lot more questions that need answering and you are going nowhere."

Evander picks his cup up and slurps his tea on purpose.

It seems to irritate Jacob.

Evander smiles.

CHAPTER FIFTY-ONE

After three more hours of interrogation, Evander finally suspends the interview for the day. Jacob is escorted to a holding cell by an officer who is not on his team. Evander goes into the observation room and is surprised to find that there are more people in there than there should be.

As well as his team and the Chief, there are four Detectives from different M.I.T teams, and one other division within Scotland Yard.

Word had spread of Evander and his twin brother and though it didn't turn into a circus, there are far too many people in the observation room for his liking. He does not like it at all.

To make matters worse Detective Eugene Wilson is in there, of course he would be, anything to watch Evander squirm. They have had conflicts in the past and Eugene and Evander will never see eye to eye.

Evander always tries to rise above the bait, but he is tired and today has been an emotional one, so he had better not push any of his buttons, or Evander will push back harder than Eugene can handle. Of course, he cannot help himself and as soon as he sees Evander, he takes a pop at him.

"Well, if it isn't Very Special Detective Chief Inspector Evander Kincaid with the murderous brother."

"How are your little bits today?" Evander says, as he wiggles his little finger with innuendo, are your operations nearly complete? You must be ready by now to change from Eugene to simple, feminine Gene, right?"

Some of the others in the room laugh, but Eugene doesn't reply. Apparently, he is lost for words again, but his face says it all. He never was any good at coming back with quick

witted remarks.
Adam rescues Evander. "Boss, before we leave the office, I found something I want you to take a look at, can you come upstairs to our office?"
"Sure Adam."
They both leave the room and the rest of the team follow them.

~~~~~~

Back up in their office space, Adam watches Evander, who sits in his office with his hands on his head, his fingers wrapped in his hair.
Adam gets up, knocks on the open door of Evander's office. Evander looks up to see him and he forces a smile.
"You okay Boss?"
"Just tired. I need to sleep. No, I need a bottle of wine, some music and then my bed, then sleep."
Evander opens his desk draw, pulls out a bottle of Jack Daniel's and two glasses, which he raises in offering a drink to Adam. Adam nods his head in approval. Evander opens the bottle and pours a double into each glass, pushes one across the desk to Adam. He puts the lid back on the bottle and returns it to the draw.
Evander picks his glass up, holds its out to Adam and they clink glasses.
"All out of ice, sorry." Evander jokes. They drink in silence, but Adam breaks it after a few seconds.
"You know if you want me to take a shift with him tomorrow, I don't mind."
"No. I told you, he isn't seeing anyone else on my team."
~~~~~~

"But I'm a big boy Boss, I can handle him. Takes a lot to rattle this Scouser."
"I know Adam. Not that I don't think you're capable of taking him on. I know you could, I just don't want him using anyone else on my team to score points. And then, there's James. I need to ask him more questions about James and the first victim."
"Boss, you know... when you first asked him about James, I really thought..."
Interrupting him, Evander says. "It's okay, I'm not going to punch his lights out while he's in interrogation, I know beating a confession out of a suspect isn't admissible as evidence and the courts would throw it out."
Adam laughs and looks down at his drink.
Evander looks over his shoulder and watches his team.
"How is Grace holding up?"
"What do you mean Boss?" Adam asks.
"Her and James, they were close, or getting closer. Is she okay?"
Adam's eyes open wide as he turns around in his seat to look at Grace, who is sat at her desk, staring out the window.
"What. Were they erm, like 'together', together?" Adam asks.
"No, I don't think it had gotten to that point, or I would have needed to move one of them to a different team if they were, you know, conflict of interest and all that, no dating co-workers on the same team, it clouds judgement."
"I didn't even see the connection Boss. You want me to check on her?"
"Yeah, but don't tease, be her big brother. If my observations are right, and they were getting close, she'll be hurting right now a bit more than the rest of us, so be kind."

"Got it." Adam says.

They drink at the same time. Evander realises he is going to need to think about replacing James at some point, but not right now. Still too raw. He looks back to Adam, he can almost see the cogs whirling in his head. "Hey, stop thinking." Evander tells him.

Sighing, Adam says. "Ohhhh, that obvious huh?"

"Yup. Get your head on right, let it go. I understand why you questioned things and put two and two together. I'd have probably come to the same conclusions."

"But Izzy knew… she didn't…"

"Adam. Stop. Don't compare your thoughts to those of Izzy. Jacob was right, she does see me like a big brother, and you know she wouldn't have a bad thing said about me… even if I did turn out to be a whack job, she'd find a loophole for me somewhere. You were just doing your job and I'd expect nothing less from my Senior Detective."

"But Boss…."

Pulling rank on him Evander says. "As my senior Detective, I'd expect you to be one step ahead of the rest of the team. Haven't we had this conversation before about why you are my Senior Detective? Why do you think I want you to take point and organise the team when I'm not around and allocate tasks and duties and keep the team purring like a well-oiled machine? I trust you to do your job and that's exactly what you were doing - your job. Let it go, you hear me? You don't need to be forgiven for doing your job, got it?"

Adam nods his head but says nothing.

"Now," he says as he finishes the last of his Jack Daniel's and puts the glass in the draw "Time for all of us to go home."

~~~~~~

The roads are busy as would be expected for London, but traffic moves quickly, and Evander arrives home in good time. He is mentally exhausted and just wants to sleep, but he needs to try and switch off first from it all and what a mind job today has been.

He hangs his jacket up and goes straight to his music. He puts the player on random. It flicks between songs from The Who, to Depeche Mode, to Queen, to The Beatles, to McCartney, to Weller, to Manilow, to Lennon.

He needs to get out of his work clothes and in the bedroom, favours jogging bottoms and a racer back T-Shirt, that he normally wears when at the gym, but chooses now for its comfort.

He goes back to the kitchen, opens a bottle of wine, takes it and a glass with him into the living room.

He pours a glass of wine as the music plays, Depeche Mode sing about enjoying the silence, something he needs to find before he can try to sleep.

Before he knows, his first glass of wine is gone, *'where did that go?'*, he wonders, didn't even touch the sides. He pours another. After he takes a second drink, he puts the glass down. He closes his eyes just to rest them, not to sleep, but finds himself thinking about his brother slurping tea to try to annoy him.

Somewhere down the road, amongst thoughts about dragons and traitors and his tea slurping murderous brother, sleep finds him.
~~~~~~

CHAPTER FIFTY-TWO

Back in interrogation the next morning, Jacob arrives at room number two in cuffs, his hair is slicked back and wet, he also chews gum.
"Where did you get the gum?" Evander asks.
"One of the female officers gave it me when I asked her for some. I think she likes me, no… wait… maybe she likes you." He winks as he sits down.
Evander opens a file in front of him and reviews evidence and his notes for what he needs to ask him.
"Now I'm in here, can I have these removed, please?" Jacob asks shaking his wrists, which causes a slight rattle from the cuffs.
Evander nods to the officer who escorted him in, once the cuffs are removed, Evander lets the officer leave. They are alone now as Evander requested.
Jacob rubs his wrists after the cuffs are removed and asks.
"Here we are again, set up for a cosy chat, but what, no tea? No full English breakfast? I'm disappointed brother." He says embellishing the pronunciation of 'brother', his bottom lip protrudes in fake disappointment.
"We're not here to play catch up. We're here to get answers to questions on you committing murder."
"Oh dear, have we forgotten our lessons from yesterday already?"
"I'm not playing your games anymore, *brother*." Evander says sarcastically.
"I'm not happy I was kept here all night. I missed a particularly important appointment last night and will have to wait months now to time it right again."

"I'm sorry Jacob, but you're not going anywhere except prison."
"Well, Dahhhh! I work there, so of course I'll be going to prison. Tell me something I don't know."
"That's not what I meant, and you know it."
"What *did* you mean?" Jacob asks, genuinely perplexed.
"Murderers don't walk out of Scotland Yard free. They go to prison."
"Were you not listening? I work there! Idiot."
"You won't be going to work, you're not a free man Jacob Caine. Not anymore. You're a murderer, you killed people, maybe you missed that part?"
Jacob ignores Evander's last comment, either by choice or ignorance. He still believes he will be free to leave any time. Jacob leans forward in his chair and with cupped hands he pleads, "Can I have tea and I'll answer your questions? Please? Pleaaaaase?"
Evander assesses his request, turns and nods to the team in the observation room.
Jacob calls out. "Evander's team, bring one for my brother too, please. In a proper cup!"
Evander reviews the file in front of him while they wait, he makes pretend notes in the margin of some of the documents, but angles the file up and away, so Jacob cannot see what he writes, which is in fact nothing, he just scrawls and doodles, but he does not want Jacob to know that. Jacob takes the bait and strains his neck to try and see what he is writing.
Something Evander does write however, is something he knows must be achieved today: '*Break him today, Confession time.*'
After some time has passed, there is a knock at the door.

Evander knows it is one of his team as he has given strict instructions to them not to enter the room and all of them are in the observation room, watching.

He does not trust Jacob at all and is admittedly perhaps a bit too overprotective of his remaining team members. Understandable. Or, at least it is as far as Evander is concerned. What if others think he is too cautious? He doesn't care.

Evander stands and puts the file on his chair. He opens the door and is presented with two mugs of tea. Izzy also has a plastic cup with water in it. Evander looks puzzled at the water and has a questioning look on his face as he looks at Izzy.

"He'll ask for it at some point no doubt to keep his hair slicked back, thought it would save any further interruptions as he seems to do it when he's feeling pressured by you. Needs to gain his confidence and he uses the water, or tea thing as a distraction to buy himself some recovery time." Izzy explains.

Evander raises an eyebrow, impressed by her observations.

"How did you..."

"I use it myself at home and you know your own tricks best don't you!" She explains.

"Indeed, we do. Thanks." He takes the water off her too and retreats into the room.

Evander places his cup on the table and pushes the water and a mug of tea towards Jacob who looks worried at the appearance of the water.

"I didn't ask for water." He notes.

"Your victims didn't ask to be slaughtered." Evander says, hoping for a reaction.

"But I didn't ask for water." He repeats. "Not yet." He is

perplexed at its appearance.
"You will eventually. No more distractions." Evander replies.
Jacob purses his lips together in a tight grimace. Son-of-a-bitch. Izzy was right.
Evander picks his cup up and sips tea. He waits for Jacob to stop sulking and pick his cup of tea up to drink before asking him questions.
Eventually, Jacob does so after he removes the gum from his mouth and sticks it to the side of the plastic up of water. Then he takes a drink.
"Now shall we begin?" Evander asks. "Who was the first one?"
Jacob rolls his eyes up to the ceiling and puts his cup down.
"Did I *not* make myself clear about this yesterday? I told you, I'll never tell you who the first was and you'll never know. I don't care what you do to me - you can lock me in solitary, put me with all the hardened criminals, torture me with anything you like. I'll never tell a soul." He folds his arms defensively, "I. Am. Not. Telling. You."
Something niggles at the back of Evander's mind, and he feels like he should '*know*' who the first victim was. It swims closely by, but just scurries beneath the surface, too far away to grasp and yet… it is there lurking like a spectre in the liquid fog that drifts into and out of focus, but then gone too quickly to grab hold of it and keep it.
"Why don't you want to talk about it?" Evander fishes.
No reply.
"Is it someone who was close to you? Someone you cared about?"
No response.
"Is it someone you trusted, but had to let them go and it was

painful for you?"
Silence as golden as the fleece of the mythical creatures from foreign lands long ago forgotten, hangs in the air. "Ohhhhh, maybe it was someone you loved and lost. Someone…" A thought crosses Evander's mind. What if… their Mother... he cannot continue his thoughts. He only vaguely remembers her. More so her laughter than anything else. She would giggle with him when they played with... played with… what? He cannot remember.

Intuitively, Jacob says. "It wasn't her… I wouldn't have…"

"Who?" Evander asks.

"You know who." Jacob admonishes.

"How do I know you're thinking of the same person?"

"Because like it or not, you're my brother and I'm yours and we'll always share things." Jacob leans forward. "I know who you're thinking of, and you *know* I know." He leans back and picks his cup up and drinks tea, quietly.

Evander weighs up what he has just said and realises he is right.

Regardless of what he has done, he is and always will be his brother. No escaping it.

"I see you believe me for once." Jacob notes, as he peers over the rim of his mug of tea at Evander. He tries to look confident, but Evander sees vulnerability masked behind his eyes.

"Brothers we may be, but that doesn't mean I trust a word you say."

Exasperated, Jacob says. "I was... *We* were four years old for goodness' sake. I already told you, I found her killer and she was avenged by me."

He has a point, Evander thinks and dismisses their Mother as

the first victim, but then, he thinks of Jasmine.
"It wasn't her either." Jacob tells him right away.
"Who am I thinking of now?"
"Your wife, Jasmine. That's how I found you, Brother." Jacob says and sounds sincere with his use of the word 'brother' in this sentence. There is compassion and sympathy there.
"I'm sorry what?"
"That's how I discovered you were still here. In London. I kept asking about you as a child, but they told me you were not here anymore. You had gone away."
"How would you... oh, wait... the media, yes?"
"Of course, good old reliable tabloids. Printing their sensational stories. They had your photo in the first article I saw. I thought it was me at first. I was ready to call them and ask how they got my photo and demand they retract it." Jacob recalls with amusement.
"I hate the Papanasty." Evander thinks out loud, honestly.
"Is that what you call them? I like it, I must remember that one, it's the perfect insult to them cowards. How appropriate. Yes, I know. I can understand your reasons and I don't blame you either. Cruel what they implied about her."
Evander is surprised to find that Jacob shares the same contempt for the media as he does, although perhaps not quite as intensely as he feels it. He is not ready however, to discuss Jasmine with his brother.
Evander changes the subject. "So, who was the first?"
"Not her and not Mother. Told you, I will never reveal who."
"You'll tell me who it wasn't, but not who it was? That doesn't make any sense."
"Makes perfect sense to me. One day, you'll understand. When you figure it out and you'll have to, as I will never tell

you of my own free will, but then you'll understand.

"Now, are we done with this? Can we move on? Ask me something I can answer so I can go home."

Evander writes a note at the side of the margin next to the words *'Who was the first victim?* 'Unidentified'.' He turns the page over.

Looking up at Jacob, he is watching him intently, observing - no studying.

Evander steels himself, ready for the next question and tries to disassociate emotions and personal feelings. He tries to make the subject of James like any other victim and part of his job.

"What happened with James?"

A saddened look crosses Jacob's face. "I know I upset you yesterday, teasing about him to a degree, that was mean of me, and I apologise. A most unfortunate series of events that was, which lead to his..." Jacob's words trail off.

"Lead to his what?" Evander prods.

"His journey with the Ferryman."

"Arranged by you."

"All journeys with the Ferryman are arranged by me, or people like me."

"What do you mean *'people like me'*? Did you have a partner in this after all?"

"No, I told you, I was the only one who wielded the sword of God."

"So, no one else committed any murders?"

"Not sure. I don't know any murderers. Do you?"

"Yes. Sitting across the table from one now."

"Well, it goes with the territory."

"What?"

"Perks of the job I guess."

"Hardly a perk."
"It's the career you chose."
"I think actually, it chose me."
"Why would you say that?" Jacob wonders genuinely interested.
This all feels too 'normal'. Evander changes the subject back to James.
" Answer the question."
"What was the question again?" Jacob asks, slurping tea.
"What happened with James? Why did you shoot him?"
"Can I have some water." Jacob asks.
Evander smiles, taps his pen against the plastic cup on the table near Jacob.
Jacob looks disconcerted. He had forgotten he already had some.
A glimpse of panic flickers in his eyes. He puts his cup down and takes the water. He removes the chewing gum from the side, pops it back in his mouth and chews.
He pours a little water in his hands and slicks them through his hair, making sure the curl is not there.
In order to bring him back into the room and keep the edge of uncertainty and not allow him any time to regroup his thoughts, Evander repeats. "What happened to James?"
Jacob puts a temporary wall up, which Evander has worked out comes from the slicked back hair. Jacob pulls on his fake persona with his reply of arrogant confidence that he can fool anyone.
"Well." Jacob says. "Given the situation, it seemed the kindest way, the quickest, most painless way. He thought I was you. Did I mention that? He thought I was you, quite ironic really. He thought I was you as he ran for his life. And failed."

"James is how we caught you."

Jacob tilts his head to one side, like a dog listening to a high-pitched whistle, or a command. Ah, something he doesn't know about. This is the way in.

"You don't know, do you?" Evander asks, a note of excitement lacing his voice.

"Know what?" Jacob asks concerned.

"James took a picture. Of you. Attacking him. He sent it to us before he died."

"How?"

"On his mobile phone."

Jacob replies quickly. "No! You lie, you didn't find his phone. You can't have found it anywhere because I..." He stops himself from saying any more.

He realises he has said too much. His eyes are fixed on the table in front of him now, they dart left to right, left to right as he frantically tries to think, to regroup the persona that he occupies when under the slicked back hair, but Evander can see it starts to fall apart. Getting closer to breaking point now.

"I didn't say we had his phone, but he sent us something from it. A photo. Of you when you attacked him. Before you shot him."

"Yes, shot... him... yes... I... yes." Jacob is distracted, he doesn't finish his sentence. He rubs his hands through his hair as he frantically tries to think. He chews the gum quickly, trying to think, think, think!

Evander has seen this plenty of times before, his brother is falling apart.

"What are you trying to remember? Can I help you try to remember?" Evander offers.

Jacob looks up at him. Evander is surprised to see a wounded little boy looking back at him. He can see it in his eyes, the little boy is evidently scared.

"Yes, help. But… how?" Jacob asks.

"Where did you find him? James, where did you come across him?"

"I didn't." Jacob begins, slowly, measured. "Actually, He found me."

"Where?"

"Lambeth."

"You went to Lambeth? Where James lived? Did you target him?"

"No! I didn't I swear. It was an accident. Him being there." He puts his hands up to his mouth, twists his hands, then he covers his mouth, then twists his hands. He looks like he is tortured. He becomes agitated.

"Jacob, take it easy, calm down, alright?" Evander notices a twang of Scouse in his accent when he tells him to *'calm down'*. Adam is rubbing off on him. He would smile if this wasn't so serious a situation.

Jacob takes a deep breath and puts his hands flat on the table in front of him.

After a minute or so, Evander resumes. "What happened in Lambeth?"

"I was in the tunnel, one of the foot tunnels near Waterloo. Had it all sectioned off for something I was planning the staging of, and I was preparing it, cleaning it ready and he saw me. Thought I was you… and…" he drifts off into the distance, his words trail away, he shakes his head remorsefully.

"What happened Jacob? It's okay, you can tell me now… no more secrets, okay? It's alright you can tell me, I'm your

brother." Evander assures him.
"Well… he thought I was you… thought there was another one you know. Came over while I was preparing the scene, just then, he saw it and he realised something was wrong. He thought I was you, he tried to run, but I caught him. He dropped his coffee, spoilt the scene, contaminated it after I'd carefully prepared it and cleaned it ready for the display, couldn't use it after that, but…" Jacob grimaces. "He spoilt it. Coffee everywhere and then he kept pleading *'Evander, please no! Evander, please stop!'* And he wouldn't shut up, so I pulled the gun out, told him to shut up, but he wouldn't *shut up*, I had no choice but to hit him, knocked him out."
"So, you didn't shoot him there."
"No! People would see me. See him. Hear the gun fire. See the body, I had to get out. Out. Out! Flee. Take them somewhere safe."
"You took him somewhere, alive?"
"Knocked him out. Put him in the van, with the other one. Got out of there. Had to rethink it all."
"Who was it?"
"Who was what?"
"The one you avenged, ready to stage the scene, who was it? Did we find him?"
"No. Therefore your figures are wrong. I couldn't present him as a dragon's avengement. He was contaminated by James stumbling across us. A most unfortunate event. Ruined a perfectly good display… it would have been glorious; the body would have descended from the oh, never mind spoiled now but… Ahhhhh the glory. What a spectacle, what a presentation that would have been."
"Why did you kill James, murder him? Shoot him?"

"He was an accident, he got in my way."
"You don't murder someone by accident. You fed him, gave him wine?"
"Yes, he deserved that."
"Why did you do that for him?"
"I didn't intend to hurt him. He was a witness to my work, there couldn't be one. Then he made a mistake by thinking I was you. I had to get rid of him don't you see?"
"Not really, tell me." Evander says.
"Compromised. I couldn't allow that to happen."
"Who was compromised?"
"I had to let him go to the Ferryman to protect you."
Evander is shocked. He was not expecting that response.
"What do you mean?" He asks.
Jacob replies with conviction. "I had to stop him from blaming you. I was looking after you, because he'd have run and told everyone it was you and you're not a bad man. Unlike me, but I can't… the feelings…" Jacobs words trail away, incomplete. He struggles with an inner demon, and he is about to crack, just needs one more push and he will be over the falls, just like Niagara.
Not that it would bring James back, but Evander wants to punch Jacob so badly. For James. He can't though, not in here. Not on camera in interrogation. One more push.
"What feelings Jacob? Tell me about your feelings? Do they hurt you?"
"You don't know what it's like to feel these feelings. Such rage burning inside me, the injustice of injustice. The feelings I have, I hate it, yet part of me loves it and I hate the part of me that loves it, but I can't stop it. Sometimes I'm in combat all over again, trying to survive and you have no idea what that's

like. You leave a part of yourself back there, but the part you bring home with you instead is alien, you don't know where it's come from, or how it got there, but it messes with your head, it fucks it all up and you have to try to trap the demon, or it will eat you alive. The pills helped for a while, and I trapped it. I try to control the feelings, but then the rage comes, and I need to release it, set it free. That's when he comes to me."

"Who?" Evander inquires.

Jacob lifts his hands to his hair he smooths it in place. "God. He asks me to be his messenger, his avenger."

"I see. What does he do, why does he take over?"

"It's the rage. The rage when I see these people, these criminals walking the streets of my city free to do whatever they want. I pray to God, tell him how angry I am about it, about the injustice. The lack of atonement, the lack of punishment, no servitude, no justice, or righting of a wrong."

Jacob talks, but it looks like he has gone off into a world inside his head as he tells Evander how he feels, what he goes through, like he recalls a memory.

"It eats my insides, crawls into my head at night and keeps me awake while it burrows and builds a nest of hatred. It crawls around in my mind and no matter how much I pray to God for guidance, he is unable to cast the thoughts away. I can't banish them. Must obey them, need to fight them. Must act but must retain humanity. It's a constant battle between good and evil, but then the Romans came along, and they gave me salvation and confirmation that I am right. I knew I must obey the thoughts of justice as I realised, I am a servant of God. I am right."

"You broke a rule." Evander observes.

"Rule? What rule?"
"One of the commandments, 'thou shall not kill'. Murder, it's a sin, is it not?"
"It is yes, but I didn't kill. The murders are not as you would think. This was an eye for an eye, a tooth for a tooth, a life for a life. That's in the scripture, that's why God sent me as an avenger, He showed me the way. That's why I'm not guilty or a rule breaker."
Jacob is quiet for a few seconds. Evander is patient this time and waits.
"I choose to put right what Lady Justice fails to". Jacob continues. "I think sometimes that's why she wears the blind fold, not to be impartial, but so she can't see the injustices when they happen. That's why you need me, God's servant. Do you know how many criminals, real criminals walk free every day? The prisoners are right, some of them don't deserve to be free and they certainly don't deserve to be walking God's green earth. Where justice fails, the Dragons prevail. Do you know how many people in our great and glorious city, the capital of England, how many of them are so bad, corrupt to the core, feeding off their fellow man and woman, and child too? Have you any idea, really, have you? It's sickening. They take from the hardworking people what they want without a thought for the consequences it has on the lives they tear apart. But there are consequences in all actions. Cause and effect."
Jacob looks up at Evander, finally his façade is down. He has admitted to murder, whether he realises it or not, he has said the words, and that he shot James and that he is metering out the dragon's justice. Got him for sure. Going to jail for life. Yet Evander feels a hint of remorse for him. He sees from his

words that he has a tortured soul, but that does not mean he is not dangerous, he is, very much so. Maybe prison, regular medication and a routine will bring him some structure and he can find himself again.

They both shared the trauma of watching their Mother murdered. Evander suppressed the memory to function, a self defense mechanism to protect himself from the horrors that he bore witness to with his brother.

Jacob however recalls the murder in detail, and though he feels that murder excites him, it is not because he gets off on it, it is because it is what feels normal to him. It tortures his mind every second to see injustice in the world of others getting away with things, when they should be punished. Getting away with the murder of their Mother, Evander realises now that this is his real reason for the dragon murders – revenge. They watched on as helpless four-year-old twin boys as they watched their Mother being taken from them, and no justice was served for it to the man who took her away from them, and them from each other. This is why Jacob found refuge in the arms of Romans 13:4; salvation and justification for being an Avenger to and for God.

Evander stands up.

"Where are you going?" Jacob asks, panic in his voice.

"To make arrangements to charge you with murder."

"No! Brother, please don't go… I, I didn't, I mean… I can't be… that person…"

Tears spring from his eyes and trail down his cheeks. He looks pleadingly to Evander.

He crumbled quicker than Evander expected.

James solved the case. He may have thought that Evander was guilty, and he was the killer, but Evander tries to take solace

from the thought that his photo, his email to Adam broke the case. Evander will see to it that James gets a posthumous bravery award. The least he can do to honour his memory.
Evander stops the interview. He takes his file with him to the bathroom and locks himself in a cubicle. He puts the lid down on the toilet, sits on it.
He cries.
For his Mother.
For Jasmine.
For James.
Surprisingly, for Jacob too.
Evander may be plagued by nightmares he never remembers, but now he knows why. Protection.
He no longer feels the need to remember the nightmares.

CHAPTER FIFTY-THREE

Seven months have passed, the trial of Jacob Caine has come to pass.
The media hacks had a field day with the story, one paper tried to gain access to Jacob to interview him and tell the world *'my story'*. Jacob refused their advances.
The Papanasty knew better than to come to Evander for 'his side of the story'.
James got a posthumous bravery award; he will be forever missed on the team. His photo hangs on a wall in the team's office. His name has been added to the National Police Memorial in London. Evander goes there more often than he will tell any of his team.
Jacob confessed to all the murders, although he did not call them that. He got a life sentence serving a minimum of 35 years, with no chance of parole, unless he appeals to the Home Secretary, which is highly unlikely.
It is also unlikely that the Home Secretary would approve the application, given that he is a serial killer and murdered an officer of the law.
Jacob had asked for a meeting with Evander before being taken to Belmarsh prison to serve his time. Evander is reluctant to engage in conversation with his estranged brother, but there is some sense of duty that compels him to swallow his anger over James and sit and talk to him - man to man. Brother to brother.
They talk for 20 minutes, and he cannot even remember the time passing, or what specifically they talked about.
Everything but the three 'M's': Mother, Marionettes and Murder.

One of the team who escorted Jacob to Belmarsh, tell them they have five minutes to wrap things up with the meeting. Evander stands to leave, but Jacob is not finished yet.

"Evander, will you do something for me?"

Evander doesn't answer.

"Please?" Jacob asks.

"What?"

"Will you come and visit me? Please?"

"Why would I want to do that?"

"Because we're brothers."

"We've gotten along without each other for this long, so why change things now."

"Because now we've found each other, we shouldn't let it go."

"There was nothing to keep hold of to begin with."

"Evander, you're my brother."

"Unfortunately, yes you are. I'm aware."

"We're all we have now. You're my family."

"What makes you think we had anything to start with? I don't think we can talk family yet."

"We were lost to each other, but now, we're found. Please come and see me. Just once a month, please."

Evander looks at him, almost at himself, but not quite. He assesses his request and is surprised to find he gives it consideration.

"I'll think about it. I'm extremely busy with my work as you are aware." Evander tells him.

Jacob smiles, accepting of the consideration, he does not push it any further.

Jacob stands and thinks... hesitates. Stops himself from speaking. He considers his train of thought again. "You know, with James, I genuinely am sorry about him."

His apology seems sincere, but it does not change anything. It won't bring him back.

Then he goes and spoils it with... "I guess he took one for the team."

His comment is flippant, insensitive and negates his apology. Now the trial is over Evander has a bit of wiggle room. Jacob infuriates Evander and he punches him, Jacob's head whips quickly to the left, but he remains standing.

"That was for James." Evander tells him as Jacob turns his head back to face Evander. He has been wanting to do that for months.

Completely unexpected, Jacob takes a step forward and throws his arms around Evander and he hugs him tightly.

This is not the reaction Evander was expecting.

Jacob releases his grip and takes a step back. "That was for Mother."

Evander is unsure what to do or say to that one. He punched Jacob who hugged him back in return, not quite the retaliation he had imagined. Maybe that is Jacob's way of accepting the punishment from his Brother. Maybe he lets it slide for that reason. The hug in return for the punch though is quite unexpected. How to react to that one.

"Please come and visit me next month. Please, say you will?" Jacob asks again as his escorts arrive cuffs in hand, to take him for transportation.

"I told you, I'll think about it."

Jacob is handcuffed and lead away. He looks back periodically over his shoulder to see if Evander is still there. Evander turns on his heel and walks away. He guesses that Jacob must have turned around and saw him walk away.

Jacob calls out. "I'm sorry Evander. Please come and visit me.

Please."
Evander does not reply as he walks away, buttoning his suit jacket as he goes.

~~~~~~

Two months have passed since Jacob was sentenced and taken away to Belmarsh prison. Evander has not been to visit him. He is still processing the request.
He has begun looking at applications for a replacement for James and that is only due to pressure from his team, as they need an extra body in the office to help with their workload, which continues to grow.
Evander sits in his office and reviews files on possible candidates, not an easy task. He has though narrowed the field down to three possibilities. Just needs to review one more file from the short list, before he calls a team meeting to discuss it with them. He doesn't have to do that; the decision would ultimately be Evander's. However, he trusts his team to be honest with him. They may see something he has missed, not the usual protocol, but then there is nothing 'usual' about Evander's team.
One month later, the appointment of not one, but two new team members has taken place. Evander could not decide between them, so some strings were pulled so he could add both. Matthew 'Matty' Goddard has taken one place, the team like him and are forming bonds already, which is good. Makes things easier when a newbie is welcomed by the team, especially when they have all selected him. He will no doubt set the girls hearts aflutter on this floor, as he looks a little bit like Will Smith, the American actor, except he has not got his
~~~~~~

quick wit, or the humour. The joker in this team is unsurprisingly, all Adam. In contrast the other appointee, Jack Marriott is the geeky side of the growing team. He is quiet to start with, but the more settled he has become with the team, the more he has opened up. There is a good rapport going with everyone now.

~~~~~~

.

Evander is at home, watching Football, the Merseyside Derby clash. Adam's fault for getting him into football. Well, he is a Scouser, so of course he would love the football.

It is a staple part of the diet in that part of England. Evander hopes Everton win, as they are Adam's team and if they lose, he will be like a bear with a proverbial sore head tomorrow at the office.

The phone rings. Evander mutes the sound on the T.V. and answers the call. It's Adam oddly enough.

"Why are you calling me and not watching the football? I am!" Evander says.

"Are you watching the news?"

"No, I just said, I'm watching the football. You do know its Derby Day, right?"

"Put the news on." The tone in Adam's voice tells Evander something is wrong.

"Why? What's wrong?"

"He's back."

"Who is?"

"Put the news on."

"What channel?"

"B.B.C. news."
~~~~~~

Evander turns the channel over and though the T.V. is still on mute, he knows instantly who Adam is talking about. "He can't be back. He's in jail." Evander says.

"He was."

"What do you mean, *was?* He should still be there."

"He escaped 24 hours ago."

"You've got to be shitting me! And no one thought to tell me? What the fuck is wrong with them? Why wasn't I told? Why weren't we told?"

"I know Boss, I'm pissed off too. I thought you may have known about it and not told the team yet."

"No, I'd have told you. Told you all. Wouldn't hide something like that from my team. I'd have told you all and of course you and Izzy were both with me then, but I'd have told the whole team. Had I known. Has the Chief been in touch with you?"

"No. How about you?

"Nothing. No."

"I Wonder if he knows?"

"Yes, of course he bloody knows…" Evander's words trail off as he watches the news coverage without sound. The murderous crow man is back on the streets.

"How many victims are there?"

"Don't know."

"Still processing evidence?"

"No Boss, that's not the problem."

"What is?"

"According to the news, they can't identify how many victims there are yet. Too many body parts."

"Not again." Evander says dismay in his voice.

"I know Boss."

"We're going to have to visit the prison, his cell. See if there

are any clues there."
"Not sure, but apparently he was pissed off with something he saw on T.V."
"What did he see?"
"Well…"
"Let me guess, you don't know?"
"No."
"Figures. How did he get out?"
"He walked out the front gate."
"What? How?"
"He wore a disguise and you're not going to like it."
"Why?"
"He knocked out the Chaplin who was visiting, undressed him swapped clothes with him and walked out the front gate. He's also been seen talking to Jacob."
"For fucks sake… are you saying my brother helped him escape?"
"No Boss, I don't think so. At least not as far as I know, don't have all the details yet. It's mostly just what was on the news report and we erm…"
"What?"
"Well Boss, will we be assigned the case?"
"Nothing mentioned to me yet, but I'm going to call the Chief."
"I was hoping you'd say that. I want this case."
"This case is ours. No one else is getting it. Call the team and get them in the Yard in the next hour. I'll call the Chief, find out what's going on. I'll speak to you later."
"Sure, Boss." Adam hangs up.
Evander turns his attention to the news as a picture of the man known under many pseudo names appears on screen, here,

the newscaster refers to him as 'The Bird Man'.

The screen changes to a split screen of a black crow and a white crow. Taking the T.V. off mute, the news reporter explains how he is killing again and how a new fear grips the nation, after he escaped by walking out of the main gate as if invisible.

It means he will have to pay a visit to prison and to his brother too.

The murderer with the crows is back and waiting to be caught by the police.

Anger twists through Evander like an oil slick spreads across water.

Aloysius De'Ath is out and back on the streets.

Evander will get him and this time he will break him.

He just needs to find him first....

DCI EVANDER KINCAID
WILL RETURN IN

A MURDER OF CROWS

REVIEWS

The story is a plethora of twists and turns, cliff hangers, suspense and many surprises. The characters are all very real and relatable and Lana has successfully turned every line into a visual treat, that has you running it through your head like a movie. Lana's attention to minute detail, research and subject matters keep the reader interested throughout and her writing style flows effortlessly through every chapter. *Rosalind Winton*

There are some people I admire greatly, for example, anyone who can play a piano well, or a guitar perhaps. Lana is one of those people! I had planned to keep going back to her book, but in the end I had to read it from start to finish in one sitting. The story hangs together well and is well thought through. What could be loose ends all get tied away neatly. The twist is kept hidden until it comes. I liked the way Lana introduces characters and there is enough depth to them to involve the reader and make them believable. she provides a flavour of the relentless grind of the investigation. She sets the scenes well and I really liked her descriptive narrative style. the test for me is always whether can I see what the subject of the narrative is seeing - and feeling? and I absolutely could. The strong first chapter draws the reader in at the start of the story and later on, the reader is given a tantalising and intriguing glimpse of the suspect, but cleverly keeps their identity hidden. *Bob Attwood.*

As a lover of Crime books the catchy title spoke to me right away. Main character Inspector Evander Kincaid comes across as a charismatic person with a great sense of justice , but also as a vulnerable soul. The story grabs you by the first chapter and makes you want to read more !! The feelings of the characters and events are described with an eye for detail and a good mix of humor , emotion and tension. Reads very well and makes curious to the sequel!! Highly recommended!!
Carla Zwackhalen

The best crime novels always start with a murder and this story is no exception. I knew right from the start it was going to be a great read and it was. I was impatient to know answers to the questions that the story raised and these were eventually answered. The story is well researched from a policing perspective, which gave the book a sense of realism. I could tell that the writer knew what they were writing about. I loved all the characters and there is witty, sarcastic, brutal banter. I just wanted to keep reading to find out what was yet to unfold. It kept me guessing and I was intrigued. Lana's incredible use of language created fear and tension. There are gruesome scenes, almost to the point where I didn't want to carry on reading, but then had to get past it to find out what happens next. It's gripping and I felt as though I was actually part of it. *Lydia Georges*

A modern thriller with lots of unexpected twists and turns that will keep you awake all night. A killer on the run with a twisted soul that is crying for attention! You won't be able to put the book down until the end but get ready for lots of unexpected twists and turns. *Ana Franco Zabala*

Printed in Great Britain
by Amazon

86882383R00214